Bird in Tree

A Novel

MICHAEL REILLY

Outskirts Press, Inc.
Denver, Colorado

Bird in Tree, A Novel
All Rights Reserved
Copyright © 2006 Michael Reilly
Cover art by Phoebe Jordan-Reilly

Outskirts Press
http://www.outskirtspress.com

ISBN-10: 1-59800-334-8
ISBN-13: 978-1-59800-334-5

Outskirts Press and the "OP" logo are trademarks belonging to
Outskirts Press, Inc.

Printed in the United States of America

for MJ

Hey, diddle diddle!
The cat and the fiddle!
The cow jumped over the moon.
The little dog laughed to see such sport,
And the dish ran away with the spoon!

—child's nursery rhyme

Prologue

Cornelius missed his first opportunity to meet up again with Valerie. He was driving on a country road in a torrential downpour. All around were nothing but soggy fields. Rain water slid down his windshield like corn syrup. The last thing he expected to see (*he almost missed her*) was a person by the roadside holding an enormous umbrella. By the time he realized she was there, he had passed and thought he could not go back.

The second chance also slipped by, this time not so easily, on board a plane from Los Angeles to Chicago.

A young woman came onto the plane at L.A. airport, carrying a violin case, and she sat beside Cornelius. Her clothes were rich in hue, her face incredibly beautiful— not for any particular physical attributes, but simply because it almost literally shone. Her eyes beamed placidly.

She was a direct contrast to him.

For by this time Cornelius had lost a lot of weight, his eyes were bloodshot, bagged and dark, and he never looked paler. He moved aside his only piece of luggage, a small wire birdcage holding an albino cockatiel, to allow her room. Next to him, she looked like a fantasy cartoon penned into a black and white "you can save little Cornelius or turn the page" ad.

Above the Rockies, she spoke to him.

Her voice was as pure and clear as spring water. She asked if they could trade seats, if he didn't mind, because she would like to look at the mountains. Cornelius grunted and obliged.

Once the mountains had passed from sight, the plane flew into some clouds, and beneath the clouds was only flat land anyway, so the young woman opened her violin case and began to play. None of the other passengers seemed to hear music, and no flight attendant came over to tell her to put the instrument away. But Cornelius heard the sonata from his first record album: the violin solo he had composed in Boston and which Andrew Healy had arranged and played on the CD. He listened with his breath drawn in as she played it perfectly, better than it had ever been played, even by Andrew.

It was as if the notes as conceived in the ideal had come to life through this woman's violin. The sonata was not being played. It was *being*

—as if it had always been.

The cockatiel began to sing along. And that is when the other passengers looked up, and they said to themselves, "My, doesn't that bird sound lovely." Yet not a one said anything about the young woman or her violin.

The plane landed at O'Hare and the woman put away her instrument without a word. Cornelius saw her once in the terminal, but when he finally got the idea to follow her, she had vanished, as a mouse does when you thought it only ran behind the couch.

The third time Cornelius saw Valerie was during one of his concerts. He had returned to the stage after a long time in the bathroom thinking he would vomit. He was very sick this time, but he could not refuse the applause, so he made up his mind to attempt one short song. Halfway through the encore he looked out at the glare of stage lights, beyond which he knew were a lot of people he couldn't see. He could never distinguish faces in that glare. But tonight—tonight he thought he did see someone with large black eyes, a beautiful face like the young woman on the airplane: Valerie's face for sure— Valerie for sure. A moment passed and he was not sure if he had seen anything.

He had a direct confrontation with her after the show. In the men's room, where she most decidedly should not have been. Cornelius had just filled the sink and dunked his head. His face came up dripping and he glimpsed her in the mirror. She smiled, and her whole form seemed to give the usually cold room its warmth and light. Cornelius looked at her and was not sick anymore. Valerie did not say a word, only touched his cheek with a hand that was soft and warm, a familiar touch, and she was gone.

Right after that someone knocked on the door and shouted his name. It was Andrew's voice and when Cornelius opened the door it turned out to be Andrew as well.

"How long were you out there?" Cornelius asked.

"About ten minutes. Did you pass out?"

"Did you see the concert?"

"Yeah," Andrew admitted.

"I was horrible. Why didn't you come up and help me out, Andrew, I needed it bad."

"Because I can't keep doing that."

Cornelius sat on the toilet lid. "And I can't keep doing this..." He sighed heavily.

Then he said, "You know Valerie was just ... on my mind."

Andrew said nothing.

Cornelius lit a cigarette. "I thought I saw her in the audience tonight. Saw her in the front row."

"Someone who looked kind o' like her," Andrew suggested.

"No, it was Valerie. She was right here in the bathroom – just before you knocked."

"Did she talk to you?" Andrew leaned against the sink and folded his arms.

3

"She didn't say anything. But she was here. I'm telling you Valerie was here...at the concert...in the...in this..."

Cornelius stood, lifted the toilet lid and threw the cigarette into the bowl. "Andrew, let's get out of here. This is finished."

PART ONE

Chapter 1

She could read music.

Her Papa played violin in the Performing Arts Center orchestra, taught music at Skidmore College, and brought symphonies into the house. So she could read notes though she could not herself play any instrument. This manuscript, done in a painstaking hand, which lay on the table before her had an influence of Beethoven but it would not sound like anything you could put in a category.

She did not know why she had come, what she was doing here holding a hot root beer on one of the hottest nights so far this summer, thinking about rats, well after two a.m., with some forty or fifty miles to drive home.

Getting into the car with him earlier—and again as she stood in that dark alleyway—the third time as they climbed the crumbling stairwell to this apartment, when her heart beat with its old anticipation, all three times she banished the feeling. She was not here for that—not anymore, not ever again—that was a different person whom she had made up her mind never to be again, never to give a single inch to, because it was a person sick.

She would not be like that anymore, and this decision would be cradled foremost in her brain, and protected.

The piano player was quiet, confident, a little unsettling to the nerves. Tonight was her first night out in months—the first she had been brave enough after her illness—and she had come out only because sitting in the television room at home, staring with acceptance at whatever came on the tube, had, in a single instant, drained itself of anything tolerable. Her Mama and Papa were in Philadelphia where her Papa was guest conductor for some occasion. She had chosen to remain home, as she had opted in all choices for the past year, but suddenly being in the large house alone made her panic. She fled, as though from a mayhem, went into the first place she came upon: that coffeehouse which had at one time, long ago, been a Catholic church. The Catholic church, in fact, where she had made her First Communion, where she had told her First Confession to Father Dimura. The booth she chose was against the wall upon which had once hung a Stations of the Cross plaque. The Fourteenth Station: Jesus dies on the cross. Was there irony to be found in the fact that Jesus was a carpenter and they nailed him to two slats of wood? Could there also be something in this former church being now a night spot for people under twenty-one? Suffer the little children and all that jazz—

Stop.

Mary Magdalene, at the foot of Jesus' cross, had wept. Valerie Mastropietro, with much too to weep about, scoffed.

No no...someone else talking.

There she had sat in the booth, nothing to eat or drink on the table before her, forehead bent into a tiny, fingernail chewed hand, wondering why the coffeehouse had no air-conditioning. Sweat oozed out of the roots of her very black hair, slid down the side of her face, around her neck, and between her never developed breasts. She had not been consciously listening to the piano music, did not become aware of it until it suddenly stopped in the middle of a measure.

8

It was the interrupted count that snapped her attention to, and she looked in the direction of the piano player.

She saw him walking toward her.

She had escaped her house—propelled by boredom—escaping lonesomeness. But she did not seek company. She prayed he would keep walking (maybe he was just going to the bathroom), but he sat down beside her. She prepared herself to hear his best pick-up line, made up her mind to ignore him, turned her face the other way.

He never said a word. Sat there like a statue. Not a carved statue, but one smoothly molded, totally at ease. The longer he said nothing, the more uneasy she grew. Finally she could stand it no longer, gave in, and turned to speak to him. That is when the piano player stood up and returned to his piano, picking up on exactly the next beat and note as if there had been no interruption.

By the time he finished his set, she was so annoyed that she stalked over to him, planted herself beside his piano and demanded to know what he was trying to prove back there. He did not answer her, only took a pair of wire-framed eyeglasses from the top of his piano and looked at her through the lenses. Valerie squirmed. Her ill-timed, early puberty had never finished what it began, leaving her more than a little self-conscious, and she could feel his scrutiny on her tangled and curlicue hair, on her flat chest, on the ever so slight baby-like pot of her belly. She hurried away from him intimidated.

Yet she encountered him again immediately outside, where he leaned against the fender of a Saratoga Springs police car, smoked a cigarette. He introduced himself as Cornelius. She found herself shivering. As stuffy outside as it had been inside, and she was cold. That was enough of an upset to her. But she found herself, also, offering him a ride home as he looked, leaning there against the police car, very much a waif. When he agreed to let her take him home, she led the way to her Toyota with a sickness in her gut at the anticipation in her heartbeat. When he told her, as she started the motor, that home for him was way down in Albany, all palpitations ceased. She wanted to throw him out of the car, if for no other reason but that he didn't forewarn her that he lived so far away. But he sat so placidly in his seat that she found herself heading down the Northway to the city of Albany.

She had grown up in nice—probably too comfortable—financial straits, and the part of Albany Cornelius lived in was like nothing Valerie had ever witnessed before. Sagging tenements and it would seem blown out warehouses surrounded on all sides. She did not want to insult a guy she had barely met, so she said nothing, but she guessed her horror showed on her face because he said to her: "You want to see the city? We'll take a little tour."

Valerie wanted to say most imperatively that no she did not want to see any more of Albany than she was presently seeing, that this was certainly an eyeful, but she did as he told her and he took her down...

Down beyond the wide, well lighted pavements of Madison Avenue, beneath the bridge of concrete steps which spanned the street and connected the New York State Museum on one side to the Empire State Plaza on the other, down into an ash pit, down into a black hole. And there were neighborhoods here. Houses crammed between one another on a steep hill, like books nobody wants to read anymore on a dusty, warping shelf.

"People live here? In these—houses?"

"They fight for the leases."

She did not want any more, she wanted to get out, but the narrow streets led only down. There was no escaping it.

Blackness and stillness banged on the hood and roof of the car.

"Turn left," Cornelius said.

The headlights swung around a corner and pulled the Toyota into an alley. About fifty yards ahead, the high beams fell on the cracked face of a brick wall. There were garbage cans overflowing, and crumpled beside one of the piles was what looked like a cat—its stomach chewed open by something. The spilled guts were dried like stuffing croutons.

"Oh my gosh! Cornelius, this is just a dead end, I think you made a wrong turn."

"You made the turn," he said.

She pressed the brake, put in the clutch, anxiously shifted to reverse.

The headlights, dashboard lights, motor all went off at once.

Cornelius sat calmly in his seat.

Valerie turned the key and nothing happened. There was a trace of panic in her voice as she said, "What's happened?" She clicked the headlight switch—on, off, on. The action became frantic.

"We'll have to get out and fix it," he said.

"It's dark," she said slowly. "I don't want to get out of the car."

"Either we try to fix it, or we walk back," he told her.

"Let's fix it."

Cornelius got out of the car. Valerie stayed put. She thought the alley was getting darker, but that had to be her imagination. She began to chew on her fingernail. A sudden tap on the side window made her bite too hard. She tasted blood.

Cornelius was at the side of the car. When she opened the window a crack, he said, "Pop the hood." She reached down with one hand, sucking on the bleeding finger of the other, and groped for the hood release.

"I need your help," he said.

"Out there?" she said with her finger in her mouth. But he did not answer because he had gone to the front of the car. Valerie opened the door reluctantly, put one sandaled foot timorously on the gravel. She worried because she could not see where she stepped. "Can you see what's the matter?" she asked him. Standing beside him, she could see only a black maw where she knew her engine was. She ought to carry a flash light in the car. A responsible person would have one.

Behind them, she knew, was the dead cat. She couldn't see it, but she knew it was there, and she could not tell if that stench was from the garbage or from the carcass.

It's garbage—just, just regular garbage like yours at home. Everybody has garbage.

Cornelius had his hands in the maw.

Valerie could see nothing. Some help she could be. She looked up at the sky. All the stars up there amazed her. Little by little her guard disintegrated, and she found her attentions wandering to adventure, the pace of her heart quickening. She and Cornelius were so far from the city lights that the stars had full bid. It was like sitting outside in her garden at home. It was beautiful...

Some *thing* ran across her feet. She felt its claws step on her toes.

Valerie leapt onto the fender. Cornelius dropped the hood at the same instant, and the bang drew out the scream stuck in her throat. She was sobbing when they got back into the car.

"Get me out of here. I hate this place. I don't know why you wanted to come here even. Get me out."

"Why don't you start the car?"

It started on the first turn. Her rear fender glanced a garbage can on the way out. She hunched over the steering wheel, hands gripping the rim so tightly that her knuckles whitened. She ran a red light.

"How can people live in a place like that?" She shuddered.

"Ever see a rat in a Skinner box?"

"In a what?"

"Electrify the floor and after a while the rat simply lays there and takes it."

Valerie looked at him puzzled. She asked if he believed in God, but he only asked in return if she meant to blame God for the places people lived. Then he directed her to Hamilton Street, where he lived, as if no further talk on the old matter should follow. The houses in his neighborhood were old and weathered, but nothing close to the likeness of the ones they had just visited. This was all a new world. Her exposure to the seedier sides of life was selective, almost elitist: high school kids who owned cars, who spent their easy money on liquor, dope, fancy ways to get into a girl's pants (or, as had been her target, into a boy's pants). Cracked stairwells and rats scampering across her toes had been filtered out. If ever there was a place for rebirth, to begin functioning in a new way, this tenement building, this city, where she was off balance, clumsy, toddling, was that place.

That is why she had come.

"Do you like it this way?" she asked Cornelius.

"What way is that?"

"Living here by yourself," she said.

"The rats and the cockroaches keep me company."

"You have rats?" She stood up from the table and shivered as she relived once more those little paws on her toes.

"Willard and Ben." He opened the window. "Want to step out onto the verandah?"

"You have a verandah?"

"It's a little cooler out here." He climbed out the window. Valerie bent through the frame and followed with her root beer. The steel slats of the platform were solid underfoot after the spongy feel of the floorboards inside. She paused with her body crouched in the window frame until her eyes adjusted to the dark. She thought she heard a sound in the alley below.

"Are there rats out here, too?"

"They have to be home at nine o'clock."

Valerie tentatively leaned against the rusted guardrail. "How do you get all the way up to Saratoga? It's a long way."

"You learn how to get around without a car."

"Life would be easier with a car."

"I have one."

"Why don't you drive it?"

"It has a burned out starter," he replied.

"That can be fixed."

"And bald tires and a broken spring, no windshield wipers and a very old muffler."

"How could you let so much go wrong with your car?"

"I bought it that way."

"You bought a car in that condition?" She fought a laugh.

"It cost a hundred dollars," he said as if proud of a good deal.

"Are you going to fix it up?" she asked, looking across at someone's laundry hanging in the night.

"Did the person who does your hair tell you that your nose would be less noticeable with that style?"

"What do you mean?" She was indeed aware of her nose, and now he had to go and mention it, making this simply a complete evening. "Who are you to make comments like that?" she demanded. "I don't even know you." As if he had said nothing, Cornelius began to scrape rust off the guardrail with his fingernail. "I have to go," Valerie decided. Cornelius scraped away without looking at her.

She climbed back through the window into his apartment, banging her head on the raised sash. She left the root beer on the table and slammed the door. Down in the car she pretended to wipe sweat from her nose as she measured its size with her fingers.

But...

In spite of that insult, she did go back to the coffeehouse the following night. All day long she told herself that this was not her plan, and when she lay down to take a nap at five-thirty, tired from being up so late on her first venture out, she said, "If I wake up, I wake up." However, she awoke with a start, confused to find herself lying on her bedspread in her bra and panties cradling a stuffed white elephant against her brown belly. Then her first clear thought bolted to the clock and the time. She claimed to herself that sleeping the evening away was unconstructive, and that was the reason she chose to go out. Walking into the smoky coffeehouse, greeted by the smells of coffee and the sounds of the piano, Valerie knew that lying to herself was a good way to end up exactly where she had been—

...where she was petrified of finding herself once more.

She hated the clothes she was wearing tonight. This peach colored blouse and printed jumper were from eighth grade. She felt she had been caught last night looking her worst in those baggy and patched blue jeans and that oversized Skidmore College t-shirt. She did not wish to appear that way a second time, but all of her clothes had grown sinister. They were too closely aligned with her days in high school. This was the only innocent outfit she owned, this outfit that underlined the fact that her body had never fully grown up.

She took a seat and listened to him play. His music was intricate—rarely with lyrics, the melodies holding her with bizarre effect. His music made her feel as she had not in a long time. It made her dream of...well, of love, and she believed in those dreams because the music made it seem likely.

Tonight when she walked up to him between sets, to offer him a ride home again, this time certain there would be no fighting with dubious expectations, he said to her, "Hi, Pinocchio."

"Please don't call me that."

He put a cigarette in his mouth but did not light it.

"That was a nice song you played," she told him diffidently. "They are all nice."

"What's the matter with you tonight, Pinocchio? Where's all that spitfire?"

"Don't call me Pinocchio."

He agreed to a ride home again, walked to her car

without smiling. She wished he would smile. He would only look at her as if he always knew exactly what she would do next. He even told a joke without smiling. He said: "Why is life like a penis?"

She admitted she did not know, and he said, "Because it's not how long it is, but what you do with it that makes people talk."

Everything would be less disturbing if he would just smile.

On the way down the Northway, Cornelius leaned into the windshield and looked at the stars. "The light from those stars is thirty years old," he said. "It takes the light from a star thirty years to get to the earth. That is thirty year old starlight we're looking at."

"I never thought of that," she said.

"How old are you?"

"Me? I'm nineteen, going on twenty."

"Everyone who is nineteen is going on twenty," he said. "That light left the stars eleven years before you were born."

Valerie thought about the starlight exploding away from its berth, embarking on its voyage across space, traveling still and only a third of the way along on the day she was born, whooshing through the essence of nothing (her ears burned with a sound like a wind tunnel) as her body hit puberty too early for anyone's own good and then balked and went the other way—as she lived out her shameful and stupid adolescence, and as she suffered the indelible consequences of those years. The starlight had sailed on, undisturbed. And now she drove down a highway and admired, when she ought to resent, the beauty of those stars: those stars which weren't even there anymore.

Tonight she found his mud-hole apartment just as hot as last, but the dishes had been done, the laundry hidden if not washed—as if Cornelius had known that she would be coming back.

She hovered near the open door, the hem of her

jumper too far above her knees with a six-year-old style, and she said, "It's kind of late, maybe I should get myself home now."

"You can't go home yet, Pinnoke." He turned to the kitchen.

"Why can't I go home yet?" she asked, finding herself coquettishly posed in the kitchen doorframe.

"Here's a root beer. But it isn't cold." He took the bottle out of the cabinet.

"Why don't you put it in your refrigerator?" Valerie said.

"It's broken."

She opened the refrigerator with idle curiosity. Frost grew out around the rim of the freezer door like a tumor. "When was the last time you defrosted this!"

"Defrost?"

"No wonder it doesn't work. Cornelius, all the coils are covered."

"It was like that when I moved in." He held the root beer out to her.

She smiled at him over the mouth of the bottle.

They went out of the kitchen. She sat at the wooden table; he sat on the floor by the window. Valerie's eyes burned for sleep. He began to work at something. She tried to see what it was, but his body blocked his hands.

"Have you ever thought this would probably be a nice apartment if you decorated it a little?"

"Decorated it?"

"Yeah. Like if you put up new wallpaper, had a carpet, maybe some plants, for example."

"Why should I do that?"

"To make it nicer to live in."

"I don't know how long I'm going to be living here," he smirked. "I would never live here at all if I could help it. I live as close as I can to wherever I can work. And I wouldn't waste my time in a dump like this if I didn't have to move around all the time. Nomads don't hang pictures on the walls."

"No, I guess not." She wandered around the room, feeling abashed. All she wanted to do now was go home and go to sleep.

He had been working on pouring little pinches of dope into papers and rolling several joints. She did not know if he intended they would both smoke

(christ i would love to get high again)

and she contracted instant nausea. Her vision turned to a rippling pool. Blood rushed in her ears. The apartment see-sawed and reeled and teetered.

"Bathroom," she gasped.

He pointed.

The floor rotated, Cornelius veered out of sight, the bathroom door swayed toward her.

Inside the bathroom she flung herself on the floor before the open toilet bowl. The urgency to vomit subsided. Panting, she sank against the radiator. Its edges dug into her back, but she did not move. She wanted to be sure she had completely recovered before going back out there. When she finally made a move to get up, she steadied herself with hands braced on the rim of the toilet. In the water she saw her reflection—more of a shadow, not detailed, a bluish suggestion of her features...

...there was a frantic banging on the door. The tall, narrow mirror jarred from its mounts and folded to the floor, its three folds shattering into a million fragments. Her reflection—the image of a sallow and horrified little body—broke into pieces inside the mirror. But the reflections were not falling as fast as the chunks of mirror. The mirror hit the floor as g=ma dictates, but the images fell more slowly. Slow motion superimposed on normal speed action.

Valerie had blood on her hands and it ran down her wrists, dripped from her elbows. It hit the floor in heavy drops and began to pulsate as if still within veins. She checked herself for cuts but it was not her blood. Still: banging on the door. Pounding. Kicking. Her high school friend George Miller screaming for her to open up.

A baby cried from somewhere, a muffled, amorphous cry.

Valerie wiped her hands on the pink curtains, got most of the blood off. She staggered to the sink, leaned on the marble of the counter. She left her fingerprints in blood. In the mirror over the sink her eyes had turned to cadaverous holes. She averted her face. Her bare feet stepped gingerly to avoid the broken glass on the floor.

The baby wailed.

Valerie opened the shower stall and turned on the water. It sprayed over her hands and arms, washing red down the drain. She yanked the curtains from the rod and threw them into the shower's stream. Her skin glistened with sweat as heat and steam rolled about the room. The mirror on the wall fogged. The little bits of mirror on the floor fogged. The window fogged. Good: no one would be able to look in and see her in this hideous state. And more importantly, the mirrors would not be able to flaunt her hideousness back at herself. George was just outside the door, still in a rage, and she did not want him to see her like this either...

...She looked away from the toilet bowl. She turned on the tap and touched her lips to a handful of water, returned to Cornelius looking like a crumpled piece of newsprint.

"I'm really sorry," Valerie said. "I just suddenly didn't feel very good."

"Do you want to lay down?"

"I don't know what happened..."

Cornelius led her by the hand into his bedroom. Valerie collapsed on the bed. He brushed her sweaty hair away from her face, and then he went to the bathroom to wet a cloth for her forehead.

"You know you haven't got any sheets on your bed?" Valerie said weakly.

"You're puking, and you're worried about sheets on

my bed? I don't know about you, Pinnoke."

"Don't call me that," she whispered, her eyes closed.

Cornelius held her cold hand. He smoothed the wrinkles in her jumper. His eyes moved up and down the short length of her figure. Her bare feet were as small as a child's and smooth like ebony wood. Around her left ankle was a finely braided gold chain.

"Maybe if you had company," she said sleepily. "A pet maybe..."

She did fall asleep, without realizing, and when she awoke the bedroom was full of daylight. Cornelius had fallen asleep on the floor—it looked accidental.

Valerie had spent the entire night here.

She leaped off the bed and ran into the living room to find her shoes. She could not, and she did not want to be here when he woke up so she left without them. She ran out of the apartment and all the way down the stairs. His apartment door had been wide open all night and she left it that way.

It was almost noon when she reached home. She went upstairs into her bedroom, took off her jumper. As she undressed to take a shower she looked at the lacey valances on her windows, at the pastel walls, and she walked across the floor feeling the soft pile of the carpet with her toes. She set right the white elephant which last night she had tossed carelessly aside, and she smoothed out her bed spread. For a moment she stood by the window, looked out over her garden, at the hedges and rose bushes, at the trellises and stone benches. Valerie realized what an alarmingly removed from the world girl's bedroom this was. Like her body, it had never stopped holding onto its own childhood.

She walked out to the hall and took a towel from inside the linen closet. Inside the bathroom, all at once, it seemed to her—it was only a tingle of a feeling, barely perceptible, certainly not a memory—something *not good* had happened to her once in this bathroom. In a harmless suburban bathroom with bright walls and

20

gleaming marble counters around smooth pink porcelain sinks, with patterned curtains forming a tasseled arch around the window, in a little room where the morning's light flooded through the nine square panes of glass and threw sunny patchwork on the floor, a nightmare had happened.

Valerie stood square in front of the mirror on the door. She took a step forward, leaned toward the reflection of her searching face. She breathed on the mirror, touched it, and placed her palm on the palm of her image. She pressed against the mirror with her body. Her little breasts flattened against the little breasts of her reflection. Thighs against thighs, knees to knees, toes to toes. Valerie looked into the blackness of her irises.

Only a flash and it would not return.

She stepped away from the door, turned on the shower, got into the stall.

There was no kidding herself about why she went back a third time to the coffeehouse she had not been to since it was a church. She looked forward to seeing Cornelius again. She thought about his hand last night guiding her to where she could lie down. He was actually very sensitive behind those intimidating glasses.

She was forced for lack of choice to wear the same jumper tonight, but at least she wore a different shirt; and she decided to test a little perfume on Cornelius tonight. She bounded to her car, drove to the coffeehouse, parked, hurried from the lot to the front door. She could feel her scent following her through the thick warm air. Her fingers wrapped around the brass doorknob and her arm tugged open the heavy door.

But Cornelius was not playing.

Instead there was another fellow, with a beard darker than his hair, seated on a stool and playing an acoustic twelve string, singing with a good voice. The piano had been rolled off the dais and put away.

Valerie sniffed her perfume as water came to her eyes. Maybe Cornelius would play after this guy. Perhaps two musicians shared the bill here each night. Quite possible, for she had not been here to catch the early part of either last night or the one before. But the piano had been rolled off the dais and put away.

The guitar player told jokes between songs.

Why hadn't Cornelius told her that he would not be working here any more? The chance had come up: last night, when he had talked about being a nomad. He ought to have said: "By the way, tomorrow don't bother to come hear me play because I won't be there." It would have been polite.

So what now? Now that the piano had been rolled off the dais and put away? Cornelius couldn't call her—he did not even know her last name.

Valerie stood there and chewed on her nails. The guitar player took a break. Then he came back and he played some more, told some more jokes. His jokes were not funny, they were stupid. They filled time while he put on a capo or tuned a string. People in the coffeehouse laughed to be polite, but Valerie didn't feel particularly polite. Who was this guy anyway? And why did he play all night long instead of yielding to a piano player?

A big piece of her nail broke off between her teeth. Valerie went home and went to bed.

Early the next morning she drove to Albany and found Cornelius' neighborhood on her own. She parked and got out of the car. As she cornered her own fender, she noticed that the car she had pulled in behind was a very beat up, gold Rambler from the late 60s—in better shape, it might be collectible for the people who liked those cars. It leaned into the curb like a bike on a kickstand. This was Cornelius' derelict car to be sure. She chuckled at the wreck, paused to lean her face against the side window for a look inside. It was not all that bad. The interior looked musty from being long enclosed, but it didn't look as terrible as she had imagined.

Yet he had bought a car that could not run.

Valerie laughed again—not at Cornelius, but at the

winsome little wreck.

She was barefoot—her shoes were still up in his place—as she climbed the front steps to the house. She went inside, wished the front door did not squeak so as it closed, slowly, very slowly, on a spring, and she climbed the three flights of rickety stairs, wary of wood splinters, to his battered door.

She knocked. The sound rattled up and down in the stairwell. What if people in the other apartments heard and thought someone was at *their* doors? What if they stuck their heads out?

Cornelius' door did not open.

Tentatively, more quietly, Valerie knocked again.

"Cornelius?" she said to the door. "Cornelius, it's Pinocchio."

All this way, braving this quasi slum on her own, thinking to surprise him, and he was out. Valerie felt foolish. She felt so foolish that she did not wait, nor did she go away with intent to return. She simply went away.

She paid no attention, with her foot to the floor, as the car flew up the Northway at one hundred miles an hour. She missed her Saratoga exit, but came to in time to get off the highway at Lake Luzerne, where her family kept a summer house.

The tiny cove that held the camp was quiet. The morning sun shone on the smooth water, and the raft out there in the middle seemed to be resting on a smooth, polished surface, not floating. Valerie stood beside her car, her little toes wrapped around the root of a tree. The scene was strange to her after being away for a year—as though she were seeing for the first time those two trees forming a *V*, that rock sloping into the water, that sandbar at the mouth of the cove. For years this had been Valerie's favorite place, summers her favorite time of year because she did not have to go to school and compare her body to her classmates. Then this place, like everything else out of the old days, had turned on her. She used to spend her days lolling naked out on the raft, letting the sun bake the pigment of her skin to the color of cream soda.

Tearing herself away, she walked toward the steps of the porch. Valerie liked the feel of pitch between her toes, and she liked the smell of pine in the air. Maybe she could convince herself that Cornelius had not really existed.

Chapter 2

Cornelius would walk to the corner of Hamilton and Lark, turn right and walk all the way to Clinton, follow Clinton up to Quail, and eventually he would come to a place where for a hundred or so rising and falling acres of trees and sand, with a pond and cattails to boot, the city would disappear. It wasn't a park—the city's main park was on the other side of town—it was more like a huge vacant lot with a view, just south of an old railroad yard. But to him, it was park-*like*.

He took a walk here every day, regardless of weather. It took about forty-five minutes to reach, and he left a trail of cigarette butts like Hansel and Gretel.

Cornelius hated cigarettes. They smelled horrendous, made him sick—even after eleven years of steady inhaling. But tobacco had an idiosyncratic effect on him. It clouded his mind, like a steady drunk. Not enough for anyone to be the wiser, but just enough to keep him like normal folks.

During times when he was really bad, he smoked pot. That was like a booster for him. Usually the tobacco did what he needed.

His first clairvoyance had been in gym class when he was ten years old. They were running the 440. Bobby Chrighton, who would have grown into a very fine athlete, popped a hamstring and fell forward, searing the skin off the left side of his face. And he died. No one would have thought it would be a fatal accident. A bad scar on his face, sure, and maybe he would not be able to run again, but—

And no one believes you when you say *I knew it was all going to happen. Just before he went down—I am the one who knew.* So Cornelius had not said one word.

Sometimes while watching Bugs Bunny cartoons, Cornelius had known what was in store for Elmer Fudd before it happened. But perhaps cartoon scripts were predicable, even for a small boy.

And people speak of prodigies so perhaps Cornelius figuring out the entire "Let's Play Piano" series in one week was not so strange. The books had been incidental to him. Music theory simply felt right, and the piano keyboard seemed to him to have the theory written all over it.

But there were other things: Knowing he had a step father even before his parents sat him down to say his real father had died in a plane crash before Cornelius' birth; knowing what a test would ask before the teacher drew it up; being able to score 800 on the SAT exam without giving a single question a moment's thought.

Yet he kept silent about it. He had to keep silent because people always say, "I had a feeling that would happen." It is only a figure of speech.

Cornelius climbed a hill. He could see the South Mall towers rising above the trees. He sat down and lit a cigarette. On ground level the air was close and hot, but up here on the precipice there was a breeze blowing his thin hair around.

He had thought that girl in his tenth grade math class had been the one. He had been waiting for her all those years. Waiting as one does for a malignancy to progress, with prayers that it would not happen. He had examined the face of every girl he passed by, strangers on the street. And then came that girl in his math class. Ellen had been her name. Pretty. He did not want her to be pretty. If it were someone ugly he might not feel the pity of it, or the shame.

But Ellen was pretty, and shy, little, and the way she carried her books into class made him sweat with dread.

So he tried to stay away from her. He knew where her locker was and he never went down that corridor. He kept the width of the classroom between himself and her. Then one day he was shut inside one of the practice rooms, playing something by Beethoven, and the door opened a crack.

"Excuse me," Ellen said timidly. "It was just so beautiful I had to see who was playing."

"Cornelius Prince," he said.

"How long have you been playing?"

"About half an hour."

"I mean in your life," Ellen said.

"My brother put a piano in my bassinette and said *play.*"

"Can I listen some more?" She asked as though she were perhaps asking audience of the Pope.

Cornelius turned back to the keyboard.

She was *not* the one.

He knew that—as soon as she had opened the door. Ellen was not the one and the waiting, then, must drag on.

At the end of his senior year he formed a band. Cornelius, a guy named Raj Hernandez, and a girl named Patti Winson called themselves Milagro Beanfield War (no "The"). Patti played bass. Cornelius thought she was the one. He believed it for a long time. All the while the band was doing concerts in local junior high schools, Cornelius was concocting schemes to escape Patti—let *her* escape. Whatever he came up with seemed to be undermined, and he realized he could never avoid her fate.

Milagro Beanfield War played once at a parochial school and was not allowed to finish the concert. Shortly after that incident, the public school principals became anxious too, and the school board forced the band to break up. Cornelius never saw Patti Winson again.

Now, today, he flopped backwards on the top of the hill and stared up at the sky. He watched the smoke from his cigarette circle before his eyes as his stomach hurt.

Here she was. No guess work involved, and all the tobacco and pot growing on God's brown earth could not turn it away. He knew even as he took that job in the coffeehouse. He knew what night she would walk in. He knew every thing about her before he knew how she would look.

Then he had seen her black eyes and that had sealed it.

He protested this. This girl, the one, had been trying so hard. So many times she had almost *given up*. She had come this far through ugly times; now she was given to hope. It was not fair to make it her. This girl, *she* would continue to try, and she would almost make it too—*almost*. Weren't victims supposed to be without blemish? Like Ellen. Ellen had been the more likely choice.

Who said anything about choice? He could see this was all laid out.

Chapter 3

She could not sleep in the summer house. It seemed emptier than home, and its unfamiliar emptiness made every thump and settling floorboard something to investigate, to fear.

So she gave in to a sleepless night, left her bedroom for the hall. She recalled that the sound of the refrigerator downstairs ought to be audible from here. This was a sound which for most of her life she had taken for granted, but now, coming here after such a peculiar interim to spend her first night alone at the lake, she found the house's silence as disconcerting as she found Cornelius'.

She began to hum to herself. No tune, she thought, just a noise to pacify, and then she realized it was the melody written out in such meticulous handwriting that she had seen on Cornelius' table. What had she come to the lake to do, for crying out loud?

(yes please someone cry out loud)

"Find something else to sing."

Walking down the stairs, one step at a time, slowly, as if there might be something dreadful at the bottom, she unconsciously toyed with the hem of her nightgown, wrung it, almost tore it.

"I never considered this house as large."

Upon saying that, Valerie realized she was talking to herself in *Italian*—a language reserved, by unspoken consensus in her family, to convey import, or displeasure, or doom. It was the language which, as a child, she was always scolded in; the language her Papa had once used to inform her that she was henceforth alone with her mistakes, that he and her Mama could no longer back her, as if they ever truly had.

"Maybe I am becoming crazy."

She went into the kitchen to see why the refrigerator was not running. If she opened the door, that would start the motor. She looked inside at shelves filled with abandoned leftovers. Her Mama and Papa had been here last about a month ago. The milk was surely sour by now, the vegetables were softening, and the covered bowl of sauce looked far from appetizing.

Valerie ripped a can of soda from the plastic ring of the six pack. She popped open the top and took a drink. It was flat. She closed the refrigerator door but the motor did not start. She walked out of the kitchen.

Here was lonesomeness again. Why is it that when you fight hard against something it only tightens, like a serpent, its hold?

She unlocked the front door and went outside. She sat on the porch rail with her soda and noticed her knees and hands. They were shaking. She looked back into the house, expecting one big bump in the night to sneak up on her.

And then suddenly she hopped from the porch rail to the ground, headed for the water. It was certainly still hot enough for swimming, and what else was there to do in the middle of the night?

Well...drown while swimming alone...

God help me, I am becoming crazy.

As she walked to the end of the dock her feet thudded on the boards and the slosh of waves underneath seemed to be caused by her footfalls. She felt the grittiness of the deck on the skin of her soles. She put her soda can down, lifted her nightgown up over her head and let it fall, sat on the edge of the dock, picked up her drink again. She rested the can between her knees and stared out at the mouth of the cove for a while. The moonlight was tarnished. It made the water like silk.

Valerie slid off the dock into the water. The cool waves lapped around her hips. The feeling made her giggle. She tried self-consciously to stifle it as she walked, fingers sieving water over her shoulders and down her back.

Holding the soda can straight up in the air, she swam on her back to the raft. She eyed the can through her splashes. The moonlight, somehow, made it look like a cardboard cutout against the starry sky.

She reached the ladder, grabbed hold of a rung. She set the can on the raft, then climbed out of the water, sat and cradled the can with her knees again.

As she sat on the raft, the palms of her hands and the soles of her feet, her fingernails, and her forehead glowed like a vision.

Valerie had redeemed her life. And she had spent a long time in that hospital and halfway house trying to decide what she wanted to exchange her soul *for*. She had spent a year, a whole year, knowing that she was better, but afraid. Now she was pretty sure she could be okay. No one again would ever make her do things she did not want to do.

Now she wanted Cornelius to be special. She knew that he would be, because it was a matter of her self respect. Yet he had disappeared without telling her. He had excited her hopes, and had then apparently taken the liberty to owe her ... nothing. Surely people, who live in the same world, must owe each other *something*.

Birds were chirping in the trees around the cove. It was closer to sunup than Valerie had thought. She gazed into the black water, and then she slipped herself into it, swam to the dock. Halfway in, she let go of the soda can. Half full, it floated like a buoy. The splashes of her wake upturned it, and it eventually sank.

She climbed onto the dock. Not quite ready to go in yet, she sat on the edge with her legs in the water. Her body was relaxed and tingling from the swim. She closed her eyes for a moment, felt a drop of water slide down her breast and hang on her nipple.

When she opened her eyes George Miller was standing on the land spit, watching her. Valerie scrambled for her nightgown, smashing her shin painfully as she twisted to reach behind herself. She crushed the nightgown to the front of her body. George was gone. Only a tree with bark a little different in color from the others remained where he had stood. Valerie tried to sigh, but it came out as a whimper.

She stood painfully, rubbed her shin. The skin was broken. She put on her nightgown and limped into the house. In the bathroom, as she put a bandage on her cut, she realized her thoughts were still coming in Italian, as she wished she had gone to Philadelphia with her parents.

The sun had risen, and Valerie made herself a cup of coffee. She made the coffee and watched the ripples on its black surface vibrate from the now running refrigerator motor. Once the coffee was cold, she took the cup to the sink, emptied it down the drain.

Today would be too hot. It was already. She hated summer for days like these. What she was sure to want today was a nice, cool air-conditioned retreat.

She could go shopping. She had been wanting to do that for a long time, to get new clothes to replace the ones from the old days. But she would have to think for that, and she did not want to think. She wanted something more passive.

A movie perhaps. People would not go to the movies on a day like this. They would all be at the beach. Valerie could buy popcorn and sit by herself without feeling funny about it. She could sink into the chair and forget that her shin hurt, forget everything. That was a terrific idea. She would find a real tear jerking movie. Something she could take a box of tissues to and use every one. That would be fun.

She tried to get the local movie schedule and showtimes on her cell phone but couldn't get a signal.

So she'd have to do it the old-fashioned way. She would buy a newspaper at Mr. Feeney's store and look in it.

"Good day, Mr. Feeney," Valerie said as she walked into the store. (Italian, still.) Mr. Feeney looked balder than she remembered him.

"Valerie Mastropietro! How are you? Haven't seen you around in a long time!"

"How's business?" Valerie said as she searched around the rearranged store for facial tissues.

"Heard you were pretty sick a while back," Mr. Feeney said. "Feelin' better now, I hope."

Something like fear stabbed Valerie's stomach when he mentioned the "illness." She hid herself behind the shelves of tea and coffee as she answered: "Much better."(In English.) She tried to think if there was anything else she needed as long as she was here.

"Still have boys swarming around you?" Feeney smiled. He reached behind himself reflexively to the cigarette rack as Valerie put the box of tissues on the counter.

"No cigarettes," she said almost rudely. She did not want to be in this store any longer. "Give me a pack of gum. And I want to get the newspaper."

Feeney's hand moved from the cigarettes to the gum. "And no boys either?" he said almost with disappointment.

"One boy," Valerie said evasively, wondering if counting Cornelius just to please Mr. Feeney was fair.

"Only one?" the proprietor's eyebrows touched his bare scalp in surprise. "Looks like somebody's growing up."

Valerie was looking at the door. "Happens even to the worst of us."

The store owner rang up Valerie's purchase on the register, took her money and made change. "Just pick up the paper there on your way out," he said. "Stop in again soon, Valerie. How come you let nearly two summers go by without me seeing you? Must be that boy, huh?"

Valerie took a paper from the stack as she left. At the car she sighed, looked back through the screen door as though at an old photograph, at a time when life did appear now to have been in black and white. She opened the gum and folded the stick over once, then twice into a pad between her fingers, popped it into her mouth. She sat behind the steering wheel and unfolded the newspaper like a road map, looked for the movie ads.

On the Arts page was a photo of Cornelius Prince. And in the caption it said where he would be playing, featuring classical and fusion jazz piano. The place was in Albany. Valerie almost swallowed her gum. Cornelius *had* been telling her he wasn't going to be in Saratoga anymore. When he had talked about living near where he could find work. Valerie was supposed to have asked if he would now be working near Hamilton Street, but she had missed her most important line. Now she had been lucky enough to discover it while stupidly looking for a movie. She had to go instead to this place in Albany.

She noted the address and phone number, folded up the newspaper, and opened her cell phone. She quickly punched in the number and listened to it ring, until a recording answered. She closed the phone and forgot about her aching shin, and everything else.

She sped home to Saratoga, went shopping for a nice outfit, and then she sat all day hoping it would cool off enough so she would not look silly dressed up. After dinner, which she prepared as busy work but was too nervous to eat, she took a shower and dressed. She did without the perfume because maybe it was bad luck.

She looked nice. She looked grown *up*. A woman in a maroon see-through top with a matching spaghetti-string camisole beneath it, and a black bra showing ever so coyly through the layers, and sleek black pants and high heeled shoes. She sat as still as possible while waiting to go, afraid she would sweat into her new clothes.

She hoped that the place where Cornelius would be was near his neighborhood so she could find it. She prayed too that it would not be in those dreadful slums. She poked around the city for a while, got confused by some one-way streets, finally asked directions from someone. The building turned out to be very near Cornelius' house—right around the corner and down the street, in fact—no wonder he had taken that apartment. Pitched his tent right by the watering hole.

As she approached the door, she peeled the wet material of her new shirt away from her sweaty back and worried about it. Just before she went in, she had a funny feeling, as if—as if she did not belong here, like someone unwelcome trying to pass into an exclusive club. She hesitated, afraid that she would find a guitar player or someone else telling stupid jokes.

Then she had the door open and she recognized Cornelius' piano music. Valerie smiled with happy relief. Very self-conscious, she grabbed the first empty seat she saw.

A waiter who was haughtier than any barman ought to be asked if she wanted anything to drink. Valerie could tell he was waiting to pounce on her for proof of her age—hoping to catch this apparent minor red handed. Valerie asked for a root beer, which he said they did not have, so she said tonic water and the waiter went away.

She broke into a frightful sweat—as if all her pores had broken and poured blood down her skin, as she realized she had almost said, *"G and T."* She shifted nervously when the waiter brought the water and set down the familiar red napkin, and then the glass with swizzle stick and a cherry.

g and t

Her hand fumbled through her purse. For money. All

she found was the gum, which reminded her of Mr. Feeney reaching for her favorite brand—formerly favorite brand—of cigarettes. The waiter was gone by the time Valerie came up with the money, and she felt dumb holding out a five dollar bill to the people at the table beside hers.

She grabbed the drink and sniffed it.

gin and tonic

No, it was just the tonic.

Cornelius had been playing when she walked in—a song without words—and then he stopped playing that song and, with no introduction, he led into a second one. He could not possibly have known that Valerie was here. He had never looked her way, his glasses were as always laid on top of the piano and his eyes were on the keys. But this new song he struck up was about her: about her whole life, her past, her present, her thoughts, her disjointed fears and hopes—her entire rotten from the outside but promising to do better existence. Nothing was exaggerated. It was simply the BALLAD OF VALERIE MASTROPIETRO, and he may as well have swung an arc lamp spot around on her.

(but how could he have known?)

She took a sip of her drink to wet the inside of her mouth. The glass slipped from her fingers, struck the table once and broke into splinters. Everyone looked at her. She wanted to get up

(she had never told him a thing)

to get up and run out, but that would only have given these accusatory eyes the confirmation of guilt they were watching for. The tonic water had soaked the tablecloth, had leaked into the lap of her new pants, but Valerie sat there and watched the dark spot grow, looked at the pieces of glass, the swizzle stick and cherry laying in the middle of the mess, did not look for a waiter to clean it up.

(there is no way he could have known)

It was as if he had interviewed her on the porch of the

summer house that summer following it all, watched with her while skeletons and ghosts and monsters with drugs and dope and alcohol did exotic dances

exotic dances

exotic dances

exotic dances

Valerie had found that the best way to get through her grandfather's wake was to come thoroughly stoned. George Miller had come too. Before it all, they had smoked some really great weed and now she felt more like someone watching all of this on a TV tube than like a participant.

There were a lot of things Valerie detested about wakes. But two stuck out worst of all. One was that she had to wear a dress and that meant she had to wear underwear, which she hated. The second thing was all the old Italian farts who got off on bawling until their eyes and noses were red and puffy. There are all kinds of old jokes about the Irish being the only people who know how to throw a good wake. At an Irish wake the only ones not having a good time are maybe the widow and the corpse. For everyone else, it's the first the family has been together since the last wake, and it's a great time to catch up on gossip and how the Dodgers are doing. After the funeral, they all go out and get really blotto, drink a million toasts to the old guy they just put in the ground. But in Valerie's family the only one *having* a good time was the corpse because he did not have to look at all the soggy handkerchiefs. Anyhow, the whole idea of a wake was ridiculous to Valerie. Lay out the body with every embellishment but a glass display case (and Nano never looked like that a day in his life) then invite everyone: *"Hey! Come see my dead grandfather!"*

George had wandered away from her. She'd been trapped too close to the bier to escape consolations from relatives she did not recognize. Actually, the worst part about Nano being dead was that everyone in every part of the family would suggest, being polite, that Nana live with them now. Nano had died of cancer of the head and it had taken him the better part of two years to do it. During that time, Nana had managed just fine. Her husband finally free of suffering, she would have to find something to do with the part of her days formerly spent at Upstate Medical. But she would go on doing all right on her own.

Valerie was beginning to feel menstrual cramps. She wanted a cigarette but she knew she couldn't light up here in front of her dead grandfather and all the dearly beloved. She looked in the general direction of the door as if she could see through the crowd of darkly dressed people. (Her own dress was bright yellow—only dress she owned—and she gleamed like the midnight sun.) She pushed through her relatives and ducked out the back of the funeral home.

On the back stoop, looking at the garage she supposed housed the Hearse, she rummaged through her purse and found her pack of cigarettes. She watched the smoke circle up and get lost in the glare of the security lamp. George Miller pinched her rear end. Valerie squawked.

"I was just looking at my smoke going up to that lamp and thinking it was Nano's soul going up to God's face," she told him.

"Ha! That's funny," he said. "Gimme a drag." He sat down with her cigarette.

She sat down hard. "I'm getting my period. I can feel it. Tomorrow I'll wake up dripping."

"How do ya feel?"

"I just told you, ya moron." Valerie laughed. "Jesus, don't you listen to anything?"

"Not when you talk, lady." George puffed complacently, now in possession of the cigarette.

"Hey, that's my butt!"

George tapped the side of her buttocks: "No, this is your butt."

"Screw you," Valerie said, getting another cigarette.

"What I meant was, how is your buzz doin'? I got more

weed if you want."

"Thanks for coming, George. I never could have taken this alone. If I hear any more Italian tonight, I'll kill."

"You're my best friend for all time. How could I not be here?"

"Best friend and drinking buddy," she winked. "That's what I could use—a good drink!"

"You always need a drink."

"It's my crutch in life." Valerie laughed. She stomped on her cigarette, reached under her hem to tug on the elastic of her underpants, which were chafing her crotch. She glanced at her fingers for any signs of blood, and then she stood up. "C'mon," she said, "we gotta go pay some respect."

Inside the funeral parlor again, George knelt at the bier and Valerie watched him pretend to say prayers. Suddenly it hit her: what would happen if her grandfather sat up? Like what if a nerve in him still had some impulse hiding in it, and what if it now fired like a spring unwinding in a broken clock, and the body were to sit up? Wouldn't that turn all their red faces white? Maybe Nano would even say, "Good evening!" to them all. He might come back to life like Lazarus. Then they could all make like the Irish and go have a beer, except they would have one up on the Irish because *their* guest of honor would be raising toasts right along with them. The whole preposterous notion tickled Valerie pink. The more she tried to suppress her giggle, the more uncontrollable it became. A gasp of laughter burst through her fighting lips and Valerie hid her face in her hands. The rest of the family thought it was a sob.

Finally George yielded the kneeling bench to her. She knelt and looked at all the flowers piled around the casket like a florist's window. She could smell them all; they smelled just like spring.

Then she looked at her grandfather's waxen skin and through the lashes of the closed eyelids she was sure she could see the white eyeball. Her cramps were turning her legs to wood, and as she knelt before her Nano she *knew* that he was gone. She wished he would indeed sit up and say good evening; tell her that when he was a schoolboy in the Old Country he used to rise with the birds to get to school on time; pick her up at the dirty Syracuse bus terminal in the middle of a blizzard when she visited; come downstairs in the morning and rub his sandpaper face on her little-girl face. She hated that, the sandpaper feel, but the absence of it made her think about how his death meant a part of her life had ended too. Valerie thought of the cigarette smoke going up to God's face, and a great wind blowing from his cheeks and pushing her fast.

The gasp that blew out of her throat this time was a sob. More of them followed. She wanted everyone else to be gone. This was her moment: her funeral: she owned it and they had no right to trespass.

She felt George's hand on her shoulder. He whispered into her ear, "How's your buzz? Got something special for later."

...monsters with drugs and dope and alcohol did exotic dances out on the raft. Cornelius simply finished the ballad as if it were easy, as if it were fun. People clapped. He started another song. Valerie knew that everyone was looking at her, expecting her to do something, and not just sit there, pinned there like a dissected animal, or a rat in a Skinner box.

She stood and weaved her way through the tables, back stiff, to the piano, to his shoulder. She watched a minute, and then her hand darted between his as they played and slammed three times on the keyboard.

People looked up.

Valerie ran out of the bar. As soon as she reached home, she regretted running. She supposed it would have been better to stand up to him, to tell him that he had absolutely no right to rip her bare and put her on display. He should be told that he could not simply do with her as he pleased. As if her life were an insignificant joke.

40

Chapter 4

C ornelius went home that night, went to sleep, and he had this dream:

He waited at an airline gate as an airplane rolled shining white to the ramp from the taxiway. In a few minutes passengers were filing off the plane. Last to emerge was Valerie, from Bermuda, and Cornelius awoke screaming.

In the morning he did not remember the dream.

Chapter 5

By the following day Valerie had decided the best thing to do would be to ignore everything Cornelius did, as she had originally intended to do. After all, those people in that bar did not know who she was. Certainly none of them had gone home with a second thought of her as a person. Valerie sat in the living room, her mind made up to stay right there. Maybe she would never go to see Cornelius again.

If her Mama ever caught her in this room, she would kill. The living room was reserved for very important occasions, *just like their Italian language.* And what was worse, Valerie was eating a piece of toast and drinking coffee while sitting on the sofa.

She was wearing a yellow strapless sundress, bought yesterday. The house's air-conditioner kept it quite cold inside, and the lack of use the living room got made it colder still, but Valerie would not get up to adjust the thermostat. Along with her toast and coffee she had brought a crocheted blanket into the room. She reached for it now and wrapped it around her shoulders, curled up in the corner of the sofa. A sunbeam through a slot in the closed curtains shined through a glass candy dish on the coffee table—landed a rainbow on the table top that also looked like a smile. Valerie looked at the smile.

"Sure, this is all very funny," she said to the rainbow and stood up, stomping her feet. Her ankle turned in the blanket and down she went. She tried to get up but her legs were tangled in the folds of the blanket, and she struggled, making the situation worse. The more she tried to free herself the more complicated she made everything.

Finally she gave up and kept the blanket. She stumbled to the door, yanked it open, and left the house with the blanket trailing colorfully from her shoulders.

Furious by the time she reached Albany, she only got angrier when Cornelius opened his apartment door before she reached the top of the stairs, as if he were expecting her.

"Hi, Pinnoke," he said.

"Who do you think you are?"

"I paid for your water."

Valerie limped past him into the living room. Her twisted ankle was killing her. "The one thing I don't understand," her colorful cloaked back to him, "is how you *knew*. I never told you anything. You never told me anything not even that you weren't working in Saratoga anymore, so I made a big jerk out of myself. But that wasn't enough for you, was it? I only found you by accident. I was going to go to the movies. So you wrote a song and I sit in a bar, when I'm not even supposed to go into them, feeling like Roberta Flack!"

"I'm on my way to the supermarket for groceries," he said. "Do you want to come along?"

"I hate you," she informed him.

"Do you want to drive?" she asked as they walked down the steps to the sidewalk.

"Drive?" he said. "It's only a few blocks away. Don't high gas prices teach you anything?"

So they walked.

And as they walked, Cornelius lit a cigarette, puffed on it, began to whistle. He whistled only parts of songs.

Bits of "Grand Old Flag" and a puff on the cigarette, "In My Merry Oldsmobile" and another puff, "Melancholy Baby," "Down in the Valley," "Yankee Doodle," and "Bye, Bye, Blackbird."

The supermarket was very crowded. Lines curved away from checkout and clogged the mouths of the aisles, while cashiers in royal blue smocks frantically scanned items, trying to stay ahead. Nine registers going *boop boop boop boop*, all at once. The people in the lines did not seem to realize, or maybe care, how foolish they looked standing behind wire shopping carts. Half of them had cell phones at their heads. "Hey, guess where I am? ...What? *What?!*"

Valerie usually did the grocery shopping for her family, but she had never experienced a supermarket like this one before. The people here were the personification of the houses Cornelius had taken them to that first night. They were not like any sort of human being she had seen before. They appeared weary, drugged, sick on their feet. Not the common chubby housewife-in-hair curlers drudges—they were fat, bloated, wrapped in clothes bought probably at this store: cheap polyester stretch pants that showed off every ripple in their spherical rumps, molded hideously to their crotches. Or else they were spindly, with clothes that hung on their frames like scarecrows' rags. Women with gobs of make-up almost dripping. Valerie and Cornelius walked by something that smelled so strongly of something like wet leaves that she almost gagged. Two girls who may have been pretty, with wild hair, very red lips, and tube tops—their nipples black circles beneath the thin cloth—picked out meat.

All these people, pushing their carts mindlessly, picking from shelves, wandering around wide-eyed, they did not look like human beings but like reflections that shine back so grotesquely funny from a carnival mirror.

"It's the lead," Cornelius said to her.

"What?"

"The pipes in the houses are old," he explained. "The lead comes off and gets in the water, and this is what becomes of the people who drink it."

"Noooooooooo..."

"Sure it is. I'll be like that soon too."

"You will not!"

"Sure I will. In a while I'll be cutting the bottoms out of my shoes and sitting in Washington Park with spittle drooling into my shirt collars."

"Don't talk like that," Valerie said. "These people have been living in this slum all their lives. You only just moved here. And you'll be moving again as soon as you get a different job."

"Oh but it doesn't take long to affect you. I'm already losing my hair."

"Do you need bread?" she said unevenly as she took the cart from him and swung it toward the bread aisle.

After they got a loaf of bread, they went to the deli. Valerie had by this time taken charge of shopping because she said Cornelius didn't "know how to get good buys." No more mention was made of the lead in the plumbing.

The deli clerk who waited on them was an elfin looking fellow with blond hair and a reddish mustache, round wire glasses. He wore his paper hat with the pointed crown crushed flat, his tie was a little crooked. Valerie instructed Cornelius to observe how she bought cold cuts. Then she asked the clerk how the roast beef was today. He showed it to her, and she said it was too rare.

"I like it rare," Cornelius said.

"That's hardly cooked," she whispered back. "I've seen cows recover from worse cuts." To the clerk: "Can I see the baked ham?" And when he showed it to her, she asked for a pound of it, cut thin.

"I don't like ham, Pinnoke," Cornelius said.

"Why didn't you say so?"

When she finished with the deli, Valerie led Cornelius

to the meat section. She began looking at cuts of steak.

"Pinnoke, I can't afford steak," he protested.

"I have some money too," she replied.

When she at last announced that they were finished, her timidity of the other shoppers surmounted by the joy of shopping, they had bought enough food to last two or three people for weeks.

Cornelius said, "I think ya got carried away, Pinnoke."

"We can always freeze it, Corey."

"My freezer is ..."

"I'll defrost it. It'll take six years but I think it can be done."

The cashier rang up the order, Cornelius paid the total, and they left the store.

"I thought you said you had money."

"Do you see me with a purse? I'll pay you when we get back home. My purse is in my car."

"You owe me at least half of this."

"I'll pay for it all, Corey. I have a lot more money than you do."

"Pinnoke..."

"I was planning on it," she said. "Or I wouldn't have bought all this. Think I would have if I had thought you were gonna have to pay?"

"I will never eat this much," he said.

"It's not that much. It's just good food. I'll bet all you eat is junk food."

"I eat food food," he said. "How come I got stuck carrying *all these bags* and you only got *one*?"

"I'm little," she answered. "And cute."

They got back to his apartment and Valerie cleared a space on the kitchen counter to put the bags down. Cornelius lit a cigarette from a new pack and said: "How about my money?"

She reached into the patch pocket on her sundress and pulled out her car keys. "My purse is in the glove compartment." She tossed the keys and he caught them, went out. When he returned, Valerie had the refrigerator door open and her head inside.

"Know what, Corey? I'm really stupid."

"I'll buy that."

"No," she said, straightening, "really...I ought to have defrosted this thing *first.* I don't know what to do with all these perishables while this is defrosting. And it's such a hot day, too. Do you have a picnic cooler?"

"Oh yeah sure. Your purse is on the table. I'm not going to fumble through it. Ya know, this ain't Saratoga Springs – you should not leave your purse in the car."

"It was in the glove compartment," Valerie said.

"It was on the floor beneath the glove compartment."

"I must have left it there last night. I was so upset."

Cornelius left the kitchen and headed for the fire escape.

"Corey, what am I going to do with all these groceries?" Valerie said.

"It is your problem. I would not have bought all that stuff." He climbed out the window.

After a few moments, she joined him. She clumsily climbed out the window, like someone not used to going out fire escapes, like someone wary of hitting her head again on the sash. Cornelius was leaning on the rail, a cigarette in one hand, fingers of the other fiddling with a coin.

"Here's your money. And the extra dollar for my drink last night. I'm real sorry about what I did."

"What did you do with the loot?" Cornelius asked.

"Somehow I fit it all into that refrigerator. I decided to defrost it another time. When it's empty again, you'd better remember to do it."

Cornelius fumbled the coin and it fell. They heard it clink on the ground. They both looked into the alley after it.

"I can't get that," Cornelius said.

"What?"

"The coin tumbling across your knuckles. I've lost a lot of quarters into that alley."

"If we went down there, we could probably get rich," Valerie smiled.

"Nah, the lead people gobble them up."

They stood side by side leaning against the rail. Neither spoke. Cornelius smoked. Valerie noted this as the first they had been together when a pause felt good, when silence did not feel like anger or some other antagonism. She felt as if Cornelius might hold her hand if she put it there on the rail. She did not dare do that, of course.

"D'ya know what, Corey?" she finally spoke.

"What's that, Pinnoke?"

"You talked more today in the supermarket than you have in all the time since we met."

"When some crazy little chick is throwing all kinds of stuff you can't afford into a basket, you gotta say something."

"Corey. Do you like me?"

He tossed his cigarette into the alley. Valerie felt herself blush. She had gone too far. That question was as bad as trying to hold hands.

"Like you said, you're cute," Cornelius said laconically.

"Y-you don't have to worry about dinner," she stammered. "I've decided what we're having, so I will cook." And the old kind of pause fell like a lead balloon again. She looked into the alley trying to locate the fallen coin. Without another word, Cornelius ducked back inside. Valerie heard piano music.

She began to plan dinner. Would going all out and making a fancy meal be appropriate? She would make it good; perhaps simple but good would be best. In her full blossomed daydream there were candies and wine on the table. But there could be no wine.

Valerie listened to his music. Cornelius was by far too good to be playing in little coffeehouses and bars. As far as she knew, he had no other jobs. He lived off his piano. She ventured over to the window and spied in. There he was, playing away—he had forgotten about everything else. There was a wall around him whenever he sat at a keyboard. And he had talked to her in the supermarket because there was no piano there.

Valerie imagined the wall, if it were visible, would look like the staves on sheet music encircling Cornelius and his keyboard. Seeing in would be easy, you could look between the lines. However, from his side of it, there would be notes and chords and dotted quarter rests, accent marks, syncopation ties, triplets, crescendo lines, the words *moderato, accelerando, allegro, forte.* There would be three-four and four-four and six-eight time signatures.

There was so much obstructing his side of the lines that it was impossible to see out.

That evening, Valerie intended to go home. She did not want to go with Cornelius to listen to him play. She was afraid of that new song. He never invited her to go back. He did, however, once mention offhandedly that this was his last night at this gig. Maybe he had tossed that out as he had, thinking that she could make up her own mind. At any rate, she weighed it lightly, but then the more she thought about it the prospect of losing track of him a second time weighed heavier. She wanted to say: "Where will you be playing next?" but she knew he would only say something about nomads and walk off, leaving her. She gave in and decided to go.

He did not play her song.

And when he played his last note, when he said, "Good-night all," and put his glasses on, she knew he would never play it – not ever again for a long time.

As they walked side by side back to his apartment, Valerie's eyes were closing. She was very, very tired—way, way too tired to drive home. Today seemed the busiest day of the summer, the fullest day of her life, although they had only gone shopping, and eaten the food together.

Her head was a beehive of daydreams, almost full

dreams as she fought sleep. The dreams inside and the events outside traded places, acted like one another, and she was not certain when she found her hand in Cornelius' that it was real.

He carried her up the stairs, put her to bed in his room. He sat on the edge of the bed and watched her. He touched her gold anklet, hooked it with his index finger, tugged lightly once, let go. In the living room, he smoked a joint, then covered himself with her crocheted blanket and lay down on the floor.

He awoke early in the morning. Light intruded on his eye with overwhelming brightness. He went into the kitchen for something to eat. The packed refrigerator took him by surprise. He reached in, took out the orange juice, drank from the carton.

Sounds beneath his floor began to rise from the apartment downstairs. Sounds of life waking up down there. Things banging, voices singing in Spanish, footfalls on sagging floors. Cornelius sat at the table and looked through the floor. He watched with absent interest those other lives as they were in this building. Their individual lives were absurd, the collective life of the family meaningless. She waddled into the bathroom and ran rusty water to brush her teeth: something to do. Dishes rotted in her sink and food was undergoing metamorphosis to mold in her broken refrigerator, and she brushed her teeth for something to do. Her husband watched television. She wandered out of the bathroom, cursed him in Spanish. He barely grunted at her. She came over to him, sat on his lap. His hand slid under her rump, squeezed her fleshy buttocks, moved up the front of her ill-proportioned torso to plant itself on her breast. Yet his eyes never moved from the mesmerizing tube. She asked him questions. Her plump arms were around his neck in a loving gesture, but her tone was abusing, demoralizing. She seemed to bawl him out with her tongue, make love to him with her disgusting body. And he seemed oblivious to both.

Enter their daughter. A twig of a thing, the face of a dart team goalie, hair like a stale mop with wax caked in its head. She stood in the middle of the room with nothing on her emaciated body but a worn towel covering her immodestly. She watched her parents fondle each other as she smoked. Money for cigarettes, money for junk food, money for Tigerhead Ale, but no money (no ambition) to get out of this stinking existence.

That was all. Cornelius came out of the floorboards.

Valerie bounced out of the bedroom, vivacious, her face a thousand smiles and her black eyes all sparkles. She sang, "Hello, Corey!" Every one of her movements was like a sped up movie. She took her purse and slung it on her shoulder. She told him that in a dream, she had come up with the most wonderful idea and she'd be back later with a surprise. With that she was out the door.

She was away most of the day. Cornelius took his ritual walk, made a point to be back before her. Shortly after he got in, he heard her coming up the stairs. He opened the door. She smiled big and swung her purse around saying: "Surprise!"

"I knew it was going to be you."

"No, no—I mean what I got. It's down in the car. I'll get it." She ran down the stairs. The door at the bottom slammed, then it squealed open again and he heard her footsteps landing more heavily as they came back up. She appeared holding with both hands a great birdcage, and inside of it was an albino cockatiel.

"Where did you get that?" Cornelius asked.

Valerie set down the cage. "Whew—that is heavy. This is the surprise," she said.

"It is? What is it?"

"A bird. He talks."

"He does, huh?"

"Well, we have to teach him first. Do you like him?"

Cornelius knelt and examined the bird. It peered back at him blankly through the bars.

"I'll teach it to say 'nevermore.' Pinnoke, what am I

51

gonna do with a bird?"

"He can keep you company. A bird doesn't take up any room like a dog or a cat, so he won't be a bother. Oh please say you like him, Corey."

Cornelius opened the cage. The bird stepped from the perch to his finger. Valerie cowered when he stood up with the free bird. "You're not supposed to take him out of the cage," she said nervously. Then the bird hopped up Cornelius' arm and stopped on his shoulder. Valerie was afraid it might bite, and then she giggled. "Now you have to keep him."

"I plan on it, Pinnoke."

"What are you going to call him?"

Cornelius turned his head and looked the bird in the eye. The two considered each other. "Clancy," Cornelius concluded.

The bird peeped and took off from Cornelius' shoulder. It flew at Valerie. She shrieked and covered her head. It bypassed her harmlessly, circled the room, landed on the table.

"Put him back in the cage," Valerie implored.

"C'mere, bird." Cornelius lifted the cage and brought it to the bird. It poked its head through the open doorway, jumped inside. Cornelius closed the door and hooked it shut.

With the bird safely behind bars again, Valerie relaxed. She walked over to the table and looked into the cage, watched. "Hello, Clancy," she said to the bird.

"For a talking bird it is pretty quiet," Cornelius said.

So, too, did the two of them become quiet. Valerie walked to the window and gazed outside. She realized, standing in the direct light, that the lightweight fabric of her yellow dress was probably virtually transparent, that her girlish figure showed through. She remained motionless with her back to Cornelius. The room remained very still.

Then Valerie was surprised by the touch of Cornelius' hands on her shoulders. The first thing she did was stiffen up. Then she reached her own hands up to his. She rubbed her fingertips back and forth, feeling the grain of the hair on the backs of his hands, probing his palms. He lowered his arms to hold her waist, and Valerie felt herself nestled into the front of his body. She felt him place his chin on top of her head.

Neither one moved. Valerie felt peculiar. Her heart bammed in her chest. She was rigid all over. As if being touched and felt by so many could be the same as never being touched at all—this was her first sexual experience.

She turned within the ring of his arms and faced him, looked up into his face, for the first time noticed the color of his eyes.

They were blue.

Blue with threads of gold surrounding each pupil, looking like the coronas of little eclipsed suns.

Time stopped. All around the city people looked at their clocks and wondered; people on the streets paused and tapped their watches, held them up to their ears for some ticking sound, and they said, "That is odd, this watch has always kept good time." Wines stopped aging and fruit stopped ripening. Valerie and Cornelius kissed. She had to stand on her toes, and he had to lean down, and they kissed.

When the kiss broke, Valerie smiled and pressed her ear against his chest for his heartbeat. He stepped away abruptly and walked across the room, jerking everything back to normal. Valerie nearly fell on her ear. She watched him light a cigarette—a run-through of motions she was beginning to despise. He went into the kitchen, opened the refrigerator and, exhaling smoke into it, he pulled out an apple and bit it.

Valerie felt as if she had suddenly vanished. She tapped on her arm to verify that she had not. The feel of the kiss totally obliterated now, she wanted to clench her fists at him, to tighten her shoulders so he would know she was furious, and yell at him. She wanted to say: *Why do you toy with me all the time? Why do you tease me and trick me into being a fool?* But that is not what she said. What she said was: "I guess maybe I should start making dinner."

So she began, and while she worked, Cornelius played Beethoven's Sixth Symphony on the keyboard. Valerie felt cheated as she imagined that wall of staves. She imagined taking a huge pair of scissors to each line, snipping them all one by one until there was a hole big enough to get through. While she thought, she pulled rice and spaghetti and a can of tuna fish from the cupboards. She pulled cream of tartar, garlic salt, oregano, a can of sliced peaches and placed them one by one on the counter. She took out a bag of chocolate cookies, a box of sugar, a canister of salt, a sack of flour, ketchup and mustard, and a can of tomato soup, put all of that on the counter too. From the refrigerator she took the orange juice, a bottle of root beer, a head of lettuce, milk, three tomatoes, an apple, and she put all of that with the rest. She had the freezer door open and a half gallon of orange sherbet in her hand when she came to. She looked at all the food sitting on the counter like a bizarre and overcrowded game of chess, and she said:

"Oh."

She tried to put everything back, but this time it did not fit as it had the first time. There remained a pile of food on the counter, and the cupboards and refrigerator were packed. Valerie sighed. Cornelius' keyboard continued to play. This was all his fault. It seemed the only recourse would be to make dinner from what could not be put away.

So they had salad and soup, instant potatoes, and peanut butter sandwiches. For dessert they had the cookies and root beer. They sat cross-legged on the floor like it was a picnic. As they ate, Valerie kept sighing, and the leaves of her lettuce kept resisting the prongs of her fork.

Finally she asked Cornelius how in the world he had been able to write the song he'd played in the bar the other night. "I mean," she said, "I just don't know how you *knew*."

"I made it up."

"You did not."

"It was just a song, Pinnoke." If he was kidding, he bluffed very well.

Valerie set her peanut butter sandwich down. "I don't believe you."

She tapped her thighs in frustration as if she did not want to be told that the song was not, after all, about her. "You weren't thinking of me when you wrote it?"

"No."

She was sorry she brought it up again. Now she could feel her face very red, and she knew he was eyeing her peculiarly even though it did not show on his face (the way *nothing* showed on his face). "I have to go to the bathroom," she said. She did not have to go to the bathroom, but she did have to get out of there. She closed the door, flushed the toilet to make it sound real, then turned on the tap and just stood there watching the water go down the rusted mouth of the drain. She listened to the chugging sound in the pipes.

(lead in the plumbing)

She looked around the bathroom and her eyes stuck on the toilet. She was stricken with the same odd feeling she'd had in her own bathroom – the feeling that something had happened here. The same feeling, the same something. Or perhaps it was, rather, some sort of link—that this bathroom and hers had something in common, something beyond what bathrooms normally share.

She looked into the mirror at herself, and it was like watching Dr. Jekyll turn into Mr. Hyde: Her hair was long and pulled into a ponytail, her nails were bright red, and her body was decorated with jewelry. She reached around to the back of her sundress and unzipped it, all the way to the base of her spine. Then, holding it up in front maybe a little lower than she could have, she opened the bathroom door and went out to Cornelius.

"Corey," she said, "can you help me here? My zipper is stuck in back." She turned her bare back to him so he could see.

Cornelius tugged on the tab of the zipper but it would not move. "It's caught but good," he said.

Valerie looked over her shoulder in surprise. "You mean you can't get it?"

"I'm trying, Pinnoke. How did you do this anyway?" He tugged up on the zipper and Valerie thought she heard threads rip.

"Don't rip my dress! Here, let me try again." She had to reach back, which meant letting go of the front of her dress with one hand, and she couldn't believe it when she discovered that the zipper really was stuck. Somehow a ploy had turned itself into a genuine problem. Valerie gritted her teeth as she tugged, and she sighed with aggravation and went "tsk" a lot, but all to no avail. She had to use both hands in her struggle, and the front of her dress fell away from her breasts. She was glad he was behind her and could not see.

"*Oohh!*" she whined and stamped a foot.

"Don't get aggravated," Cornelius said.

"This is a brand new dress."

"We'll fix it. Take it off so we can see better what we're trying to accomplish here and I don't have to worry about pinching you in it."

"As you can see, I don't have much else on. What am I gonna wear?"

"Go into the bathroom and hand it out to me."

"Can't I go into the bedroom? I don't like the bathroom."

"I don't care where you go, just get."

Valerie walked slowly into the bedroom and closed the door. She dropped the sundress to her ankles. She gave it a good kick across the dusty floor. She stared in disbelief at the snagged zipper, then opened the door a crack and handed the dress to Cornelius. She felt very stupid sitting there on his bed naked except for her underpants, waiting for him. She could imagine him out there, bent over the dumb dress, picking threads out of the zipper tracks, trying to free the tab. Probably he was grumbling to himself and thinking what an idiot she was, and how could she get her zipper so thoroughly screwed up (which was a very good question) and why did he even bother with her?

The oldest trick in the book had backfired. She fell face down on the mattress and pouted. Three little holes in the wall looked like an upside down face, also pouting. And the two pouting faces had a staring contest for what seemed like ages.

Cornelius tapped on the bedroom door, said "Pinnoke," then he went into the room when she did not answer. The living room had faded to blue as dusk fell and the bedroom was even darker. Valerie had fallen asleep.

"Hey, Pinnoke, I fixed your dress."

Her eyelids fluttered and she looked up into his face. She felt very groggy, as though she had been sleeping soundly. She could not have been out for more than five minutes.

"It's fixed, no tears." He showed her the sundress.

"Oh good," she said. She stretched on the mattress, smiled as her arms reached to clasp around his neck. Didn't think about the fact that she was nearly naked. That he could plainly see she had no real breasts—that he didn't care about that.

She closed her eyes again, fell asleep in the middle of a kiss.

The next morning Cornelius informed her that he had to go out for a while, and then he went out for a while. Valerie finally got up, took a shower, used some of his spray deodorant, and put on a Potsdam State t-shirt she found in one of his drawers. The shirt covered her to the bottom of her thighs.

So Cornelius had gone to college in Potsdam? She thought about him in college, wondered what he was like then, how long ago it was, and that led her to think about him as a high school boy, which made her wonder what he had been doing the whole time starlight was tearing through space and she was messing up at growing up. She knew nothing personal about him, yet he was able to write songs about her.

With him out of the house, she could investigate his apartment. She searched through all of his bedroom drawers, checked underneath his underwear and socks, peered into his closet. She did not know what she was looking for—clues about what went on in his head— pictures or keepsakes. But Cornelius owned very little.

Her nosing around discovered one thing: the apartment was in worse shape than she had originally thought. In the bathroom the caulk was green, the enamel flaked off the toilet seat showing the wood grain, something slippery coated the tub. There were muddy corners behind radiators, rippled floorboards. It made her sick. But then, nomads don't take care of their houses, and all that.

However, she would not spend another minute in a hovel. She would have to clean today, while he was gone and could not get in her way. If he did not like it, too bad, she supposed he would like hepatitis or typhoid better.

She scrubbed the bathroom most of the day. It was difficult to clean well because he had few tools to use, and what he did have was old and caked, discarded here most likely by the former tenants. When she finished, her hands were chalky, her knuckles and knees scraped, the soles of her feet black, but civilization had triumphed. She wiped shiny the faucets as a final touch and admired her work. She was satisfied that the whole apartment even smelled healthy now.

"Tomorrow," she said to the bird, "I am going to buy

some disinfectant and a pail and a mop. This place is not done yet, and Cornelius is going to help me."

Cornelius came in. "Help with what?" he asked.

She greeted him with a kiss. "Hi, Corey," she said. "How was your day? Where did you go?"

"I had some errands."

That was exactly what her Mama and Papa would say to her whenever either of them would disappear: *I had some errands.*

"That's my shirt," Cornelius said.

"I hope you don't mind me wearing it. Did you go to Potsdam State?"

"I spent some time in the town. I didn't go to college."

"Not at all?"

"Pinnoke, if you're going to stay here, we should go up to your house and pack you some clothes so you don't have to wear mine."

"I had an idea," Valerie said. "Do you think maybe we could both go up to my family's camp at Lake Luzerne? It's pretty up there and no one is using it right now. This city is such a dreary, hot old place—and you aren't working now."

"I have to find a job."

"You have earned a vacation. It's on Papa."

Cornelius went into the bathroom. "What happened in here?" He closed the door.

"I cleaned it. I washed the kitchen too. Doesn't it look nice?"

"Looks beautiful," but his voice sounded sarcastic. He came out of the bathroom. She was standing by the door so she reached up and kissed him.

"Can we go to the lake?"

"I don't want to," Cornelius said.

"Why not?"

"I have stuff to do."

"What kind of stuff. I'll bet it's not important."

"Stuff."

"You just don't want to go."

"I said that."

"But you didn't say why."

"Yes I did."

"Oh—real particular: stuff. Cornelius, you're a poop. Please, can't we go?"

"Yes, we can't go."

"Oh—" she stomped her foot, "you are such a stick in the mud. I'm gonna take a shower." She went into the clean bathroom and closed the door, not a slam but firmly. Then she opened it again. She tore Cornelius' t-shirt over her head, ripping the seam in the shoulder, and threw it on the floor. Naked, she kicked it across the floor. "Here's your shirt," she said and turned back into the bathroom.

The shower calmed her, and by the time she emerged, wrapped in a towel, the idea to take him to Lake Luzerne seemed like an attempt to play out a fantasy anyhow, something that ought to be abandoned. She looked for Cornelius, thought he had left again, and then realized he had gone out onto the fire escape. She put on her sundress and joined him out there. He was rolling a coin over his knuckles. It dropped into the alley.

He watched it fall and muttered something. It sounded like "Feed the birds."

"I'm nice and clean now," Valerie said.

"You ready to go?"

"Go where?"

"To your house to get your clothes."

"I guess."

He turned toward the window.

"Are you mad at me?" she asked him.

"Are you mad at you?"

"No, I'm not mad," she said.

"Then why did you ask if I am?"

"You drive me crazy."

"And you drive us to Saratoga." He ducked through the window.

Valerie banged her head on the window again as she

went through. "I *hate* that thing."

When they reached her house, seeing it made her uneasy, knowing how the neighborhood of wide, well-trimmed lawns, sweeping drives, stands of birch and huge shade trees compared with his. She did not like showing her bedroom either. He knew too much about her already. That white elephant on the bedspread was too much.

She thought he was crazy when he began to insist she pack warm clothing. It was July and he was throwing sweaters and corduroys into her suitcase. She wanted only t-shirts and gym shorts, and only the new ones she had just bought, and he was packing her for the arctic.

"Corey, it's a heat wave."

"Not for long," he said.

"In the summer? You're nuts. Get out of my way so I can do this."

"You'll be freezing."

"I do not freeze at 70 degrees. That is how cold it's apt to get."

"We'll only be coming back," he insisted.

She allowed him one sweater and one pair of corduroys, but she would not take her own. She took her Mama's from her parents' closet. They were a size or so too large but had no associations.

As they got into the car and drove off, she wished there were a way to white out the car windows so the neighborhood could not look in so smugly.

Do you believe in God?
Do you want to blame God for the way people live?

And Moses said, "The people of Israel will want to know what is your name? What shall I say to them?"
I AM

It rained. It was the kind of summer storm that poured over the horizon like the murky foam of a wave, darkened a sky only moments before clear, and poured down. There was wind, there was thunder.

A loud crack of thunder awoke Valerie in the middle of the night. She sat up on the mattress and looked around. A flash of lightning showed her Cornelius still asleep.

She wondered what his dreams were like.

She got out of bed and walked quietly, although the storm was not making any effort to be silent, into the living room. The window was open. Wind blew water onto the floor. Lightning lit up the room for a second, and then it was dark again. Between flashes, it was very very dark. The temperature had dropped. It was by no means cold, as Cornelius had predicted, but it was no longer stifling inside. She almost smashed into the keyboard, but the lightning saved her. She stood still. During another instant of light, she saw the Potsdam t-shirt laying on the floor where she had kicked it. She put the shirt on, went to the window to close it; instead, she put her leg through the frame, stuck her head out. The rain was not unpleasant although it came down hard. It was like a warm, strong shower. Valerie went out onto the fire escape. Maybe a bad idea to stand on something metal in a thunderstorm, but there she was.

Cornelius awoke with a start and found himself alone in the bedroom. He got up and walked into the living room. Several rapid flashes of lightning lit the room like a strobe, a loud bang of thunder drew his eyes to the window. He saw Valerie out there, standing by the guardrail, the rain pouring over her, soaking her hair. In another whip of lightning he noticed the t-shirt, its torn seam low off her brown shoulder. He crossed the room to the open window. Streams of water rolled down the glass, in each second of lightning the streams glistened. Valerie did not turn around. She did not hear him or sense him there.

She was twelve years away, sitting in church, on the day of her First Communion.

Her legs were too short and her feet dangled above the

floor. She crossed them nicely at the ankles, in obedience to the nuns who offered that as an alternative to their directions to sit with feet flat on floor. Her frilly white dress was too short, and every time she slid forward off the pew to stand or kneel, the wood rubbed on the back of her legs and burned. She clutched the plastic handle of her little white pocketbook, trying to keep her white-gloved hands folded reverently at the same time.

Valerie hated to go to church. It was boring because she was too little to see over anyone's head to know what was happening. And it was too long to sit on a hard wooden bench—and she hated most kneeling for so long while the priest said all those prayers to turn the wine and bread into Jesus. Now the nuns told her that after today she would be lucky enough to be able to go to church every Sunday. And, of course, if she did not she would go to hell and never see God.

That was blackmail.

At this moment the priest was involved with telling them what a big occasion in their lives this day was. But it was a lot more interesting to look around at all the other kids in her class in their white clothes with their hair combed and done at the hair dresser's in ways they never usually wore their hair. Most looked pretty funny. And most interesting of all were the picture plaques on the walls around the church of Jesus' Stations of the Cross.

Whenever Valerie's Mama and Papa took her to church, she liked to examine those pictures. Each was carved from wood, the figures painted bright colors. The first station was "Jesus is Condemned to Death on the Cross." Valerie could read only some of the captions, others had big words in them, but she knew them all to repeat from Fridays in Lent when the whole school would get out of class to go to Stations of the Cross. In Stations of the Cross the altar boys would go into the aisles with a big gold cross and stand opposite one of the pictures while one of the favorite kids in school would read: "The first station of the cross: Jesus is Condemned to Death on the Cross." Then the whole school would say prayers together, and the altar boys would carry the gold cross to the next picture. Her favorite pictures were the ones with soldiers in them, because the soldiers were brightly painted silver, with red dresses and red capes. And of course Jesus would be in the picture with a bright yellow circle around His head and His dark brown beard and white dress.

Valerie looked around at the pictures instead of listening to the priest. She did not understand why this was a big occasion if it meant she *had* to go to church every Sunday unless she was sick—God always knew if she was really sick or not so she could not pretend—or else she would have to tell it in Confession.

Yesterday, Valerie and her class had gone together to their First Confession. No parents had come to see that as they had come today. First Confession had been a more casual affair. Father Dimura had come into their classroom at the beginning of religion class and told them that today, instead of Sister teaching, they were going to go over to the church to receive the sacrament of Penance for the first time. It had not been a surprise. They had all known that the date was coming and had rehearsed the event, gone through the motions with Sister. They had each gone into the little booth of the confessional as Sister sat on the other side of the screen pretending she was Father. And each of them had practiced reviewing their consciences, going down the list of the Ten Commandments to make sure none had been violated. And finally, each of them had secretly prepared a list of their sins so they would be ready for the real Father and the real occasion. But now that the time had come, the class' collective heart skipped a beat, and at once no one could remember a single sin on his or her prepared list. No one could remember, either, the "Act of Contrition" prayer, which Father Dimura was apt to ask them to recite in the confessional.

Very nervous, the class assembled in two lines—boys in one line, girls in the other—according to height, as Sister had arranged them. Valerie was first in her line and she was petrified that she'd stumble on the way over to church and topple everyone behind her like dominos. She hated being the leader. She would be the first girl to go into the booth for confession, and Father Dimura was sure to remember Valerie Mastropietro had headed the line and would be the first girl's voice he heard.

But she did not stumble, no one did, and the lines proceeded smoothly and reverently into God's house. When Valerie and the shortest boy were each abreast of the first pew, and the whole class behind was inside the church, Sister stood in front of them all and clapped her hands as a signal. On that signal the class genuflected in unison, and then Valerie and the shortest boy each led their lines into the pews on different sides of the center aisle.

Sister had a great system for keeping the confessions secret and private between each kid and God. Valerie's pew did not line up first beside the confessional booth. A pew of girls from the center of the church went first, and an equally arbitrarily chosen group of boys stood on the other side of Father Dimura's confessional. He would not be able to guess whose confession he was hearing.

This system as well increased the individual suffering of each of them, for no pew knew exactly when they would be chosen.

When Valerie was finally tapped, she was so startled that she let out a gasp that echoed all the way to the back of God's silent house. Then, as she rose from her aching knees, the hem of her uniform jumper caught on the corner of the kneeler and yanked her back down. The girl beside her tripped over her, and down went the whole pew with a loud bang, echoing all the way to heaven. Sister frowned fretfully, and Valerie thought she was going to get punched. But she was helped to her feet and pointed in the proper direction.

The inside of the booth was silent, dark, and filled with a strange odor—like papier mache paste. There was a little crucifix on the wall and the tarnished figure of Jesus stared at her. When the door of the screen slid open with a dull thud, Valerie jumped and gasped again. Her mind raced, and breathless, she rambled her sins softly. Father Dimura stopped her in mid sin and asked her to begin again, to speak up a bit.

Valerie hesitated.

Sister had cautioned them all to be quiet in the confessional box. A confession is private, and if anybody besides a priest listens, except in an emergency of life and death, it is a mortal sin and they will go to hell and never see God. Valerie did not want to talk so loud she'd be responsible for sending thirty-seven kids to hell.

When she finished her sins, Father Dimura didn't ask for an "Act of Contrition." He said a prayer and told her she was forgiven, gave her "Three Glory Bees" to say as penance for her wrongdoings. Pretty easy going, Valerie thought—you could do anything and pay for it with a mere "Three Glory Bees"

—which meant you could skip church once in a while without worrying about it, unless you got killed before you could get to confession. So Valerie felt a little better about making her First Communion. She really was not as cornered as it seemed. The priest had finished his sermon, and now the class was standing. Valerie snapped to, slid off the bench to her feet. She was sure her short skirt had flipped up and all of London had been shown to the girls behind her.

When it was First Communion time, they did go pew by pew, so Valerie was the first to receive the Holy Eucharist. She carried the bread wafer on her tongue back to her place, trying to dissolve it with her saliva because Sister had warned her not to chew the bread because she would be chewing Jesus. Chewing Jesus was probably also a mortal sin. The wafer stuck like a piece of wet paper to the roof of her mouth, and she spent the rest of the Mass trying to peel it off with her tongue.

Now she became aware of her Mama and Papa in the back of the church, craning their necks to see her take First Communion, proud of their only child. Valerie dared to turn around and look down the aisle to find them. She began to smile when she thought about them. She could not help the warm feeling, the glow, the great big grin. She looked up to heaven, and the lights of the church seemed to her like Jesus coming down and wrapping her in a big hug. She decided that she would gladly come back every Sunday as long as she did not have to wear this dumb white dress, and as long as she could sit with her Mama and Papa.

That is not exactly how it had happened. What had happened that day as she received Holy Communion was nothing. Valerie *wished* it had happened the other way, but she had continued to worry about her dress, had wondered why she did not feel any different, had felt ripped off.

Valerie broke her reverie, and no longer did the rain feel nice. It came down with so much force, and the wind seemed strong enough to blow her off the fire escape. With thinking like this, she would get hit by lightning. She pulled the sopped shirt away from her skin and it made a most distasteful sucking sound. She looked back through the window and saw Cornelius in the darkness of the apartment. He looked sad in a glimmer of lightning, but as soon as Valerie thought that was what the expression in his eyes had been, the lightning was over. He turned away and went back into the bedroom.

She climbed back in, went to the bathroom to dry herself off. She could barely sense the beginnings of menstrual cramps, sighed at the thought of the next several days.

Once dry, she went back to bed, lay curled beside Cornelius while thinking quietly. Then she sighed. "Oh Cornelius," she said forlornly, "I did everything so wrong."

She took his hand and put it to her breast, kept it anchored there with her own hand.

Chapter 6

Day after day there pass a million possibilities which can only be identified by the people involved through hindsight, when the subjunctive voice takes over: What if this...supposing that...speculation in reverse is an amazing force.

Which choice taken was the crucial one?

Even looking back, is there a way to know?

Valerie and Cornelius may never have gone to Boston together if events had not been channeled as they had, if—at the critical moment—Valerie had walked out instead of him, he may have taken the trip alone—things may have been different.

...Maybe not.

Dawn came late and Valerie awoke around that time to get the crocheted blanket. She huddled close to Cornelius for more warmth. She thought about shivering, wondered if that would wake him as she had by now burrowed almost beneath him, and if she shivered she would be like a vibrating mattress. Finally she dozed off again, and when she awoke the storm was quiet. Her skin was bumpy from the cold.

"In July?" she said aloud, afraid to move away from Cornelius' body, for exposure to the air would certainly mean frostbite.

She heard the release of pumps and water gurgling through pipes, muffled voices, and Spanish folk songs as the family downstairs began to wake up. Valerie wondered how they could stand to move around so much in such a cold building. Or perhaps they had the right idea. The sooner they were up and circulating, the warmer they would be. Valerie stayed put in bed and listened. The sounds she heard were not unlike what she would hear in her own house on mornings when she lay in her own bed upstairs. She was able in her mind to give shape to the unseen activity going on below her. Like looking at an anthill after owning an ant farm. Valerie did not have to imagine an apartment much like this one, a bathroom medicine chest shared with silverfish and cockroaches. She could lay with her eyes closed and imagine a comfortable home, a family who did not have to worry much about gasoline prices or healthcare costs, who compared prices in the supermarket for satisfaction, not survival.

She decided to follow the downstairs neighbors' example and get out of bed. She ran to the bathroom, closed the door. She turned on the shower so the steam would heat the room. It took a long, chilly time for the hot water tank in the basement to pump water to the third floor. Valerie hopped up and down to warm up.

She realized she had forgotten her overnight bag in the bedroom, and as she ran through the living room, whispering a low *"Aaaaaaaaah"* all the way there and back with the bag, her breath poured out in February clouds.

She stayed in the shower a long time. The longer she let the water pour over her body, the less she wanted to step out into the cold. Finally, the water that poured over her was no longer hot. It faded steadily to lukewarm, then dropped off to cold—she had exhausted the hot water tank, and now she had to get out.

While she was dressing, there came a loud knock on

the door.

"Who is it?" she said.

"Who is it? Get out of there. You've been in there forever."

She supposed he was right. "It is too cold out there," she said in a small voice.

"Out—*now*!"

Valerie giggled. "Not by the hair of my chinny-chin-chin."

But she opened the door and let him in. He closed her out, and in a couple of seconds she heard him say: "Ye-ow!" and she remembered that there was no hot water left for him.

It was still raining, but it came down in very fine, icy sheets. Silent but steady. Yesterday she had made up her mind to spend this day cleaning, but she had her period now, and she did not feel like doing much of anything. She got the blanket and wrapped herself in it, sat on his old couch beside an exposed spring in the upholstery. She turned up the cuffs of her Mama's corduroy jeans. She glumly thought about being imprisoned by the rain, inside this cracker box with nothing to do. He would play the keyboard all day and her menstrual cramps would make it all miserable. She wished they had gone to the lake, because up there rain did not always seem gloomy. At the lake, Valerie sometimes liked the rain. Especially at night—to hear the sound of it on the roof, and on the dock, and on the water, while they had a fire and maybe hot chocolate inside.

Valerie sat there and thought about the early days at the camp, when the family had just returned to Saratoga after her Papa's sabbatical. Those summers when she and her Mama used to live at the lake while her Papa commuted back and forth whenever he could, because he was playing in the orchestra at the Performing Arts Center. In those early days, Valerie thought now, she had missed the chances she could have used to grow close to her parents. Because while they went through the motions of playing backgammon and of making trips to Mr. Feeney's store, of excitedly awaiting her Papa's visits, they always seemed to be just that: the motions of passing time.

And inside herself Valerie had pondered too many questions about the funny things happening to her body—but not to her classmates'—yet she and her Mama always walked in silence, played games with perfunctory groans and squeals. The longer Valerie harbored all her questions to herself, the deeper entrapped those questions became, until they could never get out.

At the end of a few summers, every one the same, Valerie concluded that she and her Mama would never discuss anything important. She watched girls on television having such *tête à têtes* with their mothers, and the younger really did seem an extension of the older. Later in her adolescence, when commercials would ask her if she remembered those heart-to-hearts she used to have with her mother, Valerie would answer aloud that all she could recall was lonely small talk to suppress things that were dying to be said.

She discovered the public library, applied for a card, started going there to look for books about growing up. She rifled through the card catalogue, covertly copied down call numbers, wandered up and down the ranges of shelves, but the books were always missing. In Mr. Feeney's store there was a paperback book that looked as if it would be of some help, but she was too embarrassed to buy it from him.

So in response to her own puberty, she was propelled by the activity around her, and all of it seemed too full of urgency and secrecy, as if she were coming down with a strange, shameful illness.

Cornelius caught her pouting on the couch. She tried to hide her mood. He looked at her, and then he went into the kitchen.

She leaped off the couch and tried to sound like a tease, "Don't drink out of the juice carton!"

There he was, placing the carton back on the refrigerator shelf, orange juice on his lips.

"What do you want to do today?" she said awkwardly.

And he said, "Why don't we teach the bird to talk?"

Chapter 7

It finally stopped raining around two in the afternoon—just about the time Valerie was ready to strangle Clancy for refusing all morning all speech lessons. The bird simply perched there in the cage as she repeated over and over again words she thought it would be fun to have Clancy say. She tried its name, she tried Cornelius' name, she tried her own name, and Cornelius threw in the name of Lou Henry Hoover as long as she was stuck on names. She tried elementary words like up, down, in, and out. She tried all the vowels, numbers one through ten in both English and Italian. Any morpheme would have made her happy, but the bird remained silent.

Valerie grew aggravated, and it wasn't fun anymore, the cramps in her uterus making the bird's stupidity intolerable. Cornelius pointed out that it had stopped raining, and suggested they take a walk.

Valerie got the idea to make spinach lasagna for dinner, for which she had not bought the ingredients the last time they'd gone shopping. So she made up a list and off they went again to the supermarket.

On top of her Mama's sweater, Valerie wore Cornelius' hooded sweatshirt, the kind with pockets in the front that are really only one pocket. She clasped her cold fingers together inside the pocket. Cornelius wore only a windbreaker, but if he was cold he did not show it.

The sky was low and white-grey. The tops of the South Mall office buildings were cut off, and the air rolled with mist. She huddled her shoulders close as they walked. He strolled as if the temperature were quite comfortable.

"Even so," she said, "I like it cold better than too hot. You can always get warm but it is hard to get cool. I like winter better than summer. The snow is pretty when it first falls. I don't ski or ice skate, do you?"

"I'm not a big fan of winter, Pinnoke," Cornelius said.

"No? I love it. It's invigorating. One winter I built a snowman bigger than me. I had a lot of trouble getting the head on, but I did it."

"Spinach lasagna is my specialty," Valerie told Cornelius as they toted more groceries back to his apartment. "It takes a long time to make the sauce, so we may not eat until a little later than usual—it'll be like in Europe—hope you don't mind." She set the bags on the kitchen counter and began to empty them. "Know what, Corey? The guy who built your kitchen could not have been Italian. There's no room for food at all. A kitchen is made for food. I am blabbering a lot, huh? I bet you think I've gone nuts or something. You hardly ever talk. I'm not crazy, really, even if I do dumb things a lot. Like my sundress getting snagged, but then, look how that turned out, not so bad, huh? When I was a little girl lots of people thought I was kind of dumb because I used to daydream a lot. Sometimes I'd go for walks and get lost because I wouldn't pay attention to where I was going. But it wasn't really my fault. Papa was on his sabbatical. We were in a strange city. I don't know how you can stand to be a nomad, as you say, I hate to move a lot. It gives me a stomachache. I was always kind of spacey—in high school especially, but I don't like to talk about high school. Anyway—I am a lot shrewder than I let on." She tapped her temple and winked.

"You haven't the right pans for this, Corey. I am going to have to make do with what is here. That, you realize, will put the outcome of this wonderful masterpiece in jeopardy. If it doesn't come out the way it's s'posed to, it will be your fault. Keep that in mind."

They never found out if it did or it didn't because she never finished. Her cramps became unbearable, and she could not stand in the tiny kitchen any longer. She left a mess of pots and pans and utensils, spices and tomato paste, spinach draining on a paper towel. Cornelius made franks and beans, but Valerie felt too defeated to eat.

She lay on the bed, shivered with cold, crumpled into a little ball. She still wore his sweatshirt, with her knees drawn up inside it so that only her feet stuck out. Cornelius brought her the blanket. Then he went away to play the keyboard.

She would have been mad; there was not a thing he could do for her physically, but he could have stayed beside the bed—but then she saw the piano chords as if they were people come softly into the bedroom. They tucked the blanket around her snuggly, kissed her on the forehead, and rubbed her head gently. Valerie fell asleep and the chords returned to the keyboard.

She slept late into the next day. She felt much better, maybe for having slept the extra time. There was no sign of Cornelius. He had gone out again, no sign of how long ago or if he had slept in the bed at all. Valerie did not like to wake up to an empty house, not knowing where everyone had gone.

The aborted lasagna lay in the kitchen, totally ruined and beginning to stink. She stared at the mess in disgust and disappointment.

She sat on the couch, looked at the bird. She considered trying to teach it to talk again. The door downstairs squealed open, closed slowly. She looked at the apartment door in anticipation of Cornelius. But no

Cornelius came up. Valerie walked to the window, looked outside. After all these days, she noticed, that laundry was still hanging. It looked colder outside today than yesterday. She wondered if the laundry might be starched with ice. And the sky actually looked the way it does in winter when it is going to snow. What if it were to snow in July? "It'll be a winter day in July before I do that!" Anyone who had ever said that would finally have to deliver.

She turned away from the window and stopped beside the keyboard. She looked at it. She turned it on. She touched middle C, kept the key down and listened to the prolonged note. Then she touched D and held it; then E and held that; she went all the way up the octave.

Clancy repeated perfectly the octave she had just played.

"Hey!" Again she went up the octave and this time Clancy hit each note along with her. She hit C an octave higher, and the bird reproduced the note. She hit the note an octave lower, and so did the bird. Valerie started to giggle. Clancy was a musical bird.

She wished she were able to play a song—perhaps the bird could learn to sing "Chopsticks," maybe "Happy Birthday." Valerie played an octave over and over again until Clancy tired of singing along. She fooled around a little longer to see if the bird would be coaxed into singing again, then she tired of the game herself and shut the piano off.

She decided that Cornelius was probably not going to come home soon. Instead of waiting for him, she ought to find something to do with the day. Doing laundry always spent time, and come to think of it, she really did not have enough clothes with her, not enough warm clothes anyway.

So she collected his clothes, which were all over his bedroom floor, bundled them up in her arms because he did not have a laundry bag or even a pillow case to put them in, and she carried them down to her car. It *was* colder than yesterday, and the heater in her car smelled stale as if it protested its use in summer. The disk jockey on the radio chattered away inanely about the weird weather.

She turned into the driveway of her house, gathered his clothes out of the passenger seat in front and walked to the front door. She dropped a few socks while fishing for her keys. Then she was amazed and worried to discover she had not locked the door the last time they were here.

She took in the mail. There was a postcard of the Liberty Bell from her Mama and Papa. She did his laundry, and while she waited on the washing machine, she went upstairs and packed more of her Mama's fall clothes. Then she opened the hall linen closet and grabbed a stack of sheets for his bed. She took her pillow too, put everything in the car, and it was past dinner time before she was on the road again.

Cornelius sat at his keyboard, said to the bird, "Okay, bird, if you won't talk, how about a song?" He played Beethoven's Sixth Symphony.

"Wait a minute—" he stopped playing abruptly "—Valerie is coming." He opened the door for her.

He had gotten a haircut and that made it look thinner than ever. He really was losing his hair. Valerie looked at him over the pillow, which she had lain atop the stack of sheets she carried, and at the same time she tried to drag in the bag of laundry. She said to Cornelius, "Please help me and take something."

He looked at her, and she watched him perform a series of movements that somehow seemed unrelated: He took out his glasses.

He unfolded the stems.

He wiped the lenses on his shirt.

He put the glasses on.

He pulled out his cigarettes.

He took one from the package.

He replaced the package in his pocket.

He lit the cigarette.

He shook out the match.

A long silence endured. She felt the weight of the sheets straining her arms. And she could feel the room grow colder as he looked at the stack of sheets, the pillow.

He did not raise his voice. "What is that?"

"Sheets...for your bed," Valerie said. The weight on her arms grew heavier. "Because I noticed...that you...don't have...any..." her voice was very small before she finished. It was obvious by the look on his face that he did not think he needed her sheets.

Still speaking too calmly to trust, he went into a list: "You cleaned my apartment...you did my laundry...you cooked all my meals...you bought my groceries...you take forever in my bathroom and use all my hot water...you wear my clothes...and you bring your mother's spare sheets to put on my bed." With each item Valerie felt her cramps return, intensify. The tendons in her arms stretched to the breaking point under the weight of the sheets. The bag of laundry slipped from her grasp and tumbled over, spilled. Valerie felt something hot bust open inside her, and her underpants sopped up what they could, the rest poured down her legs and she began to cry.

"If you didn't want me to do it all, you should have said something." She felt utterly miserable, shameful. "You never say anything. You just let me go ahead and talk and do everything I do so I make a fool out of myself."

"If I want you to do something, Pinnoke," he said, still not raising his voice, "I will ask for your help. If I don't say it, don't do it."

"Yeah, sure, and in the meantime I will sit on the shelf, okay? I am not your puppet, Cornelius! And I do have feelings which you do not seem to care about anyone's but your own!" She did say more, but it all came out in Italian. By now her corduroys were heavy and wet along the inseams and she was afraid to look as the pungent scent of her own menstrual blood reached her nostrils. She dropped the sheets. The Italian words poured out of her mouth, even she did not know what she had said to him.

"I had everything the way I want it," Cornelius said, talking as she spoke too, "and you came along and rearranged my cupboards, talked about putting pictures on my wall—"

Her English returned, but just one letter: "Oh—!" she cried, and she ran away from him into the bathroom. She heard him go out quietly, listened to his footsteps echo down the stairwell, and then it was silent, he was gone.

Slowly, feeling utterly sick, Valerie cleaned herself up and put on her nightgown. She took some Midol and left her underpants to soak in the sink. She put the corduroys outside on the fire escape. Then she slinked into the bedroom and crawled onto the bed.

If only she did not feel so bad, she would go home and never come back—she hadn't asked to come here—but that would probably bother him little. He might miss her for as long as it took to notice he didn't have to wait for the bathroom anymore. Valerie wondered why people bothered. No one really cares about anyone except how it reflects on them. That is what she had learned from her rotten adolescence, and if she had been looking to contradict that here, she'd been in the wrong place.

Yet she was still in this place, lying on this bed like it was her own, and Cornelius had walked out, not her. And when he came back she would not go home. She knew that. She could lay here as angry as she was with him, and she could fantasize about walking out, but she could not get beyond the what happens next. Because she knew she would never even get that far.

And Cornelius would only light a cigarette and look at her exactly as if he had known what she was going to do, to say. Valerie began to shiver. She could have attributed it to the cold, but she knew it was not that. The shivering became uncontrollable

(i wish i had a drink)

and it scared her.

Hours passed. Hours of silence and trembling. It had gone dark a long time ago. Now and again she would hear Clancy fluttering in the cage, and when she did not hear anything, she would strain her ears for just that tiny noise. It meant she was not fully alone. After a while she figured the bird had gone to sleep. She did not want to sleep. Sleep can be the most frightening place to go.

After midnight she got up to take another Midol, and while she stood in the kitchen drinking a glass of water, she heard the door open downstairs. She hurried to the apartment door, opened it, flipped on the light at the top of the stairs.

The stairwell was freezing. It was so cold that frost covered each step. He appeared on the lower landing and Valerie could tell he was tripping. She felt his drug slithering around his corpuscles, stopping up his synapses. Her knees weakened, her stomach squashed. She hated knowing what drug he had probably taken.

She looked hopelessly at him as the cold floor stabbed into her bare feet. She said, "Cornelius?" wondered if he could hear her.

He stood at the bottom of the stairs and looked up at her. The light bulb behind her head looked like a corona surrounding her tiny, tiny body. She was burning, on fire, but she was not being consumed. She was like the burning bush in Exodus. She came down the stairs, one step at a time, lowering one fiery foot and then the other. She reached an arm of flames down to him, and foggily he took her hand. It did not burn him. She led him up the stairs and brought him into the apartment which she now owned. She sat him on the couch and held onto him. He clung so tightly her skin dissolved as did his, their blood vessels came unraveled from their individual bodies and wove together. He hugged her so tightly their bones fused and their fleshes melded into one.

Cornelius awoke first in the morning, staggered into the kitchen. He touched the door frame to stop it from spinning. He leaned over the sink and threw up. He vomited and vomited, and it all came up pink from the two bottles of Pepto-Bismol he'd downed the night before. Valerie appeared, tired looking. She watched him sadly, but she said nothing.

"We have to go to Boston," Cornelius muttered with pink lips. "I got a job."

Chapter 8

They didn't speak. Valerie packed their clothes, although she did not even know how long she was packing for, while Cornelius lay on the bed with his arm across his eyes. Now and again she would glance over her shoulder at him, one time with consternation, another with compunction, but she did not speak...she was afraid to speak. She took refuge in the silence, and the longer it droned, the deeper into it she crawled. She was afraid of words.

At last she was ready to go. She put the suitcase by the door, and then turned to get Clancy. Cornelius stood up and walked uneasily out of the bedroom. His face was like paper. She wanted to touch it, but she did not. He picked up the suitcase and took it down to the car. Valerie followed with the birdcage.

She found him checking her oil, her battery cables, her fan belt. She put Clancy in the back seat and sat in the front seat, in the passenger seat. She stared at the raised hood, which blocked all else out.

Then the hood dropped with a bang. She jumped. Clancy peeped. A D minor. Then she watched Cornelius go back into the house. In a few moments, he returned carrying the keyboard in a gig bag. He put it into the back seat, on the floor, and then got into the car behind the wheel. Valerie had stuck the key in the ignition. He now turned it. And for the three and one half hour trip to Boston, there were only two sounds: that of the motor and tires, and the rain, which began to come down as they came upon West Springfield.

Valerie daydreamed and looked out the window. She thought about turning on the radio, but she did not do it. Her period bothered her. She reached into her purse and took a Midol. She swallowed it dry, and her mouth was chalky the rest of the drive.

They stayed in a house as beaten as Cornelius'. It was Boston architecture rather than old Dutch, but there was no difference in the two. Valerie wondered if everyone Cornelius associated with lived in squalor.

But she was excited to meet, finally, one of his friends. It would be a telltale, something better than any old photograph, or a t-shirt. And perhaps such a person could give her a few personal details about him.

She was convinced, from the moment she laid eyes on him, that this guy Porter was the embodiment of the soul inside Cornelius. He was short, his hair was a little shaggy over his collar, and his blond beard was short but not evenly trimmed. His corduroy jeans were wrinkled, just out of the dryer and not ironed, and his herringbone jacket was old. He kept his hands in his pockets when he was not playing his guitar, which he played so sweetly it made Valerie feel melancholy. He was soft-spoken, diffident. She had read in a magazine once about twins who had been separated living their lives like they were the same person, a theory of genetics that they *are* actually the same—in this way too were Porter and Cornelius the same person. They both had the same eyes: blue with the eclipsed suns.

There existed a quality within both of these people that she had yearned for, sweated and bled for, duped herself for, chased after by wandering in tangential directions, for nineteen going on twenty years.

And any fool could see that these two guys were the

same person – the interior and exterior of the same person.

There were also two other people in the apartment. They were not Porter's roommates. His roommates were not at home for the entire weekend. One of the people there was a scruffy looking saxophone player (she supposed it made sense they'd all be musicians—her Papa's friends were all musicians, too) named Derek. He was a riot because his Boston accent was so thick. It was exactly the accent people affect when they parody Bostonians: he said *Bahston*, Red *Sawks*, and he called soda *tawnic*. The other person there was a girl—a woman—whatever...Her name was Cindi. She was Porter's girlfriend, but they did not seem very intimate. No wonder. They were not at all alike. She had a Boston accent too, but it was not hers; it was Derek's, stolen. No doubt she felt that if she was going to live in this city she had to sound like it. And she was overly sophisticated. Valerie wondered what it must be like to live day to day, minute to minute, as someone else, maybe worried that at any time your real self might show.

(didn't she know?)

She did not like Cindi, who had bright blue eyes, full red lips, and nice round breasts that floated in her sweater.

The first thing they all did once the suitcase, the keyboard, and the bird were up in the third floor flat, was eat dinner. Cindi was the cook. She was horrible: tasteless soup, a big salad made with all the wrong greens, pita bread stuffed with plain cheddar cheese. Valerie could have done better with no notice.

Dessert was vanilla bean ice cream – and honey. Who on earth puts honey on ice cream, of any flavor?

After dinner they sat around the living room with a bottle of wine. Valerie felt a strong twinge of fear in her stomach. She did not want any, would never say that she *could not* have any—she was intimidated by that woman with such blond hair and ivory skin.

Porter, unprompted, said: "I have Coke, if you want Coke."

"Sure, there's *tawnic*," Derek said. "In fact, get me a *tawnic* too."

Valerie giggled. She told Porter that she wanted the soda. "Thank you," she said, as she was sure Cindi turned up her nose. Nothing delighted Valerie more than to be in this person's disdain. She went on smiling as Porter handed her a bottle of Coke.

(It was hot.)

When there are three musicians in a room, a keyboard, a guitar, and Derek just happening to have his saxophone with him, there is of course going to be music.

Here was the wondrous thing: the trio played Porter's music, original music, tunes Cornelius had never heard in his life. Valerie knew that, because he asked to hear a few bars before he started to play. But once he did, he played as though he were the composer. He even took the lead away from Porter for a number of measures, then handed it over to Derek perfectly for him to play a saxophone solo.

Valerie hid the tears in her eyes, because she knew Cindi would scoff at her. Cindi sat there intellectually analyzing every sound. It was not music to her, merely a series of tones – playing with theory.

To Valerie, this was the most beautiful phenomenon alive, and the most beautiful place to be.

The guys took a break, and that was when Cindi pulled out the powder. Boldly, like it was nothing, she cut it into lines on the coffee table. Valerie bolted to the window. Her knees shook. Outside, it had stopped raining. She snatched Cornelius' sweatshirt and ran out the door. On her way down the stairs, she looked at the wall boards showing in the gaps of crumbled plaster, and she *hated* these old buildings.

She sat on the damp stoop between a couple of puddles.

Then Porter came out.

"I don't like it either," he said to her.

He sat down too, his herringbone jacket laid across his knees.

"Corey knows I despise it," she said.

"Cindi knows I do. For one thing, it's illegal. Sometimes I think she does it only to irritate me. But she's into it, and people do things."

"I know," she moped. "But I have experience with this stuff. It's not a moral thing. It's experience, and it's bad."

Porter said, "You're shivering." He put his jacket on her shoulders. "It is chilly, huh? Want to walk?"

She nodded.

They headed up the street.

"Glad it stopped raining," Porter said. "It's rained here for three days straight."

"We were having a heat wave at home—until it got so cold."

"Do you want to go have a cup of coffee somewhere?" he asked. "Or how about something to eat? Cindi's so called dinners never fill me up."

Valerie smiled wide. "I would love a pizza."

"The very thing," Porter grinned.

"Aren't you cold without your coat?"

"I'm fine."

"I'm not cold, really," Valerie said. "I was just upset. I shiver when I get upset."

They walked in silence. Easy silence. They walked to a place that smelled satisfyingly of pizza in the rainy air. Inside it was warm and bright.

"How long have you known Cornelius?" It seemed a terrible thing to talk about Cornelius to Porter. She knew that she only had to be with him, to talk about anything at all, and she would know Cornelius better as a result. But Cornelius was what they shared in common.

"I knew him in college."

"He said he didn't go."

"He didn't. I did. I went to Potsdam State for a fiasco. Dropped out after three semesters and went home to

Schenectady—"

"Schenectady! I know where that is. I live in Saratoga Springs."

He smiled.

"How come you came to Boston?" she asked.

"I don't know." But he did. He had a reason, and it was a strong one, but he held it back.

"How did you meet Cindi?"

"Don't let Cindi bother you. She's trying to be preppie. Actually, she's a country girl from Connecticut and doesn't know anything about being a Harvard student."

"I might have known she was a Harvard student. Oh—you don't go to Harvard too, do you?" She blushed. "I don't want to insult anyone."

"I met her on a subway platform. I play guitar at Harvard Station a lot—"

"Doesn't that make you nervous? Playing on a subway platform, where everyone *looks* at you?" she wondered. The playing seemed okay to her. It was the looking that bothered her.

"At first. I came here with my guitar bound to make it a living, but I didn't know what to do. I was nineteen, and to me, then, Boston seemed like where you went to make a living. I saw these guys playing on the platforms a lot, so I thought I'd try it. But to just take out your guitar and begin to play—I was afraid people wouldn't want to hear it. But they do. You would be surprised. Sorry, I'm talking on and on."

"I want to hear. Where does Cindi come in?"

"One day she let five trains go by just to listen. I got a boost out of it, but what a flake she was—like a groupie. She started talking to me. A bit odd, perhaps, but she amused me. She was a cheerfulness I needed at the time. If you talk about it now, she makes believe it never happened that way. She won't admit to it."

"Do you still like her? I'm sorry, very bold question."

"I like her very much, yes."

"I am afraid sometimes that Corey doesn't like me.

We're not speaking, in case you have not noticed. We had kind of a fight, and—well, I don't know, we aren't fighting now but it's all out of control. He's a wonderful piano player, don't you think?"

"In Potsdam he was very big. He's known in Boston, too—you'll see tomorrow night. The place will be full. Newspapers don't write about him. He kind of flies below the radar."

"At home he seems like a nobody. But he is so good. He should be recording."

Porter smiled wryly and sighed.

"I know, I know," Valerie said. "Any jammoke with a horn and a lap top can record these days. Getting heard is something else. I've been through it with Papa's pupils. But Cornelius is one who should. So are you. I'm not being like Cindi, either. All three of you guys are great. You could make a band. I don't know how Corey does it—blends in so well with you."

"He improvises. He says it's easy. I was never very good at music theory, but Cornelius is out ahead of it. Derek is pretty good at jamming too. He goes to MIT. He's started a company to develop algorithms that analyze music to see if a song will be a hit. He says it's right almost all of the time."

"Porter, tell me why you left home after you went back. I need to know."

He smiled dryly. "Why else?"

"Ah ha! I knew it."

"It was stupid. I knew her in high school. To remove the emotion from a sappy story: she broke up with me and I took it hard. Off I went to college, but she was still with me, in a manner of speaking. So I gave in and went home—to face her, you might say—that old story. Then I ran away to here...The things a nineteen year old kid thinks are urgent are really mind numbing when you're not nineteen anymore."

"I'm nineteen," she said flatly.

"Um..."

Valerie smiled. "What was her name?"

"Ronnie. She had long red hair and freckles, these little round glasses, and great big green eyes. I still think I loved her."

"We're very alike," Valerie said. "Yet different."

"How so?"

"We are both of us stuck in our past, frightened of it, but perhaps more frightened of this—of...I don't know...you know..."

He blinked.

"If I were ever to become the person I was once—it seems a long time ago, but when I wake up in the morning it seems like only the night before—I could not go back to that—" her voice broke; the break had sneaked up on her, taken her by surprise, "...if I ever was, I would, rather not be alive anymore."

The pizza was gone. There was nowhere to hide, no last slice of pizza to grab, no more soda to drink. They looked at each other.

"Do you want to go home?" Valerie asked.

"Yes. It's late, and I think they'll be wondering about us."

On the way out the door, Valerie touched Porter's arm. He placed his hand on her back.

"Take your coat back," she said. "You'll catch cold." Her breath came out in puffs. The temperature had plummeted while they were eating the pizza.

They had walked a long way to get here, too far to care to walk home, and the trolley they waited on was late in coming. Finally they got home. The apartment windows were dark. A puddle on the front stoop had frozen. Valerie put her foot on it, and it was solid.

"Do you believe it?" she said.

Up in the apartment, Cornelius and Cindi had gone to sleep, she in Porter's bed and he in one of the roommate's rooms; Derek had gone home.

So Valerie and Porter sat up for a while, and they had the living room lights off. They did not talk. Clancy was restless in the cage. Little by little, Valerie dozed. Her head nodded into his lap. He put his hand across her shoulders. She was never fully asleep; she felt warm and swaddled, safe and relaxed, but she was aware of his touch. She wrapped her arm around his leg.

A light in the hall came on and split everything. Valerie sat up fast, making her head swim, as Cindi entered the room. Cindi was cloaked in a bed sheet, and it was obvious she was naked underneath it. The hall light behind her spotted much.

Valerie was not sure if they had been discovered. Cindi showed no signs of having seen Porter cradling her. "You're back," she said sleepily. "We were about to call out the *cawps*." That accent again.

Porter said, "Did we wake you coming in?"

"No," she answered, "I couldn't sleep. Are you coming to bed, Porter?"

"In a minute or so."

"Got real cold," Cindi said.

"Yes."

Then she went into the bathroom, the bed sheet billowing behind her as she walked.

Porter said, "You had best get some sleep. Think I'm about to catch hell."

"I'm sorry. See you in the morning."

She wanted so much to be kissed good-night. But he only stood gently, as if sudden movement would shake her out of the drowsiness she had found, and he went into his bedroom. Their mood had snapped. She was sad.

Then Cindi did a very weird thing. She came out of the bathroom, and she did not go back to bed to give Porter hell. She came into the living room and sat down. She made little effort to keep the sheet over herself. Her nipples and pubic hair were the color of the honey she'd dripped on the ice cream. Cindi didn't trim her pubic hair. Valerie wondered why Cindi had sat down. Surely not to show off....

Then she realized Cindi was probably still coasting on

coke, which made her more uncomfortable than the nudism. After a moment, Cindi asked, "Where did you guys go tonight?"

Valerie hesitated while deciding whether there was any prodding or jealousy in the question, but there did not seem to be. "We went for pizza," she said.

"Your boyfriend is a very good musician," Cindi said.

"Yes," Valerie said.

What was this? Girl talk in the middle of the night? Valerie wished Cindi would cover herself and go away.

"I felt sort of a third thumb without another woman around. Wish you'd a stayed."

"I wanted to walk. I'd been in a car all day."

"How long a drive is it from Albany to *Bahston*?" Cindi asked.

"I don't know. Thirteen years."

"Are you from Albany too?"

"Too?" Valerie said. "I'm from Saratoga Springs and Cornelius only lives in Albany today. He isn't from anywhere. He's a nomad."

"How did you meet him?"

"Hmm?"

"I said, how did you two meet?" Cindi said again.

"He was playing in a coffeehouse."

"Don't tell me you just fell in love with his music."

"His music is good, but I hate it."

"*Beweh-ah* musicians," she said. "You can't tell them anything."

"Words of wisdom from the Harvard girl," Valerie muttered.

"I'm sorry?"

"I'm real tired, Cindi. Please excuse me if I go to sleep, okay?" she said, still trying to avoid the view.

"Sure."

Valerie left the room, almost running. She went first into the bedroom where Cornelius slept, but she did not stay there long. She went into the bathroom so it would seem to Cindi as if she were readying for bed. With the door slightly open, she spied through the crack at Cindi who sat still in the living room. From here Valerie could see only Cindi's toes and a little of the bed sheet. It felt like a long time to Valerie before Cindi decided to go back to bed, but she finally stood, allowing the sheet to fall off altogether. She left it behind and walked back into Porter's bedroom. Now Valerie could return to the living room.

She sat on the floor beside Clancy's cage and stared at the sleeping bird. Cindi's sheet was rolled up near the couch. It held a fragrance like tobacco ashes and Ivory soap. Valerie could smell it from where she lay. She curled up by the cage and fell asleep eventually.

A baby cried in a dream she had, cried in horrible pain, and she shook herself awake. She sat up in terror as the baby's cry continued. The cry turned out to be some cat outside in the cold, meowing like the sound of a child calling "he-e-lp, he-e-lp." Valerie shuddered. Her period needed tending, and she got up to take care of it, then took a Midol.

As she stood in the dark kitchen, in a strange house, she chalked up her bad dream to a first night in an unfamiliar city. She wanted Porter to come out of his bedroom. She looked wistfully at his closed door as she passed, and then she lay on the couch. Outside it was grey, as dawn came up. She watched the window grow slowly lighter. She shivered.

When she looked outside, all the puddles had frozen, cars were covered with frost. In fact, the frost had killed the grass and leaves on trees were curling.

"But it's July," Valerie complained to the glaze of white outside.

No sun came out to melt the ice and it stayed all day. People did not have ice scrapers, and many drivers peered through small round holes they rubbed out with their fists or melted with cigarette lighters. Others just stayed home.

During the afternoon, Valerie, Porter, and Cindi got

on the trolley to Cambridge to take Cindi home. Wrapped in a bundle of assorted borrowed, oversized clothing, Valerie followed Porter and Cindi up out of Harvard Station. Porter and Cindi never once touched each other. Nevertheless, Valerie felt like a tag along on a brother's date. She could not wait to get Cindi home.

Cindi's apartment was a cold walk from Harvard Square. No one had heat, naturally, so it was not much warmer once they were inside. The apartment was very small—supposedly three girls lived in it. The biggest room was the kitchen, not saying much, and in a little nook off of it there were two bunks like in a submarine. The third girl was the lucky one with her own room, but everyone, including company, passed through it to get to the bathroom. The living room was actually a converted porch, furnished sparsely as there was little available space.

Cindi invited them for lunch. Valerie wished she were free to decline. Porter accepted. He was too much at home here for Valerie's comfort. She wondered if he sometimes slept here in this supreme absence of privacy.

Lunch was no surprise. It was tea with honey (ugh, honey!) and some kind of coarse, homemade bread with *un*homemade jam on it—that was all, end of meal. Valerie finished in no time flat but she did not ask for more. Time stretched on in the Gulag. She sat there, still hungry, thinking of another pizza.

Finally they had served their time and they left. They walked most of the way back to the square in silence. Valerie thought about what it would be like to walk hand in hand. She reviewed her old tricks of getting a guy to touch her first, kept walking, hands in pockets.

"Porter—" she said suddenly, timidly. "You know last night?"

"Yes?"

She wished she had not begun, now she would have to follow through. "You know how we were before Cindi

94

woke up and came out? Was that an accident?"

please say yes

"We were getting to know each other and that is a special moment."

"Oh." Her voice fell like a dull thud. "And that moment is over?" She did not know if she wanted it to be, or not.

"No, not over."

"Oh," again.

He put his arm around her shoulder, squeezed once, took his arm away.

"It's just I noticed you never kiss Cindi or anything," Valerie said.

Porter shrugged. "That's the way it has always been."

"Even during your special moment?"

"We still have those moments. They don't stop happening."

"Porter...do you know what love is?"

"No, Valerie, I don't."

They went down into the kiosk and went down to the subway station, through the turnstiles.

There was a guy playing his guitar on the platform, just the way Porter said he sometimes did. Valerie dug into her purse and threw a few dollars into the guy's open guitar case. There was an odd familiarity about him. A train squealed up, and she and Porter boarded. The doors closed out the music, but Valerie could still see the guy. As the train began to pull away, she realized that he was the guitar player who'd been in the coffeehouse the night Cornelius hadn't been.

She watched the platform slide away, replaced by blackness.

Porter was right, Cornelius drew an impressive audience. Valerie wondered if Cornelius might be originally from Boston. It would explain his local fame. Yet he did not talk like Derek. He did not have any type of accent at all. He really did seem to be from nowhere.

During his break, he sat with them and talked with

Derek and Porter. It hit Valerie that she and Cornelius had not exchanged a single word since their fight. And the ice grew ever thicker. It would take a great heave to break through it.

Or maybe just I'm sorry.

Derek left first. Valerie and Porter remained until the end. Then they went back to Porter's and Valerie went straight to bed. She took the second roommate's room, knowing Cornelius would go into the other, and she closed the door and lay there with the light on all night. On the wall was a poster of a nude woman in a pose too gross to be provocative. Valerie wished she could be held by Porter. It was not sexual desire—it was simple human yearning. She needed to feel something so that she would not feel alone.

The night passed, and she did not think she slept at all. But at some time it had begun to rain again, and she could not recall hearing the first drops. She did not remember, either, when Cornelius' piano had begun to play.

He was writing a new song. Valerie could not hear Porter at all. Perhaps he had gone out. She had no clock, did not know if it was late enough to be up and about. There was nothing to stop Valerie from going out there to put her arms around Cornelius. She could end all of this. But she did not have any scissors. She could not snip through the wall of staves. So she simply lay there, alone, felt helpless, while his new song took shape on the inside of his wall.

When she heard other voices in the apartment, Valerie got up. She went out in her nightgown to find Porter and Cindi. Cornelius continued to play. He was blurred by a cloud of cigarette smoke.

They had not spoken to one another for fifty-three hours.

She sat meekly by Clancy's cage, hugged her knees, and she looked at the bird although she listened to Cornelius' song. It was a beautiful sonata: part sad and lonely, part happy, part haunting – or haunt*ed*. She listened carefully but could not choose.

"You are going home today," Porter informed her.

Valerie nodded, and then she found herself forcing back tears. Something had begun here, she did not even know what it was, but it had begun, and it ought to have the opportunity to finish. Such an opportunity would never be.

They packed up the car the same as they had back in Albany—in silence. And while Valerie tried to take her time, it was finished quickly. The rain poured down outside and they ducked back into the foyer for the farewells and the next-time-you're-in-towns.

Cindi said: "It was nice to meet you," and Valerie could only try to figure out what that was supposed to mean.

And then Valerie and Cornelius were inside her Toyota on the way to the turnpike. As soon as Boston was out of view behind them, she closed her eyes, fell asleep before they reached the toll, and she did not awaken until Stockbridge.

Chapter 9

Valerie awakened and found that they had passed out of the rain. The sun shined and the roads were dry. She looked around the inside of the car as though exploring it for the first time. After she saw Clancy, she looked askance at Cornelius. Finally she said:

"It was a good holiday, wasn't it?"

And he answered, "Yes, it was, Pinnoke."

"I am sorry," she told him.

And he said, "I am sorry too, Pinnoke."

Valerie had one week remaining before her parents returned. She planned to spend all of it with Cornelius.

On the first day, Cornelius had his dream. It startled him awake, in an indefinable panic. And without breathing, he looked at Valerie in the room with him. He looked at the window, at the door. He got out of bed suddenly, dressed slowly but deliberately in the dark, opened the window, then the bedroom door, walked into the living room. He opened the living room window also.

Valerie had been awakened by his movement, and she lay trying to feign sleep. Her eyes were half open in the dark as she watched him, wondered what he was up to. She heard him go out of the apartment, got up quickly and ran downstairs in her nightgown.

She reached the front stoop in time to see him walking, already far off down the sidewalk. She shivered as she watched him pass beneath a streetlamp, and then she went back inside and up to the apartment. It was cold in there now with the windows open. She closed them in a puzzlement, went back to sleep.

On the second day, Cornelius decided that if Clancy was going to be of any use at all, the bird would have to learn to do something. If not talk, then sing. So he sat down at his piano with Clancy's cage on top of it, and he began to play Beethoven. He played only the Sixth Symphony, over and over again, until at last the bird got the feel of the opus and began to sing along. The bird would never utter a single word, but would go on to become a virtuoso of the Sixth Symphony of Beethoven.

Cards from a deck of Disney World playing cards were the foundation of the whole elaborate edifice Cornelius built. They leaned against one another like lean-tos set up in a row. Laid flat atop their peaks was a bridge of cards from a different deck, one with blue backs. The second level on top of that was made of cards with red and blue backs. Another span of cards was laid flat across the second level, and so on upward.

The shadow of the card house beneath the overhead light bulb was an asymmetrical configuration on the table top. Cornelius leaned his face down to the level of the Disney World foundation. He rested his chin on the table. The smoke from his cigarette breathed through the huge card structure and came out in smoke triangles.

Each triangle rose slowly and joined in space with another. They all hooked together like skydivers falling upward. The card house was nearly replicated in smoke, but that one of the skydivers could not catch the rest, and it all broke up before finished. A shapeless ghost of smoke gathered around the light bulb. With a casual wave of his arm, Cornelius knocked apart the cards.

On the third day, a dreadful thing happened. Valerie had to go up to Saratoga to check the house. She wanted Cornelius to accompany her, but he would not. Once she had made certain that everything inside the house was secure, she got back into the car and turned the key.

Nothing happened.

She did not understand how the car could operate fine only five minutes before, then turn up dead. She got out and opened the hood. She knew nothing about a car except that when you turn the key, it is supposed to start. She needed Cornelius. She ran her hands along tubes and wires, covered her arms with grease, but she was helpless. If she did not return to Albany, Cornelius would not know the reason. There was no way to contact him. She was stranded, and she was alone, and he would probably believe that this time it was she who had deserted him. He would not know what to believe.

She opened her cell phone and called her Papa's auto club. In a while a tow truck came around, and the men tried to jump her battery. They tried a few other common remedies for cars that won't start, while Valerie looked on feeling increasingly desperate, but *nothing worked*. Valerie watched the back end of her Toyota lifted by the truck, the men got into the cab, and she watched them drag her car away.

Late in the afternoon her cell rang, and the voice on the phone said that her battery was not holding a charge. That, she was told, did not necessarily indicate a bad battery. "What might it indicate?" she asked. There was no way to be certain, it could still be a lot of things. Until the battery would hold a charge, the problem could not be determined.

"So put in a new battery," Valerie said, and snapped the phone shut.

There was no chance of getting back to Cornelius today. He might think she had been in an accident, but more likely he would think she was still angry with him for what happened before their Boston weekend. There was no way to know what he would think.

She turned on the television, but she could not watch. She got out the telephone book and looked for Cornelius' name—perhaps he had a telephone hidden in his apartment somewhere. She even called the information operator, but as soon as she heard a voice say "What city please," she hung up. Cornelius did not have a phone in his apartment. She knew that. And if he had a cell phone, she had never seen him use it.

It was not even dark outside yet, but she went up to her bedroom, undressed, and got into bed. She pulled the blanket up to her ear. The bed grew warmer, and her depression enabled her to fall asleep. The phone began to ring, but she was too settled to get out of bed to answer it. It stopped ringing, and then it occurred to her that it might have been Cornelius. She whined, reached for the stuffed white elephant, and was asleep a few minutes later.

More than likely that phone call had been the garage, so in the morning Valerie checked the caller ID. Sure enough. But the mechanic who had been working on it was out sick now, and no one else there knew anything about it. "Is someone else going to look at it?" she asked.

"We'll get to it."

"Yes, I am certain that you will get to it," Valerie said in Italian, and hung up.

She did not even dress that day. She took a long shower only because standing under the water created a limbo in which she had to neither plan nor do. When she turned off the shower, she dried herself and took her time wandering from the bathroom to her bedroom, back to the bathroom to brush her hair, back to her bedroom – not until she was dressed would she have to do anything.

She simply did not know what to do.

Finally she put on her robe and quit, went downstairs to the television room and clicked on the tube. She used to watch all the soaps, every day, but now she felt like a prisoner condemned to watch them, either the soaps, or else all of the talk shows.

She picked up a magazine and hurled it at the wall. Its pages fluttered. There had to be some way to let Cornelius know of this fine mess she was in. She stood up and retrieved the magazine, sat on the couch again, flipped through the wrinkled pages.

Her Mama and Papa came home three days early. And they found her sitting in the television room in her robe, looking at the pictures and browsing through the recipes in a magazine—exactly as they had left her.

Valerie began to read, rather than watch television all day. And then, in ultimate boredom, she turned to letter writing, something she never did. She wrote a letter to her Nana, one to her cousin Gina, and then she wrote a letter to Cornelius. It was a long, sentimentally sloppy letter which she was not brave enough to send once it was finished. So she wrote another one, a letter which simply explained the trouble she was having with her car, and she sent that one. But a little later she grew bold again and she sent the original letter.

Writing to Cornelius appealed to Valerie so much that he began to receive letters every day from her. Sometimes he would find two on the same day. Valerie buried herself in her room, taking all her meals there, perpetually writing to Cornelius on stationery with little yellow ducks in the corner. She wrote everything and anything that came to mind as she sat there on her bed, and she looked out the window at her garden as she lay on the carpet beside the air-conditioning vent. Every last thought was consigned to paper, some in words, some in pictures, and some as mere scribbles of color.

Two and a half days later Valerie emerged in the same clothes she had gone in wearing, the cloth now stiff and dried with sweat. Her curlicue hair was a flattened, itching mass hanging into her face and on her shoulders. Her legs and her underarms were black from not shaving. She carried a tome of every thought and feeling, logged by hour and by day, which she brought to the post office in a manila envelope. She paid an impressive postage and mailed it.

Then, when she got home, she returned to her bedroom, locked the door again, and wrote some more. Cornelius took each of her letters as they arrived and tacked them page by page like a story board on the walls of his apartment. Day by day the wall space filled in until all around was Valerie's careful handwriting with duck after cute little duck on each page.

At long last the cell phone rang with word that her car was fixed. By this time, beneath her eyes were circles black as her irises, her face was pale, and her right arm was cramped from elbow to fingers so that she could not use it for a week. She carried one last letter to the post office. Then she returned home, removed her clothes like cardboard from her body, and she went into the bathroom to take a shower.

She rejoined her parents at the dinner table, all showered and shaved, in fresh clothes and perfumed. She wore her hair in a short ponytail, as it was now just long enough to tie with a yellow ribbon,

"Did you finish what you have been working on?" her Mama asked.

"I met a boy," Valerie said in Italian. "I mean a man. He is really nice, too, I'm sure you would like him—not like the others. I was writing letters to him."

"Where does he live that you have to write to him?"

"He lives down in Albany. His name is Cornelius Prince. He plays the piano."

"He is not an Italian."

"Mama, what does that matter? Papa, do you know any people in the record business?"

Her Papa chuckled and said in English, "You want me to get one of them to let your new boyfriend make a CD?"

"He is not a boyfriend, Papa," she answered in Italian.

"You do know people who could help him?"

"Perhaps I do," said her Papa, in English. "Do you want me to discover him?"

Valerie, in Italian: *"This is not a game, Papa."*

"How old is this musician who is not your boyfriend?" her Papa inquired in Italian.

"I am not sure," she said in English. "He never told me. He might be about twenty-five. Maybe he's twenty-six. But he is very talented. His age isn't important. And you would love his music. He plays Beethoven."

"A classical pianist?" Now her Papa looked interested.

"And jazz. He is very serious about his work," Valerie assured him. "He practices all the time. All he needs is the help of someone who knows people. And I thought that perhaps you would know some people."

"I would like to meet him."

"Does that mean you will help?"

"It means I would like to meet him. Where is he working now, we could hear him play."

"Umm...he's not. He's out of work right now." Valerie feared this would be a big point against Cornelius. "But he just finished a real good gig in Boston."

"Will he come here?" her Papa asked.

"But we don't have a piano," Valerie said.

"He must have one. We will go to his house."

Valerie envisioned her Papa's face when he saw Cornelius' neighborhood. "On second thought, Papa, Corey's piano is portable, maybe he should bring it here."

"A portable piano?"

"It's electric."

"Electric pianos are for rock and roll, not for Beethoven."

"He plays a lot of different music. Mostly jazz and classical though—trust me, Papa, you will like him."

"Can he come to dinner tomorrow night?"

Valerie squealed. "Oh! I am certain he can! I'll go see him tonight and invite him. Do you know some people who can help him, Papa?"

"I will see how the boy plays first." said her Papa in Italian.

She could not pick up her car until the next day, but she was too excited to wait, so she borrowed her Mama's car and drove to Albany to tell Cornelius what her Papa had said.

Cornelius said he did not want to go.

"What do you mean!" Valerie said.

"You did not tell me you were going to do this, Pinnoke."

"I wanted it to be a surprise."

"You don't even realize what you have done," he said.

"I think you got cold feet. Tell me you wouldn't love a recording contract. I bet you even have picked out the song you would want to do."

"Producer does that."

"And Papa could help you get a producer. Corey, you have to do this. I've arranged it with Papa. What would he think if you didn't come?"

"It is not my problem."

"God, Cornelius, I can't figure you out. What in the world are you afraid of?"

"You know," he said point blank.

"Good Lord, *look* at this place you live in. Do you want to always live this way?"

"If you were not so determined to look out for me, you would be freer to look out for yourself."

Valerie opened her mouth, but she said nothing. She had an eerie feeling that he was speaking of something else. And he had that look in his eyes, like he knew what she would say next.

She made herself smile, placed his hands precisely on her hips, and she said to him: "You cannot resist an Italian's stubbornness, ya know. If you don't come to dinner tomorrow, I will come down here with Papa."

Cornelius stepped away. "You do not understand, Pinnoke, but if I told you, you still would not. So I will come, and I will play my heart out."

She stepped up to him and kissed him. "I understand that you are nervous. It's natural. I will see you tomorrow. I will pick you up at five-thirty. And wear a tie. Oh—and play Beethoven. I told him you play Beethoven, and he likes Beethoven."

She turned to go, then she looked back at him and grinned. *"By the way,"* she said in Italian, *"I love your new wallpaper."* And feeling very nearly on top of the world, she went out.

Valerie's Papa did not sit and listen to Cornelius play. He ran out of the room where Cornelius had set up his piano and amp and then he ran back in with his violin, opened the case, and began to play.

"Do you have a demo CD?" her Papa asked him when they finished.

"No, I've sort of been waiting for this," Cornelius replied.

Then her Papa promised to contact one Edgar Pufknack, who would be able to set up studio time for Cornelius to make his demo.

As she drove toward Albany, however, Valerie could sense that Cornelius did not feel triumph. He said nothing, even when she spoke to him. And as they went up the stairs in his building, the door still squeaking slowly closed behind them, she said, "This calls for celebration," and he responded, "Why is that?"

"Let's break out the root beer," she said as he unlocked the apartment door.

"If you say so, Pinnoke."

"Corey, Papa doesn't get out his violin for just anyone. And if he says he will call Edgar Pufknack, I know that he will do it. Papa is a man of his word."

Cornelius gave her a root beer and they went out on the fire escape.

"Can't you let yourself get excited about anything?"

He took out a coin and began to roll it over his

knuckles.

She put her arm around his waist. "What the heck is bothering you?"

"Pinnoke, you should get home. It's late, and it is a long drive."

"Would you like me to stay the night?" she offered. "I could. They will have gone straight to bed. They don't wait for me."

"I think we ought to both be alone tonight," he said.

"Okay. I'll see you tomorrow."

"Thank you for the ride home, Pinnoke."

She kissed him good-bye and went out. When she got down to her car, got in, and turned the key in the ignition, it did not start. It was supposed to be as good as new, and it had died again. She thought about going back up to his apartment, but he had asked to be alone, and although she could not understand what his problem was, she had to honor his wish. So she curled up in the back seat, with the doors locked, and she fell asleep there.

A street cleaner, with its lights flashing, passed around her car, and the noise woke her up. She sat up quickly, not knowing what was happening to her, or where she was. It was still dark, no signs of dawn. The street cleaner was down the street now, and she remembered why she was asleep in her car.

She got out of the car and noticed that the temperature had begun to go back up. Perhaps by morning, it would be summer again. Then she got into the front seat and tried the engine again. This time it started. She pulled away from the curb, turned on her headlights, and headed for home. There was a parking ticket on her windshield.

She pulled through a drive-thru and bought a cup of coffee, and then headed up the Northway, sipping the coffee and feeling troubled. Now that she was fully awake, she thought about Cornelius' strange view of opportunity knocking. The radio told her the late night headlines: an automobile accident, caused by drunk driving, had killed three; a tornado in the central part of the country had turned a whole town into a pile of scattered playing cards; oil prices were, again, higher than ever; economic indicators were inconclusive. She wondered where all the news of happy people was.

Perhaps Cornelius was plain nervous.

She reached home and it was still dark. She must have slept a very short time in the back of her car. But thanks to the coffee, she was wide awake now. Instead of going into the house, Valerie sat outside in her garden. The air was pleasant, summer was indeed coming back. She could smell the flowers around her as she sat on the bench.

No lights were on inside. The garden was totally dark. She could not see the flowers that she smelled or the trellises or the hedges, she could not see her own writer's cramped hand before her face.

There was no moon or stars.

Valerie sat there in blindness; and then the crickets stopped their noise, and the sounds of traffic from routes 50 and 9, not far off, ceased. She sat there in abject silence; and then the smells of the flowers and of the grass and hedges no longer reached her nostrils. Then her seat was numb and she could not feel the bench beneath herself, nor could her feet feel the softness of the grass.

For a moment, all she had were her thoughts and her dreams, her hopes for a future. She felt like screaming out. And so, in fear, she went into the house.

Chapter 10

"What is the matter now!" Valerie asked, practically kicking the door open as Cornelius unlocked it.

He followed her into his apartment, flicked on the light, and closed the door. "I don't know, Pinnoke," he said, "what is the matter?"

"I mean with *you*," she said, throwing her purse on the couch. She tossed up her arms. "Maybe you didn't understand Mr. Pufknack. He said he wants you to go to New York."

"Sure I understood him, Pinnoke."

"Don't you want to go to New York?"

His eyes flashed in an ambivalent way. He said, "What's the best way to get to Carnegie Hall?"

"*What?!*"

"We have arrived at a critical point."

"Yes, we have," she agreed. "But for heaven's sake, it's good, isn't it? I don't think you think so."

"Practice," he said. "The answer is practice. ...I can't fight it now. The hero has his big break, and the only thing remaining to finish is for him to get the girl."

Valerie blushed. "Well...you have the girl," she stammered.

"I mean for keeps," he told her.

"You mean...like in, uh, getting...mar-ried?"

"Okay."

"Oh my God—do you mean it?"

"Of course."

"Yes! Oh yes!" she shouted. "Yes yes yes yes yes yes yes yes yes yes," she said yes four hundred and thirty-seven times, all the while laughing, crying, giggling uncontrollably, jumping up and down, squealing. Then she stopped it all suddenly to say: "But you don't mean tonight, do you?"

"I thought we might wait a little while," Cornelius said.

Like until after the demo was made.

However, people began to wonder, when Edgar Pufknack dropped off the face of the planet for two and a half months, if there would ever really be a demo at all. Valerie's Papa did not know what had happened to him, neither did Metacarpal Records, the studio Edgar Pufknack represented.

Summer ended immediately after Labor Day. The leaves turned color, the wind took them off the trees, and before that day was over, it was autumn. Valerie's Papa had his classes again, and with each additional day of Edgar Pufknack's absence, as he returned home at night, he met his daughter with increasing chagrin. He promised to try to reach Edgar Pufknack again, and if he could not locate him, he would see what he could do about finding someone else.

By Valerie's twentieth birthday, most everyone had given up. Valerie became anxious that Cornelius would change his mind about marrying her. She feared that he would feel that as a poor man he would not be able to support her properly as a husband should. On the afternoon of her birthday, they walked through Washington Park in Albany, kicking through piles of shriveled, fallen leaves. As they walked, Valerie linked her arm through his and said she was sorry to have put him through all of this, only to end with disappointment. She loved him, no matter what, she said, and even if they had to eat scrambled eggs every day for eight and a half years, she would still marry him.

Cornelius was the only one who had not gone off into a tizzy these two and a half months. "Of course we are going to marry, Pinnoke," he said. "We have to. And I am not worried about scrambled eggs."

"That would never happen. I was just being romantic. My family has too much money."

They sat on the ground and Cornelius lit a cigarette. The wind snatched the smoke away before it left his lips. Valerie sat beside him with her knees drawn to her chest, and her feet together. She stared at the toes of her shoes.

"I will never leave you, Cornelius," she said suddenly.

He looked at her.

"No matter what," she promised. "No matter how bad things might get for us—I'll love you forever. But things will never get bad for us because we'll live on love. And I will always make you happy. We'll be together forever and ever—until the cows come home."

"The day will come," he said cryptically, "when you will leave me in the most selfish way possible."

"*Oh no, Corey! Never!*" she sprang to her knees, clutched his arm urgently, "How can you say that?" she demanded, fighting tears.

Cornelius crushed his cigarette beneath his boot. "Pinnoke..." he said softly, and it was the first time she had ever heard him speak with so much emotion. "Pinnoke..." he put his arms around her. "Valerie," he whispered, and for a moment he looked like a different man, like a weak man—an old and tired man looking back on a lifetime of sweat and bleeding, with his heart aching.

"I will never leave you," Valerie said.

He kissed her. She simply could not imagine what would make him say such a terrible thing when she had promised to be his wife.

"Shhh, Pinnoke, it's your birthday."

The very next day, Edgar Pufknack reappeared. Just like that. Turned out he had been traveling near and far looking for musicians good enough to play back-up for Cornelius. It had not been an easy search, but he managed to find, after traipsing from one end of the continent to the other, two guys who were nearby after all.

He had a drummer named Daniel Serahuli from Buffalo, but the real find was a musical wizard from New Jersey named Andrew Healy. Andrew was twenty-three years old; he played the keyboards, any kind of guitar, the flute, stringed instruments, saxophone, even a cittern, all as if he were born especially for each. He was a likeable looking fellow, with reddish hair and a brown mustache. His eyes had a perpetual sleepy look, so that no matter where he was or what he did, he looked as if he wanted to be somewhere else.

They finally made the demo. By the end of the winter of that year, they made an album. The CD was released with the private joke of a title: *The Milagro Beanfield Truce*. On the cover was a picture of a grand piano with an arrow piercing it like a valentine. Daniel Serahuli played drums; Cornelius had a field day in the studio with several different types of keyboards; and Andrew filled in all the other parts playing violins, flutes, and, the liner notes said, "Thirteen hundred and two guitars."

The album was mainly instrumental, but there was one song releasable as a single. It hit the charts at 94 and got downloaded onto a few hard drives before moving, only once, to 96 before vanishing.

The longest track took up most of the CD. It was the sonata Cornelius had begun work on in Boston, changed somewhat, with strings added and arranged by Andrew. An abbreviated version of it got some airplay on college radio stations. It was titled "Valerie."

During the long making of the album, Valerie ran

around Manhattan—her first time ever in the City—a little child turned loose in a concrete candy factory. She visited the top of the Empire State Building, she walked down the narrow streets of the financial district but avoided the site of "ground zero." She ice skated at Rockefeller Center, and she went into Saint Patrick's Cathedral.

She wandered down the wide center aisle, looked closely at the Stations of the Cross, peered inside an empty confessional booth. She had not been to church in years (but God understands when you are truly sick). She had returned, finally, as a tourist.

Valerie reached the studio on 52nd Street while Cornelius, Andrew, Daniel, and the rest of the crew stood around listening to the mix of Andrew's saxophone track. She walked past the receptionist, down the hall and found the control booth, and she pulled open the heavy door. She carried her coat over her arm. Her hair, growing quite long and straightening out these days, was tied into a ponytail with a yellow ribbon. The ribbon was loose by now and her hair looked disheveled from a busy day on Fifth Avenue. She wore a white embroidered ski sweater, which accented her perpetual tan.

It was when she had the door open that the sax mix hit her ears, and she suddenly felt like crying. She fought that feeling, and smiled at a woman whom she realized was the mix engineer, and at Edgar Pufknak, who were busy listening.

So Valerie looked through the glass at the microphones and the chrome trusses, which reflected the work lights, and at the wires and the monitors, and at her husband-to-be leaning against the baby grand. Andrew cradled his sax, Daniel sat beside some woman who had a clipboard. Valerie's own reflection distracted her in the glass like an apparition.

When the recorded sax stopped, she shyly asked to go in to talk to Cornelius. The mix engineer touched a button and told Valerie simply to talk.

"Ummm...Corey?" Valerie said, and everyone beyond her reflection turned toward the booth. She said self-consciously, "Hi," and blushed at the sound of her own voice coming through speakers all around. "How's everything?"

To the engineer and Edgar Pufknack, she said, "Will I be able to hear him if he talks back?"

"Only if you listen very carefully," Cornelius said.

"Oh! Umm, I just wanted to say hi. I went shopping today. I bought this sweater; and I got something else, too, that is *really* dumb. I'll show it to you later. I don't know why I even bought it—and you'll see why when you see what it is—but it was on sale and I couldn't resist the impulse. Sightseeing does strange things to a person. Well, you are busy, so I'll see you later at the hotel."

"Right, Pinnoke."

"Ummm...it's a wrap." She giggled and left the booth.

"Who was that?" Andrew asked.

"That is Pinnoke," said Cornelius.

Later on, when Cornelius returned to their hotel room, he found Valerie asleep on the bedspread. He sat beside her, ran his hand softly down her back, waited, as if for an elevator, for the dream she was having to finish before he woke her. She lifted her head slowly, recognized Cornelius before she recognized the room, kissed him hello. Still filled with sleep, she remembered that he was busy making a CD and asked if it was finished yet. He said no.

"Do you want to see what I bought today?" she said.

Reaching into a bag, she drew out a burgundy colored bathing suit which, in her hands, did not look big enough to fit a doll. She withdrew to the bathroom to put it on.

With a flourishing "Da-daah!" she stepped out wearing it, assumed a solicitous pose in the doorframe.

The color looked very good on her dark body. The leg

holes of the suit arched very high over her hipbones so that it plunged up obscenely from between her legs in front, left most of her bottom bare. The suit had no back, and with very little material it crossed over itself in front, and if her breasts had been of any size they'd have been tumbling out. As it was, the way the scant material stretched, every line of her body was enhanced, and the bulges of her nipples could not be ignored.

"That isn't really designed for swimming, is it?" Cornelius said.

"I will never *dare* wear it," she said. "It was on sale for half off. Hee hee – you could say it is half off when it's on. Ya gotta love New York, because there was a whole rack of bathing suits in my size—which is extremely rare. Don't worry. I bought one that's more modest and tame, too."

"I'm not worried, Pinnoke."

"It's yellow. Want to see it?" She reached into the bag again and pulled out a bright yellow maillot suitable for a public beach. "Isn't it pretty? I almost bought a third one, but I bought the sweater instead. Do you like the sweater?"

"Yes."

"Want me to model the yellow bathing suit for you?" She untied the string behind her neck and peeled off the burgundy suit, such as it was. She had one leg into the yellow one when Cornelius grabbed her with a hand on each of her hips and lifted her up like a potted plant.

He lowered her onto the bed, kissed her for the rest of the night.

"I am planning a very big wedding," She said to him as they lay in bed in the morning. "Papa would not have it any other way. Especially since I'm his only daughter."

"I'd prefer a small wedding, Pinnoke."

"There is no such thing in an Italian family. You're going to be an honorary Italian from now on. We've got to have lots of food and dancing...and more food...and after that more food."

"Who can eat that much?"

"They'll all be too drunk to notice."

"All the more reason not to be able to eat," Cornelius said.

"Don't worry. We can leave. We're only the bride and groom—we don't count. I can't drink, and I hate a lot of drunk people—especially relatives. Soon as no one is looking," she moved her face real close to his and said conspiratorially, "we will slip away and go get a pizza. Where do you want to go on our honeymoon?"

"Cohoes."

"I'm serious."

"Pinnoke, I don't like all this wedding stuff. That's up to your father—I don't have any money. Anyway, right now we have to get this album done, and I am late for the session."

"You take all the fun out of getting married. Well, don't worry, at least the wedding party will be small. I'm only having my cousin, Gina, as my maid of honor. So you only need to have a best man, and you don't have to worry about ushers."

Cornelius got out of bed. "I'm not worried about ushers. Am I the family black sheep-to-be because I never gave you an engagement ring?"

"Who cares about that," she shrugged.

Then she said: "Cornelius...you know what you said on my birthday about me leaving you? What did you mean by that?"

"Your birthday is over, Valerie. Think about today." He went into the bathroom to shower.

"I love you!" Valerie called to him as she lay there in the bed. Somehow it sounded like a threat.

The sound of the shower came out of the bathroom. Valerie got out of bed, too, picked up her new bathing suits, stuck them back into the bag. She sat at the dressing table and began to brush her hair, so it would continue to straighten as it was doing—a little more each day.

PART TWO

Chapter 1

On the day of the wedding, in the middle of the reception, Cornelius would walk out of the Italian-American Center, stroll on down the street, turn a corner, and continue into a hamburger stand. He would step to the counter in his blue-grey tuxedo, the striped tie unknotted and the collar open, and none of the adolescent girls in their pajama-like uniforms, nor the small family in the back of the lobby, nor the old man with no teeth who shuffled his feet beneath his table, would notice. When Cornelius left the hamburger stand, he would walk down the street and think about the wedding blaring away in what he believed to be drunkenly overstated fervor, the preparations of which he had nothing to do with.

It was taken for granted by Valerie's Papa that there would be an open bar, wine with the meal, a champagne toast. At first, she merely stipulated that her own glass be filled with ginger ale for the toast, thus solving any problems—but the more she thought about it, the more she did not want anyone at all to be drinking at her wedding.

She told her Papa at dinner one night that she

wanted the toasts raised with root beers—in bottles, she decided at that moment. Her parents thought she was joking, and they laughed out loud.

"*It is no joke, Papa,*" Valerie said in Italian.

"You will have ginger ale, or root beer, or whatever you want," her Papa chuckled in English, "but do you want all your relatives to be angry at your Mama and Papa when they have come to have a good time?"

"*Why do you think that they will have anger?*"

"A wedding is a happy time," he said incredulously, "and it is a sacrament—and you want to make a joke of it with root beer toasts?"

"If it is a sacrament, I wish to keep it sacred. Please, Papa, do not have the open bar and do not have the wine. It is *my* wedding, Papa."

"*The reception is for the guests,*" said her Papa, now in Italian. "*They will want to celebrate.*"

"I want them to celebrate," Valerie agreed, "and I want them to mean it."

"Of course they will mean it," Valerie's Mama said.

"My marriage will not be an excuse for drunkenness," Valerie said firmly. "And you know that it will become one."

"A wedding is not an excuse for drunkenness—it is a reason," her Papa said. "It is a celebration—not a wake for the dead."

"*Papa!*" Valerie's hand slammed on the table so that the dishes rattled, and the wine in her parents' glasses swilled about. "I have said no; you will do it my way."

"*How dare you speak this way to your Papa?*" said her Mama. "*You are the child. And you have yet to ask for your Papa's permission to marry this boy. Your Papa has charge of your wedding. He is paying for it.*"

"And I have nothing to do or say?" Valerie switched back to English. "I'm just supposed to get married and smile pretty for the family album, and be a good little girl, right?"

"You are the child until you walk away from the

altar."

"Why are you making such a problem of this?" her Papa said calmly.

"Because it's important to me, Papa. It's my day, and I want to be spared the sight of sloshing glasses, and red eyes, and slaps on the rear with insincere congratulations. I want people to be happy because I have done something grand, and not because they want to make the hangover they are in for worth the misery. If they are happy, they will have fun no matter what they drink. And if they don't care, I *want* them to sit around bored silly."

"And do you want me to cancel the band too, and while I'm at it the hall, and we'll have the reception in the back yard?" her Papa said.

"In the back yard would be kind of nice, Papa." Valerie stood up and walked out of the dining room.

Valerie's Mama looked at her husband sadly, and he said:

"She already is not her Papa's daughter."

Valerie left her house and drove down to Albany to be with Cornelius. That is when she discovered that it was Cornelius' turn to disappear. His apartment door was open, and everything looked fine from the stairs as she walked up. But when she reached the landing and peered in, she found the piano and the birdcage missing.

She sat on the couch beside the exposed spring. She looked at the space where the piano had been set up, and she knew that its absence meant he had not simply gone to the store for milk. Clancy's absence portended that everyone would be gone for quite a while—possibly for good.

Valerie was too stunned to do anything. To feel anything. To observe her, it would seem that she had retreated from her body altogether—Only the empty works of a human organism fired its nerve endings, pumped its blood, took in oxygen and respirated carbon dioxide, kept itself in service, in the event that the person it housed should return.

Cornelius stayed away for one month.

During that time, Valerie's body walked around, ate, slept, did as it was asked by its parents, spoke to people when spoken to, and even sat in front of the television. One day Andrew Healy came to visit Valerie's body, because he was supposed to be Cornelius' best man and he too had discovered the would-be groom missing.

"He is gone," her body said to him.

"Do you know where?"

"He took Clancy with him," the body reported. "I do not know where they went. I do not know if they are coming back."

"Would Cornelius just abandon you a month before the wedding, without telling anyone?" Andrew wondered.

"He is a nomad."

"He must be coming back. I can't believe he would do this. There's still time before the wedding. Maybe he just needed a vacation. To think things out." Andrew paced nervously, angrily. He thought of all the places Cornelius might have gone, considered whether it was worth looking for him. "That isn't unreasonable. So don't worry."

"I am not worried," said the body.

The wedding plans flowed along, uninterrupted. No one had informed the bride's parents that there existed the possibility of the lack of a groom. Winter ended in late March, the snow melted, the ground sopped and filled the air with the smell of damp earth, buds appeared on branches. Andrew returned to New York City to see if Edgar Pufknack or anyone at Metacarpal Records had heard from Cornelius.

No one had.

Valerie's parents began to suspect their daughter's sudden cooperation. They feared she was up to something. Possibly she planned to elope. Anyone who remained capable of feeling became tense and edgy. Valerie's body remained passive. Everything was about to explode and come down on Valerie's body, which merely sat and looked at magazines, when the doorbell rang.

Parcel post with a very large package for Valerie.

The package was singing Beethoven's Sixth Symphony.

Valerie thought Clancy's return was meant to end the engagement. She ripped open the package in a fury, wanting to scream, to cry, but unable to call up either. However, when she had the package open, there was Clancy, chirping away, with an engagement ring around his ankle. Valerie gazed at the diamond for a long time, watched it reflect the light in the front hall as the bird hopped around the cage. With the open box and the torn brown wrappings around her feet, Valerie stood up and looked about like someone who had been asleep a long time, who had awakened to find everything changed, and she observed:

"It's spring."

The next day, Cornelius was back in his apartment. He had gone north to Potsdam and joined a guitarist named Martin O'Kelly, a horn player named Alvin Haynes, and a bass viol player named Gene Bienvenue, who populated a band called Next Tuesday. Cornelius had used the money from those gigs to buy the engagement ring and have it shipped to Valerie. He had played once more with the band to get fare home, then he bid them good-bye and left. Valerie was ready to kill him, engagement ring or no engagement ring.

She found him smoking a cigarette in his apartment. She plopped herself down and did not speak, did not even look at him. But he ignored her too, and the two of them sat there not paying any attention to each other for a long time. Valerie recalled the day they met and she felt like laughing. She was determined not to break, though, so she sat there biting her lip with her arms folded indignantly, watching him out of the sides of her eyes. He smoked quietly as if he and the bird were the only ones in the room. Finally Valerie couldn't stand it anymore. She said:

"You could at least say hello."

"Your hair's grown pretty long, Pinnoke," he said.

She touched her hair, now down to her shoulder blades, very thick, its weight pulling the curl out, and she said, "Surprised it's not grey from wondering where the devil you have been for a month. Do you like my hair long?"

"It looks good."

"I didn't even realize it had gotten this long. But I like it too. It's straight. It has never been straight before, even when I used to wear it long."

She looked at the little suns in his eyes and she smiled, unable to be angry with him. He had a young face in spite of his thin hair. He was only a little boy. He was frightened to death like a little boy.

And, no wonder. The wedding was in a huge church with towering stained glass windows – a long, high Mass said in Italian. The bride's family filled every pew available to it, and then some. Cornelius' side of the church was empty. Valerie trembled down the aisle with her Papa, attended by her cousin Gina.

There is no intrinsic drama to a wedding ceremony, despite the theatrics of it. They all pretty much start out and turn out the same. Valerie looked beautiful in her white dress and veil, with her dark face framed by her rich black hair. Cornelius watched from beside the altar as she approached, and he thought that she looked like a child playing in her mother's wedding dress. He did not understand any of the Italian. When the priest addressed him, the only clue was that all eyes in the church were on him. He said "I do" when he judged that to be the appropriate response.

At the reception, Valerie was greatly distressed to

discover real champagne in her glass. She looked at her
Papa with a frown, and during the toast she blatantly did
not raise her glass.

Everyone swarmed over Valerie and it bothered her
that they seemed to forget she had not married herself.
She spied Cornelius standing off by himself on one side
of the hall, alone, while guests danced and flirted with
the bride. And then, he was not there anymore.

That was when he slipped out and went to the burger
stand.

Imagine a line.
It cannot be done.

For each time the mind tries, it must begin with
something – but except for length, a line has no concrete
dimension. A line is endless in two directions, and yet
the mind is forced to originate it with a point and extend
from there. And too, the human vantage does not
consider naturally that space is curved and every line
will eventually loop back on itself. A line is the closest
entity to eternity, both straight and curved at once, and
it cannot be understood in its true nature by the human
mind. Two lines will form a plane, and upon a plane the
first cell of life was placed, like an egg, to start the motion
that separates time from the infinite.

As he walked in the opposite direction from the
Italian-American Center, a paper cup in one hand, the
crumpled wrapping of a cheeseburger in the other,
Cornelius remembered the day Valerie walked into that
coffeehouse. He could not be surprised by a thing which
followed, not even this wedding. Lately, his clairvoyance
held a closer resemblance to a perpetual *déjà vu*. With
the April sunlight slanting between buildings, the evening
turning cool, Cornelius began to sweat. He felt his legs
weaken

(i will never leave you)

and he had to stop walking. Sitting on the curb, he
wiped sweat from his face with his sleeve. Light skidded

off passing cars, dashed brightly in every direction. The effect gave him a headache. In just one spot. An intense pain where a lightning bolt might have gone into his skull.

He squinted at all the street motion: automobiles, people walking, shop doors opening and closing, dogs wandering, children laughing and carrying balloons from the park, chasing pigeons. Sirens wailed far away, sirens wailed closer, they were coming down this street. Cars pulled over, people stood and stared in their tracks, dogs howled painfully, children with their balloons chased the red fire trucks. Cornelius watched as the scene was absorbed by the light

(but it was almost dusk)

into a kaleidoscope of confusion. People opened and closed, shop doors wandered, pigeons chased fire trucks, dogs carried balloons and laughed, children howled painfully.

Cornelius' stomach and head pounded. He began to hiccup. The sweat he wiped from his brow was red. He stared at the back of his hand and saw beads of red rise from each of his pores. He wiped the red away, watched more ooze out. He wiped his brow a second time, and again his fingers came down red. It was blood, squeezing from his pores with his sweat—*like* sweat.

His *déjà vu* was turning on him and showing him that which was out of his power to turn around. These were events that could not surprise him.

Cornelius lay in the gutter, his tuxedo drenched with his bloody sweat. He hauled himself to his knees, looked about at the people passing. He walked every day to get ideas for his music. Everything led to an idea, this one useful, that one not. He walked all over every city he'd ever lived in, and he had watched. But he wished he had never taken this particular walk.

He dusted off his clothes, wondered what to do about the stains. The sun had gone down. Beneath the streetlamps Cornelius walked back to the reception. He found Valerie sitting outside, her veil discarded, her hair flowing down her back, her legs folded inside the skirts of her wedding dress. She saw him coming far off, and when he drew close enough for the stains on his clothes to show, she gasped. "Oh my God, Corey! What happened to you?"

"Mud. A truck ran through a puddle."

"Andrew told me you went for a walk. They wanted to cut the cake."

Cornelius sat down beside her. "Sorry, Pinnoke. I hadn't planned to be gone long."

"Apologize to Papa—he's the one's mad. No one else really cares. They cut the cake anyhow."

Cornelius took her hand. Her very tiny hand, like a rabbit's foot. "You are the only one I care about," he said. "I am saying I'm sorry to you."

"I don't blame you for leaving. I came out here for the same reason. Everybody's drunk—just what I was afraid of. I'm furious With Papa. Only reason I'm mad at you is we said we'd go for a walk together, and you left me stranded."

"I needed to be alone, Pinnoke."

"So did I. I understand. All that going on in there? That's all *wrong*. We just did a scary thing, and they don't care." Valerie stared at Cornelius, squeezed what she could of his hand. "I am Valerie Prince now, huh?"

"You are still Pinnoke to me."

"But what does it mean?" she said to him. "We got to help each other now—forever. We have to work like hell every day of our lives...I will never leave you, Corey."

"I love you, Valerie."

She started to cry. At first she fought it, but then she let go. Cornelius cuddled her and she sobbed against his bloody vest. Then she looked up at him with puffy eyes. She blew her nose, wiped her cheeks dry, kissed him. She said: "When we get home to your silly little apartment I am going to love you like you've never been loved. Right now, let's go back in there and laugh at them. Because they don't even know what's going on."

So they went back in, and a sentimental tenor was singing an Italian love song. Some people were dancing, drunkenly holding one another up. Valerie and Cornelius walked over to the ravaged wedding cake and, with no one and no cameras watching, they each picked up a piece and fed each other.

Chapter 2

The apartment always swelled of raw gas – so thick that eyes watered. The old man fumbled his keys with age spotted hands, unlocked the door. He heaved the brass goose-necked lamp over the threshold, left it just inside the door. He shuffled into the kitchen and lit a burner. The gas first hissed, pumping more fumes into the air, then the flame caught. He lit a cigar off the stove, coughed as the smoke scraped down his windpipe. It was a damp cough, a cough that brought phlegm into the back of his throat, that yanked on his diaphragm. He had learned to live with the cough, until he would eventually die with it.

His elbow knocked a sauce pan off the counter, and it clanked and banged loudly, tumbled under the sink pipes. He grunted, strained to get down on his knees, looked at the rust-eaten pipes, reached for the pan. He dragged it over the rippled floor and hauled himself up awkwardly. He coughed again, dumped the loose ash of his cigar into the sink, and placed the sauce pan on the blue gas flame. He opened a can of corned beef hash. The hash slid from its aluminum mold, retained its vacuum packed shape until the heat broke it down.

The old man shuffled back to his living room. All of his furniture was covered by yellowed sheets. He ran his hand up and down the stand of the goose-necked lamp. He might have purchased a telephone table, a pewter pot, or an alarm clock

(what use did he have for time?)

or a rug, but he already had plenty of those. He dragged the lamp farther into the apartment. He had a lot of lamps, too, but this was the only one like it. Arranged as if by category around the room were the myriad purchases from a hundred garage sales, porch sales, lawn sales, Salvation Army thrift stores. The old man lived alone, collected as though priceless the furniture outgrown by other lives.

Cornelius refocused his eyes so that the wood grain would close—now he only stared over the edge of the bed at solid floorboards. He believed Valerie to be still asleep, until she asked him what he was looking at.

"The lamp," he replied.

She perched her head on his shoulder and peered at the boards he looked at. "What lamp?"

"More lead people."

"Huh?"

"Nothing...I was just thinking."

"About what? Corey, did you ever know we were going to get married?"

"Uh-huh. Right after you said yes."

"I mean way back in the beginning."

"In the beginning..."

"I'm not sure if I knew or not," Valerie said. "After all I've been through, I guess I might have been thinking I'd probably not know what love was, even if I found it. But then, I guess I always believed my prince would come yet—get it? My prince would come and your name is Prince? This is no time for joking. I should get up now."

Valerie rolled back to her portion of the skinny bed. She looked into the small mirror she'd bought and brushed her long hair. Then she put on her robe and went to the kitchen.

While stirring up pancake batter, cooking sausage,

making orange juice, cracking eggs, Valerie sang this song, which her Mama used to sing:

I love you—
a bushel and a peck,
a bushel and a peck,
a bushel and a peck.
I love you—
a bushel and a peck.

Summer brought the disappointing results of the album sales. Valerie was angry, but Cornelius appeared unfazed. "That's the way it goes. Ninety-nine cents a download," he said.

No talk came from Metacarpal Records of another CD. And Edgar Pufknack was nice to them, but he did not talk about trying to convince the studio not to give up on Cornelius Prince.

Valerie and Cornelius moved out of the Hamilton Street building, on her money, uptown to a little apartment in a nice house where they knew their landlady, and where they even had a back yard. The kitchen was huge compared to the closet Valerie had grown accustomed to working in. As wedding presents, she had been given ice cream blenders—one from every person who brought a gift—everyone had given her a General Electric blender. Valerie exchanged each in turn for a toaster oven, an electric mixer, a carving knife, cutting board, can opener, and other useful items until her new kitchen was equipped as she liked it. Their new bedroom was big enough for a full size bed, and they bought a living room set. No broken springs.

Yet Cornelius was still playing one-horse bars and traveling to cities like Hartford, Syracuse, and Poughkeepsie for jobs. Valerie grew to hate travel as she never had, and after a while she stayed home. Anyway, a single motel room cost less than a double.

She made a little garden in the backyard. It was

131

considerably smaller than the one she had left at home, but she made it just as nice. She spent every day tending it. Clancy in his cage would sit on the back porch and sing as Valerie worked.

Valerie loved gardens. She loved the feel of the cool earth as her knees and toes sank into the soft soil, she loved the heat of the sun on her shoulders.

Only when she came back inside, with black crescents under her fingernails, the skin of her shoulders and of her calves stinging warmly, did she think about Cornelius far away in some city she could not begin to picture. The new apartment was a home, the one on Hamilton could never have been, but nomads wander.

Valerie could not romanticize his absence. She knew that he was not working hard to make ends meet, cradling her face in his mind each minute to maintain his stamina as he drove from town to town. He was working hard, with a fence of music staves around him, because it was what he did. Nights in bed, she would place two pillows on his side of the mattress. It was not a dummy to fill in for him. It was a filling, for a cavity that Valerie otherwise stuck her foot into, as if she were probing a bad tooth. She longed for her single bed where there were no nerves to touch.

One day, as she pulled weeds from between stems of flowers, she felt something grab her rump. Her heart jumped and she screamed. It had been so quiet, even the bird had not been singing, and she had heard no one walk up. She fell forward into the flower bed, rolled over and looked up to see Cornelius standing over her, looking like a giant.

"You scared me," she said.

He had been on a long trip—a string of one-night stands with tedious drives between, and he looked every mile. He was gaunt, pale, an untended beard growing wild on his face, and the little suns in his eyes had gone grey.

"I thought you weren't coming home until the end of

the week," she said.

"The map was wrong, and I ended up here." He reached for her hand and pulled her to her feet.

She kissed his scruffy cheek. "Oooooh—tickles. Corey, you look real tired. Come inside and I'll make you some dinner."

He followed her inside, but he told her he only wanted coffee.

"That may be all you want, but you're getting more."

"Just a sandwich then."

Once she made the sandwich and put it in front of him, she told him to eat and then she went to shower the earth off her skin. When she came out of the bathroom, wrapped in a towel, she found him lying on the bed beside the two pillows.

"Pinnoke, have you thrown me over for a pillow?"

"I'm glad you're back," she said.

"Was I away long?"

"Too long. Couldn't you stay home a while? We don't need the money that bad, and there must be gigs in Albany."

"You should come with me."

"We tried that."

"Your car needs a tune up. I think it's burning oil too."

"Our car." Valerie moved the pillows and sat on the edge of the bed. "Please stay home with me for the rest of the summer. Or let's go on a vacation."

"Pinnoke—"

"Papa and Mama think you hate them. They are your family as much as I am, and we never visit them."

"Pinnoke, you gotta understand."

Yet he knew the absurdity of that statement. He knew what this would eventually do to her, and here he was asking her to understand?

"But admit you're tired," she said. "You should see how you look. Why you want to do *this* to yourself is what I don't understand."

He looked at her, at her black hair tumbling down the

front of her shoulders, at her dark thigh slipping through the slit in the towel. She appeared as frayed as he, and it sounded like such a simple thing to choose another path, to remain at home, which was all she asked.

"I talked to Edgar Pufknack," he said.

"Oh?"

"He's up for another album."

"I thought they wouldn't let you do another."

"It's not a question of letting me, Pinnoke. They'd let me if the CD could sell. Pufknack thinks we could do a different format. Maybe that would persuade them to take another chance."

"Can we not talk about it now?" Valerie said.

"I need to know what you think of the idea."

"I think that if you can make a million with another album and save going on all these trips and never being home, I'm for it. Besides, I was the one who helped you get to record the first one, remember? I think that one was terrific and the studio just didn't try to sell it. It would let Papa down if you gave up. What kind of new format?"

"Larger back-up band, fewer instrumentals, more techno."

"You *hate* that kind of thing."

"I am going to pick the band."

"How about Porter and Derek – or Andrew?"

"Andrew is a studio musician, and making top dollar doing it. He has no interest in joining a band."

"Find whomever you want. And if you stay home to write the songs, I'll be a supportive wife." She pushed him backward and climbed on top of him. She unbuckled his belt. "Now that's decided, let's forget it for tonight." She undressed him and then she lay down beside him and they went to sleep, skin to skin.

Valerie dreamed about going back to New York City, and in her dream she thought she could feel his dream going on simultaneously with her own. The feeling that resulted was dread.

Here, again, is what Cornelius dreamed: Valerie merely

got off a plane. The airport was JFK, and she was returning from a trip to Bermuda. Her skin was tanned browner than ever, and she looked very happy and rested. The dream terrified Cornelius. He could not say why. Nothing happened, she only came down the Jetway, but there was a feeling within it—this perfectly ordinary homecoming carried a threat of—of what? trial? challenge? It presented a question that he could not within the short reel of the dream grasp—it was, indeed, terrifying.

Valerie got out of bed after a night of not very satisfying sleep. She moved quietly to avoid waking her husband; he did not appear to be sleeping well either. She left the bedroom and went to the kitchen. She ground the coffee beans, and then there was a knock on the door.

It was Mrs. O'Connell, their landlady. Mrs. O'Connell was a short woman, in her mid forties, with a husky Irish brogue. She too was in her housecoat, so Valerie did not feel so embarrassed.

"Good marnin' Mrs. Prince," Mrs. O'Connell said. "That's yer car out by the carb, isn't it?" She was referring to Cornelius' old Rambler, which still did not run.

"Yes, it is," Valerie replied.

"The third garage stall is not in use fer now. I was noticin' you might want to get it away from the street because the children were playin' on't this marnin'."

Valerie said, "We aren't paying rent for the third stall, though."

"Don't warry," Mrs. O'Connell said. "I doubt if anyone'll be usin't soon. You can borrow it. I wouldn't want anyone to get hart."

"Thank you. My husband will move the car."

"Oh, yer husband is home then now?"

"Yes. He got home yesterday."

"That is nice. I'm shore you were missin' him. If there are any other problems, you let me know right away then. G'marnin'."

It was kind of Mrs. O'Connell to let them use the third garage stall, but actually Valerie wanted to get rid of that old car. She had no idea why they kept it.

(*It's a classic!*)

She picked up Cornelius' suitcase by the door, brought it into the bedroom. He was up now, in the bathroom with the shower running. Valerie listened to the sound of the water. She liked the sound of not being alone. She opened the suitcase. All of his clothes had been rolled up and stuffed inside. She chuckled and shook her head as she pulled them out. The shower stopped running. "Corey, breakfast," she called to him.

She sat at her vanity and brushed her hair. In the mirror she watched Cornelius come out of the bathroom naked and holding a toothbrush.

"We have to go to Potsdam," he told Valerie.

She watched his reflection rummage through the suitcase for underwear.

"Don't wear those clothes, Cornelius, they're ready for the laundry. In your drawer you have underwear." She watched his thin body cross the room. "Now that you are home for a while, I can fatten you up with my spinach lasagna."

"And then turn me into gingerbread?"

"Into what?"

"I know who my band is going to be. They are up in Potsdam. We have to go get them." He began to dress with urgency, as if he intended to leave immediately.

Valerie put down her brush and stood up. "I am not going anywhere. You promised last night you were going to stay home."

"Don't you want to hear the band I'm going to sell out with?"

"You have to play with them."

Cornelius walked out of the bedroom. She followed.

"We're leaving today," he said in the kitchen.

"Have a nice trip. Better check the oil in my car first."

Cornelius sat at the table. Valerie poured two cups of

coffee.

"I don't want to fight, Corey," she said. "Why can't we put aside this trip for just a day?"

He sipped on his coffee. "Is there sugar?"

Valerie walked out of the kitchen. She closed up the suitcase in the bedroom and swung it into the corner, left it there. She went into the bathroom and slammed the door. She knew she would be in Potsdam tonight, but she wanted so much to fight it—or at least make it her own choice.

She brushed her teeth. Aggravated, she pushed the toothbrush very fast inside her mouth. She brushed so hard her gums bled. She filled the glass with water and rinsed. She spit red back into the glass.

Potsdam, New York, is a small college town in the northwestern part of the state. It is secluded from the rest of the planet. Part of the ride from Albany is through the Adirondack Mountains, and that part is pretty with lakes and mountains. But most of the ride stretches across stark fields. It is boring. And the town itself is not much. Houses, some bars, two colleges—when the students go home, Potsdam turns to nothing, and in the summer, most of them had gone.

Valerie lay beside Cornelius on a tennis court on the State College campus. There was not another body about. She looked straight ahead; lying on her back, straight ahead was at the night sky. There was no moon, but there were so many stars that the sky was bright from their light alone.

"Those guys rock," she said.

"I know."

"It ought to be a good album. The guitar player is real good."

"He's a jerk."

"You don't like him?"

"I like the way he plays. That's all I care about."

"I'm excited about it now," Valerie admitted.

The sky grew brighter still with flashes of light from the horizon. Valerie watched the Aurora Borealis shoot out of the north: a wild, swirling display of electric color—the more it raged, snuffing out the stars, the smaller she felt as she lay on the clay court, the smaller the court became, the smaller the trees and the red brick buildings around. "The sky is *so* much bigger up here," she said in awe.

"The horizon is never very far away."

"Cornelius, how come you always talk so I can never understand?"

"Why do you try so?" he said.

"I think you are crazy." She patted his leg.

"Not crazy, Pinnoke."

"I've never seen the northern lights like this. We used to see them up at the lake, but they only lasted a few minutes. This is like fireworks. They are pretty." She sat up suddenly, looked at Cornelius' face. "Don't you think?"

"Yes. It's an unusually active sun that's the cause. Sunspots become unstable and explode."

She lay down again. The clay of the court was damp against her back. She felt the dampness crawling through her shirt into her skin. The sky exploded with intense, skywide swirls of luminescent green, like the handwriting getting written on the wall.

Chapter 3

The ride down to New Jersey and Andrew Healy's house had been dreadful. It had poured rain from door to door, and Valerie's car had broken down four times on the Thruway. It finally died altogether on the Jersey Turnpike and Andrew had to rescue them. Valerie had been nagged by a pain in her lower back since that night on the tennis court. At first she figured it to be from menstrual cramps, but then her period came and went, yet the back pains remained. Sitting for so long in a car that kept breaking down had aggravated the pain, and by the time they pulled in front of Andrew's brownstone apartment building in Jersey City, Valerie could barely make it up the stairs to his flat.

Now the rain had stopped. But the last few days had been mournfully grey. Valerie sat by the window and looked out at the dull street. Andrew and Cornelius had not been home in days. They were in New York City somewhere, presumably that same recording studio, working on the album with Daniel Serahuli, The Next Tuesday Band, Edgar Pufknack, and the rest of Metacarpal Records.

Andrew's sister, Eileen, had come to the apartment to keep Valerie company. Eileen and Andrew were twins, but you wouldn't know it to look at them. Andrew was short and a little stocky like a barrel, Eileen was tall and willowy. She had his red hair, but not his sleepy look. When Valerie first met her, she liked her little. But that was because Valerie's back had been killing her, the car lay dead on a highway, and Eileen had bounced vivaciously out of the kitchen all smiles and sunshine while outside it rained. The mood had been all wrong. Now, Valerie loved Eileen, and thanked God for some company while her husband was wrapped up in recording sessions.

"I got lunch," Eileen said.

Valerie did not turn from the window to look at her. "Okay."

"How is your back?"

Valerie waddled into the kitchen. "I'm getting used to it," she said as she sat slowly.

"Maybe you should see a doctor."

"If it doesn't get better, I guess I will. My body has always been tricky on me. My Mama says I was born with a head shaped like a banana. Even my grandparents wouldn't come to see me when they brought me home from the hospital—and no one would take any pictures of me because they were afraid the camera would crack."

Eileen laughed.

"I'm serious," Valerie said. "Mama kept the sunbonnet on the baby carriage even in cloudy weather. Papa took us away from home to escape embarrassment. Then, after we moved back to Saratoga, I started puberty before everyone else in my class. They called me lumpy."

"Oh dear," Eileen smiled.

"Yeah, but my body atoned. It stopped. I was halfway finished with growing up, and everyone else passed me. They all grew into little women and I've stayed a child all my life. I don't get along well with my body."

"Do you want milk, or pop?" Eileen asked.

"I'll have milk. I can get it." Valerie got up and turned toward the refrigerator. Just to watch her was painful. She felt a pain like her spine snapped and she toppled to the floor. "Oh rats," she moaned as she looked at the ceiling.

"What happened?" Eileen knelt beside her.

"I can't get up."

"Valerie, how did you do this to yourself?"

"Blame it on the unusually active sun. Oddly, it does not hurt anymore—but I can't get up."

"Should I carry you? I'm not sure I should touch you."

"I can't stay here!"

Eileen collected Valerie's limbs and lifted her in a bundle. She was amazed at how heavy a little body could be. Valerie apologized for being no help at all, and Eileen carried her to the bedroom.

"Shouldn't you be stretched out?" Eileen said.

"I don't know." She was folded in half across the pillow.

"Does it hurt?" Eileen gently straightened one of Valerie's legs.

"Nothing hurts. That's what's scary, Eileen." She paused in terror and said: "Eileen, do you think I could be paralyzed?"

"No."

"But I can't feel." Wondering what life would be like without feeling choked Valerie's throat and dried her tongue. "Oh my God, Eileen, I'm scared." But she was not crying.

"Valerie, you are not paralyzed. I'll call the doctor. See what he says."

"Don't call Corey."

"Why not?"

"I don't know. I don't want him to know about this."

Eileen looked at Valerie lying on the bed in a most uncomfortable looking position, and then she went to call the doctor.

Valerie moved her eyes around the room and tried to see what her feet were doing. Ten minutes ago her back had been hurting, but at least she could walk. Now she felt nothing (except blood rushing to her head from being tilted like this) but she was unable to move. Which was worse? Her fingers were near her mouth; she began to chew a nail.

She did not know why she didn't want Cornelius told. Maybe she was afraid he would leave the recording studio and come home. Or perhaps she was afraid he would not.

Eileen came back. "The doctor wants you to come in tomorrow if you are still in pain. You can go to the ER, he said, if you think you need to."

"Did you tell him I can't move?"

"He said he's certain it is a spasm that will relax by tomorrow. I'm supposed to put you in the tub."

"I'll drown!"

"I'll hold your head above water."

"What will the tub do?"

"Relax your muscles. Don't get uptight about this, Val—that'll only make you feel worse."

Valerie tried to see the bedroom door. It seemed a long way off. The bathroom was steps farther down the hall. Eileen would have to carry her again. And Eileen would have to undress her too.

"Ready?" Eileen bent down to lift Valerie from the bed.

"Do we have to do it now?"

"Unless you want to lay like a Bavarian pretzel all the rest of the day."

Valerie sighed. "I guess not."

Eileen lugged Valerie into the hall. She had to stop to rest.

"I'm sorry I'm so heavy," Valerie said.

"It isn't that you're heavy. It's just that you're like dead weight."

Valerie was inclined to feel insulted at that.

Eileen hoisted her up and this time slung her body on her shoulder like a sack. "Ugh!" Valerie said. "If nothing really is injured, this will take care of that!" She looked at Eileen's heels and felt really stupid.

The tub was a large soaker tub, and it took a long time to fill up with water.

Eileen squatted before Valerie's ragdoll body and began to unbutton her shirt. She pulled the shirt tail out of Valerie's jeans, yanked the shirt off. She rolled Valerie over, turned her this way and that, lifted her limbs, bent her at the knees, tugged at pant legs. She was not as gentle as Valerie would have liked, and it felt like some perverse game of dress-up. She reached for the clasp of Valerie's bra strap, unhooked it.

Valerie caught the cups before they fell away. "Can I keep my underwear on, Eileen?" she said suddenly.

"You want to go in the water with your underwear on?"

Valerie nodded.

Eileen looked puzzled a second, then said, "All right." She lifted Valerie into the tub. They sat in silence for a while, Valerie half floated, half sat in the big tub. Eileen sat on the toilet lid.

Then Eileen said: "How's it feel? Do you want the jets on?"

"Not so bad," Valerie answered. "It may work. No to the jets."

They sat for a while longer. Eileen took up a brush and ran it through her hair. She polished her glasses with toilet paper.

"Eileen?"

"Mm?" moving the brush through her hair again.

"I'm sorry I didn't want you to take my underwear off."

Eileen looked into the mirror at Valerie's head sticking out of the tub, then she turned around and eyed her strangely.

"It was just skeeving me out."

She realized that what it really had done was remind her of something, of the way her clothes were always coming off in other people's hands as she lay there not doing anything to stop them.

"I think I know how you feel," Eileen said.

"I'm...not sure you do."

"I would never wear a bikini because I thought my belly button stuck out too far."

Valerie thought she ought to ask: "Does it?"

"I still think so. But my boyfriend says it's cute."

"What is your boyfriend's name?"

"Simon."

"And he thinks you have a cute belly button?"

"Yeah, well he's sort of strange anyhow—Now *I'm* embarrassed."

"I think I can move," Valerie said. She straightened herself slowly. "Eileen, I'm not paralyzed!"

"Terrific." Eileen helped Valerie to her feet and wrapped her in a towel. Valerie walked stiffly alongside Eileen to the bedroom.

Valerie said timidly, "Would you, sort of, like turn around, or not look?"

"Oh—sure." Eileen obliged. Valerie dropped the towel and took off her underwear, dried her skin quickly and got into bed, pulled the sheet up.

"Want to finish lunch?" Eileen said. "I could bring it to you."

"No thanks. I think I want to sleep for a while."

"All right." Eileen picked up the towel and Valerie's sopped underwear. "I will put these in the laundry."

She smiled with reassurance and walked out.

Eileen's doctor prescribed a muscle relaxer, and recommended Valerie continue to sit in the warm baths. He told Eileen she could massage Valerie's back should the pain become too bad, then he bid them off. Valerie's palm was sweaty holding the prescription slip as she thought about having to ingest a drug. The most horrifying part was that she knew this drug.

For a few minutes, she entertained the thought of not filling the prescription.

Back at home, Valerie put on her nightgown and got into bed. Eileen sat on the edge beside her.

"Andrew and Cornelius haven't been home for two days,"

Valerie said. "I miss them."

"Andrew is never home. I don't know why he bothers to have this flat."

"Is he always working?"

"Life of a studio musician."

"Do you have an apartment too?"

"I live with my parents officially," Eileen said. "But I'm here as often. Maybe more. Andrew and I are very close, but we were never too close to our parents, I guess. Everybody in our house always sort of did what they wanted."

"Do you have a big family?"

"Four of us live at home. There are nine altogether." She looked embarrassed. As if that were something obscene. "We're Catholic."

"So are we," said Valerie. "But there's only me and Mama and Papa."

"Andrew has lived here since he was eighteen. My parents couldn't stand him practicing all the time."

"So they threw him out?"

"He volunteered. I went with him, but I had to go home because I don't have a job. I'm going to move out as soon as I graduate."

"I don't go to college. I barely made it through high school—through every fault of my own. What are you studying?"

"Microbiology. Pharmacology."

"I don't do anything. I'm just Cornelius' wife. Sometimes I don't even feel like that."

"Hey—" Eileen said imperatively, "don't start getting bummed, Valerie. When they finish this album he'll be home more. He loves you to death. I can tell."

"I know. Where's Clancy?"

"Out in the living room. Want me to bring him in?"

"Sure!"

Eileen went out and returned with the bird. It began to sing when she set the cage down.

"Are you going to marry Simon?" Valerie asked.

"No."

"Do you love him?"

"Yes, but we won't get married."

"Why not?"

"I am not marrying material," Eileen said.

"Maybe you are. Maybe when you get older."

Eileen's gaze was suddenly far away. "No, Val; I don't think so."

Clancy continued to sing. Valerie listened, but Eileen looked as if her mind were somewhere else. On Simon perhaps. Yet in her eyes there was the slightest, noticeable expression of pain.

Wondering about that pain, Valerie fell asleep.

When she awoke she was alone and the room was dark. Her back ached again. She sat up and reached for the bedside lamp. She looked at the phial of pills and read the label with her name on it. She would not take a single pill unless the pain were intolerable. No—it would have to be worse than that: unearthly.

She thought about lying with Cornelius on the damp clay of that court, which was the start of this. She was in too much pain to ponder Cornelius.

Eileen came into the room. "I saw the light on. Do you want to eat?"

"What time is it?"

"Ten-thirty."

"Corey come home?"

"Andrew called."

"Eileen, do you think we could put me in the tub again? My back hurts awful bad."

"Did you take your medicine?"

"I want to try the bath first."

Eileen helped her out of bed and into the bathroom. When the tub was filled, Valerie hesitated, blushed, smiled uneasily. Eileen said: "Can you get in all right? I could go out."

Valerie shrugged. She said slowly, as she thought about it: "No, I might need help." She reached for the hem of her nightgown, pulled it over her head. She turned her back to conceal herself, glanced nervously at the mirror to see if Eileen was looking. Then she got into the tub as quickly as her pain would allow, feeling like a sideshow.

"Okay?" said Eileen. "Call me when you need help to get out."

"No, Eileen, stay and talk to me. It's okay. It doesn't bother me too much."

Eileen leaned against the counter. "Does the water feel good?"

"Feels fine. But my back doesn't. Do you think you could rub it like the doctor said?"

Eileen got down on her knees beside the bathtub.

"Stupid thing to lay on a tennis court all night," Valerie pouted.

"How do I do this?" Eileen touched Valerie's back gingerly.

"I'll tell you if it hurts."

"You'll tell me if it hurts?"

"It hurts—"

"Sorry!"

Valerie started to laugh. "This reminds me of when I was a little girl and Mama would give me baths...Sorry. Not that you are my mother..."

"They used to put Andrew and me in the tub and we'd try to drown each other."

"You took baths with your brother?"

"When we were both very small."

"Why don't you come on in?"

"In the tub?"

"Sure, there's lots of room. I won't stare at your belly button."

She gave it some thought. Then she stood up and began taking off her clothes. Her freckles were all over her body, even on her bottom, and her full breasts turned up at the nipples. Her pubic hair was a thick tuft of reddish brown below her domed navel. She pushed her strewn clothes into the corner with her toe. "I feel silly. But communal bathing is an ordinary custom in Japan."

147

She sat across from Valerie and under the water her fingers clasped conveniently over her abdomen.

"Eileen, what does Simon do?"

"He's a student too. He wants to be a writer."

"I'll bet he's really nice."

"He's terrific."

"What's his last name?"

"Wolfe."

"Simon Wolfe. Sounds like a writer. Don't you want to be married to a writer? Can't be any worse than being married to a piano player."

"If I got married, Valerie, I would marry Simon."

"So maybe when you get a little older, and you graduate—"

"I am dying, Valerie."

Valerie felt a contraction of her uterus. Her hand splashed under water, darted to her abdomen in pain reflex. The sound from her throat was: "Hee—" like a laugh, not a groan. "You can't be." Anything said would be clumsy, so she might as well go ahead and say that stupid thing.

"I have leukemia."

"You sound so calm."

Eileen shifted in the tub, water sloshed around; she drew her knees up, as if to cover herself. "I've had it—well, I've known about it for three years. I was in remission, but I just had some tests and, and it's back."

"But you look healthy. And you were carrying me around."

Eileen hugged her legs, lowered her chin to her knees. Her hair hung over her shins and the ends floated on the water. Into the hollow between her long, folded legs and her huddled torso, she said:

"Certain things make me very tired."

"Maybe you'll get better."

Eileen smiled wanly. "How does your back feel? It's getting late, maybe we should sleep."

She stood. Water beaded and dripped off her skin. She lifted one foot over the side of the tub, placed it on the floor, stretched out for a towel. Her body looked strong, and all of her movements were graceful. The figure of her body was smooth and pretty. On top of that, it now appeared to be quite fragile, and every motion of her body looked different than it had just one moment ago.

Eileen helped Valerie out of the tub. Valerie hobbled back to her room, said good-night, crawled into bed. The house fell silent, and dark when she turned out her lamp. Valerie wanted to get up and go back to Eileen. But she was afraid she would not make it across the room.

As dawn lit the window, Valerie lay on the mattress wondering if she had remained awake all night. The bed sheet was knotted at the foot of the bed, but she did not remember kicking it down. She lifted her head and looked the length of her body to her feet. Her gaze landed on that gold chain on her ankle.

She raised her hands before her eyes. These feet and hands had once belonged to a baby. She looked at her right hand, turned it over, made a fist. It was yet a young hand, but someday it would be wrinkled, warped with arthritis perhaps, though she hoped not. She opened her fist and examined her fingerprints.

Valerie closed her eyes and felt her hand from inside its skin, from beneath its muscles. The hand slowly traced her body. Eyes still closed, she moved the hand up the outside of her left leg, over her hip, into the curve at her waist. The right hand touched the knuckles of the left one, the fingers, it found the cold metal of her wedding ring, slid over the hairs on her forearm to the smoothness of her left shoulder. The fingers of both hands probed over the bump of her collarbone, down the front of her body, cupped the soft mounds of her small breasts, traced the raised circles of her areolas.

Her heart beat behind her sternum. When it is another's heartbeat, the feeling is soothing, when it is your own heart, its beat is frightening. Her hands continued across her navel to the sparse tendrils of her pubic hair, finally traced the insides of her legs back to her feet. She touched the gold chain, and stopped.

After Valerie had traced the limits of her small body, she lay frozen with her eyes closed, and after that, terror shot through her bare limbs and her heart broke like a fortune cookie.

When her eyes opened, Eileen was in the room.

"The sun is out today." She crossed to the window and raised the shade. When the direct sun fell on Clancy's cage, the bird began to sing. "Doesn't he sound nice." Eileen sat on the bed.

"Andrew called," she said.

"Are they coming home?"

"For a day or so. They aren't finished, but tempers are flaring. Do you know they haven't cut a single track yet?"

"Why not?"

"Still writing the songs. Andrew told me one of the guys—didn't say who—was being a real pain in the patoot."

"Martin," Valerie said.

"You know him?"

"Cornelius said he would be a bother. I'll bet it's him. Anyway, I'm glad they're coming home. That doesn't mean you'll be leaving, does it?"

"No."

"Oh good."

"How's the back today? Wanna get dressed and have breakfast?"

"Yeah...sure..."

Eileen walked out of the room. Valerie did not watch her go. She stared at her pillow until she heard the door close. Eileen could not be dying. Valerie rolled off the bed and landed prone on the floor, lay there staring at the dust underneath the box spring. Eileen was barely twenty-five years old. She was a pretty young woman in love with a splendid writer. Valerie dragged herself to her feet painfully. She grabbed the birdcage by the wire bars, wound up, flung it at the wall. It struck and smashed open, sending Clancy reeling head over tail, squawking in F major, flailing his wings.

Then Valerie crumpled in pain.

Chapter 4

The album was finished on Valerie's twenty-first
birthday. She was madder than a hornet when the CD
came out around Christmas time and she saw what
had happened. The album was supposed to be called:
*Cornelius Prince and The Next Tuesday Band: See Me Next
Tuesday!*—but the CD art was the work of a graphic
designer who had not been quite clear on the distinction
between Cornelius, and the purpose of the band behind
him. No one caught the mistake (or maybe they hadn't
cared about the mistake), and the cover of the CD read:
"The Next Tuesday Band: See Me Next Tuesday!"

If this CD had sold with the lack of success that
Cornelius' first had, it would have been an insignificant
insult. But the album hit the top ten and the jaunty rock
and roll title cut was heading for number one for the
month of January. The liner notes threw Cornelius' name
in with the rest of the band members. Anyone who looked
for it would find his name beside all of the songs, but Martin
O'Kelly had done as many vocals as Cornelius had written,
so Cornelius was lost.

Valerie would hold the jewel case in her hands in
record stores and glare, knowing he had been railroaded.
She'd stop people as they browsed and tell them: "This
was supposed to be my husband's CD." They would all

look over their shoulders at her, then walk away to look someplace else.

Valerie also called Edgar Pufknack on her cell phone and scathed him for allowing this atrocity. She wanted new art designed and all the CDs recalled. However, Metacarpal Records was too happy with the sales of the album under its inadvertent title. They were delighted for the mistake and planned to hire the artist again.

"You're going to be a rich girl," Edgar Pufknack's voice buzzed like the wind on the other end of the wireless connection.

"I already *am* a rich girl!" Valerie shouted. "Corey worked hard on this album, and he did it your way too, and you stole it from him."

Cornelius never said a word about the entire mishap.

"This was no mistake!" Valerie protested still to Eileen one late night in Andrew's kitchen. "I'm sure of it."

Andrew was in New York sitting in for another session man who had not been able to do the gig. Cornelius was asleep in the bedroom. This was one of the times when Eileen felt tired. Since October, in fact, she'd felt cranky and weak. Valerie realized that Eileen's periodic errands were chemo treatments. She found a sickness in her stomach, pretended not to notice.

"It's too bad," Eileen said. "But they won't change it now...You seem tired."

"I guess I am," Valerie admitted. "Maybe I'll go to bed. Will you? You look like you need some rest."

"I'll sit up a little longer. Andrew might call. It is Christmas Eve after all."

"Christmas Day now—it's after midnight."

Eileen smiled at Valerie. "Do me a favor and turn off the tree lights on your way in?"

Valerie chewed her lip and said: "You feelin' okay?"

"I'm fine, Val. I've got some medicine that helps offset it."

Valerie hesitated, thought about saying something, then said, "Merry Christmas."

"You too."

Valerie crawled behind the tree in the living room and pulled the plug. As she stood, she paused by the window and looked outside. New Jersey did not get nearly as much snow as Saratoga. Every Christmas Eve her Mama had the family over. They cooked a huge buffet: sausage and sauce, ziti, and they baked trays and trays of cookies. This was the first Christmas Valerie had not been sitting in the living room with her family. She went in to bed.

She cuddled next to Cornelius. Her back did not hurt as much or as often anymore. They had bought one of those visco-elastic foam toppers for the mattress to help. She liked it because she could take it with her when they were on the road. Tonight, Valerie could not sleep and she imagined, until she finally felt, an ache, in order to blame a pain in her back.

Chapter 5

Eileen took off her gloves in the dark of the kitchen and dropped them on the center of the table. She flipped a wall switch; the fluorescent tube over the sink flickered, blinked, came on. The cold light reached halfway across the counter, touched the edge of the table. She heard a sound in the bedroom.

"Andrew?" She lifted the lid off the jar of tea bags, took one out.

Andrew wandered into the kitchen, shirt and shoes off.

"I put them on the bus," Eileen said.

"Still snowing out," he commented.

Eileen filled the tea kettle with water.

"Water for me too. I'm gonna have coffee."

"More coffee. Why don't you leave the caffeine and go to sleep for once?"

"Marvin's supposed to call. I have to stay awake." Andrew sat.

"He will call at four in the morning again and want you to be in the city at four-thirty."

"Probably."

"So why not sleep until then—it's a few hours anyhow."

"I don't need sleep," Andrew snapped.

"Course not—you just take a pill."

She poured the kettle out over the tea bag, watched the water in the cup turn orange to brown.

"Are you staying here tonight, or going home?"

"I guess I'm staying."

"Why don't you take off your coat then?"

"I'm chilled." She placed a cup of black coffee in front of Andrew. "It's cold in here. It is cold, right?"

He sniffed the coffee, drank it still very hot. That was the way he liked it, always took it, hot enough to scald anyone else's throat. Eileen sat across from her brother.

"How you feelin'?" he asked.

She removed her glasses. "A little tired." Then she perked herself up. "Don't worry, I'm okay." She sipped her tea. A little bit spilled over the lip of the cup when she set it back in the saucer.

"I'm glad they stayed through Christmas," she said.

Andrew grunted his agreement.

"She's a very lonely and dear girl," Eileen said.

"You mean Valerie? How so?" Andrew stood to make a second cup of coffee.

"She wants so much to be loved."

"You don't think Cornelius loves her?"

"He does. But I don't think she's certain of it."

"He told me—Eileen, this is decaf!" he said, as if she were trying to poison him.

"I know."

"Is there any of the other stuff left?"

"Andrew, what would happen if you weren't here for Marvin's call?"

"I wouldn't get the job. He'd most likely call George and their saxophone track would sound pretty poor." He pushed jars and cans in the overhead cabinet out of the way, looking for coffee that was not decaffeinated.

Eileen stood behind him and put her hands on his shoulders. "Let's get out of here," she said.

"What did you do? Throw out the real coffee?"

"It's in the other cabinet." She turned away.

156

Andrew found his coffee and turned to her as he opened the jar. "Where do you want to go at one o'clock in the morning?"

"For a drive."

"It's snowing like crazy."

"Andrew, I just wanna get out of here—it will not hurt to miss one job, will it?"

"If I skip this one, they'll think twice about calling me for the next—and for the one after that."

"That is stupid paranoia. You're too good for anyone to pass up. You could tell Marvin to stuff it when he calls and he would call you right back."

Andrew sat with his second cup of steaming coffee.

"You *know* that I'm right. Do this for your sister, okay? Turn down a job for once? If you're not available, Marvin will only figure someone else got to you first."

"You wanna go for a drive."

"I wanna go to the mountains."

"As you said, they'll want me in the studio within half an hour. Can't stray too far. What's up there?"

"We'll find out when we get there."

"Maybe I could call Marvin now. Could be they won't need me." He opened his cell phone.

Eileen snatched it from his hand. "No, Andrew, I'm kidnapping you. You can call from the car. Get your coat on. Wear boots, there'll probably be a lot of snow up there. Now do as I say. I'm the older one."

"Okay, older sister by two and a half minutes. You win. But give me the phone so I can call Marvin. Wake him for once, and tell him to stuff it so he can call me right back."

"You can call him from the car as soon as we're out of range," Eileen said firmly.

Andrew got his coat and they went down to the car. The snow had stopped but for a few stray flecks. They got into Andrew's very old, restored VW bug. He could have bought a new car – he could have bought a Lamborghini. But he liked "to keep things simple." Eileen sat with her long legs folded up on the seat. She shivered. How simple was life in a car with no working heater?

"Go faster," she said.

"There's ice on the road."

"I wanna go to Pennsylvania. I wanna go all the way to Pittsburgh and I want to be there before dawn."

"We'll never get there at all if I go too fast."

"Be careful, but go faster."

The sky was lightening by the time they reached the mountains. The snow on the road was heavy and unplowed. It was about dawn when drifts prevented them from going any farther.

"We'll never make Pittsburgh now," Andrew said.

"Get out here." Eileen opened her door.

Andrew stood beside the car and looked down the hill at a smooth snow. It was broken only by two lines of tire tracks. It was silent and very cold. He wondered how he would get the car back down the mountain.

His sister had walked up the road. She was at the crest of the hill. Andrew walked inside her footprints. The buried road curved around and there was a cliff falling off ahead. Nearby, a spring trickled over rocks from two directions, joined and leaked across more rocks. The flowing water prevented ice from forming, eroded patches of the snow. Andrew reached his sister at the guardrail.

Stretching from the base of the cliff below, grey patches of tree branches poked above the snow. The rising sun's rays broke a hole in the overcast and shined across the trees. Andrew looked at Eileen's face. It had a reddish hue as the sun hit her. The mist of her breath floated into the sunbeams. Far behind them, the light green bug sat up to its running boards in snow. As the sun blared fully risen through a break in the clouds, the crystals of snow sparkled. A coat of frost on the bug's windshield burned blue and orange.

"This is where I'll be, Andrew." Eileen's voice seemed muffled by the mountain silence. "Come here and talk to me sometimes."

Andrew put his arm around his sister—like a pal—

but then he grabbed her, and he held her body close to his as if clutching and surrounding her could put off the inevitable. It began to snow again on the mountain, although on the horizon the sun continued to shine through its slot in the clouds.

"She's dying, you know. She has leukemia."

"Andrew told me."

Valerie turned back to the black mirror of the bus window and stared at their reflections. The Greyhound bounced roughly up the Thruway. They were halfway home.

"I would be afraid," Valerie said. "Eileen doesn't seem afraid. I would be afraid."

"Are you afraid now?" Cornelius asked.

"I am afraid for Eileen." Valerie rested her chin in her hand.

"For yourself?"

"Why should I be afraid for myself?" She spoke to his reflection in the bus window.

"Maybe you will be dead before Eileen. It's snowing. Maybe this bus will skid and roll over and everyone in it will die. Maybe an airplane will land on the highway and we'll smack into it. Eileen knows how she will most likely die...we do not."

"Corey, please don't talk anymore, 'kay?"

"It's not going to happen," he said.

"Which, you not talking anymore, or us dying on the bus?"

He paused as if thinking for a second. "Either one."

PART THREE

Chapter 1

A ndrew found him in the smoking area by the ER curb. Simon stood next to an ashtray filled with ashes and flattened filters and dirty sand. He was holding a book as he stared at the building wall. Andrew couldn't see which book. He walked over to him.

"Hiya," Andrew said.

Simon looked startled. "Have you seen her yet?"

"Looked in on her. She's asleep."

"They won't let me see her. I'm not family." He said it blandly, but the way he worked his cigarette into the ashtray showed his anger.

"She's fine. She was all curled up and the blankets were pulled up to her nose. Like looking in on a sleeping kid."

Except for the dripping tubes and the beeping monitors.

That afternoon had been Eileen's first day at a new job. She was hoping to make enough money to get a place of her own. So she went out searching, and she found a job in a delicatessen. Halfway through her shift, a customer ordered a corned beef and Swiss sandwich. Eileen went into the back room to make it. She took a long time—even for a new clerk—to put together one sandwich. At the customer's prompting, the other clerk went back and she found Eileen fallen over the sandwich board; the ketchup had spilled.

"Eileen!"

It was not ketchup, it was blood.

Eileen had fainted onto the blade of the sandwich knife. It turned out the knife had scraped her spleen, but nothing inside was actually ruptured. The emergency room stitched her up, and she was in intensive care for the night.

Simon was wearing a grey turtleneck and blue jeans. He looked wrinkled and tossed together. He had driven all day to get here, and then he had been told to go home.

"She's going to be all right," Andrew assured him.

He wondered if Eileen had told Simon yet about the leukemia. Andrew kept quiet about what the intern had said to him:

"You're closer to your sister than anyone. Has she ever talked about suicide?"

Suicide

The answer was no, of course. Eileen was going to school. She was matriculated, and she had every intention of graduating. She was a rock.

"The doctor told me so," Andrew said to Simon.

Simon lit another cigarette. "Hospitals have stupid rules. Family only. Thank you, HIPAA."

"It's getting close to the end of visiting hours," Andrew said. "They're gonna give us the boot anyway, so let's go quietly. You'll be able to see her tomorrow when she's out of intensive care. And I bet she'll be smiling."

They turned back to go inside the building.

"Do you need to pick up your coat or anything?" he asked Simon.

"No, I'm good."

They headed through the corridors for the parking-garage elevator.

Suicide

The doors opened after a long wait. The elevator car was crowded. Every visitor was on the way out. Andrew and Simon squeezed on.

164

Suicide
And the doors closed.

Simon pushed open the wooden door, afraid of what he might see. But it was only Eileen – asleep in a bed. He had expected tubes and monitors. But, except for an antibiotic drip because they were still concerned about infection, those were gone. She was curled up as Andrew had described her, but the blankets were knotted up below her feet. She wore one of those blue-grey hospital gowns with the slit down the back, and in her sleep she was mooning anyone who walked in.

Simon sat on the folding chair beside her bed. The nurse who had directed him to the room had remained in the nurse's station. They were alone. For a while, he was content to sit by her and listen to the sound of the heating vent. Then he decided to wake her.

She stirred only a little when he pinched her behind.

"Wake up, Shamrocks," he said.

Her head moved from the pillow. She started to look around, then plopped her head down again.

Simon grabbed her buttock and pinched harder, not letting go.

"Hey, Shamrocks, it's time to get up," he said a little louder.

This time she did awaken. And then he watched in horror as she turned over slowly, wincing, sweating from her forehead, tears squeezing from her eyes—it seemed forever before she was on her back.

Sleeping kid.

He wiped the tears off her pale cheek. Coherence returned to her very slowly. She seemed to recognize him before she did the room.

"I got a boo-boo at work," she said hoarsely. "Wanna see?" She pulled the hem of her hospital gown over her hips, but he stopped her from going any farther. He did not want to see the stitches, or even the bandages.

"When did you get here?" she asked.

"Last night."

"What time is it now? Is it tomorrow?"

"If it wasn't tomorrow, I couldn't be here. Yes. I stayed with your brother last night. He had to go into the city today. He's doing a commercial."

"My brother's a real sympathizer... You have classes today!"

"When your mother called and said you had an accident at work, I didn't think about that much."

"Is my mother here? How is your book coming?"

"Slow this semester. I got a lot of work to do."

"I think I'm probably going to miss a lot of school now. Don't know how I could be so clumsy as to stab—"

Simon stood up. "Want me to open these drapes?" They were heavy curtains that kept out all of the daylight. "It's a sunny day and it'll be better than these fluorescents."

He opened them and sunlight fell on her face. The warmth felt good. Eileen thought of the day Valerie had been bedridden with her back, the morning after Eileen had told her that she was dying. The same day everything between them had turned peculiar—like the kind of conversation you strike up with someone while waiting in a dentist's office. Like pulling teeth.

She watched Simon at the window—the sunshine so rich that he was just a silhouette. Suddenly she wanted to make love with him. Wasn't that a laugh? A line of thread holding her together right where all the hip-action came from, and she was having erotic fantasies.

She wondered if she should ever tell Simon why she had fallen on that knife.

"I'm not wearing anything under this starched gown," she said, "and I ain't got no roommate."

Simon turned around as if he had not heard what she said.

"Come over here," she said.

Simon sat on the folding chair again.

"No—on the bed."

166

He moved. The hospital bed squeaked when he sat.

"If ya turn me real gently," Eileen smiled, "all ya have to do is pull the three strings back there."

Simon blushed and touched her arm softly. "Eileen, this is a hospital. A nurse could come in any time."

She frowned. "I know. It was just a thought. They make these gowns so convenient, but it's just a waste."

"Are you in any pain?"

"They've got me pumped with drugs. That's why I feel okay, I guess. No wonder my brother never believes he's tired."

"What does Andrew have to do with you hurting?"

"Andrew is doing a commercial today. Tonight he's probably doing something else. Last night he had some kind of job—"

"He was here last night."

"Anyway, he gets by with a little help from his pharma friends."

"Eileen—"

"Anytime I want him to relax, he refuses. Go go go. When he sleeps it is only because his body is finally so exhausted that even drugs can't pull him up. Last month I wrenched him away from the house, got him to miss a phone call, but it was not easy. He's not even twenty-five yet and did you ever really look at him? He looks forty. I can't get him to stop, Simon. Even by stabbing myself in the stomach I can't get him to leave his work long enough to just sit here with me."

"You did not stab yourself," Simon said looking a little pale. "It was an accident."

"Simon, I am not talking about what I did. Didn't you listen to me? My brother is *sick*."

"Shamrocks, he's a musician."

"Maybe that's the same thing."

"Look: I write all the time. If you were at school with me, you'd go crazy. I would be sitting there with my laptop all night long while you sat alone with candlelight and a glass of wine."

"But when you heard I was in the hospital, you left your laptop at home."

"He's your brother. If you were my sister, I'd type you a get-well card. That is the way brothers are. Fiancés are not like brothers—and you ought to be glad..." He reached under her back and pulled the top string. Now her gown was loose enough for him to slip his hand down the front to caress her. "Because brothers don't do this."

The door opened and a nurse came in. Simon yanked his hand back, but he was sure the nurse had seen. She only smiled, but Simon retreated to face the window to wait for his blush to fade.

Eileen watched him in front of all that sunshine and wondered how long she should go on letting him use that word. Fiancé.

Andrew was the last to leave the studio. It was two a.m. They had wrapped up the commercial. Now that stupid jingle was prancing through his brain, running at top speed, and he could not get off the track.

He got into his car and drove out of the parking garage. He detested commercials because this happened every time. He turned the car radio on to block out the jingle. What do you know—the radio played a song from *See Me Next Tuesday*! Andrew could pick out his bass line, and it made him cringe. In his opinion, they ought to have tried another take. Any monkey with a banana could hear it was off.

But the rabble was pleased. This song was number five last month. Lots of downloads. Even some chat rooms and links from blogs. And the CD was doing incredibly well, too. People were thinking—Eileen especially—why did he have to continue to do these sessions? He was associated with a surprisingly popular new band. He'd had the opportunity to tour with that band. Daniel Serahuli had taken that opportunity, why hadn't he? The answer was that he liked what he was doing. What was so bad about that? Eileen said she was concerned about how busy he was, but wrongly so. Touring with the same band, working with the same people, and if it all goes down the tubes, so do you. Not for him. He was run ragged, sure, but he was *working*. He was the best session man around—he would never be out of work.

Yessir, that was success—you bet. And most guys his age were just out of college and soliciting insurance companies.

The jingle played on and on in his head. On and on.

Her parents were visiting. Her father stood by the window same as Simon had (only now it was dark outside), hands behind his back, a cigarette between his thumb and forefinger even though smoking was not allowed. He was dressed, as always, in work clothes and work boots. He was a welder, and his bald spot shined beneath the fluorescents like hot metal. Her mother sat on the folding chair, stockings bagged at the ankles. Her cardigan covered her shoulders, was buttoned only at the top. The blouse she wore, as usual, did not match the sweater.

Eileen's stitches felt like a caterpillar crawling through her skin.

Walter Healy turned, smoked one last puff and dropped his cigarette on the floor, walked on it as he crossed the room. Walter rarely talked. Tonight he said: "It's supposed to snow." Small talk from a man who made every word count. That had to mean something.

They were not a particularly close family, but maybe a daughter fainting onto a knife can change things.

"Does Simon have to drive all the way back tonight?" Aggie Healy asked.

"He's got classes tomorrow. He missed two days already," Eileen said listlessly.

While Simon was here, she felt fine; with her parents here, she hurt.

Walter stood at the foot of her bed. His frame and stature were the mold for Andrew. In the dark, they would look the same. Except you'd no doubt see that Andrew had long hair. Eileen wished it was her brother standing there. Simon had said he was here last night.

"Maybe if it snows, he should wait another day," Aggie said.

"He probably will," Eileen said absently.

Up on that mountain last month, watching the sun rise through falling snow, Andrew had been with her. Really with her—probably for the first time since they shared the womb of the woman sitting beside this hospital bed.

The fainting spell had taken Eileen by surprise. She could still remember the fuzziness of the sandwich board as she laid the corned beef on the bread, could remember the way the room had teetered, and how she had looked toward the cooler door to see if it was open when she felt that chill. Then, funny how it really does happen in slow motion, she swooned forward. She tried to drop the knife. She knew it would go into her. She heard it tear her smock, felt the point prick her skin and thought:

If I could just let go of the handle it would still fall to the floor, and then the pain and a sound just like when the same knife cut into roast beef—finally she was unconscious. She could remember it all with amazing detachment. It had happened to her, but she did not take it personally.

When she came to on the brown industrial tile floor, she thought very lucidly:

There: I have stabbed myself. I am bleeding and maybe I am dying. Maybe Andrew will give up a session for his twin sister.

But she was not going to die. Not from this.

Yet her last fainting spell (which she had kept secret) had not been too long ago. Like labor pains, they were coming closer together.

She had to tell Simon soon. She was not going to let it—

(What "it"? She'd never shrank from a phrase before,

had no trouble telling Valerie. Now she substituted "it"?)

—to let it take Simon by surprise. That would certainly let him know he could not use that word anymore, wouldn't it?

Up on that mountain last month, she had not been afraid. She had looked out at the snow and the valley, and known for one split second—but it was long enough—that it was only a child's fear of the dark. But Andrew had been with her then.

Walter had moved from the foot of the bed. He was taking his parka out of the closet. Aggie was standing too. "Are you going home?" Eileen asked.

"You *are* still awake. Yes, we have to go now. We'll be back tomorrow," Aggie told her.

A moment later, Eileen was alone with the lights off. Afraid of the dark.

Andrew couldn't sleep. This time, no chemical working in his body kept him awake. He just plain could not sleep.

He blamed it on that stupid commercial jingle. It was still rampant inside his head. Even his heart kept the beat.

The usual insomnia hallucinations plagued him. The window frame wavered up and down; shadows on the wall looked like monsters; the bedposts coiled like snakes. Then as the night (which would be short, thank God, because he had to be up at six) wore on, these hallucinations became more concrete. Eventually he watched a silent masque parade in front of his bed. The Next Tuesday Band playing a soundless concert. Edgar Pufknack. That bird of Cornelius', Clancy. Valerie, lying in a bed with a bad back. Cornelius, mouthing the words "That's Pinnoke." They all showed up and hung around. It was turning into a real party here. Then they began to float about the room and swirl above his head, around and around like the folks inside the Wizard of Oz twister.

Except that when the house landed, these people were not going to vanish. Andrew sat up in bed. This was crazy. Insomnia could not do *this*. He pushed aside the blanket and placed his feet on Eileen's body. She lay on his floor in a hospital gown that tied up the back.

Andrew fell back on the pillow.

This was why he preferred to keep going, to stay awake. Whenever he tried to sleep, he would have a lot of weird dreams. Let's not actually call them nightmares, let's just stick with the word weird.

He looked at the floor again and Eileen shoved a knife into her gut.

Now let's call it a nightmare.

When he turned on the light, the masque ended.

His sister lay in a hospital bed right now, staring at the ceiling with the lights off, wishing that she could walk so she could get up to turn them on. His sister was there because she had fainted onto the point of a sandwich knife.

That word stuck itself in: *suicide.*

Before this year was out, Eileen would be dead.

And he had spent the day with a song for anti-aging cream.

His cell phone, on the bedside table, rang, and nearly stopped his heart. He jumped on it. At the same time he saw the clock. It was three-forty.

"Yeah."

"This is George. Generation Why needs a guitar."

"What time?"

"Three o'clock this afternoon."

"All right. It'll be tight, but I guess I can make it. Tell them I will do it."

Chapter 2

The door stuck. Andrew put his boot heel against the side of the car and tugged. The door was frozen and his foot only pushed another dent into the VW. The snow that was supposed to have come last night had been frozen rain instead. This morning his VW was goose-bumped with ice. Andrew tried the other door. It was also frozen.

He pulled out his lighter. But while he was bent beside the rocker panels, the puny flame to the rim of the car door, he realized trying to melt into the car was as dumb as the commercial.

He put away the lighter. He hated the thought of canceling. He was playing violin for this kid named Avchen Neumann this morning. Edgar Pufknack had found her somewhere in Pennsylvania, and she was said to be incredible—for looks and talent. Andrew had been looking forward to this demo, but the train would take so long to get him to midtown, he may as well give it up.

He yanked on the door again. It gave a little. "Ah-ha!" He put his heel up again, pulled. He heard the ice crackle. "C'mon, you bas—" Then the door broke open and sent him flying backward into a snow bank.

Off to a great start.

And sure enough he was late for the session. He found the studio as quiet as a church. George sat off in a corner, looking lost. Will Dana sat behind his drums, but he looked removed. Edgar Pufknack was visible in the booth talking to a technician. Someone else had the phone in his hand, but looked as if he'd forgotten how to use it.

And across the room, reclining in an old armchair like the choice wine saved for last, was the girl, Avchen Neumann.

The most unkind thing to do to an awakening person is flick on a bright light; the most unkind thing to do to a person entering a commonplace room he frequents daily is to place something, or in this case someone, quite beyond ordinary, in it.

The girl was transfixing, commanding at once all attention and at the same time demanding none. People said things to Andrew, he could not respond. His violin was given to him—a foreign object—and he almost asked what this thing was for, but he could not think of the words to voice the question.

It was said of Avchen that as a baby she'd been so beautiful that doctors who saw her in the nursery went straight to the father with proposals of marriage. As she grew, her beauty did also, and her maturation to womanhood was more like a transfiguration. She had only to walk down the street and boys, young men, even octogenarians fell at once in love with her. Her name was written on every men's room wall in her home town—but not within the usual bathroom limericks; rather the most illiterate male was inspired to write flawless Petrarchian sonnets to her.

Almost physically trembling, Andrew took up his bow. Avchen sat in the chair. The other musicians assumed postures to begin, but not an attention in the room could settle itself. They attempted one take. It was horrible. They tried again. It was as bad. They decided to record Avchen's part, before wasting any more time.

She moved to the microphone, put the headphones on and stood waiting to begin. For reassurance, Andrew looked to see what the others were doing. They were transfixed as well.

Avchen put all the energy of a live performance into the first take. She could dance and leap and move and float. If the musicians could get their part right, this demo was certain to turn out a record. The girl was more than special. Maybe they ought to just record the song *a capella.*

Her part done, she walked out of the room. Andrew feared she was going home. The thought of speaking to her was terrifying, but the thought of not speaking to her was worse. Because he worried about this all morning, it took that long for him and the band to get the instrumentals right.

As soon as they had laid something respectable down, Andrew bolted for the studio door. He found an empty hall, and he was sure the empty hall meant that Avchen was no longer anywhere in the building.

Then she came out of the women's room at the end of the hall.

She walked toward him, on her way back into the studio. "Hi," he choked out, and that was all he could bring himself to say, so he had to keep walking.

She replied with a shy smile that caught his attention because in front of that mic there had been no signs of diffidence.

All he had to do was stop his legs from moving, to say to those muscles, "Stop moving." But even though he thought about it, he continued to walk in the wrong direction—he ought to be going back after her.

He could pretend he had forgotten something. That might even fool himself and permit him to return to the studio.

But there were far too many people in there.

Where was his adrenalin when he needed it?

It was propelling him away, working very hard—

smarter than he was.

"Hey!" someone called out, and upon examination, Andrew realized it was himself.

Avchen turned. "Yes?"

"Yes?"

"Did you say something?"

"I don't know…I mean, yes, of course I did—well, not of course—but certainly. I am quite sure that I did."

(What a jerk, right?)

"I beg your pardon?" she said.

"I did speak," Andrew affirmed, more to himself than her.

"Did you call me a jerk?" she inquired with sort of a smile.

"No—I'm the jerk. But did I say that out loud? I didn't think that I did."

"Well, you did."

"Which way are you going?" he asked. "I mean, can I give you a lift?"

"I can get a ride," she answered.

"Umm…you want to go have a cup of coffee?"

She considered it.

"I don't drink coffee," she finally said.

"Tea then, lemonade, milk of magnesia."

That was not at all witty.

"I could be talked into lunch."

"Come closer then, so I don't have to do my persuading from way down the hall."

"You are the suitor—you come."

Andrew felt his face on fire. He walked up to her, his boot heels clicking on the floor. "Would you like to have lunch?" he requested.

Avchen Neumann turned out to have been born, raised, and lived in western Pennsylvania, near Pittsburgh. Her father was a steel worker. (There, their fathers had a lot of working class in common.) She provided other small personal details about herself—but upon trying to remember any, Andrew found that what she told him was all mixed up in his head. He thought he remembered something about not finishing high school—or maybe it was that she *had* finished—it must be one or the other, right? She was either eighteen or seventeen years old. Some vague recollection of figuring told him that was not such an age difference—it presented itself thus: if he were three (or four) years younger, and she were three (or four) years older, they would be the same age. She had said, too, something about not really wanting to be a singer, but doing this demo for her father, who hoped for that more than anything in the world. She wanted to be a mountain climber—or was it just get married and raise a family?

Here are some clips of other things they talked about, but even these are not reliable:

"Where are you staying?" Andrew asked.

"Mr. Pufknack got me a hotel room."

"Don't take it."

"Why not?"

"Because," he said, "they set all of this up for you and you give yourself to them. Once they got you, they do with you what they want. I seen a friend of mine get his name taken off his own album and replaced with the name of the band who backed him. Now they're big—"

It seemed to him that he had almost used a more crass expression, but found the word could not come out in her presence— "news and he is just another member of the band."

"I don't want to be famous."

"All the more reason then that you should not take anything. Because they will give you all this opportunity, and then if they wanna stiff you, they do, but if they wanna make you do something in return, they hold it over your head."

"What would they want to make me do?"

"Make them a *ton* of money."

And something like this exchange had taken place also:

"Do you have anything to do this afternoon?" Andrew asked.

"No."

"Why don't you hang out, and when I finish the session I have this afternoon, we could go have a beer."

"I'm not old enough to go have a beer," she said.

"What, you wanna go through this again? I am trying to ask you for a date."

"We already are having one."

"I'm more charming on the second one."

"All right. What time?"

"Hmmm...hard to say," Andrew admitted. "Why don't you tell me where you're staying and I'll come by when I'm through."

She told him, and they parted company.

Andrew thought about all of this as the elevator lifted him toward her hotel room. It was like recalling a bunch of dreams. He hoped that what he believed to be her room number, written on his hand, was indeed that and not something else, confused with his imagination. It was two a.m. If he was wrong, whoever was in the room would kill him.

It was Avchen's hotel, her room, but she was no more pleased than a stranger would have been. "I don't believe you came," she said.

"Sorry I'm late. I didn't want to stand you up and you didn't give me a phone number."

"I'm in my nightclothes."

"Yes, I can see that."

"I do not want to go out anymore."

Andrew was still in the hall. Avchen had not yet opened the door completely, and she did not look as if she planned to.

"I don't want to go out either," he said. "Just I didn't want you to think I purposely stood you up. I'm sorry, okay?"

"Yeah, it's okay." But it did not appear to be.

"I'll see ya later, all right?"

"I still don't believe you came. What time is it anyway?"

"Late. I don't know. We got out real late."

"Come in," she said and held open the door. "You woke me up and I won't be able to go back to sleep, so you may as well come in for a bit."

Andrew stepped in; everything became like a figment. Indeed the bed was so disheveled, the sheets torn completely off, the mattress askew from the box-spring, that only in a dream could there be such evidence of a person who had not been sleeping well.

"Want a cup of coffee?" she asked.

She walked to the dresser where the coffee maker was, her figure in soft focus, the furniture in soft focus, the coffee maker floating effortlessly out into her hands. Andrew watched her bend over as she set the thing up by the only outlet in the room, her light and nearly transparent nightgown stretching (no panty lines) over her behind.

"I guess I've gotten a reputation for being late," he said.

"Sort of one step behind," she smiled. "Like most people would have gotten around to taking off their coat by now."

She took his coat from him and hung it in the closet. Also she took out her robe while she was over there, and she put that on. Eventually they were both sitting among the ruins of the bed, each holding a mug of coffee.

Avchen said, "I was thinking about what you said today. You know, about Mr. Pufknack wanting my soul? I had fun today, and I really think I do want to be a singer after all. My father wants it very badly. Maybe that is why I decided that I want to. Is it wrong to do something because someone else thinks it is important, do you think?"

"You have to look out for yourself."

Being here ought to have been growing steadily easier,

179

things settling down, but the reverse was happening, and things were further departing from reality. But that, he felt, was the only way such a woman as this could be dealt with—at an arm's length, wonderland perspective.

"I know," Avchen said, " but my father did that for me all my life so far. I feel I should do something for him."

She set her coffee on the rug, leaned back against the inclined mattress. "That is what I think," she said.

Andrew started to say something, but he realized that she would not have heard. The date was over. Avchen had fallen asleep. He wondered if he should awaken her to rebuild the bed, and to say good-night, but he decided against it. He looked at the clock. By the time he reached his house, he would only have to turn around and come back into the city.

And besides, Avchen was asleep, looking fragile as porcelain, and someone had to guard her.

Andrew looked at her face and marveled that a witch could be more powerful asleep than awake.

The only part of his body that enjoyed a decent night's sleep was his arm. Avchen had rolled against him, pinning the arm, and she had not moved through morning. As soon as it was light, Andrew gently lifted her and rolled free. His leg itched, and he thought he was scratching it until he looked down and saw that the arm still hung limp, unresponsive to all impulses from his brain. He stood up, lifted his numb arm with the other, let it drop. It flopped to his side like putty.

Andrew went into the bathroom, and as soon as he locked the door, life became real again. There was his familiar morning face—cheeks white, chin rough with stubble, eyes sunken and red, no one in there.

He ventured back out to get a bottle of pills and his eye drops, and then he returned to reality again. He took off his shirt and splashed water on himself. A few drops in both peepers, and today's Benzedrine.

He turned on the shower, took off his clothes, glanced in

the steamed mirror to see if the eye drops and drugs were working yet. Then he stepped under the rain of water.

"You make yourself at home pretty good, huh?" Avchen's voice cut into the sound of the shower rapping on his skull.

"You fell asleep. I didn't want to leave without saying good-bye."

"Let me know when you're done. I want to use my bathroom." He heard the door open, then close again.

He shut off the water, dressed again quickly, and got out of the bathroom. Avchen was sitting beside the window, looking out in general direction of where the World Trade Center had stood. She turned her head when she heard the hinges of the bathroom door squeak. Andrew said nothing to her, he just left.

At the elevator he was feeling awake. He felt his pockets for his pills and discovered he'd left them in her bathroom. The elevator car rattled into position behind the gate. He opened it and got on, watched the floor slide upward and out of sight.

When Andrew returned to his car at the end of the day, he found a note under the windshield wiper:

Dear Andrew,

Mr. Pufknack called me today and he wants me to do another session. I thought about what you said again. You left your medicine in my hotel room. And you owe me one decent 2nd date plus one shower.

Signed, Avchen Neumann

Chapter 3

ileen lay naked on her belly on the bottom bunk in Simon's dorm room. The television was on—by the sound, an Ed, Edd, and Eddy cartoon. Eileen could see blurs of color from where she lay, but could not watch without her glasses.

Simon was in the bathroom. He'd been in the bathroom a long time. For a little while, Eileen had heard the shower, but she had known that was only to fool her.

The doctor sure had done a nice job with the stitches. The scar now was not as bad as an appendix scar would have been. Just a thin, pinkish silver line you could hardly notice. Thank God the knife had been nice and sharp—had done such a neat job. In a few years the scar would probably be so faded...in a few years...

Simon knew. Eileen had to admit she had chosen a poor time to tell him, but he had begun using that word again.

Now he was holed up in the bathroom.

She reached for her glasses, stood up and draped the bed sheet around her body. What a great feeling—a warm, slightly moist wrap, smelling subliminally of sweat and sex against her bare skin—God what a feeling. She walked across the floor feeling the rug with her bare toes. When she turned off Ed, Edd, and Eddy, the remote control was smooth and cool in her hand.

She did not want to die.

She sat in the armchair and curled up inside the bed sheet. Caterpillars weave cocoons and when they emerge they can fly with pied wings. A coffin kind of resembles a cocoon. It's even lined with silk. Eileen wondered if caterpillars were afraid of cocoons.

She let the bed sheet slip off her shoulders and there she was. All her, not even jewelry or make-up, just the freckles, the outsy belly button, and now the newest addition.

Why couldn't that knife have cut a little more to either side?

(Back in New York City, Andrew lost his breath and fumbled his flute to the floor in the middle of a take. Out of nowhere that word had jumped into his head.

Suicide.)

Her skin was smooth, and soft. Her breasts were full, but they would never nurse—and her uterus would never bear a child. She was not life. She was not the future. She was the memory that those who knew her would cherish a while.

She held up her hand. This hand would never even have the chance to be wrinkled, or to hurt from arthritis. This hand would never have the chance to perform the millions of tasks it was designed to perform. Simon said that her hands were beautiful—but they were ugly. An old person has beautiful hands. A baby does. These hands were not beautiful.

The bathroom door opened and Simon came out. He had been crying, weeping bitterly in fact. Now he tried to cover for himself. He stood there in his underpants. Simon always wore colored bikini underwear. It looked out of sorts on his body. He was thin, and he was virtually hairless—without shaving—not like the broad shouldered, buff models in the underwear ads. Eileen thought the bikinis looked hot on him. But let's face it, anyone being objective would simply laugh. Frankly, Simon was a geek.

The contrast between the geekiness of the writer and the bikini underwear was what appealed to her. She raced over to him and hugged him. He held her now as if she might crumble like brittle clay. Eileen supposed she ought to get used to that. Just the same, she squeezed back real tight to prove there was life in the ol' girl yet. "It's spring," Simon said, "and we are hiding in a dorm room with the curtains closed." He drew open the curtains.

"Simon, I'm naked in here!" She sidestepped out of the window.

"So everyone will get a nice show."

She cloaked herself in the bed sheet again.

"Let's go for a walk," Simon said.

"Don't you have classes?"

"No one goes to class at this school once spring begins. Get dressed."

Eileen reached for her suitcase off the top bunk.

Simon yanked the sheet from her body like an artist unveiling a statue. She, in full view of the window again, dove onto the bottom bunk to hide. Simon grinned impishly in his little underwear, and Eileen sat on the bunk looking out at him. She watched his smile fade and the bed sheet drop from his hands. Inside his underpants he was aroused, but in his head, he was terrified.

Something occurred to Eileen. She tried to dismiss the thought, but she knew Simon too well. Hadn't this been a cute little scene? Wasn't the little lovers' frolic ironic? Wouldn't this be a perfectly pathetic chapter for a novel?

She doubled over and vomited. It happened so quickly she couldn't get to the bathroom. She buried her face against the pillow and choked up a stomach full of yellow-brown stuff. When the convulsions subsided, she lifted her head with vomit smeared around her mouth and nose like baby food, and she looked at Simon.

He was pegged to the same spot.

It was now her turn to hide in the bathroom. She stood

up painfully and ran in there. Simon pulled the pillow out of the soaked pillowcase, balled up the linen to put it into the laundry. But instead, he opened the window, and dropped it out. The pillowcase fell three floors to the sidewalk.

"Let's try to be objective about this."

They walked across the campus, holding hands. Eileen walked barefoot. It was still early in the season, and there was yet a chill in the grass, but she did not care.

"What, exactly, are you scared of?"

"What do you mean, what am I scared of? What did you just tell me this morning?"

"Say it."

"Say what?"

"Repeat what I told you this morning."

"That you're sick."

"That is not exact."

"You have leukemia."

"Which means...?"

"Shamrocks, what are you getting at?"

"Simon, *say* what I said this morning."

"You are dying."

"Say it again."

"Oh, Jesus, Eileen, why don't you make a game out of this?"

"Once more, say it."

Simon hesitated. "You are dying," he said with finality.

"Now tell me what you're scared of."

"Sham..."

"Afraid of me dying? Afraid of not being able to call me or send me a text message? Of not being able to visit me when you come home from school? Of having all your plans screwed up? Let's face it, Simon, you are not scared. You are angry. You are really pissed off because we aren't going to be married and live happily ever after in the country with a willow tree, an Irish Setter, and a hearth you can lean against while smoking."

"You're wrong. I'm scared—"

"How can you be scared? I only told you this morning. I found out three years ago and I'm still not beyond anger."

"You've had this for three years?"

"Maybe longer. See, Simon, it isn't like on television or in one of your books where they say: You have three months to live."

"How long do you have?"

"As long as it takes, Simon."

He looked at the ground.

"See: you're angry again," she said. "You don't have a timetable so you can figure it out. Let's see, it is Monday, so she has two more weeks."

"You're being cruel, ya know."

"The doctors are thinking of giving a bone marrow transplant a try, if they can find a donor."

"I could do it?"

"You're not my type," she said wryly.

"What about chemo?"

"I'm doing it. Been doing it."

"I can't believe I never noticed the signs. You haven't lost your hair!" He said it as if that was proof of hope.

"You're kind of focusing too much on the details here."

"This morning you told me you are dying— Give me a minute to get over *that* detail."

"I am dying, Simon. When I fainted on that knife last month it was not because I skipped breakfast. And I have had fainting spells since, too."

"When?" Simon was pale. "You never told me."

"Will you please listen to what I am saying. It doesn't matter when, just that it's happening."

"I don't know what to think. I can't follow. First you tell me you are dying; then you tell me the transplant might cure you; then you're telling me you think it's going to happen soon?"

"That's the way it is," Eileen said quietly. "But let's call our feelings anger, okay? Not fear."

"You're right—I'm pissed. You're only twenty-four years old!"

She shrugged.

Simon stopped walking.

Back in the dorm room, Eileen pretended to read the newspaper while he clicked away on his laptop. Simon pretended to type while Eileen read the paper. His roommate was returning today. Eileen was leaving. In a little while they would go to the train station. Simon had asked Eileen if she minded if he wrote a bit, and she'd said no. She had already settled down with a newspaper and a beer. So they sat in the room, he with his laptop, she in the armchair, and this way they did not have to talk about anything. But if Eileen had stood at Simon's shoulder and looked at his screen, she would have seen nonsense. And if Simon had peered at the newspaper, he would have seen that she'd been reading the same full page advertisement for half an hour. Heh. A Botox ad.

Occasionally Simon would stop typing, stand, and pace the floor, ostensibly to think about what he would write next. He lit a cigarette and glanced at the headlines facing him, at Eileen's legs and feet sticking out from below, her fingers wrapped around the edges of the newsprint, the rest of her hidden behind it. He didn't suppose he would go to her wake. He knew every inch of that body too well. He had listened up close too many times to the sound of a living heart and breathing lungs and loved them. He could not stand beside this body as it lay in a coffin and know that everything he loved inside and out had stopped. He would not go to her funeral either. Perhaps he would be able, after a while, to visit her grave.

He bent down to the refrigerator to get a beer. They say those things like wakes and funerals and visiting headstones make a person's death easier to accept. But Simon believed he would rather live out his life expecting her to return from wherever she had run off to. He did not want to find himself living through a day when he accepted that they would never be together again.

He turned away from the refrigerator empty handed. He leaned over his laptop, clicked on select all, and deleted everything on the screen. He sat down to more nonsense.

"Do we have to leave soon?" Eileen said.

"Yeah. Better get ready."

Chapter 4

He fell head over heels, and as he landed his legs slammed against the side of the couch. He heard something tear and he felt a burning pain move across his calf. Slowly, Andrew regained himself and crawled to the light. Once it was on, he saw he'd tripped over a carton in the middle of the living room. He had torn his pant leg and scraped his skin on the nail sticking out of the couch's frame.

The carton was unopened. The packing label had Avchen's name on it. Andrew pushed it out of the way. As he stood up, he saw Avchen standing in the hallway.

"I almost killed myself," he told her. "What is this?"

"My parents sent it to me. I don't know what it is yet. I was waiting for you to come home so we could open it together."

What fun.

Andrew walked into the bathroom and took off his pants. He could probably easily mend them (or Avchen would be just delighted to do it for him), and they were not new anyway. He could buy a new pair. He could buy 100 new pairs if he felt like it. He tossed them into the corner and examined his leg. For a small scrape it sure hurt enough. He'd live.

He ran water in the sink to wash his face. Four o'clock

in the morning and she wants to open a box together. Avchen was having a wonderful time playing house since she moved in. She did the grocery shopping (do you need anything special—i'11 bring you a surprise) and the laundry, and she cleaned the flat and insisted on eating breakfast together. And now she almost kills me with a box she wants us to open as a team.

He left the bathroom. "What did mom and dad send, dear?" he asked on his way into the kitchen.

"I didn't open it yet," Avchen said.

Andrew got a beer from the refrigerator. "You didn't? What on earth are you waiting for?"

"Don't you wanna watch?"

"Oh, yeah, sure." He returned to the living room.

Avchen, crouched on her haunches, struggled with the packing tape and staples, tugged and ripped, and finally opened the carton. It was a table lamp.

"I have plenty of lamps," Andrew said. He sat on the couch.

"I told my father I had an apartment—he probably figured I didn't have much furniture."

"You don't have an apartment—I do."

"I couldn't tell him I'm living with you." She sat beside him, admired the lamp which she had set in the center of the floor. "How do you like it?"

"Terrific."

"Want to see if it works? Do you have a light bulb?"

"In the kitchen drawer there's one." He raised the beer to his mouth.

"Blech! How can you drink beer now? You drink too much beer." She patted his belly in a cutesy way. "You're getting a pot."

"Go get the light bulb," he said irritably.

She ran into the kitchen, the hem of her nightgown dancing up and down to bare her bare behind. He waited to get this over with. She returned with the bulb, knelt beside the lamp, and carefully screwed it in. She attached the shade, and then she was set to test the lamp's illuminative powers. She plugged it in and turned the switch. When the light came on she was simply thrilled.

"Came all the way from Pittsburgh and it still works."

"How about that."

"Where do you want to put it?"

That is a loaded question at four in the morning.

"I'll decide tomorrow." He finished off his beer.

"You want to go to bed now?" Avchen asked.

"Were you waiting up?"

"I was dozing. I got home late tonight too."

"How's the record coming?"

"Okay. I don't know. I just sing. Mr. Pufknack is nice to me, but he doesn't tell me much. Do you suppose he's insulted because I told him I wanted to stay with you instead of in the hotel he got for me?"

"I doubt it. Now get to bed, babe. I'll be right in."

Andrew took the empty bottle into the kitchen to throw in the recycle bin. A month ago he'd have left it on the end table, perhaps for weeks. Avchen was beginning to influence his behavior.

Back in the living room, he paused over the still lighted lamp, looked at it.

He grabbed it by the neck and held it up, yanked the cord out of the wall. Sparks spit from the socket. He began to coil the cord. Where would he put another lamp?

She told her parents she had an apartment.

Andrew tensed the cord, tore it out of the base of the lamp.

"They don't make lamps like they used to," he said, and inserted the frayed end of the wire back into the little hole in the lamp's base. He left it sitting beside the couch looking as if it were still in one piece, went into the bedroom.

Avchen sat in the bed with the sheet pulled up to her chin.

"What took you so long?" she said.

"I don't know." Andrew took off his shirt and dropped it over the bedpost. He reached for the corner of the covers to pull them back, but Avchen clung to them.

"Password?"

Andrew tested his patience.

"I've been warming up," she said, and when she dropped the sheet from her chin she was naked.

"Can I get in? I'm getting cold out here."

"Strange...I've gotten myself really hot."

Andrew put one leg into bed.

"No—those come off first."

Andrew removed his underpants and got into bed. Her hand immediately moved for him. It was fairly obvious what she wanted, again; Andrew resisted...again. She made noises like squeals, or painful winces, and rubbed her body against his.

"Avchen—"

She stopped and opened her eyes. "Andrew," she whined, "I'm ready. I'm ready and I want to do it."

He interrupted. "I don't think you know what you're doing."

"What do you want to do? Call time out to debate abstinence?"

"Look: we can have as much fun as you want, but you are talking serious now."

"I am not talking—you are."

"You're only seventeen." And I'm too young to go to jail.

She was insulted. "I am a woman," she asserted. "A *real*, human woman. Do you think I don't know what I do to people? Everybody acts the same way—even other girls—like they can't even come near me or talk to me. People are afraid of the way I look. I have feelings, Andrew; it's okay to touch me. I *want* to be touched."

Andrew grimaced. He tried to think of something to say but he was on the spot.

"This is so lame!" Avchen almost shouted as if in pain. "How can a guy be such a loser? You don't know me that good."

"Maybe that's my strongest argument."

"Maybe. Let's find out." She climbed on top of him. Her

192

thighs did feel soft and invitingly warm straddling his legs.

"Avchen—the first day I saw you and every day since, you've been part seductress, part child. Maybe Edgar Pufknack and Metacarpal Records have you feeling more and more the former, but I have been seeing more and more of the latter desperately trying to hold on." Besides, they'd kill me if I did their golden girl.

"Andrew, I am sick of playing with myself!" She reached for him again, and he did like the feeling when she held on.

Still, he buried his face in the crook of his arm. "Why now? I have to go out in two hours, and you pick now to start this."

"You know I've wanted this a long time."

"So, want it a little longer. Because I don't want you hating everything about living when it's over."

"I won't, Andrew, I promise—"

But I will. "Do you love me?"

"I don't know. We haven't known each other that long. After I do you, maybe I'll know. Were you in love with the first girl you did it with?"

"You sound like you're talking about making pancakes. And yes, I was in love."

"What was her name?" Avchen let go of him and flowed back to her side of the bed like water. She leaned on her elbow and reminded Andrew, not of art, but of a gossiping girl at a slumber party.

"That's irrelevant."

"How long ago did you know her?"

"It doesn't matter."

"Why don't you go out with her now?"

"Sheesh."

"If you want to convince me I should be in love with you first, you gotta tell me what it feels like when ya are."

Andrew sighed heavily. "It was not all that long ago. I don't like to talk about it."

Avchen got out of bed and walked naked across the floor, hypnosis in motion.

"You're still not over her? How romantic."

She prowled slowly around the room. The muscles under her skin were strong, shaped, smoothed nicely by femininity.

"Can I ask you a question?" she said.

"You've asked a million already."

She paused a step in front of the tall mirror on the inside of the open closet door. There was that strangeness about her reflection. He had noticed it once before when she had brushed her hair before the bathroom mirror, had seen it the last time they walked together passed a reflecting store window: It was a slight shimmer of image, as if the mirror were shining back more than it could handle. And so she stood, all her beauty not in one form, but in twin forms. It was mind boggling, and Andrew could not remember his train of thought,

"Is she the reason you are a workaholic?"

Andrew closed his eyes. He pinched the bridge of his nose between his thumb and forefinger. "Wait a minute...I must be getting tired." He opened one eye. "What did you say?"

"Is this girl the reason you're a workaholic?"

"Who?" he had to ask.

"Was there a girl, or wasn't there?" the twin Avchens asked.

Andrew forced his thoughts.

They were talking about Janie.

"I am not a workaholic," he said.

"Andrew: you are a workaholic. I've lived with you long enough to know that. And you're kind of a real, like, type A++, too. Is this girl the reason?"

"I don't believe in that."

"What?"

"That one bad thing happening to you can mess you up for life."

The reflection walked away in the mirror, Avchen walked toward him. She came back to bed where there was only one of her again. "I'm still hot," she whispered.

She drew him close, rubbed against him. Her thighs surrounded him again and clamped onto him. He struggled a little, but she would not release him. He had no idea how long she held onto him—long enough for her to finish.

Then she pushed the covers back and got out of bed. She put on her robe and walked out, her beauty following her like a flare. Andrew felt sick. He didn't really think he could go to jail, but he felt like he was already there. When the alarm rang at that moment, it startled him. He shut if off. Another day on no sleep at all. He got out of bed too and went to see where Avchen had gone.

She was making breakfast. The lamp was on the table with its broken cord laid out next to it.

"My lamp broke," she said sadly.

"What happened?" Andrew examined the cord.

"I don't know. It worked last night—you saw it. Then just now that cord broke off so easily—it was pretty cheaply made. My father will be crushed."

"It probably came loose during shipping, and we handled it just enough last night to disconnect it altogether. Just tell your father it works great. You don't have to say anything."

"I'm boiling coffee."

"Okay."

"Yeah, well, go get dressed. I won't have you sitting at the table with nothing on. We aren't animals."

He had a retort, but held it. He left the kitchen for a shower. In the bathroom, he swallowed an upper and took a few eye drops, as always. His stomach was still upset—it hurt, in fact. He did not want breakfast.

"Do you want a ride into the city?" he asked when he walked, fully clothed, back into the kitchen.

"Yes, please...Here is your coffee."

"Did you put it in a tin cup?"

"What?" she said.

They sat down to breakfast. The lamp was still on the table—an odd white elephant in the room.

"I'm so disappointed about this thing," Avchen sighed. "My father probably went through a lot of trouble picking it out."

"I told you," Andrew said simply, "don't say anything. Let him think it's bringing you hours of pleasure."

"It worked fine last night, you saw."

"We'd better hurry or I'll be late. Go get dressed, babe."

"Can't I finish my breakfast? It's the most important meal—"

"—of the day, right," Andrew said. "Yeah, but let's move it up a little, okay?"

It was raining, the kind of day when animals crawl into holes and hibernate, and when people want to follow the same instinct. It was the kind of day when all the Benzedrine in the world could not help.

The Next Tuesday Band was waiting around for Andrew when he arrived. He brightened when he recognized them. "I forgot it was you guys I was sitting in with today. How ya doing?"

Cornelius nodded, threw away his cigarette and sat at his piano.

"What are you guys into these days, big money, huh?" Andrew said.

"Yep, big money."

"How is Pinnoke? How's her back?"

"She's cool. Doin' good."

"Tell her Eileen sends her love."

"Heard Eileen had an accident," Daniel Serahuli said.

"She cut herself with a knife—she's okay though. It was a while ago."

"We picked up another guitarist," Cornelius said. "Raj Hernandez. That's him."

"So who's missing?" Andrew wondered. "You got one extra, what am I doing here?"

"We need big orchestral backing on this album," Daniel said. "That's you."

"I am the orchestra?"

"You are it," Cornelius said.

"Let's get to it," Andrew said.

When Andrew returned home, before midnight for once, he found Simon sitting in his living room, smoking while he waited. "Your roommate let me in," Simon explained.

Andrew wondered whose word "roommate" had been—Avchen's, or Simon's.

"What's doin'?" Andrew said. "Is Avchen home?"

"She went to the supermarket."

"How's my sister?"

"She's dying."

Andrew sat down. He did not say anything for a long, long time, and when he spoke all he could think of to say was: "I know," in a small, defeated voice.

"You've known for a long time."

"We've all known for years."

"Not me."

"Simon, you've only known her about a year."

"Why didn't you visit her in the hospital?"

Andrew sat back in his seat and let out a long exhale. "Simon, I was there, you talked to me."

"But she didn't. She never even saw you. She was looking for you the whole time—but you never came."

"I was very busy." Something inside did say that was a lame excuse, but he would never acknowledge it.

"She might have died then," Simon said.

"She might have, but she didn't. Look, Simon, I am sorry everyone kept a secret from you for so long and now you're feeling left out. But I am not the one who kept it from you. Now do you want a beer, because I'm gonna have a beer."

"I do not want a beer. I want to know what's the matter with you."

"I'm tired. It's raining. I've been filling in for the New York Philharmonic all day, and I am beat. I have to be back in the studio tomorrow at eight."

"She's your twin. I defended you when she was upset that you didn't come, but I don't know why."

"I was there, Simon. And I thought about her and worried about her. Why do I have to account to you?"

"What would you have done if she had died?"

"She was not dying!" Andrew raised his voice, and he felt foolish even arguing this. "I knew that from what the doctor told me. On the day she is in the hospital and really dying, we will all know it, be certain of it, and I will be there every second."

Simon was up and pacing. He spoke methodically: "You are her own flesh, Andrew—her twin. There has not been a day since you were conceived you have not shared. You owe her more than you're giving her, far more. She is scared. She needs support. When she is gone, you are the half that will carry on. You have a responsibility to her to demonstrate that you will do that."

Andrew watched Simon pace. Back and forth, back and forth, his gestures contrived and planned. It struck him that Simon had quite a flare for dramatics. And then he had to laugh. He went into the kitchen so he would not laugh at Simon to his face.

Simon followed. "I'm serious," he said.

Andrew reached into the refrigerator and took out two beers. He handed one to Simon who received it dumbly. "My sister and I have never considered ourselves to be one in the same. We are very close and she means the world to me—but I do not think she expects me to take up and carry her cross as well as my own once she's dead," Andrew said.

"Simon, let's admit something: you're pissed because you didn't know. And you feel like everyone knew but you. What do you think we had going? A secret club that met every Wednesday when you had class? She didn't tell you, I'm sure, because she didn't want you to worry."

"I wouldn't have worried." Simon sat at the table. He pushed the unopened beer away from himself.

"Evidently she thought you would. You're worried now.

But it doesn't make sense to worry about what you can't control. My sister is going to die. It is going to happen and it is beyond our control."

"Don't say that!"

"Get *used* to a fact, Simon! The rest of us had to. Since you found out a little later than us, you're running a little behind. But you had better catch up because you are the only one crying about it. Including Eileen. People die—it's the coldest, hardest fact of life."

Avchen came home then, struggling with two armfuls of groceries and a dripping umbrella. Simon, about to say something, something important—about Andrew's attitude, he thought, but he couldn't be sure—found himself unable even to think plainly. Just as when this girl had opened the door earlier tonight, the second he looked at her his mind was a blank. She had stood at the door smiling at him, wondering who he was, and he could not tell her, could not say why he had come. An embarrassing game of twenty questions had followed. And it was the same now as she placed the groceries on the counter. His mind was lost, his point was lost, and so was he.

Frustrating him further, when he eked out a thought, was how Andrew could appear so unfazed.

"Andrew, will you go out to the cab and get the other two bags? And pay the driver too—I didn't have any money left and I told him you would be right out."

"Sure."

And he went out.

Avchen said to Simon: "Will you be staying here tonight?"

"What?" he had to ask.

"It's so late," she said. "Do you want me to run out and tell the taxi you need it, or are you planning to stay?"

"I don't know."

"We have extra room," Avchen said. "You may as well stay."

Andrew returned with the rest of the groceries. Avchen

went out to put linens on Simon's bed.

Meanwhile, Simon wanted Andrew to say something like "are you all right?" and then he would know Andrew did care about his sister, about what her illness was certain to do to those who loved her. But Andrew tore a paper towel from the roll and dried the rain from his face, saying: "How's school?"

Simon almost said, "Are you crazy? Eileen is dying and you think I'm even thinking of school?" and he wanted to slam his hand on the table top when he said it, but Avchen walked back into the room and confused him again.

She might have said, something like, "I made up your bed. Andrew and I usually have to get up early, but you don't have to." Then she and Andrew left and Simon remembered a hundred things he ought to have said.

Simon walked up and down in front of the Atlantic Ocean. He had gotten up early, earlier than Andrew or Avchen, dressed and left their house while it was still dark. He had slept very little to pass the night. A nightmare woke him screaming bloody blue murder and drenched in sweat. Neither of his hosts, apparently, had heard him, or else they had not cared enough to investigate.

After the nightmare, his sleep had been in fits and starts. He decided he should try to make classes in spite of everything. If he got up and left right away, he would make it to school in time for his first class, even a shower to boot.

But on his way, he changed his mind again, veered off the highway suddenly enough to surprise even himself, and he headed for the ocean.

This beach was crescent shaped, sandy for the most part, but bordered by piled rocks. He walked as far as the rocks would allow on one end, turned and walked back as far as the rocks would permit at the other end. The waves washed up around his feet, soaking his sneakers and pants. The water was frigid although spring was fast turning to summer, and his feet cramped from the drenching.

Occasionally he would stop in the middle of the beach, gaze out at the horizon. The sun had risen. Simon was sure it had been down when he'd first stepped out of his car, yet he did not remember the sunrise. Sunrises were supposed to be spectacular sights filled with God's grandeur—the kind of thing you could not help marvel at—and he had missed it. He was sorry. He would have liked to take on God face to face.

The tide was going out. Simon noticed less water reached his sneakers. The breakers were tame white curls. The white curls had come all the way from that line where sea meets sky. And from beyond. The water washing his feet now had at some time washed the cliffs of Dover. He stopped in the middle of his walk again.

If you were to watch a boat sail outward, it would appear to sink. The last thing to go down would be the tip of its mainmast. This is, of course, a trick contrived by the curve of the earth to fool you into being afraid to go too far from home. Sailors in history feared this kind of sinking more than anything else, so they stayed within view of land. Except a few, of course, there are always a few.

But you cannot really fault people for fearing what they do not know.

One thing Simon knew: right now, in those classes he had chosen to miss, final exams were coming up. He would surely fail if he did not get back to work.

Big deal.

Simon thought he used to like Andrew, but after last night, he no longer could.

People die—it's the coldest, hardest fact of life.

"There is no such thing as a fact!" Simon argued aloud.

That was a stupid thing to say. It was a fact that people died. But why did that have to mean you should take a passive stance against the death of a girl only twenty-four years old, the death of a pretty and bright girl, the death of someone you love very much?

(you're angry you are really pissed off because we aren't going to get married and live happily ever after in the country with a willow tree and Irish setter and a hearth)

The tide was way out now. No water came anywhere near his feet, and sand bars were forming.

Simon wondered if, at low tide, sailors were willing to go a little farther out.

Chapter 5

A rather unfortunate thing happened.

The best defense against Avchen driving Andrew totally crazy had been spending time at work, away from her. But while he was being mixed in as Next Tuesday's orchestra, someone came up with the idea to have a female vocal on a few particular tracks—songs which not Raj Hernandez, Martin O'Kelly, Cornelius Prince, nor any male voice, could do justice. Edgar Pufknack saw the opportunity to make use of his new talent, and Avchen was brought in to try the part. Naturally her voice was bewitchingly sultry and perfect, as was her person. Hired.

Avchen did not like it too much because she now worked on her own album in one studio, The Next Tuesday Band's album in a second, and after all that she was expected to appear as the sensual and titillating focal point of photos for album hype. That photographer was inept anyhow, could not take a good picture to save his life, but she had to do everything as he said.

Andrew did not like working with her on top of living with her. Her brain-stopping beauty only barely made tolerable her cutesy-pie juvenile manner and, now, her crankiness and childish temper tantrums.

Avchen still wanted to take care of the flat, wash the

dishes and do the cooking, go grocery shopping after midnight. She forced herself to run on three hours of sleep each night. Yet Andrew was the one she claimed was not taking proper care.

All of a sudden, Avchen had added one more annoyance to her already varied repertoire. She had begun to nag. Andrew had left home at eighteen to escape nagging. He did not need it from Avchen.

"I'm a studio musician," he told her flatly. "And if I don't continue to work, I will stop altogether. That phone will stop ringing and I won't be worth a thing to anyone."

"You're beat, Andrew. You can't keep forcing yourself to keep up. Only reason you don't know you're tired is you are too full of speed."

They were sitting in bed. The next day was Sunday and Next Tuesday was not planning to record. Andrew had taken another job in the meantime.

"And you're ill, but you don't know it," Avchen said.

"If I were sick, I would know."

"At night you can hardly breathe. I hear you."

"Don't listen and then you won't."

"Gimme a break," Avchen sighed.

"So I have a little cold."

She tried to feel his forehead for fever, but he impatiently turned his head.

"Who knows if a fever would show in you anyhow. Andrew, tomorrow I want you to stay in bed."

"I can't."

"You can, and you will if I have to sit on you to make sure."

"Avchen, do me a favor," he said and he sounded calm.

"What?"

"Get out."

She balked. She did not know if he meant out of the room or out of the apartment.

He meant out of the room and he told her so.

"I'm not into sleeping with my mother."

"I'm just saying this stuff because I don't want you to

kill yourself."

"I am not killing myself!" he shouted. "Why does everyone think I'm killing myself!"

suicide

Avchen drew back. "All right," she said. "I meant it as a figure of speech."

"Leave me alone!" Andrew got out of bed.

"What's the matter with you? I thought I was temperamental."

"The matter with me is *you*. You drive me crazy. I don't care how pretty you are. I live the way I want to live, and I am not going to change for a pubescent lovely who plays wife cleaning and cooking and shopping in the middle of the bloody night."

"I'm sorry. I was trying to help. You don't appreciate anything."

"I don't appreciate a seventeen-year-old child who just wants to get laid so she can say she went to the big city for adventure and found it."

"I am not a child," she said softly.

"You are a child. A child who can't handle herself to save her life."

"You're a very selfish person."

"You hit the nail on the head, babe," he said pointing his finger. "I'm very selfish and I want to run my own life. So leave me alone and don't help me anymore." Then he went into the other bedroom.

He forgot to bring his cell phone, leaving her in control of it and the alarm clock.

And she turned both of them off.

Avchen knew she had touched a nerve. She tried to remember everything she had just said, tried to identify what could have set him off.

In the morning, a great weight was piled on Andrew's chest. Someone was placing rocks there.

Admit it: you are a bastard.

He awoke with Avchen's hair dangling in his face. She

knelt astride him, pinning him. She was naked and Andrew's first thought was of how nice a picture the narrow landing strip of hair below her navel made as it curved down into the hair of his own chest. He tried to reach up to her and found she held his hands down too.

"What are you doing?" he inquired.

"Making certain you stay in bed," she replied.

"What time is it?"

"Ten o'clock."

"In the morning?" He tried to sit up, but she really had him quite well pinned. The round goes to Avchen. "I'm late, why didn't the alarm go off?" he said.

"Because you pouted off into this room last night. You missed it."

"Didn't anyone call?"

"No."

He squirmed to free himself, but she would not yield.

"I gotta get going," he said.

"Forget it. I am staying right here."

"Oh come on. "

"Whoever's on top is in control." She smiled. A lovely, startlingly haunting, siren song of a parting of the lips, and her breasts pressed softly on his heart.

Andrew struggled against her hold, but she really was very strong. She was right, she was in control, and he was not going anywhere. "Why are you doing this?" He went on struggling.

"You know why. Don't you look silly. And to think you can't even out wrestle a child."

"Is that why you're doing this, Avchen, because I called you a child?"

"No. Because you're sick and you need rest. We're making plenty of money from the one album we're working on, and you don't need to work today."

"What did I say last night? You don't listen too good."

"Neither do you. I'll get off you if you promise to stay home."

"What else can I do now? I'm sure that if it's ten o'clock and I'm not there, they've called another guy. I don't understand why no one called me."

Avchen freed his hands. Andrew put them on her hips.

"You're a pain in the neck, know that?" he said.

"Yep. But so are you. We make a good pair. Do you surrender?"

"I do."

"Want me to make breakfast?"

"Sure."

Avchen rolled off his chest and stretched out beside him on the bed.

"Single beds aren't as easy to fit two people in side by side," she said.

"Not unless one is on top of the other."

"What do you want for breakfast? And don't say me because that's corny."

And it's not true. "It doesn't matter. Coffee."

"You always have that. Ya gotta eat something with it." She stood. "I'll surprise you." She turned and walked out. Andrew watched her as she left the room.

In the other bedroom Avchen put on her robe, then she went to the kitchen to start breakfast.

Andrew could not believe he was taking a shower at ten-thirty. He could not believe he was even at home so late in the day. His own bathroom looked strange to him in broad daylight.

He walked into their—his—bedroom and sat on the bed. He fished in the night-stand drawer for his uppers and he took one dry. It was slow going down, and he kept reswallowing the lumpy traces in his throat. As he sat with his hair still wet and a towel around his waist, gulping again and again, he noticed the cell phone, open, screen blank, on the nightstand. He seized it and stared at the off switch.

"That little bitch."

Avchen's stomach did a somersault when Andrew appeared stark naked in the kitchen doorway, brandishing the telephone as if he meant to beat her with it.

He didn't. "Get out," he said to her.

Chapter 6

The final time Eileen went into the hospital, it was not for leukemia, but pneumonia.

Andrew met Simon in the lounge on the thirteenth floor. Andrew had been in his sister's room, just sitting there, and then their parents had come to visit. Resenting the intrusion, he left. He would wait here until he could be alone with her again. He was surprised to find Simon. Simon had not yet been into the room, had not even been to the hospital before today as far as Andrew knew. The tables had turned, and a lot could be said about that, but Andrew saw no point in saying it.

Simon did not even look at him when he sat down. But he was not ignoring Andrew—he really did not seem to notice anyone had come along. The fact was, Simon was asleep. His eyes were open, but he was so exhausted that his brain finally said no more of this, and went to sleep.

Looking at him, it struck Andrew how young Simon was. All of them were young. Children making believe they knew enough about the world to control it. Everyone was getting a very stern lesson.

Simon moved. Then he discovered Andrew's presence.

"Have you seen her yet?" Andrew tried not to show that he already knew the answer.

"No," Simon said.

"She's awake if you want to go in. Her parents are there though."

"Maybe when they leave. How come you don't have to work today?"

"I just don't."

"This is it, huh?" Simon said morosely.

"This is what?"

"Forget it."

"I'm gonna get a soda from the machine downstairs. Want one?"

"Yeah."

"You'll be here?"

"Where else."

Andrew left for the elevator. Simon stayed put. But then his mouth tasted bad, and he could not wait for the soda to come back. He went down the hall to the water cooler. Eileen's room number was 1317. He knew that. The cooler was next to room 1315. Simon turned back toward the lounge, but then he turned back for another drink of water, and after that, went into Eileen's room.

He found a crowd. Eileen's parents, plus the visitors of the other person in the room. A cloth screen on an aluminum frame divided the room not well.

How's the food here?

Are you keeping the nurses on their toes?

Want to watch television?

You look much better today.

There is plenty of light in here at least.

What banal things people talk about in hospitals.

Today, there were tubes and monitors. Simon's stomach hurt and his mouth still tasted bad—worse. Maybe they designed hospital beds overly large purposely to make anybody in one look frail.

He said hello to Walter and Aggie Healy. He hoped they would have the decency to leave for a while, but they stayed on. Simon walked to the window. Eileen appeared to be asleep. He could not bear to stand beside the bed and look at that respirator or whatever the hell it was, and that inverted bottle dripping like the water cooler into a tube running into her arm.

One hundred years ago, when people died, they did so in their homes with a certain amount of self-respect. Even an elephant is allowed by its herd to die in peace. In modern times, when they supposedly have more tricks up their sleeves, a young girl still dies, but now it is in a hospital that looks more like the cause of death than the illness

(AUTOPSY REPORT: cause of death listed as despair from looking at pale green plaster walls and waxed, dappled grey linoleum corridors)

with a lot of tubes connected to her person. Simon guessed that soon Eileen would be consigned to hospice care and would, perhaps, get to die her own bed, smelling the smells of home.

The baby has two more teeth, said one of the roommate's visitors.

Simon looked out the window and was surprised. It seemed the first time he had ever looked out to discover the world.

There it was.

The whole surface of the planet curved off in every direction until it finally formed a sphere. A little more egg-shaped than round. And this hospital was a tiny block, like a memory sticking up from the landscape on top of the sphere. It would be a little to one side of top, actually, about forty-nine degrees. Latitude and longitude were thought of in order to facilitate a search for life. It was for convenience. It had everything to do with human identity and nothing at all to do with the planet, or with the air around the planet, or the space beyond.

What existed not by the hand of man existed by pure chance.

What do you know.

One day nothing, next day something. (Or do you suppose it really did take seven days?) An accident was responsible for all of this. Some accident—

Whoops!

There were no leaves on the trees. It was late autumn. Come to think of it, Simon wore a coat these days. He did not remember the first day he had put it on, or how long he had been putting it on every day, but yes, he was wearing a coat now. And he did remember the last time he and Eileen had gone to the beach—it was long ago. Their final summer hadn't been the big to do that he had planned. She had been too tired all summer to do anything. And there was that lousy summer cold she'd had also. They had gone to the beach only a few times. Usually by the end of summer the freckles on her skin had multiplied by the hundreds, darkened to a very healthy color. This summer she more or less kept her winter complexion. Yes, Simon could remember those little events that pass the seasons, but he had not been aware of them. Now the trees were bare, and it was cold outside, and sooner or later, it would snow.

He heard a noise and turned toward it. Walter and Aggie Healy were preparing to leave. Simon tried to conceal his relief. "You going home?"

"We're going to get something to eat," Aggie said. "Want to come?"

"No thanks," he answered, swallowing the urgency he felt for their absence.

Finally they were gone. Aggie's coat, however, remained as a retainer. Now, if only the bodies of those ridiculous voices behind that screen would also leave. Simon went to the bedside and sat on the folding chair.

He thought about holding her hand, but imagined it might be cold. He did not want to hold a cold hand. Then he decided he was being absurd and grabbed her hand as if capturing it. He told himself that of course her skin would be warm—hot even, from fever—but he was nevertheless surprised to find it the same soft, smooth and warm hand he had held a thousand times.

Eileen opened her eyes. She did not move her head,

but recognized him out of the corner of her vision. When she spoke her voice was nasal, probably from that thing leading into her nostrils. "Hey," she said.

"I'm here," he told her.

"It's about time you joined us after sitting at the end of the hall all day."

"Who told you?" Simon wondered. No one had known he was out there until Andrew.

"I knew you were there. It's something you would do."

"Your mother and father went to eat. I guess your brother did too." The conversation on the opposite side of the divider had ceased. Simon felt that no matter how low he whispered, those people eavesdropped on every word. Eileen could not speak loudly, and they would hear only his voice—like hearing one party on a phone call. They would be making a game of guessing what the other one said. He wished they would start talking again. Of what interest to them could he possibly be?

"How do you feel?" he asked.

"Same."

"I don't know how 'same' is. I haven't been here, remember?"

"Same is my chest hurts and I'm exhausted."

"How long do you have to stay here?" Simon's mouth tasted bad still. He thought his breath must be horrible in Eileen's face.

"I don't know."

As long as it takes.

"I finished my novel," Simon said quickly.

"Great."

"I'm afraid I don't like it much."

She muttered something he didn't catch.

"What?"

"I said you're your own worst critic."

If only that were true. Instead, a sort of odd corollary was true. He was the world's worst critic. He had always used his writing to scream and tell the world how bad off it was. His themes were not subtle: Society stinks. Society breeds contempt, confusion, competition. Solitary people trying not to know one another, because it's harder to compete and win in a free market until your adversary is just a cartoon. Republicans vs. Democrats; neo-cons vs. libs; evangelicals vs. everybody; man against himself with predatory desires surrounded by a rhetoric of goodness and sincerity so sincere, it just *has* to be genuine—has to be. Have the terrorists really won?

Thus Spoke Zarathustra...

Who had nothing to say.

Only now had Simon become aware that it was not he who should point this out. Here he was a twenty-four-year-old kid—maybe not a full member of the society his writing was at odds with, though certainly as much of a pledge as anyone—but here he was a twenty-four-year-old boy, and he had noticed only today that the earth is round.

He squeezed Eileen's hand and she had quite enough strength to squeeze firmly back. "How do you feel?" she asked him weakly.

"Scared," he replied.

"Angry?"

He thought for a moment. The voices on the other side of the screen began to chatter again.

"I think it's going to snow early this year," Simon said.

On the other side of the screen, a voice said: "It's quite cold outside today."

"You haven't even had Thanksgiving yet," Eileen said with great effort.

"Don't talk," Simon advised. "We'll just sit here a while, okay? But rest your voice."

She nodded, ever so slightly.

There was a coat of perspiration between the skins of their hands. One of them was sweating.

No one at all spoke in the room now. Heat came through the vent with a sudden, rising whoosh, and the steady hum then followed as the only noise in the room.

It grew dark, and after some time the other visitors

appeared from behind the screen. They were on their way home, just passing through Eileen's side of the room. Normal seeming folks, tired and drawn looking, but not monsters or peculiars. They smiled at Simon and said hello. His eyes caught theirs. They were an older man, a woman probably his daughter from the resemblance, a second man most likely her husband, two little girls—not so little—early teenagers. Simon kept his eyes on their faces longer than he needed. He and they were just a group of people with maybe nothing else in common but that someone they loved was sick enough to be in a hospital. The group went out and Simon looked behind their screen. He expected an old woman, the older man's wife, but he found a sleeping girl younger than Eileen.

PART FOUR

Chapter 1

Christmas was coming; it would be here soon. The anxiety in all the media was rising by the day. From newspapers and local news spots, drive-time talk-radio shows, all the way to web site home pages, the constant chatter about the fate of retailers if people didn't step up the buying was a vale of tears. Soon there would be no shopping days till Christmas, and it would all be over for consumer confidence.

But this was a lazy day. Valerie sat in front of her vanity mirror, ran a comb through her short, wet hair. She had liked it long, but she had suddenly desired a drastic change. So after her shower she wiped a circle in the steamed mirror, took scissors in hand, and snip snip here, snip snip there. Now her hair only brushed her shoulders. It did make her look closer to her age, she had to give it that. Something had to be done—she was so weary of herself.

She dried her hair, curled a little flounce in the ends, and then went downstairs. In the kitchen, she dragged a step stool to the counter in order to reach the overhead cabinet. The architect of this house must have had gripes against short people. She took a box of cereal down and put it on the table. Nothing commanded her to keep her cabinets arranged this way, she was free to move things about, but it seemed no matter what, there was always more room in those high overhead cabinets than in the ones underfoot. You just couldn't win.

Valerie took her breakfast into the living room. Her Mama would have a baby if she ever knew Valerie brought food into this room with all its fancy furnishings. But Valerie had picked out this deep, soft carpet perfect for burying her toes in, and it was a cold morning—too cold. She liked the carpet, warm on her feet. When she finished eating, she set the dishes aside and stretched out on the floor. The morning sun had been coming through the window, heating this patch of floor. It was the only warm spot in the house.

Yes, today was a lazy day.

Every day was a lazy day—and not of her choosing either.

Actually, Valerie had no Christmas shopping done. She put it off. Excuses are easy to find when you don't want to do something. Christmas would not be Christmas with Cornelius in Buffalo and she alone here in a suburb of Albany.

She took a magazine from the holder and thumbed through it. The pictures struck her funny. Her own living room looked like these in the magazine. She hated it. It was her upbringing, so she had continued it, but now the absurdity of showroom houses struck her. This was no home. Their apartment in Albany had been a home. The personality of their marriage could be found in every corner, doorway, window sash, and in every piece of furniture in that apartment. Valerie wished they had never bought this house. It was big, familiar in that way, but without character, and cold.

Her whole life was like that. Cold. Always cold, whenever it ought to have been warm. Just like that time there was frost in July.

She whipped the magazine across the room, thought she felt her back creak as she stood. Since winter had begun, the darn thing threatened to give out again. She stooped for the dishes and straightened carefully.

The kitchen sink was stacked with dishes, filthy. Yes, children would be born if her Mama ever got a look at this housekeeping. Valerie left the sink as it was. She turned on her soap opera but that bored her. She turned on the radio. Then she turned that off in favor of a CD.

She had bought Cornelius' first album—the one that had not sold—and she'd bought the second one, which had made him into The Next Tuesday Band. And she had bought Cornelius' third one, which would be the band's second—should have been only its first. It was the one Avchen Neumann sang on for the first time. Avchen was now considered a member of the band.

Avchen's debut album had gone over fabulously. But it was probably that nearly nude glam shot of her on the inside of the jewel case that sold it. That picture was not even a good one. It was fuzzy, washed out, her body lost in so much excess light. Only a vague form could be distinguished in there. That, of course, is what made it interesting. And it had all been an accident. They had tried to take clear, cover-girl photographs, they had tried many times, but not a one came out. The original photographer was fired. The second encountered the same problems. There was nothing wrong with his camera, with his lighting, or his talent. There was something wrong with Avchen.

Avchen was simply too beautiful to photograph.

Valerie, however, knew a secret. Last summer, the whole band had gone to the beach on a day off, and Valerie had seen Avchen in the locker room. Her perfectly marvelous and voluptuous body, when naked with all its mystery removed, was actually flawed. A pink rash of teenage acne was beginning to sprout on her precious behind. Take that.

Rather than a Next Tuesday album, Valerie chose one of her old CDs, then went upstairs. She wandered around on the second floor for a while, then decided to take another shower. It was cold in the house, would be warm in the shower. But this second shower of the day was really more of a time killer than a bastion against cold.

As water slipped over her bare skin, slid warmly down her legs, Valerie closed her eyes and savored the feeling. She wanted to make love, but, again, there was no one to make love with.

She finished the marathon shower and sat on her bed. Her body was delicately fragrant, her hair smelled like lavender. She discovered that if she lolled her head back the ends of her newly cut hair could sweep her shoulder blades. It felt nice. And *her* bottom was smooth!

She did not dress again. She sat around in her robe the rest of the day, looked at magazines, picked lint out of the carpet, had the TV on, clicked on a few web sites, had something to eat, and went to bed early.

With the lights off, she huddled into a little ball, waited for the bed to warm up. One last shiver—or a shudder to ward off a sob—as it occurred to her that again Cornelius had not called.

And this had been a *good* day.

A bad day went something like this.

Valerie awoke. Warm air inside the blankets cradled her body. She knew it was cold outside the bed, did not want to get up to endure it. So she didn't. Instead she remained in bed and thought about things.

These are some of the things she passed the day thinking about.

She was twenty-two years old and married almost two years already. She did not have a career, did not go to school. No excuses. She had no girlfriends, she never went out. She had spent more than her share of "fun" and made it a trial even to go into a bar now. She had even made it impossible for herself to have a baby.

She was twenty-two years old and all her choices were already made.

And the bedroom grew lighter as the sun moved

directly into the window, and the bedroom grew darker as the sun set, like one inhale and one exhale of time.

Here are some things Valerie had taken for granted all her life.

A big house, a nice car of her own, new clothes whenever she wanted them. No sweat. Then she saw people living in ways and doing things she simply could not comprehend. She had slowly—very slowly—begun to appreciate a struggle. The "lead people," as Cornelius called them, had one up on her. They got along, and they hadn't grown up expecting unreasonable things from life. Valerie had perhaps been right in taking her world for granted; she had been wrong in doing so without knowing why she did. The house, the car, the clothes were all worth nothing. Except as a firm restraint.

She had taken her Mama's best spare sheets and put them on Cornelius' bed. She had written letters to him every day while her car was in the shop. She had gone to New York with him to make the demo. As Corey's life had bloomed, so had her own, in a new way, so that it was true they had been struggling together. It was romantic, and she had been a captive of that romance.

Now she struggled in a private way and no one would ever go through this with her.

Today Valerie got out of the shower, sprinkled her body with powder. She dressed up, if only to please herself. She even put on a little make-up. She drew on panty hose and a skirt. And she had this red sweater she liked because it went nicely with her skin coloring, as well as made her breasts look more womanly. She looked at herself in the mirror and discovered a kind of glow about her face.

She looked good.

Valerie left the bedroom. At the top of the stairs she had a hallucination. She thought she was standing on the landing in Cornelius' house back on Hamilton Street—looking down that stairwell on the night they had argued. She saw him down there, looking dopily up at her, unreachable. It was two years ago, but somehow when the thought entered her mind, she stuck to that moment, the awful dread, as if glued.

And it hurt. The pain *hurt*. Like it was still there.

She shook herself all over and looked around to be sure no one was there.

She thought of George Miller and the night he may have seen her swimming naked

(he was not seeing you naked—no one at all was around)

up at the lake that night.

Valerie ran downstairs as fast as she could and turned the radio on.

It was time to get out of the house. There was shopping to be done.

The car was covered with snow from the season's first a few days ago. She could not keep this car in the garage because Cornelius' "classic" Rambler was in there. Valerie brushed the snow off the new Mercedes SLK350 and got inside. She sat in the driveway a while, shivering, with the defroster blowing cold air on the windshield.

First, Valerie bought groceries. She drove into Albany to the supermarket Cornelius and she had first gone to together, home of the lead people. As she pushed her cart up and down the aisles, she watched the other people with awe this time. She wondered how they did it, how they sorted things out of what had to be for them— despite never knowing differently beyond vicarious television experience—an indigent life. She made believe she was shopping for a family whose man came home every night at six o'clock. She bought Cornelius' preferred foods. Then she pushed her cart to the check-out and became part of a line of single mothers and grandmothers who appeared worn, broken, angry at the world. Old coats and overshoes.

And here she was all dressed up like she had someplace to go.

Chapter 2

Andrew chose a table in the coffee bar across the street from the recording studio. On the table was an unused napkin with the name Jackie written on it in felt tip marker. Beside the napkin was an empty Styrofoam cup with coffee residue sticking inside, and on the opposite side of the napkin an empty plastic juice bottle lay on its side. It reminded Andrew of a still life painting. He wondered who it might have been that drank that coffee, drained the plastic bottle and tipped it over, wrote "Jackie" on the napkin for what reason.

People die—it's the coldest, hardest fact of life.

Andrew himself had a chicken sandwich and coffee. He was tired. Name a part of his life, he was tired of it. Tired of going into that recording studio each day; tired of people telling him to quit; tired of taking drugs to keep up with himself; tired of the nightmares.

People die—

(suicide)

—it's the coldest, hardest fact of life

The nightmares had been around too long. Waking him up in the middle of what would have been a mere four hours sleep. At first he figured it was the speed doing it, thought he would eventually get used to long waking hours, short sleeping hours. The nightmares weren't bad back then, so he could set himself to wait them out. He did not want to give up his work.

The nightmares did not go away.

And now they prevented him from sleeping at all. It was not even a plural anymore—it was the same dream nightly. Like TiVo run amok. He could count on watching Eileen walk into his room and stab herself with a deli knife. Carve herself up is what she did.

Then she would say: "Save the pieces. You will need them."

Andrew did not go to sleep anymore.

Peculiar was that the last time he had endured the dream, Eileen never showed up. That made it worse. The dream was the same, except he waited, knowing, expecting, and no one appeared. He heard footsteps— footsteps of a staggering person, as they always were. He waited for his sister. The footfalls stumbled closer. Andrew wanted to end the anticipation, to look around the doorway, but he could not get out of bed. Eileen never showed. At any second, she could have come around the doorjamb, knife poised, but she never did.

Andrew hoped to drink enough coffee to make sleep absolutely unnecessary. Instead he felt greasy inside— and exhausted.

If he walked into that studio to play one more commercial jingle, he'd surely go mad.

He wanted to be at the hospital. He really did. But every time he went there, he felt strange:

Shame. That is what it was.

He did not understand it, but certainly shame was his feeling. He'd pushed himself to stay as long as he could stand it—but he had to give it up. Maybe if he could have Eileen to himself while she died, maybe if nurses and doctors and parents and Simons didn't come in and out all the time, maybe if he knew what the hell to say to her, he could go through it.

He was not abandoning her.

He was not.

227

Yet he could not, for shame, go back to the recording studio. And he could not drink another cup of coffee. He could not rise from this table and walk out of this coffee bar and continue with life as before.

People die—it's the coldest, hardest fact of life.

He wished all the people around him would vanish. He wished that when he did leave the coffee bar, he would walk out onto the streets of a ghost town. All across Manhattan, uptown and down, there would be no one. Cars abandoned in the streets. Buildings empty. He could walk from one end of the island to the other, never see another human being. He could go through the Lincoln Tunnel back to Jersey and find no one there as well. Or anywhere.

If he were the only person in the world, he would have to be responsible only to that one. It was a job difficult enough—he could not deal with further responsibility on top of it. It was asking too much.

Eileen is dying.
Janie is dead.
Eileen is dying.
Janie is dead.
Eileen is

The others in the coffee bar heard a loud crash. As they looked up, they saw a ragged haired boy with a mustache and three days growth of beard stand—maybe homeless?—and upturn his table in one motion, snatch the plastic juice bottle up in his hand. Crouching behind the table as if he believed it were a shield on some battlefield, he hurled the bottle like a grenade at the wall. It being plastic, it did not break, but bounced back onto the floor. He leapt the edge of the table and ran out the door.

Andrew did not return to the studio. Probably now he *would* go to jail for disturbing the peace or whatever. He ran to his car, drove to the exit of the parking garage and paid the attendant. Shortly thereafter, his green VW carried him north up the Thruway. He drove very fast, watched the rearview mirror like the fugitive he thought he'd probably be. He felt as if he were running, as if he needed to hide, but not from the coffee-bar police.

Near Poughkeepsie he got off the Thruway, headed east on I-84, toward Hartford. Eileen appeared in his passenger seat, dressed in a hospital shift that tied up the back and slipped off her shoulders, and Andrew knew that his sister had finished dying.

Chapter 3

At Christmas time, taking needed room away from the shopping-mall mobs, were real reindeer, young women dressed as elves at work on balloon animals, and of course Santa himself sitting inside a forty foot tree, with a maze of velvet ropes guiding a line of children to his knee.

Valerie walked into the mall and shocked herself. Perhaps she had been at home too long. She was gripped by fear—a panic inspired by all this heedless activity. She almost fled. Everyone looked at her. What was so peculiar about a girl doing her shopping, she could not guess. There was no way to concentrate on Christmas presents in this profound paranoia.

She put forth the effort as long as she could, then went to get a coffee. She ducked through the crowd in the shop, juggling packages, and once inside she realized it may have been a dumb idea. There were no seats, the wait would be long, and getting out looked more difficult than getting in. Her whole body was taut. She looked toward the mouth of the shop to the mall, could not see it. It was hot. She took off her coat. But then she was forced to hold it with her packages. What a day.

A man with a beard darker than his hair wanted to get by her. She moved some of her packages from his path, inhaled to let him squeeze by.

The man paused and said to her: "You have very pretty eyes."

Valerie blushed, began to look away, then she responded with a harried thank you.

"Merry Christmas," the man said and moved on.

Valerie called after him, "Merry Christmas to you too." The man, however, had vanished. Into the crowd or somewhere, anyhow he was gone.

A seat opened up for Valerie.

The empty, silent house was a refuge. Valerie slammed the door, dropped all her packages, finally breathed. She threw off her coat and boots and collapsed on the sofa. She tore off her panty hose and began to scream. She screamed until she began to sob, until the sobs became heaving gasps.

She lay there in the dark, did not want ever to leave the house again, and whimpered. From the kitchen, Clancy sang.

Her shopping was not finished. She still had absolutely no idea what to give Cornelius.

It was an unmeasured time before she dragged herself into the kitchen. She flipped on the light, poured bird food into the feeder on the bars of Clancy's cage. "Don't you know you're supposed to talk," she said to the bird. "You were guaranteed. Why didn't you ever learn?"

The bird answered with four more bars of the Sixth.

Valerie returned to the living room. She put on a CD without looking at it. Then she lay on the floor amid her discarded clothing, stretched her arms and legs. Her muscles crackled.

Garbled, muted voices from the stereo speakers, difficult to make out:

okay, let's go—one two three
wait a minute
what

Valerie looked at the speaker, puzzled, almost frightened, for a second, and then she realized what album she had inadvertently selected.

anyone seen my scimitar?

Silence.

It was the second album by The Next Tuesday Band. Cornelius' piano began with a syncopated beat; a few measures and the drums picked up; the rest of the band followed; Avchen began to sing.

The band's music had undergone some strange changes for this record. Valerie remembered that Cornelius had said they were going to have an orchestra as back up, but only one song had that backing. The others had been modified when the idea to employ Avchen had been thought of. Two of the songs on the album had Valerie's name in the lyrics. That was spooky. Like being in two places at once. Cornelius still wrote most of the songs the band performed, but Valerie liked his old style better.

She made herself something to eat, sat to watch television. A magazine lay open on her lap. The page was a travel advertisement for Bermuda. It showed a beautiful and shapely woman in a nothing-at-all bikini standing in hip deep water. The water was so clear you could see the toes of her feet on the sandy bottom, and the small dark stone beside them. The little waves dazzled with sunlight and the sky was a sharp, cloudless blue.

Very inviting in the middle of an Albany winter.

Her cell phone rang. Unknown ID. She almost didn't answer. "Hello?"

"Hi, Pinnoke. Can I speak to the bird?"

"Very funny. Where are you?"

"Rochester."

"Are you coming home?" she asked.

"Eventually."

"What does that mean?"

"It is the adverb form of the adjective eventual."

"Corey, I miss you. Why can't you come home for

Christmas?"

"It's not on our tour."

"I am going to spend Christmas with Mama and Papa, but I want you there too. Please come home—I want to have a baby album. Where are you staying?"

"In a hotel."

"What about Avchen?" Valerie inquired.

"You want to talk to her?"

"Is she staying with you guys?"

"She has her own room, Pinnoke. Don't worry, no nookie-nookie."

"I want to go to Bermuda," Valerie said.

Silence for a moment from the other end of the call. "Why do you want to go to Bermuda?"

"It's warm there. I can't stand being cold. So let's go to Bermuda."

More silence. Longer silence.

"Pinnoke—we can't." That quaver she did not notice in his voice was terror.

"Why not? We're rich. Cornelius, I need a change."

"You said you were going to mama and papa's house."

"I want a real change," she moaned. "I want a husband who comes home every night and who'll make love and be there to have a family with, who wears ties or some other fool thing I could give him for Christmas."

"Why don't you go to the lake?" A few months back, the band had purchased a large brownstone house near Ticonderoga, on Lake George. It stood on a hill on a broad overlook of the lake, secluded from all else, used as a practice retreat between tours. "We're not using it right now," Cornelius told her.

"Corey..." she whined.

Longest silence yet.

"Sorry, Pinnoke. There's nothing I can do to change this."

"Why did you call?" she asked, sounding to herself like the biggest baby.

"To say hello," he answered.

"Oh. Well, hello. Why didn't you come home to say it?"

"I have to go now, Pinnoke."

"Good-bye." She hung up without waiting for a reply. "Why don't you go to the lake," she mimicked aloud. "Why don't you go *jump* in the lake." She stared wistfully into her lap at the Bermuda ad. Maybe going to the lake was not such a stupid idea. There would not be any people around. It would be a change of scenery. That was a nice view they had from the front porch. Bermuda, she guessed, was impractical, but Lake George was doable.

Perhaps she *was* being a baby. Cornelius' hands were tied. She knew that. He could not drop everything in the middle of a holiday tour and run home to a wife—even if that wife was bored and lonely. He had said something about starting a new album.

Life goes on and on.

But not here—

She did not want to spend another day here. She stood up resolutely. If she did not like it at Lake George, she was free to come home. The drive, anyway, would be nice. It would kill two and a half hours.

She would leave immediately. No time like the present. Don't they say that?

Don't they say a lot of things.

She ran upstairs to her bedroom and changed her clothes. She packed a suitcase, paying little attention to what went into it. Within half an hour Valerie put the suitcase along with Clancy into the Mercedes, backed out of the drive, headed for the Northway to Lake George. She never saw the house in the suburbs again.

Cornelius lit a cigarette as he lay on his bed in the hotel room. He did not look at the telephone receiver he had just replaced. He reached blindly for matches from the bed table, grasped them, and lit the cigarette. The end of it burned a red point in the darkness.

It had begun.

Now it would finish.

He was powerless. (*the weather report*) He could not be with his wife until Martin left the band. And he had no idea how that would come about, or when, only that it would. Martin would leave the band and, as if he were the cohesive force, they would disband. Then Cornelius could go to Valerie.

Would it be so difficult to go to her now? Would it be so impossible?

(*but the weather report*)

The snowball was rolling.

By the time it got to the bottom of the hill, it would be as big, as heavy, as the weight on Atlas' shoulders.

Clancy had a strange reaction to the Lake George house. As Valerie shifted down to second gear to climb the steep hill, the bird began to flutter anxiously about its cage. It ran its beak along the bars like a prisoner. The house in sight, huge and almost regal, on the top of the hill, the bird squawked and squealed, hit the side of the cage so hard it toppled off the seat and rolled into the hollow beneath the dashboard.

"Clancy, what a commotion," Valerie said, trying to ignore the foreboding it suggested.

The tires plowed through snow and the engine revved. She watched the edge of the road nervously. Drifts had buried the guardrail and a nice take off ramp of ice had built up. She stopped safely in the unshoveled driveway.

As she carried the birdcage through the snow to the front porch, she began to feel that same twinge of bad feeling Clancy must have felt. The flat brownstone face and squared roof looked offensively smug. The window shades were drawn for the winter, the rooms black behind them. On the concrete floor of the porch, Valerie stamped the snow from her boots and looked at the frozen postcard view.

Unbelievable silence.

In summer, sailboats from a yacht club not far up the lake swarmed over the blue water. The mountains across were two-toned green, and vacation sounds rose from the public park and beach way down there. Today, in winter, it looked as if paint drop cloths had been thrown on everything. In fact, the porch furniture actually was covered by tarpaulins and tied down.

Valerie opened the blue wood-frame screen door and reached the key toward the lock. Before she inserted it, the door fell open, unlocked.

She stuck her head inside, peered around the front room.

"Well, they just left it open—all winter, but that's like Cornelius." She could see her breath in the air. "It's almost colder in here than outside, huh, Clancy?"

The bird moved about nervously. Valerie set the cage on the table in the front room. "I'll start a fire," she said.

She went to the shed between the house and garage where she found a fresh cut pile of wood, some of the logs not yet dry. She examined it uneasily, found two dry logs, and when she reached for them the entire cord collapsed. Logs rolled and clattered woodenly every which way. Valerie snatched her selected firewood and ran back into the house.

Shortly thereafter, the fireplace in the front room blazed. Valerie removed her coat and sweater, her boots and the soaked socks underneath. She had yet to bring in her suitcase, but she was not certain she would stay. For now she was tired. She curled on the floor before the fire and slept.

George Miller was back. She had not included him in a dream in a very long time, but he rang the doorbell and said:

"Did you miss me?"

Valerie told him he was not welcome anymore.

"I may not be welcome, but you'll thank me anyway," he said. They walked along a beach, both of them barefoot, as the sun set. George put his arm around Valerie. She knew they were going to have sex. She did not want that-—she wanted to make love. But she was not sure there was a difference. She wanted to make love so badly that it hurt. Cornelius did not exist yet. She was only sixteen years old. George was still her best friend, and they were going to have sex.

"You are very lonely, huh?" George said.

"Cornelius won't come home."

"Not to worry about him. I am back."

Valerie waded into the turquoise water. She heard music, and the music seemed to want to tell her something, but she did not understand it. She did not have any pants on. She wore a T-shirt, but nothing else. George waded in after her. His eyes appeared empty. He dug his fingers into her thin pubic hair.

"George, I really did get pregnant. I just didn't tell anyone because I was afraid. Now I'll never be able to have a baby at all," she confessed.

A star shined in the sky. It was really the planet Venus—but Valerie wished on it as the first star of the night.

George looked really strange. He was changing. Valerie could not tell into what, but he was chilling to look at.

He was not her best friend anymore.

She was not sixteen anymore.

She had married Cornelius.

Her choices were made.

"You decide what happens next," George Miller said. "All you have to do is spin the wheel."

"I am so lonely, Corey."

Now she knew what was happening to George Miller. His skin was melting like a crayon in the sun, his eyeballs were boiling, his muscles slipping off— He was turning into a living skeleton. His face grinned as a skull does, and the bones fishing around in her crotch hurt like razors.

Valerie told him he wasn't welcome anymore.

He told her she would be seeing him around, and then he was gone.

Valerie, alone on the beach, looked at the planet Venus and believed quite certainly that wishes did not come true.

Music up and over, and fade.

The fireplace was dark but for a few embers. It was the middle of the night. Valerie was a ball of stiff muscle on the floor. She stood. Wind must have pushed the front door open. She closed it, turned on some lights.

She turned on the radio too. There were not too many stations up here. Sometimes, if the weather was right, WPTR from Albany reached this far. At rare times the signal was even strong. They didn't have cable or satellite TV, either, because the band didn't think there was any point, given the house's intended use, so television signals were unpredictable too. Tonight music reached her radio, but with much static. The disc jockey cheerfully announced that a huge snowfall was on its way from Buffalo. Then he put on Bing Crosby singing "White Christmas." Valerie wondered if she should get back in the car and go home. A blizzard would snow her in, make her a prisoner no better than the one she was at home.

If Buffalo was snowed in, maybe Cornelius would not go there, but would come home instead.

She opened the door to the band's rehearsal studio. This room was the reason for buying this particular house. It was two stories high, a balcony at one end, a huge window at the other. There was a second, unused, fireplace in here. It was a better fireplace than the one used in the front room. Valerie thought that the whole room was wasted. The band had it cluttered with microphones and mix equipment, amplifiers and musical instruments. And they had rigged videotape cameras at various angles about the room: straight on, from above on the balcony, from behind. There was a screen for each camera so Avchen could monitor her dance undulations from all sides.

Valerie climbed the spiral staircase to the balcony. She

looked down on the studio, everything set up as though the band would arrive any minute. The feeling inside her was definitely jealously, but she was not sure where it was projected.

A door from the balcony let into the second floor of the rest of the house. Valerie headed for her bedroom. On the way, she passed Avchen's bedroom. This was something Valerie hated: that Avchen had to sleep here too whenever the band used the studio. Each of them had a room. The guys shared because there were only five bedrooms, Cornelius shared with his wife, but Avchen had her own, private room.

Valerie opened Avchen's door.

What if Avchen were in there, sleeping, or in the middle of dressing, brushing her hair, or whatever secret things eighteen year old vamps do in their rooms? What if Valerie walked in and violated that?

She flicked on the light.

But the room was empty, the shade drawn.

Valerie expected a big, soft bed, fancy curtains, brightly painted walls. But the only furniture was a bed barely more than a cot, and a wardrobe cabinet. No curtains on the window, a bare wood floor, the walls painted dark lavender, the color there when the house had been purchased. Avchen had no knick-knacks or trinkets, stuffed animals or decorations of any kind.

Valerie put her hands on her hips. What was Avchen trying to prove? She opened the wardrobe cabinet. Its shelves and drawers were filled with Avchen's clothes. She owned a lot of fancy clothes. Valerie browsed through the dresses hanging, rippled through all the sweaters and pants on the shelves like someone shopping.

She took off her own clothes and laid them on the bed. She put on a gauze peasant blouse, put on Avchen's tight leather pants, not tight on her because Avchen was not as small as she. Then Valerie looked at herself in the mirrors on the back of the wardrobe doors.

Avchen's mirrors were tinted black. They reflected

almost as well as normal mirrors, but inside, the reflection was perpetual night.

Valerie opened a drawer. On top of all Avchen's underwear was a chunk of glass about the size of Valerie's fist. She lifted it out. It was a prism. The room light refracted through it and filled Valerie's palms with little rainbows. Looking through it transformed the room into a kaleidoscope. Patterns from drab and plain colors were laced and outlined with the cheery colors of the spectrum. Valerie liked that. She took the prism with her, maneuvered her way down the hall with refracted vision as she held the prism before her eyes.

She crashed into the side of her bedroom door—hard. The prism jarred from her hand, bounced on her bare foot, and one of the corners cut her toes. She felt her back give way a little. She prepared to topple, but she did not go down. Painfully she bent to pick up the prism. Her foot was covered with blood, and the blood dripped around her instep and arch onto the bedroom carpet. Valerie stared at the sight through the prism. The red blood, the brown skin, the beige carpet shattered into a rainbow. Red-Orange–Yellow-Green-Blue-Indigo-Violet; a.k.a. ROY G BIV. She turned the prism to move the kaleidoscope. Her blood stained the carpet around her foot, left an outline when she stepped away. It looked very pretty through the effects of the prism.

Chapter 4

While Valerie and Clancy were on their way to Lake George, Andrew Healy found himself heading north via Route 7 through Massachusetts to St. Albans in northern Vermont.

He got a room in a motel, not knowing how long he would remain. He stood in the motel room bathroom and ran his hand over his chin. His beard was growing fast, untrained. He looked ragged—dark circles below his bloodshot eyes, his face thin—no eye drops and no speed. He felt as if he was going to explode, or collapse inward. Even after a shower he felt disintegrated, lost, a wisp of himself.

Or was *this* the self squelched underneath the pills, the condition he had been in for a long time, yet unable to feel? The condition Eileen and Avchen told him he was in.

He got a job running a cash register at a self-serve gas station. He filled out his application as Walter Healy. The job was good because he was protected inside a glass booth. Most people used the pay-at-the-pump option. The rest told him through a microphone how much gasoline they needed; their money was placed in a metal tray Andrew extended to them and then retracted into his booth. He was untouched by human hands. He worked the late shift, lived off candy bars, which the station also vended, and he was unbothered.

One night when he returned to his room, he found a letter placed on his bed by the maid service. It was addressed to him by his real name. There was no return address on it. He opened it, discovered it to be from Avchen. He had no idea how she had tracked him to Vermont, but somehow she had found him, just as she'd found his car in a parking garage to put a note on the windshield. This letter said:

I know that you are probably wondering why I'm writing. I do not seem to be free of you. It seems that whatever I do, wherever I go, no matter how much I try, you own everything that I am.

—Avchen

Andrew crumpled the letter and tossed it into a wastebasket. He realized he had left his room door open, and it was cold, so he shut it.

These days Andrew usually slept until afternoon. But this morning he awoke just before dawn. He could hear church bells. Suddenly he sat up in bed, leapt to the window and threw up the shade.

It was Christmas Day.

The parking lot below was deserted. Snow had fallen all night, still fell, and the cars down there were just smooth white lumps in the blue sunrise light. In houses all over New England, little kids were dragging their parents out of bed to see what Santa had brought. Families were on their way to early Mass. Scrooge was realizing that the spirits had done all their work in one short night.

There came a knock on the door.

"Who is it?" Andrew said.

"Open the door and find out."

Andrew unbolted the door and opened it. He found Cornelius. "Hey!" He threw his arms around him. "Merry Christmas."

"Don't get dressed for me," Cornelius said.

Andrew was wearing his underwear. "I just woke up. I forgot it was even Christmas. What are you doing here? How did you find me?"

"I found you."

Andrew put on his jeans and T-shirt. "The band in town?"

"I'm here on my own. I've a mission for you."

"A what?"

"Valerie is in trouble," Cornelius said.

"Pinnoke? What's the matter?"

"She is alone at the lake. You must go there. She needs you."

"Why don't you go?" Andrew disliked the word *need*.

"I can't go. It is not time."

"Corey, she is your wife."

"Andrew, do you ever watch the weather report?"

"Huh? I guess, like most people, if I see the news, I—"

"Every night they predict the weather—but they can never control it."

"What's Valerie's problem?"

"She needs."

"Corey, my sister died."

"She no longer needs you."

"How'm I gonna get there? I'm sure they towed my car from where I left it, which is far from here."

"You'll take a bus," Cornelius said. "You must leave today."

Andrew sighed heavily. "Okay. I'll go. But what can I do?"

Chapter 5

Valerie pushed the blankets down to her ankles, sat up in bed. She looked at the windows. The glass had frozen over and Jack Frost was nipping at her nose. Someone had come during the night with frozen hands to finger paint on the pane. The designs suggested a crowd. A large, moving crowd, like in a shopping mall, or at Disney Land—or better yet, the World's Fair in Paris, 1889. She could see the Eiffel Tower. And the ladies in their long skirts, twirling parasols, wearing their hats with chiffon scarves tied under their chins. And gentlemen in waistcoats and top hats, tipping their walking sticks to the brims of their hats and bowing. Everybody strolling around, chattering, laughing formally, each individual veering and weaving his and her own way and somehow all of this movement blended into a harmonized perpetual motion.

Behind the glass, in the twenty-first century, snow drifts had piled above the height of these second story windows.

Yet there was plenty of light in the bedroom. A strange light, watery like sunlight shining into an aquarium—from nowhere and from everywhere. Valerie unknotted her feet from the covers, got out of bed. She wrapped herself in an oversized terry-cloth robe (which, as far as she could remember, she did not own).

On the way downstairs, the oak treads were smooth and frigid on the soles of her bare feet. At the bottom of the staircase she dug her toes into the carpet and rubbed her feet warm. Music played from somewhere—the band's studio. They played "White Christmas," but Bing Crosby was doing the vocals rather than Avchen. That was good. Valerie always liked Bing. He was a favorite of hers, and of her Papa. Avchen was not.

Each of the windows downstairs was frozen too, snow of course piled against them too. Valerie checked all the doors in the house and found not a one would open. All were iced over.

The house was entirely buried—up to its roof in snow.

She hurried up to the third floor attic room, opened the door and ran onto the roof. She stood at the parapet, stared out at the lake.

It was not there.

The houses were not there, the trees were not there—only the summits of mountains were there, surfacing out of the snow like the backs of white hippos. During the night, the blizzard had covered the world. The snow leveled at the parapet, a soft, fine powder, smooth and flat as a plain, stretching far and away in every direction, broken only by the humps of the mountains. The clouds which had dumped all this snow had gone. The sky was an open, pure blue, filled with the sun. Light dazzled off the white, turned the picture her brain received from her eyes to an overexposed glare.

Only skiers could be happy with this much snow. Valerie hated to shovel.

She leaned her hands on the parapet. It was not too cold to touch. She put one knee up, then the other, finally stood on the wall. She stepped onto the snow. Her body was so small and light that she could walk on it with no footprints. It did not feel cold, even to bare feet. It was like walking on talc.

She walked a long distance out, to the spot beneath which was buried, and frozen solid, the lake—and all the fish in it, all the lakeweed, the stones on the bottom, sand on the beaches around the water, trees bordering the beaches, cars, houses...and people. Valerie was the only one above the snow. She wondered what life was like for all those creatures of Pompeii down there.

Valerie came upon a garden of crocuses peeking out of the snow. They were wilting, surrounded by weeds. She dropped to her knees to pick out the weeds. As she worked, she lifted her chin and looked back across the snow the way she had come. The glare of the sun swallowed everything. Through her snow blindness, all she could see was unbroken white.

She stood, green weeds clasped in her fingers, black soil on her knees. She stood all alone and freezing, shivering in this too thin robe.

"No busses going out today."

"None at all?" Andrew said.

The ticket vendor vaguely indicated the window. "Even a bus couldn't get through this."

"Will there be a bus later?"

"Where are you going?"

Andrew checked the piece of paper in his hand. "Hague, New York."

"Doubt it. It's Christmas. I'm sure they're not making the route across the lake a priority. Everyone is already wherever they want to be."

"Well, I'm not." Andrew was half sorry he had let Cornelius down, but half relieved to be free of the responsibility. It was out of his hands. He crumpled the paper in his fist and headed for the door of the empty station. He buttoned his coat and forced himself against the wind like a paratrooper as he stepped outside. The snow blew so hard he could not see ten feet. Cornelius could hardly blame him for not going to Valerie. Now he was going back to the motel to tell Cornelius he had done his best and go back to bed.

A horse hauling a sleigh almost ran him over in the street.

"Merry Christmas!" shouted the people in the sleigh.

Andrew watched the sleigh as the blizzard swallowed it up.

Andrew began walking again. He walked a long way, and his feet were freezing off, when he realized that he was lost. That sleigh must have turned him around in the blizzard, and he had wandered unawares. He stopped in the middle of the street. The snow was mixed with hail, and the wind blew it against his face.

Andrew's beard and hair were frozen. Maybe his eyelashes too—even his eyes were cold. He realized he had been walking north when he wanted to be going south. Now too far from the bus station to take cover, he began to look around for another shelter until this storm abated. For a moment he ducked into a bus stop shelter to get out of the stinging hail.

Where was he going to go on Christmas Day to get inside and warm, in a small town where nothing stayed open?

He sat on the bench in the shelter, shivered, tugged at the ice in his beard, listened to the hailstones on the roof.

There was a simply printed poster, made on someone's computer, tacked to the bus shelter wall:

HAVE AN OLD FASHIONED YULETIDE!
Trees!!!!!
Wreaths!!!!
Sleigh Rentals!!!!
VETERANS OF FOREIGN WARS: Post 18

Don't get any ideas. Especially not ones that are fool-hardy.

A sleigh could make it over the mountains.

Yeah, right. A sleigh could, but even if a horse from this one-horse town could get through this weather, the driver never would.

Now he really *had* thought of everything.

He looked out the front of the shelter, saw that the wind seemed to be dying. He could actually see down the street, decided to set out again.

That is when he heard a sound in the street like thunder.

It was a state snowplow, emerging out of the shadow of the blowing snow, coming toward him like a huge forest-green carving knife. To see what would happen, Andrew put his hand up as if hailing a cab in Manhattan and, what do you know, the mammoth truck stopped. He stepped up and pulled open the passenger-side door. Inside the cab it smelled like coffee. The coffee smelled really good. "What the heck are you doing walking around in a storm?" said the driver, who was not wearing his coat but had leather gloves and a ski hat on.

"How far are you plowing toward the bridge," Andrew said. "My sister is across the lake, and she's sick. I can't get a bus."

"I don't plow all the way across the bridge," said the driver, who Andrew would soon learn was named Mac Macgillicuddy (yes, really). "Someone else does that."

"Can you let me ride with you to the bridge?" Andrew was improvising. He had no idea what he'd do when he got to the bridge. It was a long bridge. "I wouldn't ask except that she's alone and not well."

The driver gripped the broad steering wheel and leaned back in his seat. The big idling engine was loud and the smell of diesel filled the air, overcoming the coffee. "It's a good thing I'm a contractor," the driver decided. "I'm not supposed to take on riders. Let's just say I'm rescuing you."

"Let's say that," said Andrew and he climbed up and into the cab, where he could smell coffee again when he pulled the door shut.

Valerie awoke and went to the window. It was still

snowing, but the world was not buried. She may have dreamed that part, or all of the snow may have melted since yesterday. There was no way to be certain.

She dressed quickly because of the cold, went downstairs to light the fire. Once that was burning, she shivered into the kitchen to put coffee water on to boil. Then she went to the band's studio to see if Bing was still singing.

She looked around and above at all the metal. The equipment gleamed in the artificial light—jeered at her from all around her. She remained stubbornly in the center of it all.

All of this was a mystery to her. That part of Cornelius' life inside the wall of staves surrounding him. She looked at the dials and buttons, the many computer keyboards and screens around the room. His piano she had played with before—back when Clancy revealed himself a singer—she turned the piano on now. The red light on its panel glowed ferociously at her. She touched a key, but it was silent. The amp would have to be on, and the amp was now plugged into a main system with all the other amps in the room. Valerie's fingers explored control panels. The result of touching one switch was an attack on her ears with an explosion of feedback. She snapped it off immediately.

She pushed a button, and she appeared on the four videotape monitors, four different angles.

Valerie looked at herself reduced to one foot high and placed inside a row of small boxes. If the songs with her name in them made her feel odd, this was worse yet. She waved at the camera. The four Valeries waved. She giggled. The four Valeries giggled.

She stumbled, surprised at her embarrassment—and wondered why the embarrassment—over to Avchen's microphone stand, stood before it. Her knees were weak and her heart thudded—just like real stage fright. She watched herself take the mic in hand. "Welcome to the Valerie Prince show," she said.

"I mean," she corrected, "welcome to the Valerie *Mastropietro* show... This is my first time on TV, and I'm scared to death. I would sing and dance and play all these wonderful instruments for you, but I don't know how to do any of that stuff..."

She turned in disgust to the amplifiers. "Can't you guys give me any more volume?" She walked to the control panel and played with the dials.

One by one the amps switched from stand-by to on, and her voice boomed all around her.

LADIES AND GENTLEMEN, THE VERY UNTALENTED VALERIE MASTROPIETRO

"...thank you, thank you...I have a great show for you tonight. I have absolutely no guests, and I'm going to stand in front of these cameras by myself and carry the whole shebang. See, my band's cashed out on me." She gestured at the unmanned instruments. "Over there, not on lead guitar is Martin O'Kelly; back there on percussion would be Daniel Serahuli; and my very talented saxophone player is Alvin Haynes; I would have Gene Bienvenue on bass; and playing a really incredible piano should be my loving and devoted husband, Cornelius— who got his start from *my* Papa. And Avchen Neumann won't be here to shake and wiggle in front of you, so I'll just have to do with what I've got."

Valerie wiped her sweating palms on her jeans and assumed a pose which she believed imitated Avchen. "How's this? Does this *work*?" she demanded angrily.

"My first song will be one inspired by myself, I am told, which Avchen now does with none of the feeling I once heard it done with. It can be found on their first album, but its original version is on Corey's first album back when he was just a nobody who nobody would spit twice at—No one even remembers that one now and it was better than any album he's put out with this band of jokers."

She began to half sing into the mic. Her whispering lilt engulfed her and she stopped dead, looked around at her voice. It was frightening.

"That's not quite right anyway," she said, intimidated. "I should be more like Avchen—heaving my pelvis into your faces, right?"

She watched herself on the screens as she did a slithering dance, Avchen Neumann style. "Yeah! Right, like that! That's what you wanna see! Jump up and down and shake your body. Dance! Dance! Dance!"

She exploded with a wild whoop. "The butt has to stick out more! Shoulders have to slink. Pucker your lips, shake that booty! Down with the neckline and let's see some of that meat!" She ripped her blouse open in the culmination of a frenetic leap across the floor.

"Yoooor all that I have everrr ne-eeded," Valerie sang in Avchen's way. "—Stupid lyrics, but I'm Avchen Neumann and I just cover them with my fabled sex appeal."

She improvised to the same melody. Her dance became a wild-eyed striptease. She wiggled her blue jeans down her thighs. "Now I'll dance for you with my thumb on my crotch so I can make a million dollars WITHOUT ANY TALENT!"

It was no longer a song. On the screens, the four Valeries screamed, shrieked, cried, tore at their clothes. She pranced totally naked, dripping sweat, over wires and between musical instruments that blared with a heavy beat. She tripped against the corner of the baby grand and threw her microphone to the floor. Its crash resounded from every speaker. Valerie bent for the mic. Her back gave out and she crumpled to the floor, panting, exhausted. The amplifiers reared up around her. The music grew louder as the lights and dials and blank computer screens leered at her. The instruments had come to life, had taken over the show—She was not the star, but a prop. They picked up her limp body and ran their cold metal lasciviously all over her bare flesh. The wires snaked around her limbs. She was tossed into the air.

Yay, Mickey

Her stomach broke with nausea. She choked back a spasm of vomit as she fell toward the floor.

Yeeaay, Mickey

The music turned to uproarious laughter and applause. They were having a high old time.

Yay, Mickey Mouse Club!

She hit the floor hard. The video pictures flickered as a cord got pulled out of the wall, left the screens snowy blue squares. Valerie rolled on her side and was sick all over the floor.

Everything was quiet again and the Valerie Mastropietro show was over.

Chapter 6

A ndrew had thought the wind during the day was bad. Now it was night, and the wind was meaner still. He himself could not see a thing. He was covered with ice. The first plow driver, on the Vermont side, had given him a blanket when they got to the bridge. That had been soaked through long ago. Its outside was slick and hard, its inside cold, and the thing gave no protection. Andrew could not feel his toes, cursed himself for not owning gloves. Yet he pushed forward, determined.

What had happened was that Andrew had been carried this far on a string of luck and the kindness of plow drivers that impressed even him. The first driver, who didn't talk much because he was so focused on keeping the truck on the winding mountain route—on seeing the winding mountain route—took him across the first bridge to the island, and went a little further than he was supposed to go, to drop Andrew at the second bridge.

The bridge to the New York side was unplowed, and that's when the driver gave Andrew the blanket, his Thermos of coffee, and wished him luck. Andrew felt uneasy as he watched the lights of the plow disappear back toward St. Albans, and then he started walking like one of Washington's men at Valley Forge across the bridge.

Now he was walking south on Route 9N. Some ways back he came to a road sign that he read through frozen eyes: "Hague 1." The coffee was gone but he was almost there.

He had the New York state plow to thank for getting him this far. He found out, when it approached him halfway across the bridge, that there is a brotherhood of plow drivers, and his first driver had radioed to the second that he'd just dropped off some desperate kid who needed to reach his sister. The New York driver picked Andrew up and took him, as the truck plowed a single lane across the bridge, as far as he could go. Which was far enough to keep Andrew from dying of hypothermia.

No one else had been on the roads since they left. Fact was, there were no roads, only smooth stretches of snow between trees that filled up with snow almost as fast as the plows could clear them. Having come this far, as he trudged through drifts looking for the houselights in the distance that would signal the village of Hague, he started thinking he was hearing voices telling him he ought to have listened to the guy at the bus station and gone back to the motel.

Especially when he realized he had just stepped into a huge drift and was sinking as if into quicksand.

Andrew hauled himself forward to free his legs. He sweated inside his clothes and was sure the sweat would freeze the cloth to his skin. He crawled forward on his belly along the top of the snow.

A cloud of breath snorted from his nostrils, and Andrew swore he saw it crystallize in the air. He ducked away as the wind threw the crystal chips toward his face.

He was free of the drift, and now too frozen to feel pain. In fact, he was beginning to warm up, to feel quite comfortable. That, he had once read, was a sure sign of hypothermia. He trudged onward toward where he knew the village must be.

The wind ran around outside like the thousands of footsteps of a rampaging army.

(let me in, you bitch!)

It swept angrily across the backyard. Valerie looked up from her magazine in fear, then looked back to the page, pretending that she did not hear the battering.

But what if the wind found a weak spot in the house?

(i'll huff and i'll puff...)

The solid brownstones did seem to quiver, the storms rattled in their frames, the front door pushed on its latch. A powerful gust broke onto the porch, ran back and forth pounding the walls, tearing the tarps off the porch furniture, scattering chairs and tables in a tantrum.

George Miller's face looked in the window.

Valerie felt her heart fold in half. It was true: he had returned for her.

Quickly she turned on the television, and the radio—loud—to compete with the noise of the wind. The howl drank from the television and added to its fury. The front door banged hard on its latch as if something were trying to get in, and the howling tore into a frenzy, beat on the walls and glass, now stomping murderously on the porch floor.

Valerie turned up the television, even though the audio was mainly static.

The wind grew.

She saw George Miller out there again, realized it was only a tarp tumbling past the window and reflecting the porch light. Her legs dissolved and she sank back into her chair.

The sounds from the television and radio were not human. They blared together and became as frightening as the wind. And now it was all around her—she had let it in.

She felt it on her skin as she helplessly gaped at Clark Gable doing some old black and white movie in dumb show on the one TV station she could get.

The gusts subsided to nothing.

Valerie lowered the volume of the TV and radio. Her heart pounded and she let her hands fall on her weakened stomach.

It had only been wind.

She picked up her magazine, but the words were scrambled and she just couldn't read it. She looked at the television even though the picture had gone snowy, and she kept the radio on too for comfort, though its signal faded in and out.

A fearsome, wailing scream outside. Everything in the house—television, radio, lights—blacked out. The porch light bulb exploded, the front door banged open. And Valerie screamed worse than the wind.

In the darkness she tripped and stumbled to the door, fought it closed, dropped the bar across the doorway. Then she felt around the living room for the hurricane lamp and some matches, found them and lit the wick. She turned the light as high as it would burn, oily smoke pouring out of the top, and she went back to the front door to examine the barricade, prayed it would hold.

"Let me in! It's not a fit night out for man nor beast!"

That was a real voice, and familiar too. Weak, speaking through uncontrolled shivers, but familiar.

"Who's there?" she sobbed, holding the hurricane lamp outstretched to see better.

"Valerie, it's Andrew Healy!"

She lifted the bar, opened the door. He was encased in ice, his nose running and freezing across his lips, freeze-dried blood on his fingers.

"Oh my God!" Valerie backed away. In the light of the hurricane lamp, he was an evil sight.

He came in. "What's the matter?" he said. "Valerie, it's Andrew, remember? Cornelius sent me. He said you were in trouble."

In the pale light, she appeared to be under a spell.

"Are you sick?" Andrew asked.

"What do you want?" she gasped.

He reached his hand out, palm up, as if to a timid puppy.

Valerie shrank away, holding the hurricane lamp between them.

"Oh, Christ," Andrew said. "I nearly killed myself getting here, and you're playing games. I don't need this." Or, Cornelius was right, and she was in bigger trouble than anyone thought.

"Andrew?" She raised the lamp closer to his face.

"Yes."

"Eileen?" She took a cautious step forward.

"Jesus. Valerie—"

The ice on Andrew had begun to melt. The carpet beneath his feet soaked up a puddle. He could almost feel the pain in his fingers. There was no point in talking to this girl now; she was sleepwalking. He closed the door again and dropped the bar into position. He dropped his coat on the wet carpet, walked away from it. As soon as the blood flowed in his hands again, those cuts were going to remind him he was alive.

He walked passed Valerie to the kitchen. He got a jug of bottled water from the pantry, filled the tea kettle and put it on the gas burner. While he waited for the water to boil, he went upstairs and rummaged in bedroom drawers until he found handkerchiefs to wrap his hands in. Valerie followed him step for step, carrying the light, like something out of a horror tale.

Chapter 7

"How did you lose your lights?"

The hurricane lamp sat on the kitchen table between them. He could see her face and her hands, all else was blackness.

Andrew sat huddled inside a dry blanket. Beneath the blanket he was naked. When he had removed his clothes, they had ripped away from his skin, leaving swathes of cloth sticking. He had been bleeding in more places than just his hands, but he did not remember getting any of those wounds.

"The storm," she answered.

"I can't believe they let the gasoline for the generator run out. What's the point of a generator?" he said. "But the lights in the village are on. It can't be a power failure. Tomorrow I'11 check the fuses."

"Corey told you to come? Where is *he*? I don't believe you came. I don't believe you made it, either."

"Neither do I. He stayed in Vermont. He said you are in trouble."

"Oh—I'm in trouble all right. But I don't know what you can do. I think I'm cracking up."

"You are not cracking up."

"I don't even know what I'm doing. I recognized you when you got here—but I didn't, you know? I can't even tell anymore if I really did something or if it was just my imagination. I don't know what day it is."

"By now it's the day after Christmas."

"Christmas Day?" she said forlornly. "Oh dear, I never even got Corey a present."

"Look: it is easy to lose track of things when you're snowed in all alone. You aren't going crazy. Probably all you need is someone to talk to."

"I have nightmares."

I have nightmares.

Perhaps it was the way she said it. "What kind of nightmares?" he asked, knowing full well that they could not really be his nightmares.

"About myself. All kinds of things. They never wake me up—maybe if they did it wouldn't be as bad—I could escape—but I have to live through these."

Andrew held his coffee in his handkerchief wrapped hands. It wasn't hot enough. "You're probably just bored. What made you come up here in the middle of the winter? You can't even get a cell phone signal here."

"Corey. The magazine. I have no idea."

"You look tired. Why don't you get some sleep."

"Maybe I will." She stood up into the darkness. "Are your hands okay?"

"They haven't completely thawed yet."

"I need the light to see."

"Take it. I can find my way."

Valerie took the lamp and went out of the room. The light quickly faded from the doorway, leaving Andrew in blackness.

After a while, he stood up and felt his way through the dark hallway to the front room. He poked the fire into a small blaze again, then headed for the stairs. He found Valerie already asleep, blankets pulled up to her ear, the lamp still burning. He picked it up. Valerie was a wash of black hair on a blue blanket. Andrew sat beside the hair and rubbed it.

And here he was: Hague, New York—snowed in until spring, without electricity, with only two fireplaces for heat, with the crazy wife of his best friend.

Valerie moaned and turned over. She grabbed his hand and held fast. Andrew was full of resentment.

She was Cornelius' wife, and she needed her husband. There was no doubt that she was cracking up. That vacant look that had greeted him was the telltale. He prayed she would not start screaming and throwing things.

Andrew took the hurricane lamp out of her bedroom and went downstairs with it. He opened the studio door and led himself in with the light. The room was in disarray. Nothing worked without power, but every switch was in the on position. He put them all off, righted a music stand.

A dark and ransacked recording studio was like a dare—could he really resist and stay away from one of these things? He climbed the percussion riser, pantomimed a drum roll. He had put the musician in himself out. It was down in New York City, walking the streets. Andrew did not know where he would go next, but he would not go back to Jersey.

Maybe he would write a book. He had gone through enough, swallowed enough alcohol and enough speed to tell a story.

Everybody thinks that. Nobody gives a hoot about your "story."

He'd had his fill of whacked-out people. This house was the last place he wanted to be.

Martin O'Kelly did not show up for the first recording session of the band's new album. Later they learned he had been picked up at a party in Poughkeepsie for possession of a controlled substance. He could not make bail and was stuck in a cell.

"I think we ought to leave him there," Raj Hernandez said.

"It is tempting. Except he wrote half the songs we're going to record," Edgar Pufknack pointed out. "I'm going to have to drive up and get him."

Cornelius crushed a cigarette with his shoe. "You won't find him," he said.

"Huh?"

"I said you won't find him." He began to put on his coat.

"Why won't I find him? Where are you going?"

"He will not be there." He headed for the door.

"Hey," Raj said, "where are you going?"

"To get a replacement." And he left.

"Cornelius! He's not dead yet!" Edgar Pufknack went out.

Avchen stood dumbly in the middle of everyone's deciding to break up for coffee. Left alone, she sat in a folding chair and lit a cigarette. Not a thing had been going right for this band since last summer. There was a lot of arguing over who was going to write songs. It was ridiculous. Tension had remained even after it was decided that Martin and Raj would each write. Cornelius never said a word about where his compositions would come in. He was right, though, whatever his reasons, it wasn't worth it. She had had the way paved for herself solo, what made her join this band of village idiots?

The studio was empty and silent. Sitting here as if waiting was bordering on the absurd. She wished she owned a dog so she could go home and kick it.

By morning the storm abated. After two hours of sleep and an unbroken chain of dreams, Andrew awoke, terrified to find himself in a music studio. Then he remembered what he was doing here, where here was. He tugged the handkerchiefs off his fingers. They stuck, pulled, tore free like Velcro.

He found Valerie sitting on the floor in the middle of the living room, playing with the bird as quietly and as intently as a child fascinated with building blocks. The bird walked up and down her arm, perched on her fingers. She held it out, looked at it, turned her hand so she could see it from many angles. Andrew said nothing to her, went upstairs to dress.

His clothes were finally thawed and dry, but they were also torn. He borrowed some clothing from Martin O'Kelly. O'Kelly was only a little taller than Andrew.

He returned downstairs. Valerie was still engrossed in the cockatiel, so much so that she did not even appear to realize Andrew was awake. Andrew went through the shed into the garage and opened the overhead door. A smooth, wind sculpted wall of snow, four feet high, blocked the garage. Valerie's Mercedes was quite snowed in.

He met Valerie in the kitchen as he walked back into the house.

"I've surveyed the damage," he said. "We're stuck."

"It looks pretty," she smiled.

Andrew considered his hands and skin along with the snow. "I guess."

"Oh dear," she said, "let me put a dressing on your hands."

"Are you supposed to cover frostbite?" Andrew said.

"I don't know. But you're bleeding."

"Not anymore."

Valerie sat at the table. Andrew cooked up some eggs and put them in front of her. He made coffee too, poured her a cup. He poured himself a cup also. The boiled bottled water made it taste awful but he drank it. It was nice and hot.

"I am so glad it's light out, so we don't have to worry. I wish we hadn't missed Christmas though." She sighed.

"We could have a belated Christmas,"

Andrew found an axe in the shed beside the woodpile. The two of them bundled up in heavy clothing, Andrew in Cornelius' too large boots and gloves, and they trekked

together up the hill into the woods. It was hard going, but
the snow, by day and without wind, was not the leviathan
it had been the night before. Covering the trees, bushes,
and shining with sunlight it was in fact, as Valerie said,
pretty.

As they walked, she lagged behind.

"C'mon, Blue!" Andrew said with the axe on his
shoulder like Paul Bunyan.

"My legs are little. Wait for me," she called.

"See what success does to a girl? Makes her soft."

Valerie scooped up a handful of snow and threw it at
him. "One thing I am not is soft!" Andrew set down his
axe and made a snowball, tossed it underhand at her. She
ducked out of the way, lost her footing and fell over.
Andrew went back to get her. She reached her hand up to
him, laying flat on her back in the snow, but she pulled
him down instead of herself up.

"Here," she laughed, "have some snow." She pushed a
handful into his mouth.

He placed a heap of snow on her head, rubbed it into
her hair like shampoo. Valerie laughed heartily. She
wrestled Andrew over and pressed him down into a mold
of himself in the snow.

Then she kissed him.

Surrounded by snow and pinned by Valerie's weight,
Andrew was taken by complete surprise. So was Valerie.
Although she had kissed him as if she intended to make
the kiss a long one, she rolled off him quickly and
blushed. She lay on her back looking at the sky.

She thought this profound silence went on forever. A
silence made of being in the wilderness, enriched by
something kind of like shame. The worst part was that
she wanted to kiss him a second time, to kiss him even
longer. She had wanted to kiss him last night, wanted to
kiss him good morning in the kitchen, and now she
wanted to kiss him again.

(lonely)

She wondered what Andrew thought of her now. After

all, she was a married woman, married to a friend of his, and here she was, wrestling him down and kissing him. She wanted to say it was an accident, but throwing a snowball seemed to her so obviously a flirt that it could not possibly have been an accident.

"That was because

(because I'm so lonely)

you rescued me from being snowbound," she told him.

Andrew said: "We're still snowbound, but at least you've got company. I couldn't leave if I wanted to."

"Right," she said, standing and reaching for his hand, "and *we* are going to have Christmas."

They retrieved the axe and headed into the woods until they came upon a suitable tree. It was short and full, its branches sparkling with snow. Andrew shook it clean, Valerie dug around the trunk so they could cut it down. Three good chops and Andrew pushed the tree over. "Okay," he said, "let me tie it to your shoulders."

"What?"

"You gotta drag the tree home, Blue."

"Yer crazy."

"How else are we gonna get it home, huh?"

"Drag it," she said. "I can't carry this tree."

"It's not that big."

"*You* carry it."

"I have to carry the axe."

"I think I know why you and my husband are friends." Valerie tramped off.

Andrew lifted the tree by the stump of its trunk and dragged it behind himself back to the house. He left it in the garage to defrost, went inside to boil more bottled water for more coffee. He found Valerie, her coat and boots already off, at the stove popping corn to string for decoration.

They placed the tree in the corner of the living room near the staircase. The strung popcorn was its only decoration, but Valerie liked it. She made a fire in the front room fireplace, sat on the couch in the living room by some candles, munched chocolate chip "Christmas cookies."

Andrew played "White Christmas" on a harmonica, sang as much as he could like Bing Crosby. Valerie laughed hard, at both his poor imitation and at the indisputable whiteness of their Christmas. He began to sing "I'll Be Home for Christmas," and Valerie's laughter was so uncontrollable that she collapsed to the floor, mouth open, no sound coming out. She laughed so hard that her chest hurt. She kept laughing until tears squeezed out of her eyes.

And then she was crying—really crying—because no one was home for Christmas and it was not even actually Christmas, but an unreasonable facsimile.

The times most inspiring to heartbreak are the times of your life when you remember the future.

Andrew stopped singing. He moved to Valerie's side. He lifted her off the floor and carried her up to her bedroom where she bawled against his chest, soaked his shirt. He felt sorry for her. At first he did not realize the irony of his songs, was amazed to see this girl laughing uproariously one second, in hysterical tears the next. He really had to watch his every step in dealing with her. He was not up to that kind of foresight.

"Why don't you get ready for bed," he suggested. "I'll come back to see if you're okay in a while."

She nodded.

Andrew went through the door to the studio balcony, down the spiral staircase to retrieve the hurricane lamp from where he had left it, lit the wick, and went into the living room. The firelight from the front room was dying and he let it. He blew out the candles and went back upstairs. No electricity yet, no way down the mountain yet. No way to contact Cornelius—the one who *should* be here with her, not him. All in all, a nice fix. Andrew was exhausted. He realized his problem. There were no foreign chemicals in his body. The numbness to his deeds was gone. He had frayed his wits, whittled away his patience, and destroyed his ability to cope with people— with himself. That's what he had left himself with: a lot of negatives.

In what felt like a dream, Valerie wore a crown of pins on her head. The points stuck into her head, but there did not seem to be any blood dripping.

She awoke, found Clancy walking on her head. The bird then hopped down to her chest, walked back and forth on her body. The tiny talons of its feet prickled her skin through the thin cloth of her nightgown. Valerie did not sit up in bed. She lay rigid as the bird strolled up and down her person.

"Clancy, what are you doing free?" she whispered.

The only light, from the nearly full moon, turned the white bird into silver. The bird eyed Valerie straight on, moved its head from side to side while staring, opened its beak.

"What's that, Clancy?" Valerie asked. She thought she heard it speak, but she knew that Clancy had never learned that trick.

The silver bird spread its wings and ruffled its cowl. Valerie looked across her breasts into its eyes. The bird then flew out the door, its wings beating like her startled heart.

A snowplow scraping up the hill woke Andrew in the morning. He ran to his bedroom window. The path carved through the snow was narrow, but it was all they needed. As soon he could dig the car out, they would be free to go.

He slipped O'Kelly's jeans on and ran down the hall to Valerie's room.

"We're home free, Pinnoke!" he said as he threw open her door.

She opened her eyes, looked at him and said, "Huh?"

266

"The plows are out. I'm going to excavate the driveway."

He ran back to his room and finished dressing, went downstairs to the garage. He found a shovel and attacked the wall of snow like he was attacking the great white whale. He sliced into its smooth face, took on heaps of snow larger than the shovel could hold. The faster he cleared the driveway, the sooner they would say adios to this place, and he could put Valerie in the care of someone responsible for her. He sank the shovel in, pushed his weight against the handle, heaved up a mound of snow. It slid off the shovel before he tossed it aside. He sank the shovel in again. The muscles in his shoulders bulged, the cords in his neck stretched, his face reddened.

The handle of the shovel bent and snapped in two.

"Oh no!"

He breathed hard and stared at the splintered shaft. He looked around the garage for another shovel, searched the shed for one. There wasn't another.

It would take longer, but perhaps he could still dig with the broken one. He held the short stump, began to scoop up snow like a child scooping sand at the beach.

And it took all day to do half the driveway. While he struggled, Valerie came into the garage. She wore only her nightgown, no shoes on her feet.

"Get back inside," he told her, "you'll get pneumonia."

"Cornelius is coming!" she said.

"Where?" He high-stepped through the snow into the street and looked.

"He isn't here yet, but he's on his way."

"Valerie, at least put shoes on if you're gonna stand there, huh? And how do you know Cornelius is on his way?"

"Clancy told me—last night."

Andrew frowned. "Oh."

"He will be here any time," she said.

Andrew picked up what was left of the shovel. "You're going to catch cold. Go inside." He went back to work.

By the end of the day the car was still swamped by drifts. Like it or not, he was stuck here for another night. He carried the broken shovel with defeat into the house.

Valerie left Andrew in the driveway. She stared forlornly at their tree in the living room. This marked the second Christmas she had not spent with her parents. Tradition was being raped, and Christmas on her own got better every year.

But Cornelius was coming. And that would make everything all right. She hurried upstairs to dress for his arrival.

He would be here for New Year's. They would share the beginning of a new year, a chance to begin again, and do things right. He would be here soon.

Her hand shook as she applied her lipstick. A line of pink skidded onto her cheek. Valerie stared at the accidental smudge in the mirror. Then she drew a circle on her cheek, colored it in. She put a circle on the other cheek, like a clown's rouge, connected the corners of her mouth to the circles for a fake smile that would never fade.

Valerie colored her fingernails with the lipstick, colored her toenails too. Then she smeared lipstick all over her palms. *Want your palm red?* And she traced a line along each of her fingers, connected the five lines on the back of her hand and continued with one long trace up her arm. She removed the good blouse she had put on so she could finish connecting the arm bone to the shoulder bone.

She reached behind her back and unhooked her bra, let the cups slip off. She reddened her nipples with the lipstick, drew circles around her breasts. She drew a broken line from the base of her throat, between her breasts, down the center of her belly. *Tear along perforation.* She took off her slacks and her underpants. Her fingers were greasy with lipstick and the little cylinder was slippery, difficult to steer. She traced lines that came out wavy instead of straight up both of her legs—so they would match her arms, and she traced the tendons of her foot. Out of the circles she had drawn around her breasts she made a bikini top, and she drew the outline of a bikini bottom too: the bathing suit marks that her skin lacked, should have had, if she had grown up like decent girls.

Valerie remained in the bathroom all day, thinking up new ways to apply her make-up. She started in full daylight but, before she knew it, the sun had gone down and she was working in total darkness. That's when she heard Andrew's voice call her name.

"Upstairs," she answered.

She heard him stumble around in the dark house, and finally he came up with the hurricane lamp. Valerie stepped out of the bathroom, into the circle of light, with her graffiti all over her skin.

"What the—!" Andrew laughed.

Valerie looked down at herself, was at once overcome by shame, and she hid her pathos behind the locked door.

Andrew knocked on the door. "Valerie, what are you doing?"

What *was* she doing? She wondered. Good question. What in the name of heaven had she done to herself? She began to cry.

"You okay?" Andrew asked from the hall.

She poured bottled water—unheated water—into the sink and began to wash the lipstick off her skin. She winced when the cold water touched her. Without any light, she could not know if she got it all. She dripped what she imagined must be red water onto the floor. She finally unlocked the door and let Andrew enter. He came in hesitantly with the lamplight low.

Valerie looked at the pink water in the basin, then at Andrew. "Guess I got a little carried away," she said and tried to smile. Andrew stared. "I'll make supper," Valerie said.

"I'll cook tonight," he said.

"No. I insist."

Her body was not dry yet, but she started anyway to dress. Andrew helped her, handing her blouse and slacks as she needed them. The clothes were stained red.

She went downstairs. Andrew looked at the water in the sink, shook his head, afraid, and then let it drain. He watched until the sink was empty before following her.

Valerie got out of bed, believing that she had to go to the bathroom, left her room without her robe and went across the hall. Her feet stepped into a warm puddle as she closed the bathroom door. She flipped on the light, found the sink filled to overflowing with blood, the unborn fetus with tangles of its umbilical cord wrapped like swaddle around its ill-proportioned head and body, heaped upon the greasy island of its afterbirth.

That's when she started screaming.

Andrew thought the sound he heard was part of a dream. He braced himself for the onslaught of his nightmare, found himself waking instead. The sound was a woman's scream.

He bolted from bed and found Valerie standing naked in the bathroom, her face screwed up in terror as she pointed at the empty sink.

"Valerie!" He shook her by the shoulders.

She screamed in greater horror.

He dragged her out of the room. She fought him all the way back to her bedroom. Her scream had evolved into the words: "The baby! The baby!"

"Valerie! It's a dream!" he shouted. "Valerie: there is no baby!"

She awoke, realized none of it had been real, that there was not even a light in the bathroom.

"A dream, Valerie—that's all," Andrew said.

With her eyes bolted open, she sank back on the pillow. "Don't leave, Andrew. Don't."

"And I thought *my* nightmares were terrifying."

She pulled his arm closer, then wrapped herself

around him. She squeezed tightly, almost too tightly. Her skin all over was sticky with sweat and the residue of lipstick. He was nervous, holding the naked wife of his best friend, being this close *to anybody*. But as much as he wanted to get away, she wanted another body touching hers.

Andrew overlooked one small fact—a fact one who had shared a womb with his twin ought to have been able to intuit—that is, to touch, to hold, confirms reality better than to see, to hear. When you cling to something, there's something that resists you—something like yourself—you know you are not alone.

"I hate it here," she whispered.

"We can leave as soon as it's light."

"I don't want to go home," she said.

"Okay, we'll stay." Then he said: "But I'm still going to finish getting the car out, and then I am going to take you to a doctor."

"Why?"

"Because it'll help the nightmares and things."

"I don't see how."

He touched her forehead. "I think you're probably sick—like with a fever. It's probably the fever."

"I don't want to go to a doctor," she argued.

"We are not going through one more day of this," he said.

"My doctor is in Albany."

"There's gotta be a walk-in medical center or something around here."

"I like only him."

"Then I will drive you to Albany—but you're going."

She fell silent. Andrew thought he would wait until she was asleep again, then return to his own room. But when he tried to slip away, she murmured "*no*" and held fast. So he made himself relax and forced himself to sleep beside her.

Chapter 8

Valerie sat on the examination table, glad she had not allowed Andrew to come here with her. A visit to the doctor was a humiliating experience. More than that, however, it brought back to her tongue the taste of her so-called salad days—rancid, with rancid dressing. She did not like the mirrors on the cabinet doors in an examination room, never had. Every time she sat on one of these tables, stripped to her underwear, those mirrors reminded her that her body looked no different this year than the year before, or the one before that—for almost twelve years.

But today she did look different. She looked exhausted, stressed out—no, that was not accurate— scared, she looked just plain scared.

The doctor found nothing physically wrong with her. And she had known he would not. She did not even have the fever Andrew had suggested. The doctor told her she was simply nervous, harried, most likely pushing herself too hard,

(but she never *did* anything)

and the best thing to do would be to calm down, take it easy.

And to help her calm down, he gave her a prescription for valium.

She took the prescription slip from him with a nervous hand. The doctor smiled at her, said "Okay?" and she nodded timidly, although it was not. She dressed, left the doctor's office, closed the door and, out on the front stoop, she faced the world again—with an old crutch.

Before she left Albany she stopped at the supermarket to buy groceries for New Year's. As she pushed her cart around the store, she debated losing the valium prescription in the frozen foods section.

But it remained safe in her purse.

She put two bags of groceries into the trunk, headed up the Northway to the lake.

Not far along, only a few miles, as the arches of the Mohawk River bridge lay ahead of her, Valerie glanced into the rearview mirror. George Miller was behind her, face pale and chalky, tongue swollen, red eyes rolled up into his brow. Valerie screamed and swerved the car. Another car passing on her left laid on its horn. She yanked her car back, turned her head around and looked into the space behind the seat.

The car might have gone off the bridge. It might have plummeted into the river, with Valerie tied inside by her seatbelts and airbags, as the muddy water bubbled up around the windows and sucked the car down head first.

Her head swam. Across the bridge, she pulled onto the shoulder, panting. She undid her seatbelts, tore her coat open, opened the window to breathe. Her chest was crushed. She tore at her blouse, afraid she would choke to death. The heaters blowing from the SLK's headrest felt like his hot breath on her neck.

He was gone now—but he had been there—he had almost killed her—again.

I'm back

A face looked in the window.

"Ohhh—my God!"

It was a state trooper.

"Trouble?" he asked.

Valerie watched the rotating red light in her rearview mirror. "I hit—some ice," she said, "kind of skidded."

"You have to be careful, miss," the trooper said. "They still don't have these roads all clear yet. Lot of black ice." He curiously eyed her torn blouse.

"I will be careful," Valerie promised.

She wanted to cry, but not in front of the policeman. She wished he would let her alone because she did not know how much longer she could hold back on what was certain to be an outburst of tsunami proportions.

"Have a nice day," the trooper said.

Valerie nodded. She closed her window, then the tears came—constipated, not the flood she had expected, hoped for. She tried to force herself to sob, but—nothing.

Everything was tumbling down, she was losing control, she had a prescription for valium in her purse, and she was too terrified even to cry.

How long would it be till it was all over this time?

Shortly after Valerie left him to go to the doctor, Andrew collapsed onto the couch in the living room, grateful for the peace of not having to worry about the girl, at least for a few hours. Let that doctor come up with some answers. He had none.

Around about that moment, Cornelius drove up in a beat up Rambler which did not look strong enough to make the hill it had just climbed.

"Your wife is not here," Andrew told him straightaway. It may have been an invitation to leave, Andrew himself was not sure. Anyway, now was a fine time for Cornelius to show up.

"I know that."

"She's in bad shape," Andrew said resentfully. "I don't know what I'm doing here. Think I'm doing more harm than good. She wants you, Cornelius."

"O'Kelly left the band," Cornelius told him.

"Cornelius, how about listening to someone else for once, you know? Can't you understand? Valerie—your wife—is cracking *up*. Wanna know what I found her doing with her lipstick? Jesus...I don't know what to do."

"I listen," Cornelius said calmly. "You must listen."

"Are you here to get Valerie or not?"

"The band needs to replace O'Kelly."

"*That's* why you're here? I thought you said you were listening. The girl is lonely—that's her problem. She's been lonely since she was ten years old. All she wants is love, you know? I can't fix that. I can't do that. What can I do?"

Cornelius lit a cigarette, looked askance at Andrew.

"How long do you figure she'll be gone?" he asked.

"Couple hours. She went to her doctor in Albany."

"Think the doc can help her?"

"I don't know. But I know you were wrong to send me. You should have come."

"I am here," Cornelius said simply.

"To tell me stories about your band. If you want me to join the band, you got the wrong guy. I don't do that anymore. If you're here to take Valerie home, then you're welcome, but if not, then get out because when she sees you, it's gonna kill her."

"I am here."

"Never a straight answer," said Andrew, exasperated.

"The band needs a lead guitar."

"I gave you my answer."

"I haven't asked a question."

"You're telling me you want me to take Martin's place. I'm telling you I won't do it."

"Do you think Valerie is safe here by herself?"

"No. I told you that I don't. And I told you what I think is wrong with her. I'm no psychiatrist. I'm just a babysitter. All I can do is keep her company and take her lipstick away from her."

"How are you fixed for money?"

"I've got plenty of money, you know that. Money will not persuade me to join your band."

"The band will make another album," Cornelius said.

"All I have to do is one album, right?"

"Only one more will be made."

"I can't play. My hands—" he held up his healing but still frostbitten fingers. "I know what you're hoping. You are hoping you can get me back into a studio and I'll be convinced to stay."

"Would you give in so easily?"

"Look: I did you this favor by coming here because you said you weren't able to. Now if I sit in and play guitar with you guys, that'd be two favors. You have to do me one."

"What?"

"Take Valerie home and take care of her, *please.*"

"Pinnoke would accompany us," Cornelius said.

"Okay. I'll do it. But I'm only sitting in, I'm not joining. This once so you can fill your contract. That is all. Okay, are you happy?"

Cornelius said nothing. But he did not appear happy. The clue on his face passed quickly, but it looked a little like (but that did not follow)...disappointment?

Cornelius lay in bed holding his wife as she slept.

He was here.

He was too late.

It was after Martin O'Kelly had left the band, as he had anticipated, and he was able to get here on the excuse that Andrew could fill in. Why had Andrew allowed himself to go where he was not needed?

What would happen if, instead of letting the course of events run its nice, neat plan, Cornelius had said no and come here sooner?

That question no longer mattered. (the weather report)

And now the course would continue.

His wife stirred in his arms and changed positions. He wondered if she was aware, if she knew exactly what was happening. Yet it would be foolish to suggest that, if she knew, she would attempt to resist—that a person would actively take a stance *against* her destiny.

If there was such a thing.

He laid his cheek against her forehead and felt the impression of her dreams. The impressions were like Plato's shadows in the cave, how well they could be trusted could not be known, but these particular shadows suggested peace. Valerie felt safe. Her husband was here, he was holding her. Her fears were allayed. God knows, she ought to quake with terror. Her dreams felt like warm sunshine, like walking barefoot through soft grass, like a warm quilt on a cold, rainy night. Remove the quilt and see your dreams.

They were off to New York City.

Chapter 9

Not only did Edgar Pufknack not find Martin O'Kelly in a jail up in Poughkeepsie, but they had never had a Martin O'Kelly in custody, never heard of anyone by that name. His stunt was plain. He had skipped town and abandoned the band. He had no interest in returning.

Andrew walked into the recording studio, following Cornelius like a show-and-tell prop. Avchen saw him and recognized him, in spite of the beard he hid behind. "Ugh, no. This is so *not* happening!" she cried and ran out of the room.

"What's the matter with her?" Edgar Pufknack said.

"I think I know," said Andrew.

Edgar Pufknack headed for the door to catch Avchen.

"Don't go," Cornelius said. "I bet she's already locked herself in the john."

"Why is everyone in this band behaving like a child all of a sudden?" Edgar Pufknack demanded. He pushed the door open, flew out in a rage after Avchen.

"Can we go to Bermuda, Corey?" Valerie asked, combing her hair at the dresser mirror in the hotel.

"What is in Bermuda?"

"It's warm. We could go, because Martin has left and you can't find him—Avchen won't sing as long as Andrew plays—we may as well just take a vacation."

"Avchen has to sing. She hasn't a choice."

"You said she wouldn't—no matter what."

Cornelius lay on the bed. He watched his wife move her comb through her hair. She had just come out of the shower, was still moist, wrapped in a towel, and her dark shoulders were bare. The little hand with the comb moved up and then downward slowly, up and downward, and her black hair swished on her shoulders at the end of each stroke. He knew she believed he was taking some magical liberty with her life, but after all, her advent had kept him at bay for more than twenty years, with so many false alarms. Could anyone really say that Cornelius was in control?

Of course not. And neither was Valerie the dominant force.

"We'll go to Bermuda," Cornelius said.

Valerie turned to him tentatively. "Really?"

"Sure, if Avchen can't be persuaded to play as long as Andrew is there, then we'll go."

"Couldn't we go anyway? We'll do what Martin did—we won't tell anyone where we went, and they'll never find us."

She got up and went over to the bed. "Corey, do you love me?" she asked.

"Yes."

"Say it."

"I love you."

"This much?" She held her hands six inches apart.

"That much."

"Or how about this much?" She widened the space between her hands.

"That much."

"Or *this* much?"

"Valerie, I love you," Cornelius said, not losing patience, as he touched her shoulder softly.

"I wish you were a real husband." Valerie laid her head on his chest.

"Pinnoke, you've got it all wrong."

"What have I got all wrong?"

"The space between your hands when you want to know how much I love you is only that: space."

"But if you put your body inside them," she said, wrapping her arms around him, "then the space is filled, see?"

Well, he certainly never expected to be here again. Tchaikovsky's 1812 Overture played on the stereo: loud. Andrew paced his living room. Back in Jersey City; back in a recording studio; back in the music business. His will power had to be admired.

He had an unfair advantage over Avchen, of course. He had known she was now a member of The Next Tuesday Band. All she had known was that Cornelius would bring back a replacement for Martin O'Kelly.

The CD player blared away at seven o'clock in the morning.

Personally, Andrew did not care if Avchen remained adamant or not. He was only doing a favor for a friend. He could just as happily, even more happily in fact, step aside and let some other person sit in for the album.

So what bothered him?

He had been a royal s.o.b. to women before. He had not been nice to a one, except for his sister, since Janie.

But none of the other women had ever come back.

He would give them the boot, they would cry and go off cursing him, he'd forget them in a wink. End of story. Avchen was the first to return and haunt him (haunt and return to him). And he could not deal with it.

He felt guilty.

He could not shrug this one off, say that if Avchen wanted to hold her breath until she turned blue, or they got rid of him, that she could go ahead. He could not say that it did not make a speck of difference to him— because it did. When she had run out of the studio, he almost went after her.

To apologize.

Andrew turned down the music just a hair.

He still felt that way—as if he had to say he was sorry. Nothing would be right until he did. He was not concerned about things being right with that band, it was with himself. He would not be at ease until he spoke to Avchen.

He turned down the music some more.

Maybe she would not see him. He could go to her hotel and knock on the door. Perhaps she would tell him through the door to drop dead. He would be absolved then, would have put forth the effort, and she could do whatever she wanted.

No, he would not be absolved, not that easily. He had to see her, to talk to her, he had to look her in the eyes and care when he said I am sorry. A mere gesture would not do, and there was a chance that even the real thing would be insufficient.

Andrew turned the 1812 Overture so low he could barely hear it.

He would go to that hotel and talk with her, not for the sake of any stalled production of some record, but for his own sake—

—or for her sake.

Andrew put on his coat to leave. He forgot about the stereo, left on, but too low to hear, right about the time the cannons fired. He was looking forward to the absolution.

Avchen surprised him by letting him in. She was up, dressed, and in fact she had obviously not been to bed at all. From the look of her clothes, complexion, and hair, Avchen had spent this and many nights drunk.

She offered him coffee.

She was not actually friendly, which relieved Andrew. If she had been so much as cordial, he would have had to leave, could not have stood it. No, the coffee was warm, but it was about the only thing there that was.

"You really knocked me on my bum yesterday," Avchen said, lighting a cigarette.

Andrew watched the match pop into flame. The cigarette too was a new touch. It was not flattering—little that she did was. He would bet they would be able to photograph her now.

"I came here to apologize."

"A year later?"

"Better late than never?"

"Heh."

"I treated you bad."

"Got that off your chest now, huh? Feel better?"

Andrew sighed. "Ever think things might have changed a little? I am sincere."

"You're telling *me* about change! Andrew, I just don't know what you expect me to do."

Neither did he. "Accept my apology, because I mean it. I do not feel good about how I treated you."

"You *shouldn't* feel good. I had been only trying to be nice, but you were so selfish, all you care about is your own life not getting screwed up." This would have been a good place for her to do something like cry, for the tension to break down, and then they would be getting somewhere. He really did want to kiss her, to kiss her and make it all better as if she were the boo-boo. But her eyes were quite dry.

"Okay—that is true." Andrew agreed. "Let's not dig it all up again—"

"I don't have to *dig it up!*"

"All right all right! Don't yell. Let's just, you know, at least be businesslike so we can do this album up."

Avchen finished her first cigarette, had lit up a second; she ground that out half consumed, immediately lit up a third. "Businesslike," she scoffed.

Andrew squinted at her, as if squinting would allow him to see her better for whatever she was up to. "I thought this was gonna be a good idea."

"It would have been a great idea—ten months ago. Do

you think it matters one bit now? Did you even know I had my appendix out? It blew up in the doctor's hand. I could have died. But you didn't even know I was sick."

"How could I?" She was not going to lay this guilt trip on him.

"All I kept thinking about was you."

"That is not my fault."

"Want to know what I was thinking? Just so you won't think I was getting sentimental under the effects of pain pills, I was thinking what a stupid loser I had to be to think you cared what happened to anyone—to think that if you even knew I was in the hospital you'd have visited me, even if only for old time's sake—because as far as you're concerned, there is no old time's sake—Or you don't want to be bothered with it anyway."

"Here I am all categorized, labeled, and neatly put away."

Here was old time's sake looking him right in the face.

He reached for her hand.

She held it away.

"I am not the naive little girl anymore you can charm into living with you," she said.

"I'm not trying to charm anything. This is probably a stupid question, but what's happened to you?"

"I'm hard now," she snapped. "Just like you."

"In imitation of me, or because of me?"

"Certainly not in imitation."

"You're not hard, Avchen. Just because you drink all night and smoke a million cigarettes and curse a blue streak don't make you hard."

"I know what I am," she asserted.

"I think that I would rather know what I'm not. More room that way."

"Okay, you be what you're not, and I'll be what I am."

"Conditions of the peace treaty?"

Avchen took a drag on her cigarette. "A peace treaty, that's so lame," she sighed, blowing smoke.

"Won't you at least do the album?"

She thought about it.

"You don't even have to talk to me if ya don't want."

"You're not joining the band, are you?"

"I'm just doing Cornelius a favor till the CD is made. I'm not even going to tour."

"All right. I will do it." She did not even say it grudgingly. She looked straight at him for the first time. "Maybe you and me could work together."

"I think we could," Andrew said.

A working relationship—that was enough—it was something anyway—only a new relationship can bury an old.

Edgar Pufknack sat in the booth and beamed. There was Avchen Neumann, in front of her mic, perhaps a bit worse for wear but as unfairly beautiful as ever, putting her all into the vocals of this song. They could most likely make up for time lost. If nothing else went wrong.

Cornelius hit an E minor chord and suddenly his head filled with pain as he had never felt it, like a hairline crack seaming his cranium, and he ceased playing. The pain was gone as instantaneously as it had struck. It would not return as long as he did not touch his piano again.

He knew what it was.

Edgar Pufknack did not. "What's the problem?"

"I have to make a phone call," Cornelius said. "Somebody give me their cell phone." Somebody did—he was not sure who—but there was no reception in the studio or the booth.

He went into the hall, pale as could be, with the memory of the headache.

Andrew followed him, saxophone and all.

"I have to call Valerie," Cornelius said, pacing with the phone, trying to find some corner where it could pick up a signal.

"Why?"

"She's done something stupid."

As Cornelius had suspected—as he had known—there was no answer in their hotel room.

"I have to leave," he told Andrew.

"What's wrong?" Andrew pleaded.

"Valerie has gone to Bermuda," he said and staggered off down the corridor like a man who did not know the building he was in.

"What's in Bermuda?" Andrew wondered.

Yet he knew why she had gone. And he realized something now, and it all made sense. Now. He understood now Cornelius' puzzling look of disappointment back at the lake when he'd asked him to join the band. Andrew was *supposed* to have told Cornelius no. There had been something he could have done, and the choice would have made so much difference. He could have said no.

The moon outside the airplane was full. Valerie sat in her seat, her belt fastened tightly, clutching her one suitcase of summer clothing she had gone out and bought somewhere she didn't remember the store now, just before she headed for the airport. She looked out the window. At 34,000 feet she looked across at the moon not up. She cruised along over clouds that appeared blue in the moonlight, looking over at a sky she used to dream under.

Once upon a time the sky had been the sky, and she had been on the earth, and the two did not seem to have much to do with each other.

When there is no moon, and the stars cream over the sky, you may drive down a highway, you may sit in a garden, you may lay on a tennis court, and they are soft and near, the stars are.

(the stars—it would be thirty years before she could look at them and know that her past was over)

When the moon is full, like that one out there now, and only a few stars can shine, few enough to count, when the moon is full and called romantic, you cannot help, even in the heated and contained cabin of an airliner, but look at each of those stars and shiver.

Chapter 10

Bermuda was better in the travel ad. In the travel ad there was no sand in the corners of the hotel room, there were no ants crawling out of wherever they came from to get inside her suitcase, into her shoes and clothing, and in the travel ad there was no unbearable heat. In the airport she had gone into the ladies' room and changed inside one of the stalls, but even in summer clothing she was too hot. She came straight from the airport to the hotel room, turned on the air-conditioner, and lay on the floor until ants began crawling into her hair. Mortified, she moved to the bed, stared out her closed window into air that rippled with heat. The beach was in view from here, possibly a lovely panorama of the ocean. Valerie wondered how those people out on that sand withstood the heat.

She missed Cornelius dreadfully.

From that moment the plane left the ground, she wanted to go home. And she could go home, nothing stopped her. But she had spent a lot of money. It was a last-minute plan, ineligible for any discount, and what a horrible waste it would be to get on the very next flight home.

Yet had she paid all this money just to lay in a hotel room and shake ants out of the folds of her clothes?

She rolled off the bed and dragged into the bathroom. The sun shone directly through the window in here, hot, too much for the air-conditioner to combat. She splashed water over her head, let it drip down her clothes, and then she filled a drinking glass and took a valium pill.

The doctor had been right about these pills. They worked. As long as she stuck to the prescription, she would feel fine. And already all her dreams were gone.

Maybe when the valium had calmed her, she would put on her bathing suit and go down to the pool. Not to the beach, she already had enough sand up here in the room, but the pool would be nice.

She walked down the stairs in her beach cover and sandals, wearing sunglasses and carrying a magazine. By the time she got to the poolside, the terry cloth was wet, her hair plastered to her forehead, rivulets of perspiration collected in the hollow of her collarbone.

But she was calm now, feeling confident that all her troubles had been left in New York City, where troubles belonged. When she went home at the end of this week, her husband would still be there, still making his music, still locked inside his music-staff cage. That is what she had left behind. She settled on a chaise lounge, checked to be sure no one would watch as she removed her cover, and she laid back. She felt tranquil. She plopped the magazine on the cement. When she could no longer stand the sweat, she would go into the pool, but until then, she would not exert any energy, not even to read. She felt very relaxed. She felt good.

A baritone voice said hello.

Valerie opened her eyes. She looked sideways past her right shoulder into a pair of sun-browned thighs and a scant blue bathing suit. Her eyes moved upward to lose the face in a glare of sun. She straightened, lifted her sunglasses to the top of her head, looked again. She was looking at a young man, more precisely still something of a boy, with perfect hair. His waist was slender, stomach taut, and his shoulders strongly broad. Sandy colored hair curled lightly out of that little bathing suit and grew nicely up his abdomen, covered his chest. The large bulge in the front of his conforming trunks made her shift in her seat.

She said, "Hello."

"My name is Gary," he said.

"Pleased to meet you, Gary," she said. She thought twice about telling him her name, did not want to encourage him, then she decided it wouldn't harm anything.

"Valerie what?" he asked.

"Mastropietro."

Now what on earth made her give him her maiden name?

He smiled. "Wow. That's quite a name, huh? My last name is Leonard. This is your first day here, isn't it?"

"Yes."

"I knew that because this is a pretty small hotel. And I knew that too because if you'd been around before today, I am certain I would have noticed."

Valerie wiped sweat from under her eye with her left hand, hoping he would see the wedding ring.

"How do you like it here?" Gary asked.

"It's hot."

"Sure is, huh? I'm from Greenwich, Connecticut, and it's winter up there right now. Actually, I go to school in Providence, and I'm on winter break. You get so used to the cold, don't you, and then it seems so hot here. Where are you from?"

"New York."

"Oh—I live right near there. I go into the city a lot on the train."

"I'm not from New York City. I'm from Saratoga. It is almost four hours from that place." That she was not from New York City, had never been there until two years ago seemed, she did not know why, an important point to emphasize.

The sun was hot, the boy an irritant. When he ran out of conversation, had nothing more to say but "I'll see you around," she was glad. Yet she watched him walk away.

She stood up, went to the diving board and sprang into the pool. The sudden slip of cold water felt wonderful over her skin. She swam a few laps, climbed out of the pool, sat on the edge with a foot in the water.

A pair of feet stood beside her, and she knew whose feet they were. This boy was beginning to frighten her. "I watched you dive," he said.

Now he would probably have some pointers for her.

"I happen to be a diver myself."

"Oh?" Valerie said.

"I'm on the swim team at school."

Valerie smoothed her wet hair back, raising the wedding ring before his eyes again. She knew the problem. This boy, about eighteen years old, had watched her walk out of the hotel, checked her out to be about his own age. It would never occur to him that a ring he saw on her finger was a wedding ring. He wanted a date. That was an innocent mistake, but he put a knot of dread inside her chest and it would not go away.

The boy did not look like George Miller, yet there was something in his eyes. He was not George Miller...he was...

(he was George Miller)

"Want to see me dive?" Gary offered.

"Sure," she said, if it would make him go away.

He ran off in his small bathing suit, climbed the ladder to the diving board. Valerie did watch, with half interest, to be polite. Gary stood on the end of the board, every muscle in his body poised. Just before he went off the board, Valerie noticed two things: the boy was gorgeous; and he had never dived before in his life.

He made a big splash when his flailing limbs hit the water.

Valerie had to laugh.

Gary's head poked out of the water by her feet.

"Bravo!" Valerie clapped, still laughing.

His perfect hair was slicked to his head, and his eyelashes dripped. He was only a boy, full of adolescent bravado, quite harmless. And hot. "Want to know something?" he said, out of breath.

"What?" Valerie continued to smile.

"I'm not on the swim team. That's the first time I ever did that."

"Want to know something?"

He hauled himself out of the pool, did not merely sit but rather he posed himself at her side. "What's that?"

"I could tell!" She started to laugh again.

Gary laughed with her.

Then they sat on the lip of the pool for a few moments as their amusement set in, made each chuckle privately a few more times. Valerie stirred the water with her foot.

Gary leaned forward and fingered the gold chain around her ankle. "This is beautiful," he said. "That is very fine gold. Where did you get it?"

"A.... someone gave it to me...a long time ago."

"Ahh, an old boyfriend?"

Valerie folded her leg beneath her haunch, hid the anklet.

"Listen," he said, "I was thinking, I got the courage to jump off a diving board, so the next part should be easy. How about having dinner with me?"

She almost said yes.

"No, I don't think I better."

He would not allow himself to display disappointment, but Valerie could see it nonetheless.

"I mean I'm busy tonight. I made plans. I'm sorry." She thought that perhaps offering an excuse, however lame, would restore his feelings.

"How long are you staying? I have another week. I could show you around the island. I've been here a week and I know all the good places. We could rent a couple of mopeds."

She did not want to say yes; she did not want to say no. Once upon a time she had been good at this, but her skill had been exorcised with her decision to eliminate the old self. "Maybe," is what she replied.

Then to avoid any pressing from him, she stood and said she was tired, and she returned to her room.

She lay on the bed, clutching her rolled up beach cover in one hand and, to her surprise, she needed another valium.

She looked at the phial on the dresser, resisted.

Gary could be company. Perhaps it had been wrong to turn him down. What harm could come from having a meal with a person and talking?

She looked again at the phial of valium, at its reflection standing right behind it in the dresser mirror. She threw the beach cover at it.

Had she not come to Bermuda to be left alone?

She was alone at home.

Valerie stood and seized the phial, unscrewed the cap, dumped a pile of pills into the palm of her hand. She looked at them, took one between her thumb and forefinger, popped it into her mouth and swallowed. Her hand shook. The other pills jittered out of her palm, hit the floor and danced severally. Valerie fell to her knees, collected the fallen pills, and dropped them one by one back into the phial.

She jumped to her feet and ran out of the room, ran all the way down the stairs in her bathing suit, through the main lobby out to the front of the hotel. She paused for a moment to see where she was, then she headed around to the back of the building where the pool was. The sidewalk was hot on her bare feet. She was glad to reach the lawn. Her head swam and she was not sure if it was the heat and sun or the second, premature dose of valium.

Gary Miller was there. He was talking to a shapely breasted girl in a nothing-at-all bikini. Valerie stood at the edge of the patio and told herself that this feeling was not jealousy.

George looked her way, it took a second, but her eye did catch his.

Valerie did know ways to beat competition. She smiled at him and he smiled back.

Once upon a time there was a girl named Valerie Madonna Maria Mastropietro who was very naughty and although she was not popular as a child she learned as an adolescent how to get boys anyway and she did indeed get a lot of boys even boys who had girlfriends and thought they were not looking for another and Valerie had many other things also too many other things whenever and whatever she wanted and the word no did not need to exist in her vocabulary.

Now the word no was Valerie Prince's only weapon.

George Miller had left his nearly naked companion and was walking toward Valerie. She wanted to run away.

"Hi," Gary said.

"Hello." Valerie realized she had brought her pills with her, and without her beach cover there was no place she could hide them. She sat on a chaise and slid the phial behind her back. "I was thinking," she said, her mouth so dry that it hurt, "that even though I may be busy for dinner—have you had lunch yet?"

"No," Gary said.

Maybe he had, maybe he hadn't.

"Neither have I."

"What to have lunch?" Gary asked, evidently forgetting his mark in the bikini across the patio.

"All right." Her voice sounded funny to her. She had a feeling of claustrophobia in her own body. "I'll go upstairs and get dressed. Give me half an hour, okay?" She stood up.

"What room are you in?"

"316."

"No kidding? I'm right down the hall. See you in one half hour."

Valerie turned around and walked. She tried not to let her behind wiggle.

Up in her room she flopped on the bed. Her head hurt, the blood pounded in her ears. Now she was afraid to go to lunch with Gary. Was she even hungry? Her stomach felt a little queasy.

That had to be nerves.

She peeled off her bathing suit and went into the bathroom to shower. She stumbled into the shower stall, let the water pour over her aching head.

The walls of the booth began to move, the floor turned slippery under her toes. Valerie leaned back against the wall before it could slide from behind her. For a second she could feel the tile smooth and wet, then her skin was numb. She slid down along the wall to sit on the floor. The water rained on her from way up there. She pushed open the door, crawled from the shower stall. The bathroom too was spinning, spinning and hot. Valerie stood up slowly, steadied herself on the sink.

She walked out of the bathroom to the closet. Her heart pounded, her breath was short. There was only one answer. She had to calm herself. She needed another pill. She put one arm into the sleeve of a blouse, put the other in, had trouble buttoning it, broke a nail trying. She left the blouse open and went to the dresser for her valium.

It was gone.

She checked the drawers. The top one with her underwear in it. The middle with T-shirts and shorts in it. The bottom which was empty. The pills were not in any of them.

Maybe the phial had fallen and rolled behind the dresser. She tried to push the dresser out from the wall, but it was too heavy. She took a hanger from the closet, untwisted it and stretched the wire out long. She peered into the shadow between wall and dresser, could see nothing. She clawed with the hook of the unbent hanger, and she retrieved from the dark hollow three pennies and a quarter, a small bar of soap wrapped in paper with the hotel's name on it, a lot of sand.

No phial of pills.

She attacked her bed, searched under the pillow, inside the bedspread, tore all the sheets off, felt between the mattress and box spring.

Nothing.

She looked in the bathroom, and when she did not find them in there she ran around the room in a panic. She stopped at the window, looked out at the ocean. She climbed onto the window sill, looking like an animal caged and in danger. Except for the unbuttoned blouse, she was naked, straddling the air-conditioning unit with her bare legs, framed in the window, hair wet, frantic over a sixteen dram phial of pills. Palms against the glass, looking at the people on the beach reminded her that she had left her pills down by the pool. In her need to get hold of herself, she had forgotten.

Knock, knock on the door.

"Just a minute, George!" she called.

She clambered out of the window frame, hoped with shame that no one out there on that beach had turned around and looked back at the hotel for any reason, and she ran to the closet. She buttoned her blouse in a hurry and pulled on a pair of jeans. She ran into the bathroom, combed her hair and started to blow dry it.

Gary appeared in the mirror.

Valerie gasped, fumbled her hair dryer.

"Ready to go?" He was dressed, hair perfect once more, looking arrogantly beautiful.

"I'm sorry I'm late. I should have said an hour."

"Not a problem." Gary disappeared out of the mirror.

Valerie decided to let the heat outside dry her hair. She put away her hair dryer and grabbed her purse off the chair beside the window. "I'm ready now," she said breathlessly.

Gary smiled.

As they walked down the hall toward the elevator, Valerie suddenly realized she had forgotten to put on both panties and bra. She had no underwear on.

"Oh!" she said aloud.

"What?"

"Urn, uh, nothing. But could we stop by the pool before we go to lunch? I think I left something there."

"Was it this?" Gary pulled the phial out of his pocket.

"Yes," she admitted, embarrassed. "Thank you." She snatched it from him and ditched it in her purse.

They had lunch in the hotel dining room, did not go outside. All through the meal her hair was soaked, tangled. She excused herself once and went to the ladies' room, looked in the mirror and saw a whorish looking mess on her head. She returned to the table as the waiter set lunch on the table.

Gary suggested they order a bottle of wine.

"No," Valerie said. "I don't really like wine."

"You haven't had good wine, that's why. I know a wine you'd like. It's very dry."

"No, Gary, really. I want only milk. You can get a glass if you want to, but I don't want any."

She excused herself again. She tried to comb her hair once more, and this time she took another valium pill before returning to the table.

By the time they finished eating, Valerie felt as if she were at the other end of a long cardboard tube, looking and speaking through it, at Gary. She felt very sick as they reached her room. She let him kiss her, felt her naked skin rustling against the insides of her clothes as his arms drew her in. She stuttered a good-bye, went into her room, and fell down on the ransacked bed.

Her hand searched in her purse until it found the valium. Her arm drew the phial out of the purse, threw it against the wall. The cap spun off in flight, and the pills scattered like bread crumbs.

But the next day, the first thing Valerie did was collect all the pills she could find, replace them in the cracked but still whole phial, and put them back on the dresser in front of the mirror.

Chapter 11

Valerie stood outside Gary's room, hesitated before knocking on the door. It was the middle of the night. The hotel corridor was lit, but behind every door the rooms were dark. Every room but Valerie's.

She had not allowed herself a pill all day long. The result now seemed to be insomnia. Not that she needed a pill to sleep, but some part of her daily ritual had been violated, and she noticed. Then she had begun to notice many other things. That she was far away from home. That she wanted to be farther. That this hotel was very quiet. That she was probably the only one in it still awake. One simple pill would not turn back this insomnia. Her day was out of kilter. Her day was out of kilter because a need had been denied.

That valium had become a need.

She continued to ignore it, knowing that one pill would not satisfy this need, only placate it, and it would be there on and on and on.

She turned on her light, put on her robe, and paced the room. She decided that now, this minute, of all times, was when she needed company. Everyone else slept. She was alone. The more she thought of that, the more she feared the urgency to take just one little valium pill, one little pill just to relax, as per instructions from kindly doctor.

She wished Gary would come along and invite her out somewhere and keep her company so she would not keep looking at the phial.

Which came first, loneliness or need?

Now she stood looking at Gary's door. She leaned her head against the doorpost, touched the doorknob. She was indeed tired, weary, in fact she had been weary for months, but need would not allow her to sleep. Looking at the numbers on the door, she began to cry.

Go back to your room. You don't belong in the hall in the middle of the night.

She knocked lightly on the door.

To her surprise, Gary responded right away. "Who is it?" He sounded startled, but not asleep.

"It's Valerie," she whispered. She hoped the whisper did not carry her weeping with it.

The door opened and there was Gary wearing his blue jeans and holding an algebra textbook. "What's the matter?" he asked.

"Are you studying?"

"Two more days and I have to go back to school."

"Oh," she said dumbly.

"What's the matter? You're crying." He touched her cheek.

"I was sort of—well, I wanted to talk—to be around some—I wanted to be with you," Valerie said.

Gary led her into the room and closed the door.

"Why are you crying?"

"I don't know—I'm dumb."

She wanted to stop crying, knew the tears were giving him wrong ideas, forcing him to second guess, and even confusing herself. She tried to stop, that made it worse. She sat pathetically on the bed.

His room was bigger than hers, more expensive. There was a little alcove with a desk for writing. He had been studying at the desk.

Gary sat beside her and put his arm around her shoulders. He must have thought this scene was nice: a little girl all upset in the middle of the night and a big strong guy to chase away her blues. She felt like a fly visiting the spider's lair.

"Do you want to go out for a drink?"

"No," she whimpered. "I'm not dressed and I don't want to go out anyway."

"What's the matter?" Gary asked.

"I don't know."

"Did you have a bad dream?"

That sounded good. "Yeah."

He kissed her on the side of the face. "It was only a dream. You're awake now, right?"

"Yes, I'm awake."

"Nothing to worry about."

He went into the bathroom and came back with a tissue. She said thank you. Gary placed his textbook on the desk. Valerie watched him, prayed that he would want to finish studying and would send her back to her own room. But he set the book there in a way that said he intended to forget it and turn his attention to other things. He walked back to her and sat down.

"All better?" he said.

Actually, she felt humiliated. Could not decide if she had humiliated herself, or if he was doing it right now. He unzipped her robe, pulled it off her limp arms and laid it aside. Valerie began to shiver in her night gown.

"You can't be cold," Gary said.

"The air-conditioner m–makes me c-cold."

He cuddled her close, rubbed her back. She wrapped her arms around him. He was warm.

"Get under the blanket," he told her.

She did so, curled up in a ball and her teeth continued to chatter. She simply could not get warm.

Gary took off his jeans and Valerie felt funny about that, turned her head. But after all, that bathing suit he had been wearing the first time she saw him showed more than his boxer shorts.

He got into bed with her, turned off the light.

Valerie did not want to get out of the bed, she did not want to go back to the silence of her own room. She had been lonely, now the need had been quelled. Without a pill she began to feel relaxed. She uncurled, felt no cold, no fear. She wanted to be sleeping with Gary. Only that: sleep. She wanted to feel another person near, to be able to reach out if she wanted to and touch another body.

There was truth in the lie that she'd had a bad dream. She'd had the worst kind of bad dream. Adolescents may dream of ideals, of poetic success, of fame. She had dreamed of doing what she wanted, when she wanted, of answering to no one, of exclusion from responsibility. She had dreamed of designing her own life with no interference from others: a very bad dream indeed.

In the morning Valerie felt Gary's kisses, hands beneath her nightgown. Not fully cognizant, she believed she was in her own bed, alone, Gary the product of a sleepy imagination. She touched him back, kissed him deeply.

"Let me get a condom," he said.

Valerie was awake in a second, pulled away. She discovered her arms out of her nightgown. The nightgown was up over her shoulders, a breath away from being slipped off altogether.

"No!" she said. "That is not—"

She put her arms back into her sleeves, covered her body. She got out of the bed.

He sat up, perfect hair still perfect, and naked. He looked frightening.

"That's really a bad idea," she said.

"Oh come on. You were really hot a minute ago," he said.

"I was *asleep* a minute ago."

"That isn't how it seemed."

Valerie tried to remember what she had been doing, but it was all on the other side of a threshold. "I didn't know where I was," she said. "I probably thought you were Cornelius."

He did not ask who Cornelius was.

He got out of bed, started walking toward her.

"George, please, no," she said. "Put something on."

Gary picked up his jeans and put them on. "Don't worry. It is just that I thought you were ready."

She put her robe on. "I won't ever be ready for that."

"You will," George Miller said.

"No. You don't understand. I'm not even who you think. I'm much older than you. I'm married."

"Okay okay. A misunderstanding." He did not believe her. "I don't want to ruin a friendship." He reached for her hands.

She did not let him touch her. She opened the door and ran into the hall. He looked at her angrily, as if any idiot could see she was being unreasonable. She flew up the hall into her room and slammed the door.

In a minute he was knocking. She locked him out, yelled for him to go away.

"Let me in!" he called; it was almost a roar.

She didn't answer, cowered into the bathroom.

"Valerie, let me in!" He slammed furiously on the door.

She shook all over. Gary continued to pound. Valerie tried to pretend she did not hear the battering.

"Let me in, you bitch!"

Valerie dispensed a pill into her hand, took it and drank some water.

"I'm going to get in anyway, you—"

"*Stop!*" she shrieked. "*Go away, Gary, please!*"

He banged so hard she thought he would split the door. "Let me in and I'll go away."

Valerie approached the door, did not open it. She said: "That doesn't make sense. Gary, please leave me alone. I don't hate you. It was a mistake, I know. Now please go away and I'll see you later, okay?"

"I'm going to wait here until you open the door."

"You'll wait all day."

"You have to come out to eat."

"I'm not hungry. Go away."

"You will be hungry."

Then it was quiet outside. She did not hear any noise

at all, pictured him crouching down by the door to wait. She picked up the phone to call the manager for help, but she did not dial the number. She set the phone down and went back to the door, sat on her side of it just as she knew he was sitting on his. And she waited.

Some time passed, she had no idea how much, but her haunches ached from squatting the while. A knock made her start. "Gary, go away!"

A woman's voice said: "Maid."

"Is there anyone else there?" Valerie asked cautiously

"No."

Valerie opened the door slowly, and sure enough it was only the maid. Valerie went into the hall to look for Gary. He had vanished.

"Did you see a boy out there?" Valerie asked the maid.

The answer was no.

"I wonder where he went," Valerie muttered.

The maid changed the bed, put new towels in the bath. Valerie said thank you and the maid left. Valerie checked the hall again. It was deserted, even the maid was gone. She went back into her room and closed the door.

She dressed quickly and hurried down the hall, hoping to get out of the hotel for the whole day and avoid Gary.

But she heard a door open behind her as she headed for the stairs, knew whose door it was. She was one flight down when her name was called. She was two flights down when his footsteps followed. He caught her at the bottom.

"Valerie, I'm sorry," he said with his sincerest face. "See: I even went away. Let me take you to dinner tonight to make it up, okay?"

"I'll have to think about it."

"I'm going home tomorrow. We'll never see each other again. Let's just have dinner."

"I don't want to answer now. I'll let you know later. I'm going to take a walk."

"Good idea. Get yourself together. I'll talk to ya later." He kissed her on the forehead and went back upstairs.

Valerie walked away from the hotel, walked down the beach, kept walking until there were no people, no beach towels or suntan oils. She took off her sandals and walked barefoot. Hers were the only footprints.

She was cold again. Not her skin—that was flushed—but her insides. The cold was deep. She kept walking, feeling the white sand slip underneath her toes and heels. She might have been the only one on the island, the island might have been ten feet wide with one palm tree like in comics. Valerie could not get warm, but she could not shiver. Gary would be gone tomorrow. Tomorrow. She was unable to think of tomorrow. She tried, but it was like pushing against a wall. There was no tomorrow within her reach. She pushed against the wall, struggled herself into a sweat.

It had to be a mirage, a mirage in the heat over the sand, like in a desert: she thought she saw Eileen walk out from behind a crag, walk up the beach toward her, red hair, freckles, and all.

Valerie turned and walked back to the hotel.

In her room, she took a valium pill. Then she took a second one with the first. She lay on her bed, thought about as many yesterdays as she could bear, since she could think of no tomorrows, and she felt very sad.

The valium helped her to relax. She did not feel warm, but she did not feel cold. She took another pill. She knew well what she was doing, but did not fight it. Feeling very calm, she changed her clothes and went down the hall to Gary.

He had ordered dinner from room service. It was there in his room, waiting for her, as though she had called ahead and said she would be right over. There was steak and champagne.

The occasion, he said, is my going away party.

Valerie stared at the champagne bottle like a scarecrow facing fire.

They sat down to eat.

Her glass stood ominously empty before her

throughout the meal.

How's the steak, he asked, I ordered it rare.

It's very good, she answered, very tender.

The champagne should also be very good.

He popped the cork off the bottle, filled her glass.

No thank you, she said.

Just a little, he said, it won't hurt you.

I don't like it.

You'll like this.

Valerie looked at the glass. Gary picked his up.

A toast? he offered.

Valerie was petrified.

I can't.

Christ, Valerie, are you still upset about this morning?

She pushed her chair back, ran into the bathroom. In a second, Gary would be there knocking. She took another valium pill and ventured back to the table.

Feeling okay? Gary asked.

Yes, she said.

They sat at the table again. Gary placed Valerie's champagne glass in her hand. Then, demonstratively, he took a sip.

See? Not poison.

Valerie sniffed the champagne, watched the bubbles.

Now, Gary said, to my departure.

Then they both drank a toast.

Valerie did not feel any different. She could not say she liked the champagne. After so long without tasting it, it seemed more bitter than she remembered. She wondered why people drank it.

Gary filled her glass again.

Can't let this stuff go to waste, he said.

Valerie drank a second glass. Her alarm systems were subdued by valium.

By now the sun had long since set, and the moon had risen. It shined through Gary's window. The clock said it was seven-thirty, but it seemed very, very late. Gary turned off the lights and let the moon light the room.

"I don't feel good," Valerie said suddenly.

"What's the matter?"

"I can't say. I just don't feel good."

"You're just drunk."

Drunk was a word she had not had to face in a nice, long time. Just drunk...Just—

"I'm cold. I've been cold all day. And it doesn't feel like anything is real anymore. I feel sad, cold, and like nothing is real."

"Do you feel like I'm not real?"

"You are not real, this hotel isn't real, Bermuda isn't real."

"Like a dream," he said in a corny, romantic way.

"No."

He put his arms around her, chuckled. "You'll be fine. It's just the champagne."

"It isn't. I've felt it before you even gave me champagne."

Gary put his hand on her tiny breast. She let it stay. It wasn't real either.

"How about a walk outside in this moonlight. It's very bright."

"Okay."

"Here's a better idea: how about a swim in the ocean?"

"All right. I'll go get my bathing suit." She stepped out of his hold. "I'll be right back."

She wandered up the hall, turned the door knob, and went into her room. She changed into her bathing suit and beach cover, paused in the bathroom and took another valium. Then she returned to Gary.

He had his bathing suit on and a tank top shirt. He brought the bottle, which still had some champagne in it.

Don't want to waste this, he said.

With his free hand, he took Valerie's, and they went to the elevator.

On the beach, he took a long drink from the bottle, handed it to Valerie.

I don't want any more, she said.

Might as well finish it, he told her.

She took the bottle, but did not drink.

Gary waded into the ocean.

It's still warm, he said.

She followed, hanging onto the neck of the champagne bottle.

The warm water lapped at the hem of Valerie's beach cover. Gary took her body in his arms, kissed her. He slipped his hand under her cover, placed it firmly over the bathing suit material that stretched across her behind. Familiar enough with that, his fingers moved up her back, then boldly plunged under the bathing suit to bare skin, rubbed.

Valerie dropped the bottle into the water. With some champagne left, it was buoyant. It floated away forgotten. Between kisses and feels, Valerie noticed a star in the sky. First star of the night. Foggily, she made a wish.

Gary removed her beach cover and untied the strings behind her neck. Her suit slipped lower on her breasts.

The two of them waded back to the beach and followed Valerie's earlier trail away from the hotel. She retraced her steps. As she walked, Gary kept feeling her behind, and she would wiggle it playfully, scoot ahead a few steps, make him run to catch up.

She began to sing:

Daddy wouldn't buy me a bow-wow
Daddy wouldn't buy me a bow-wow—wow
I have a little cat
And I'm mighty fond of that
But Daddy wouldn't buy me a bow-wow

Gary caught her again, turned her around and kissed her. The bathing suit dropped below her nipples. She giggled and covered up with her hands. He pried away her hands. Her skin was faintly damp with sweat. She rubbed against him, tugged at his tank top.

Have to take this off so we can be even, she giggled.

He did, and they walked some more. Valerie had given up trying to walk in her own footsteps. She walked too unsteadily now, could hardly navigate. Her old tracks stopped and turned around.

I bet if we stopped here to rest, Gary dared, what happened this morning isn't about to happen again.

I bet not, she said.

You bet not what? That it would or wouldn't happen.

I'm not that easy.

He halted and touched her breasts again, ran his fingers down the front of her bare torso toward her crotch.

Oooop! No, she laughed, and danced away.

Are you only going to tease me? You know you want it.

Want what? she asked coyly.

He grabbed her shoulders with what was intended to be a gentle touch, but it was so sudden that it hurt her. He prompted her down to the sand, reached for her bathing suit, to pull it off her hips, pull it down her legs, take it out of his way. This reminded Valerie of diapering a baby.

Her baby.

Her baby who would have had life through this body. This body which right now was in a dire mess. The baby who probably could have done a better job with that life than Valerie had done with hers. Who probably had more right to a life than she. Perhaps restitutions could be made. It was fair justice. A drunken, drugged-up, defeated body was at least better than none. Perhaps the baby would take better care of this body than the mama.

As Gary watched, Valerie's arms pulled in, her hands and feet curled, her legs began to kick lightly at the knees. Innocence and bewilderment poured into the eyes, babble came from the mouth. Gary drew back in astonishment.

"Valerie," he said nervously.

She did not even know him. Her infantile motions were frightening. He backed away, gaped at her transfiguring, was far too spooked to hang around. He stumbled once, turned, and he ran as fast as he was able.

They found the infant dead of abandonment the next morning. The coroner's report put the cause of death at "the lethal mixture of alcohol and benzodiazepines." But that was wrong: it was abandonment.

**"As one is
So one sees"**

—William Blake

PART FIVE

Chapter 1

Andrew slammed his refrigerator door. He heard the bottles rattle inside. He turned away with a beer in his hand, walked into the living room, and sat.

He did not turn on the lights.

He had waited in the back of the church so that if Cornelius did come in, he would be the first to see him, pull him into the pew by the arm. But Cornelius had never shown, which had been a shock to the Mastropietros but not to Andrew. Cornelius was still missing. That day he ran out on the recording session was the last Andrew, or anyone Andrew knew, had seen of him.

What followed: there was no album made.

The Next Tuesday Band returned to little bars in Potsdam, New York.

Avchen went back to Pennsylvania. (At least she said good-bye, had coffee with Andrew before leaving, promised to write a letter sometime.)

Andrew came back here.

The phone did not ring.

No—the phone did ring, once—and when he answered it, hoping it would be Cornelius, there was nothing on the line. No dial tone. Not even the sound of dead air.

There was no doubt about one thing. No matter what time it had been when Valerie died, no matter where she had been when it happened, at the moment he snapped the cell phone closed, Cornelius had known.

Andrew gulped down half the beer. He did not know what he himself would do next. He was out of the music business, that much was sure. This time, instead of tearing up a coffee bar and jumping into a car, the conclusion was deliberate. He did not need to convince himself he would not go back.

Maybe if he had been more firm the first time, as Cornelius, although he had been testing, had hoped he would be, Valerie might still be alive.

Sure. And maybe if he had done some thing or other—whatever it was she had wanted whoever to do—Janie would still be alive.

Some things would be.

Some things would not be.

He finished off the beer and decided to go to bed.

Cornelius and Clancy got into the beat-up Rambler and drove across mountains and plains and mountains and desert to New Mexico. The name of Cornelius Prince back east had enjoyed no more fame than a name on an album jacket, and in the southwest, where if it isn't country-western it is not apt to make it, Cornelius returned to being just another thin, balding guy playing the wrong kind of music in little bars on Sunday nights.

His last fit of extraordinary knowledge, his last grand *déjà vu*, had been holding that phone in the corridor outside the recording studio.

He now tried to force its return, sat for hours, not smoking, like a blind man trying to will back his sight. But it was gone. He was just like normal folks.

He almost willingly adopted the cliché of a ruined man. He played piano in some sleazy little bar with smoke swirling all around him and would-be cowboys yelling things at him, came home to another dilapidated

314

apartment (nomads don't hang pictures), sat up, unable to sleep, not smoking for there was no need for that anymore, not doing anything at all—just sitting there.

He became acquainted with emotional states he had never known before. Restlessness, the inscrutable pain of depression, a supreme loneliness that came for him at its worst in the dead of night, while he sat up as if waiting, and terrified him.

The terror was the dénouement of that vague and amorphous feeling that had seized him, had clung sometimes until morning, with that recurring dream of Valerie getting off a plane from Bermuda. A dream he no longer had.

At dawn, Clancy would begin the birdsong rendition of Beethoven, and then Cornelius would go to bed, whatever he had been waiting for again not having shown, and he would sleep until afternoon.

He never took his ritual walks now. There was no need.

He believed it was all over. No longer could he see, therefore there must be nothing to be seen. It would all wind down rather quickly, then it would stop. He really did not know what to do next. If he did, he would have done it, would have taken action—for he remembered once knowing that the most preternatural knowledge would have trouble inspiring anyone toward change. He had gone on to prove that by this example of his own. He would have done anything to unprove himself.

For a long time, as he had scoffed, he had never been able to appreciate the awesome challenge of faith, of being forced to rely on any kind of faith, in any thing.

Now he saw things he had never seen before.

So, as he waited, every night without fail, for whatever he waited for, he began the habit of buying a six-pack on his way home, of passing the night-time hours of absurd vigilance with the beer. This way he did not have to look at a thing.

Clancy chirped away the Pastoral symphony while

Cornelius drank, indeed adding to it a frenetic urgency, changing altogether the mood of the piece. *A capriccio.* In older days Cornelius may have anticipated that already he had taken decisive action. He would have sat back in complacency rather than drunkenness and realized that it was not the end at all. Rather it was the beginning of a concatenation of events that would lead not only him, but another as well, to the faith he did not now believe in.

He took a job in a nondescript bar in the basement of a former church. He had not written a new song since Martin O'Kelly and Raj Hernandez had taken over in that capacity for the last recording. So his repertoire for this particular job consisted of his high school (post Milagro Beanfield times) and other early works. He played them with a kind of nostalgia, a flavor injected unlike the style of any other small time musician. During one of his breaks, as Cornelius warmed up at the bar for his overnight vigil, a punk but pretty black woman with a blood-red belly jewel and low-slung jeans approached him. She sat down, and he put on his glasses and stared at her through thumb-smeared lenses. She smiled a million dollar smile. The little diamond stud on her nose twinkled as her nostrils flared.

"My name's Jamie Banks," she said as if he'd know the name. Her voice was soft, husky.

Cornelius lifted his glasses thinking he'd see her better without the thumbprints in the way.

"Who's your friend?" Jamie Banks, whoever she was, asked about the albino cockatiel on his shoulder.

"Name's Clancy," Cornelius drank down his draft.

"Quite a gimmick."

"Maybe a gimmick. But not my gimmick. My wife gave it to me a long time ago."

"Does he talk?"

"Sings."

"And through your act he just perches there on your shoulder, eh?"

"Tap dances sometimes."

Jamie leaned forward on the bar, ordered a gin and tonic, then turned her head to Cornelius, leaning still on the bar in a conspiratorial way. "Cornelius, I'll be blunt: you are too good to be playing in a church catacomb with a bird perched on your shoulder like a circus act, and you know it."

Cornelius looked at her blandly, through his thumbprinted eyeglasses, resigned that he would not see her clearly no matter what.

"I want you to join us," Jamie Banks said.

"Who's us?"

"Creole Swampland," she said as if of course he should know.

And of course he should have. He had only the night before walked into a supermarket where rock and roll played instead of country-western, and Creole Swampland had been singing their latest hit single. Cornelius had thought to himself that Avchen Neumann had a better voice than the girl in this tune, paid for his six-pack, and walked out.

"I don't want to join a band," he told her.

"All right, don't join—tour with us. We'll feature you."

"You mean the warm-up act everyone throws groceries at."

"No," Jamie said, "you tour with us and we'll bring you out in the middle of the act. Play your own stuff, we'll back you."

It sounded like a good idea, and since he had nothing else to do, he agreed.

"Wait until you tell your wife this when she asks you and Clancy there how work went," Jamie said.

"I can't. My wife is dead."

Valerie sat serenely on the lawn in Washington Park. Across the way, masses of kids, their black skins shining in the sunlight, climbed on playground equipment. Not far off there were a couple of teenagers. The boy sat and strummed his guitar, the girl lay in gym shorts and bikini top hoping the sun might brown her winter skin to the color of those kids on the swing sets and seesaws. To all of them, Valerie was the feel of the bright sunshine, the Carolina blue of the sky, the breeze that combed the dewy grass and sifted through the budded branches. Except for secure feelings of well-being, their senses could not tell them that she was present.

An old wino strolled across the grass toward Valerie. The cuff of one of his wool pant legs had come apart, his shirt was a chambray worn tissue thin. He had a silver dollar birthmark emblazoned on his cheek. The kids on the playground were too involved to be aware when the old guy dropped his pants to urinate on the roots of a tree. The teenage boy stopped strumming, glanced at his girlfriend to make sure she did not see the wino shake his penis dry. Two college kids who had been playing ultimate Frisbee got the laugh of their lives.

The wino's thoughts were fuzz. His brain and liver were too clouded with alcohol to think in language. Impressions tumbled in his head, like a lost animal trying to get home. There was a hall above the butcher shop. A well kept lawn somewhere. A radiator. An alley running behind the bus station in Schenectady. There was the slender, long necked bottle and the smooth feel of glass in his sweating palm.

Valerie rose from her place on the lawn and went to the man. She helped him lift his pants and fasten them, guided him to a bench where there was shade. She touched him and he slept. His bottle was empty and he had no money. When he awoke, the man would be almost sober. The painful void in his memories told her that a worse effect would come from allowing that, than from warding off its inevitability. Like a medic doing triage, she took his bottle to the lake and filled it with water, and then she returned to him. When the man awoke, he would find his bottle filled with wine—better wine than he could appreciate—better wine than he'd had in his

318

life, and enough to numb his noggin again.

The children laughed and shouted; the teenage girl turned onto her stomach and her boyfriend rubbed her back, his guitar laid aside with its polished body gleaming in the sun; the college kids tossed their Frisbee.

Cornelius was not in Albany. The house was empty, up for auction by the bank that held the mortgage. No wonder no one had answered the telephone.

Chapter 2

There is something inside which will always say, "Go home," and keep repeating it until you finally realize where home is, and you go—in spite of differences, awkwardness—you go there.

Andrew slept in Eileen's bedroom, and sometimes...sometimes...

Right now the television was on, a program about lizards in the Mojave Desert. His father watched but Andrew paid it little attention. His mother and younger sisters and brother had gone shopping. It was only he and his father. They did not talk, just sat and watched, or pretended to watch, television.

Andrew had moved here early in February. Now it was April. He had fended off two and a half months' worth of inquiries, maintained his patience whenever he answered whoever it was who asked whatever they asked, slept in his sister's bedroom, and waited, wondering more strongly than any of them with their idly curious questions what he would do next.

While he sat in the living room. with his father, he found an answer. Something said to him, simply occurred to him as his thoughts lazily day dreamed: *Creole Swampland is in town. Why don't you go see them?*

He thought it was a notion out of the blue, and then he realized there was a commercial for the concert on the tube. For Creole Swampland and their Special Guest. Andrew did not know why he would think about going to see Creole Swampland. He had heard them on the radio, considered them to be limited-range alt-rock, no surprises. But perhaps the singles released as chart candidates were, as is often the case, not representative of the band's music. It had happened to The Next Tuesday Band. Andrew had never done a session with Creole Swampland (never been asked), so who knows. Sitting there, as the commercial ended and the lizard program returned, Andrew talked himself into going to see Creole Swampland and their Special Guest.

His seat was on the second balcony. The members of the band were tiny figures way down there. Creole Swampland appeared in a drift of fog and blue light. The crowd, most of them—at least the ones around Andrew—sixteen years old, cheered madly.

Jamie Banks sang with a lot of heart, but no one could beat Avchen Neumann—Avchen Neumann who had gone back home to get married and have babies as all of her sisters before her had. She would have bewitchingly beautiful babies, no doubt. (No baby pictures there.)

Then Jamie announced that in a little bar in Santa Fe she had stumbled onto this truly exciting piano player, and as the singer spoke, she nodded to the Creole Swampland pianist to go into the wing, and then Jamie Banks requested a warm welcome for Cornelius Prince.

And he came out.

Andrew was standing, not clapping, but staring in amazement, down two levels at the micro-Cornelius who took his place at the grand piano.

That is when the whole concert changed.

Hunched over the keys, corduroy jacket from a thrift store over dark football jersey, Cornelius played alone. The kids around Andrew appeared surprised at themselves for their own reactions. They sat mesmerized by the music as it drifted through the silent hall up to their ears. The next song was one from the first Next Tuesday CD, and enough people recognized it to break into applause. But the hush returned, a granite stillness, almost as if something were wrong, and surely as if this were nothing they'd expected.

Andrew did not realize it at first, because the smoke in the air irritated his eyes to begin with, but he was crying. This was the first he had known of Cornelius since Valerie's death, and the man had been changed by all those weeks of hibernation. The change, his descent into a very deep hole, was evident even from this elevation. Creole Swampland backed him on his third song, and it was sorcery. Andrew could not identify the new element in Cornelius' talent, but it was far beyond finesse, beyond precision. Meanwhile, Cornelius was himself the opposite of the music. He was derelict.

Andrew pushed his way to the aisle, headed for the exit. He ran down six flights of stairs to the lobby, peered down the main center aisle as Cornelius played on. Andrew had to get backstage. He ran outside, ran through the delivery alley, around back to the loading dock. He leaped up the steps and tugged on the door. It was locked. The sounds of the piano came through, muted.

Andrew knocked, loud.

A guard opened the door immediately.

"Ya gotta let me in," Andrew said.

"Who are you?"

"Name's Andrew Healy. I'm a friend of Cornelius Prince."

The guard was very big, obese, wearing mutton chops but with a shaved head. "Really?" he said dubiously. "I pity you."

Andrew pulled out his musician's union card. "Here," he said. "I played with him and The Next Tuesday Band."

The guard examined the card. "Yeah, but this ain't no

322

pass," he said. "I shouldn't let ya in, but if you weren't a friend of that guy I'm sure ya wouldn't say you were. He don't need a friend though, he needs a shrink. Carries this bird around—"

"You gonna let me in, or what?"

"Keep it down. Okay, c'mon in."

Andrew ran down the hall into the backstage area. Bright yellow light spilled through smoke and dust into the wings. Creole Swampland's piano player stood half lit by the spill, smoked a cigarette while she waited to go back onstage. Andrew hurried to her, looked out onto the stage at Cornelius.

A roadie handed Creole Swampland's pianist a beer. She put one in Andrew's hand too.

"Do you think I could go out there?" Andrew asked the piano player. "I'm a friend of your special guest there, and he'd freak if I went out there."

"He's pretty freaked already. He won't go anywhere without that bird." She pointed to the corner by the dimmer board where Clancy stood freely on a high stool. "Surprised he doesn't take it onstage with him."

"Just let me go out there. I haven't seen the guy in ages." Then he got an idea. "Get someone's attention—let me relieve your guitar player."

"You play?"

"Yeah."

The piano player considered it. "Can't do it."

"I'm Andrew Healy," he said as if pulling out a trump card.

"*You* are."

"If you're any kind of musician, ya at least know the name. Wanna see my card? Let me go out there, huh?"

The piano player said: "He talks about you." And she stepped onto the stage, stole around the percussion riser to Jamie. Andrew watched them talk, watched both of them motion to their guitarist, and the piano player in turn looked Andrew's way. She returned to the wing.

"Go ahead," she told Andrew. "Jamie says you can ad lib anything."

"You kidding? I *know* these songs." And with a big wide grin Andrew strolled onto the stage, took the guitar and began to play.

Cornelius noticed the few dropped measures during the exchange of guitarists, glanced over to see what was what. There was Andrew, smiling as if at a private joke, and then Cornelius smiled too.

They finished the song.

"That guy lurking back there with the guitar is Andrew Healy," Cornelius said to the audience. "I dragged him into making an album with my old band, then I ran out. Guess he got angry and he's come to drag me back." Then he got up from the piano, went over to Andrew and hugged him.

"Where have you been, huh?" Andrew said under his breath.

"I'm heading down while I'm heading up again. How's the band?"

"Broke up. Corey, we gotta play something. It's awful quiet in here and everyone is lookin' at us," Andrew said.

Cornelius broke the embrace and went back to the piano.

"Wanna use that violin over there?" he said to Andrew, the microphone picking him up once more. "I believe you know this one."

Cornelius played the sonata named for Valerie.

Andrew played his string arrangement.

They made that the last song, walked together off the stage. Creole Swampland resumed their concert, and the audience regressed to their rowdy selves, waving their cell-phone screens in the air.

Cornelius went straight to the men's room and threw up.

"What's the matter?" Andrew went in to help him.

"I got nervous," Cornelius said, shocked, hunkered over the toilet bowl. "Tonight was my first concert since...I don't think I can do it anymore."

"Sure you can," Andrew said.

"I never got nervous before."

"Maybe it was me showing up. I took ya by surprise. Something just said go see Creole Swampland tonight. Couldn't even get a date, but still I had to come. Then I couldn't believe it when you walked out there."

Cornelius stood slowly. His face was flushed, his lips cracked. The sound of Creole Swampland made its way into the bathroom. Cornelius patted water onto his forehead.

"You were real good out there," Andrew said. "Like you been practicing real hard."

"That's my old music. I'm more comfortable with my old music. That's my old music."

"You made Creole Swampland look bad."

Cornelius shook his head at the mirror. "I can't do it anymore."

"You can do it," Andrew said. "Sure you can."

Cornelius took out a cigarette and lit it. "I'd quit these things; there wasn't any need anymore, but there's no need for a lot of things."

Andrew accompanied Creole Swampland and Cornelius on the rest of that tour, along for the ride. Cornelius' music continued to tap the audience so that every breath remained drawn, every eye fixed. Cornelius himself grew sicker with each performance. Like the music was unstringing his very heart. He maintained that he could no longer stand the drain of performing, that whatever it took to get up in front of a mob of people—regardless of how transfixed they were— because they were still *people*—he had lost it.

Andrew was distressed at Cornelius' degeneration. Perhaps Cornelius had suffered, however quietly, some kind of nervous breakdown, even a stroke, after Valerie's death.

The vital part of his music was, in a sense, drawn not

from any audience, but from Valerie. He would play each song as though she could hear, as though its melody might sound so sweet to her that she would return to him. As if the intricacies of musical formulae could undo the intricacies of the past, render it as present once more for a second chance. And then, so exhausted from the energy he expended in this, so dismayed by the absurdity of it, he would race to the bathroom. And he would blame it on stage fright.

Cornelius Prince became a controversial figure in the music business when, during a particular concert, he spontaneously chose not to play the usual songs. He walked onto the stage, sat, and looked at the keyboard. And he simply looked. Silent anticipation turned to restlessness, to nervousness out in the house, and he knew that he had to play something. He could not sit there and do nothing. They would not understand. So he began to play songs written by the long-lost Martin O'Kelly, and songs by Raj Hernandez, planned for the album that never was. Discovering that these impersonal tunes did not bring on the cadre of loss and nausea, Cornelius decided to make them his new act.

Which was fine. Although the music could not mesmerize an audience, he had become popular enough that no one lost interest and began to heckle. People showed enthusiasm for the new music with customary concert manners. In other words, they screamed.

Thus Cornelius was free, not entirely of his bereavement, nor of the absurdity of rethinking the past, but at least of the hold they had on him. And that was fine...for a time.

Creole Swampland ended their tour. Cornelius went on to share double bills with Generation Why. He was not considered an opening, audience warmer; many went to see *him*, planned to leave when Generation Why came on. Edgar Pufknack was one of those.

And he recognized each and every song as the property of someone else. Not once did Cornelius credit the composer. Edgar Pufknack made his way backstage, furious.

Cornelius lit a cigarette, with Generation Why's music piped into the dressing room, and he looked at Edgar Pufknack as if he had no idea what the man was talking about. He did not claim that the songs were his, they clearly were not, but he did not understand why they could not be performed—other than contractually—a contract long ago torn up—in concert.

Had that album ever been produced, the rights would have belonged to the whole band, because that is how The Next Tuesday Band had always done it, and Cornelius was not only a member, but leader, of that band.

He said: "It hurts too much to do my own stuff."

Edgar Pufknack put it in a humanitarian way: "You are making money off of something that does not belong to you," he said. "It is the same as stealing. Worse, it is even lower than stealing, because it is easier to get away with. It's like downloading from a pirate web site. All we're talking about here is giving credit to Martin, wherever he is, and to Chris. Or else write your own stuff."

"It has gone out of me. I can't write anymore."

Clancy walked up and down Cornelius' arm.

Edgar Pufknack regarded Cornelius, his bloodshot eyes, his wizened body, the bird on his arm, and said: "Perhaps you've burned yourself out."

"It is too late. I had my chance but I listened wrong."

The bird perched on the crown of his nearly bald head.

"What the hell are you talking about? Cornelius, you have to stop doing these songs without permission. And I am denying you that permission."

"How about if I go out and buy the sheet music? Then you get your cut of the royalties."

"Don't make me get the lawyers to do this."

Cornelius did not reply. But he did not stop using the

songs, the songs having become like morphine, and a lawsuit ensued. The scandalous publicity, as such publicity may tend to do, increased the popularity of Cornelius Prince, and by autumn he was able to tour alone on the bill. But he had yet to make a new CD. No label would touch him with Metacarpal Records after him in court. Knowing that Cornelius was beginning to founder in a bad business, Andrew advised him to stop doing the songs, at least until the lawsuit was over.

"If you want, I'll write for you. I don't care about credit or copyrights," Andrew said. "I'll be a ghost writer."

Cornelius considered it.

"This is getting worse. There is no way it will go in your favor and you're gonna get blown away."

"I can't do the old stuff. And I can't write anymore."

"But I can, Cornelius. Look: cancel your next concert. I'11 write some new songs. If you don't like them, then go ahead and do whatever you want, but at least let me see if I can do something."

Cornelius agreed.

The next time Cornelius Prince appeared in concert, after the hiatus, it was with the new songs written by Andrew, and he had never sounded worse.

Here is the way Cornelius would do a concert: it was just himself, a grand piano, Hammond organ, and his electric keyboard, which had been with him since the beginning. It lent a cabaret atmosphere to his act, made it more intimate even in the largest of halls, However, it could also backfire and sound quite insubstantial. He played each of Andrew's songs like an amateur trying to sight read music he'd never looked at before. And he experimented on the stage, often making garbled messes out of the simplest of tunes. It was embarrassing for Andrew.

Not because it was his music, but because it was his friend.

He knew the talent that had forsaken itself. When

each concert was over, Andrew would make his way backstage, praying that Cornelius would not attempt an encore.

"You gotta get out of this," Andrew said to Cornelius, even as the audience still applauded out there, waved their cell phones and called for his reappearance.

Cornelius took Clancy toward the dressing room, knowing well that an encore would not be a good idea. "What would I do?" he said. "Go back to Albany and work for the highway department?"

He did not give it up. People showed up at his next gig, still wild with support and bravos for him. Andrew left his seat and walked straight onto the stage, forced himself through the roadies who tried to hold him back, sat at the grand piano and began to play. Cornelius on the Hammond, they played a duet, and Andrew's piano made up for the gaps and stumbles of Cornelius. The sound was better, though not perfect, so Andrew crutched Cornelius to the end of the performance.

He supported Cornelius in this fashion on two or three other occasions, and then he realized he was doing more harm than good, providing the wrong kind of support, and in the end making the wrong kind of difference.

One last time he pleaded with Cornelius to retire. He came right out and said: "You are not well, Cornelius. You had a breakdown and you don't even realize it. It is understandable, but I can't believe the personality change. You are feeding on the fame."

Cornelius looked at him straight, said with a somber sanity not seen in a long time: "It's all gone, but a man goes on living, regardless of what happens, life goes on, even when it does not."

It was only one week later that Cornelius claimed to see Valerie at his concert in Chicago. Andrew drove him back to the hotel after that one, and in the morning Cornelius had checked out, disappeared again.

Chapter 3

Avchen Neumann was not at home when Andrew rang the doorbell. Her father answered the door. He was huge. Andrew being short, almost anyone seemed tall, but Avchen's father had to beat six-three, with broad shoulders, the muscles built from years of very hard work. His head was squared, exaggeratedly so by the close crew cut that he wore, hair still blond although the man was probably in his fifties. His eyes, however, a quiet blue, canceled the fearsomeness of his bulk, were definitely the eyes of a man who would want more than anything for his youngest daughter to become a singer, of a man who would shop until he found the perfect lamp for her little apartment.

He told Andrew that Avchen was at work, and Andrew held up the gaily wrapped large box he had brought along.

"I'm Andrew Healy. I brought her a present."

"Come in," Avchen's father said. "She'll be home any time."

Andrew stepped into the living room, toting the present, wondering what kind of job Avchen would have these days. She had never mentioned a job in her email notes.

Her father, for all his awesome and ungainly structure, did not seem incongruous with a woman like Avchen. Yet somehow her house, her hometown, did. Both were small, honest, simple. It seemed a far more grand achievement to produce such beauty as Avchen Neumann than this mundane middle America setting could dream of. The living room of this house was not unlike that in his own parents' house. In spite of her stories about her home, Andrew's imagination had always seen Avchen coming out of a palace, pumpkin coach and white-mice footmen and all.

Her father offered him a beer and said, "So yer one of them musicians too, heh?"

"I play some," Andrew said. "Don't think I'm going to make a life of it."

"The guys down to the plant were real impressed by the records you and Avchen did. They never heard any of 'em, but they still think it's good, ya know?"

"Yeah."

"Avchen was real unhappy though. Guess I was wrong to push her."

"She has a lot of talent," Andrew said.

"Yeah. She could do good out there, I'm sure. But it's her talent, and she can decide she wants to use it, or she doesn't, and that's up to her. Say, what d'ya got in that box?"

"It's a surprise."

"She'll be real happy to see you, that I know."

When Avchen did come home, wearing a waitress uniform, she was indeed happy to see Andrew. She gave him a big kiss. Andrew had forgotten exactly how beautiful she was. It was a beauty easy to forget, as it was not easy to believe it could exist in the first place.

"What did you bring me?" she asked.

"Open it," Andrew said.

They were alone in the living room now. Avchen knelt beside the wrapped package, picked at the tape with her fingernails.

"Just open it," Andrew grinned. "The heck with saving the stupid paper."

Avchen let out a short giggle and tore excitedly at the ribbon and wrap. She ripped open the top of the carton and peered in.

It was a lamp.

"I delivered it myself so it wouldn't be damaged," Andrew said.

She said, "Oh Andrew!" and hugged him for a long time.

"There's a question that goes with that."

"What is the question?"

"Marry me?"

She drew back to arms length to judge whether or not he was serious. He was.

"Andrew, I don't want to be a singer anymore," she said. "I don't like what it showed me about myself. I even like this dumb job I got. The people are nice."

"Avchen, I know. I don't want that either. I just want to be *dull*."

She was not sure how to interpret that.

"I mean I don't want all that stuff. I just want to marry you and live a quiet life, you know?"

"You love me?"

"Yes. I do. Please think about it, huh?"

"Can I think about it for a little while?"

"I want you to."

She hugged him and then said, "So how'd you get here anyway? Did you eat yet? I'm starving, how about if we have something to eat?"

"That would be good."

As a boy, when Andrew rode around on the New York City subways, he used to like to sit in the first car of the train and look out the front window into the black tunnel. He could spot the stations as the train approached them. First the platform would be a small yellow square of light floating on either side of the black.

It would rapidly stretch to a rectangle. Then he would see it had depth, he would see people standing on it. He used to think about the people: where they were going, where they had come down into the station from, what happened to each of them, what kinds of things did they talk about, outside of the short, depthless window he had on their lives. Finally light would race around the front of the car and the train would pause inside the platform.

On a train that raced across the state of Pennsylvania, the engine blocked the first car, there was no front view available. And of the people around you, you could ask all those questions, but you did not. Andrew sat and stared out the side window, watched the mountains rush by as rain slanted down. The dreariness of the weather and the lights on inside the car presented him with a double image: his own reflection—and the shapes of mountains, landscapes, other people's cities sweeping along. When he was a boy, one single year, that many days between birthdays, seemed a long time. Today, it had been four years since a man named Edgar Pufknack had recruited him to play on the demo CD of some guy named Cornelius Prince. Four years did not even feel like what one year had once seemed. Too much gets smaller, shorter, lower, flatter, less wondrous as you mature. It is too easy to allow everything this diminution, never realizing that some things must be preserved through the eyes of a child.

Andrew wondered where Cornelius might have gone now. The man had whittled himself down. Lost and bumbling because he had discovered a condition he had never known before. Andrew thought that could be called pathetic...but then perhaps it could not be. If he was not playing piano somewhere, if he still swore that he could not write, then he was wrong. He had a talent, and his talent had not died, just his wife. Death makes life feel very strange. Andrew was too tired to chase Cornelius down anymore, too tired to try to convince him to—

Actually, the truth was Andrew did not know what

Cornelius needed to be convinced *of*. Was there a lesson
to be learned, the moral of the story? Andrew turned
away from the train window, sat back in his seat and
breathed a sigh he might have pinned on a need for
sleep, or on bewilderment.

A child's eyes

When he was a small boy and fell down, scraping his
knee, all his mother needed to do was smile, kiss it, and
it was all better...no more danger, no threat of infection,
no worries about scarring...to the child, so simple. That
winter, when Janie's car dubiously went off the road and
rolled on itself

(not just her dying but her being there, freezing in the
snow and sleet, not missed, for days, presumed alive, for
days)

life and death began to feel like the same thing, but
the child had sought only to be held, had sought only a
smile of comfort and a kiss.

Then Andrew knew where Cornelius would be: where
every child goes—home. He made a connection in New
York City, got on a northbound train to Albany.

But it was a big city. He took a city bus from the train
station, across the river, got off and walked around
downtown. He bought a newspaper, looked in it for any
calendar of music that might include something about
Cornelius. He dumped the newspaper in a wire litter
basket on a street corner, walked around in the rain, as
if he would certainly bump into Cornelius at any time. He
walked past a bar and decided to go in and sit in a dry
place for a while. While he sat there, he got an idea, and
he asked the bartender if there was a telephone directory
he could look at. The bartender looked around behind
the bar, looking as if no one had ever asked for a phone
book before, as if he didn't care whether he found
anything or not, but then he came up with an old, dog-
eared stack of pages, barely together in book form.
Andrew looked in it to see if Cornelius was listed.

He was. But even as Andrew hurriedly scribbled the address on a cocktail napkin, he realized that it was an old address. Cornelius wasn't going to live there now.

But Andrew got on another city bus, rode it to the edge of the city, and then walked until he found himself looking at a nice white aluminum sided house with a grey flagstone front, light blue shutters. There was no point in ringing the bell. Whoever lived there now would not know Cornelius.

Andrew then went to a hotel, took a room, and went to sleep wondering how Cornelius had found *him*, how Avchen too had known where he was hiding, when he was in St. Albans. He awoke the next day. The rain had let up but the sky was still heavy, and he prepared to hit the streets again.

He was certain that Cornelius was in this city.

He thought of Clancy. Cornelius would have to feed that bird something, he would never allow that bird to starve. Andrew looked in the night stand and found a phone directory. He realized this would be the latest edition of the directory and, if Cornelius were listed, he'd be in here. But he didn't even look as he realized there was little chance he had a phone these days. He copied the addresses of all the local pet stores. Then he bought a map of the streets of Albany. This was a long shot, but there was nothing else.

"This guy you would have remembered," Andrew told each clerk he talked to. "He would have brought the bird into the store with him."

Someone actually remembered him—a dark girl who had to be older than the age she looked. "He comes in a lot," she said.

Which had to mean Cornelius was near. It would not make sense to patronize a pet shop blocks and blocks from home. And this old neighborhood looked exactly like Cornelius' mood when Andrew had last seen him—when he had been raving some nonsense about Valerie in the men's room.

All that Andrew had to do was comb these few streets for a gold Rambler.

And late in the afternoon he found the car. He did not know what else to do, having actually made it this far on nothing but luck. The Rambler might be parked right in front of the house, or it might be parked down the street from it.

He tried to open the car door so he could look in the glove compartment for the registration or insurance card, anything that would have the right address on it, but the door was locked.

So, out of ideas, Andrew just stood beside the car and began to yell Cornelius' name. People looked at him, but he did not care. His feet hurt from walking all over this city, only a miracle had discovered this car, and now only a miracle would help him complete this ridiculous quest. He called out, and the calls turned to cries, and the cries echoed off the slumping facades of the houses.

It turned abruptly silent, deathly silent for a city, as if every car on every block had come to a halt at a traffic light at once and all pedestrians waited at "Don't Walk" signs, and that is when Andrew heard birdsongs.

There was no mistaking that melody.

Andrew followed the sound to the front stoop of a very old house, up the steps and into the hall. Only one mailbox had a name on it, and that name was "Sanders." Nevertheless, Clancy was in the building. Andrew tested the staircase, judged it sturdy, and went up to the apartment where this supposed Sanders lived. The bird sang from in there.

Andrew knocked.
No answer.

He knocked again, listened, then turned the door knob and found the door unlocked. He started to go in, almost afraid of what he would find when he got there.

The shades were drawn. The apartment was dark and absolutely freezing. It was crammed with furniture—old furniture, two or three of everything imaginable. Some of the furniture was draped with white linen. Amidst it all, sitting upon an unraveling fanback wicker chair, was Cornelius. His feet and torso were bare, his blue jeans were tattered. The bird hopped from Cornelius' shoulder to the arm of the wicker chair, sang away. Cornelius did not appear to notice that anyone had come in. Too, the electric piano was buried in the collection, covered with dust and surrounded by cobwebs.

Andrew wondered how Cornelius could stand this cold with so little clothing. Even in his buttoned coat, Andrew shivered. Cornelius' body was pale, not blue, not goose-fleshed. "Cornelius," Andrew said. Clancy stopped the song. "I don't want to tell you what I went through to find you," Andrew said. He pushed furniture out of his path as he crossed the room.

"I thought I locked the door," Cornelius said blankly.

"It turned easily. It wasn't locked."

"I thought I locked the door."

"No, you didn't. Are you okay?"

"I don't know how the locked door opened."

"Don't you want to know how I found you?" Andrew said, growing nervous. "It was pretty clever, I think. I found the store where you buy food for Clancy."

"I never go out. The bird eats whatever it finds."

"You must go out sometimes. The clerk remembered you."

"No."

Andrew took Cornelius by the chin, looked in his eyes to see if he may have taken something. The eyes were grey, did not appear to have anyone behind them, but they were clear.

"Cornelius, what are you doing to yourself anyway?" He had a whole lot he wanted to say. He couldn't think of a way to say any of it. He didn't want to say it anyhow, if it wasn't going to make a difference. He looked around the room as if for cue cards. "Look," he said at last, "I have been searching for you for two days. I'm starving, my feet hurt, and right now I have to go to the bathroom. After I do, we are gonna go out and get food." He looked for the bathroom, found it behind an armchair, and went in.

As soon as Andrew closed the bathroom door, Cornelius heard footsteps on the stairs. Then Valerie, so sweet, so beautiful, so unable to be touched, came in. The gold chain was gone from her ankle. She was light on her feet, a light in the room, light in the sky. "You certainly make it difficult to catch up with you," she said as she opened the shade, opened the window.

Clancy flew across the room and landed on her arm. "Hello, Clancy," she said.

"Andrew is here," Cornelius told her.

"Yes, I know. I wish to speak with you alone first. There is much you do not understand. I cannot make you understand, that is your will or not, but perhaps I can help. Would you like a root beer?" She went into the kitchen. At the same time, the bird spread its wings, ruffled its cowl, and then flew out the window, landing just beyond the fire escape in a tree whose trunk had 30 rings. Valerie appeared with two root beers in bottles from the kitchen, gave one to him. "We should go out there with Clancy, onto the fire escape? It's warmer out here." Valerie crawled through the window, Cornelius followed with his root beer. She leaned against the guardrail, gazed at him across the mouth of her bottle.

"Andrew will be back soon," Cornelius said. "We don't have much time."

"Don't worry," she said. "There is no time."

"Pinnoke...I'm stuck. I can't tell what's going to happen anymore. I've lost that gift, and I don't know how—don't know what to do next anymore."

"Was that really a gift, Corey?" Valerie said. "You wanted it to be one."

"I had it all my life," he said.

"For a reason that was not yours." Her voice was gentle, filled with reassurance, not reprimand. "And that reason may not yet be fulfilled, but the time has changed, as the key of your music may change." Valerie drank from her root beer.

"I wasn't prepared for this," Cornelius admitted.

"Corey," she said, "you have never been lost at all before; and so there was a lot you did not prepare for."

"If you mean you, Pinnoke, I do love..."

She shook her head importantly. "I'm not here to haunt you, Cornelius. I am here to help, if I can." She frowned—a beatific frown: "When you see dark clouds in the sky, and the wind blows," she said looking out at the wind, "don't you anticipate a storm? You must be open, Cornelius, and not *only* through your eyes. You had no ability before which you do not still have."

The sound Andrew heard was a rush of a great wind, as if this wind filled the entire house, strong enough to shake up its termite-eaten frame. Yet not a thing was disturbed. Worried, he yanked open the door and rushed out. Bright, yellow sunlight filled the room, and the apartment was warm. Cornelius sat at his piano, the dust and the cobwebs gone, and he played...

Beautifully! While Clancy stood poised and silent in a tree just beyond the window, gazing out at the surface of the world as it curved off in every direction into a sphere, a little more egg-shaped than round—letting his symphonic songs out across an unimaginable wilderness; mountains that rose up from ancient ripples in the mud, a tide that rose and fell like prayers, surrounded by billowing clouds; bright blue air that made a shield against the burning circle of the sun, shining out over the impossibly large loops of planetary orbits, to the implausible swirls of space, moving like ripples on the sea outward from the big bang, so that the starlight could bounce back, skipping like a stone, for a whole decade, for two, or three...

Cornelius' playing went on. And Andrew knew. "She's here...right now...isn't she? With us."